Paulina Chiziane

THE FIRST WIFE

A TALE OF POLYGAMY

Translated from the Portuguese by David Brookshaw

archipelago books

By arrangement with Literarische Agentur Mertin Inh. Nicole Witt e. K.,
Frankfurt am Main, Germany

LIBRARY OF CONGRESS CATALOGING-IN-PUBLICATION DATA
Names: Chiziane, Paulina, 1955– author. | Brookshaw, David, translator.
Title: The first wife / Paulina Chiziane ;
translated from the Portuguese by David Brookshaw.
Other titles: Niketche. English
Description: First Archipelago Books edition. |
Brooklyn, NY : Archipelago Books, 2016.
Identifiers: LCCN 2015049933 | ISBN 9780914671480 (pbk.)
Classification: LCC PQ9939.C45 N5513 2016 | DDC 869.3/42—dc23
LC record available at http://lccn.loc.gov/2015049933

Archipelago Books
232 Third Street #A111, Brooklyn, NY 11215
www.archipelagobooks.org

Distributed by Penguin Random House: www.penguinrandomhouse.com

Cover art by Merikokeb Berhanu

Archipelago Books is grateful for the generous support of
the Lannan Foundation, the National Endowment for the Arts,
the New York City Department of Cultural Affairs,
and the New York State Council on the Arts, a state agency.

PRINTED IN THE UNITED STATES OF AMERICA

With Leontina dos Muchangos,
I travel through the world of a woman,
that unknown soul where I discovered
sleeping powers

and

With Alcinda de Abreu,
I stroll until the sun goes down and the sun comes up,
through the most extraordinary landscape
of a woman's world

A woman is earth. If you don't sow her, or water her, she will produce nothing.

(A proverb from Zambézia)

1

An explosion can be heard somewhere over there. A bomb. A landmine. It must be the war returning once again.

I think of hiding. Of running away. The explosion scares the birds that seek refuge in the heavens. No. It can't be the sound of a gunshot. Maybe it's two cars colliding somewhere on the road. I look down the road out of curiosity. I can't see anything. Only silence. I feel a faint fluttering in my breast and remain motionless for a minute. A crowd of neighbors is walking toward me.

"Rami!"

"What was it?"

"The car."

Their arms are moving like gentle waves, ready to quell the uproar. There is feeling in every gesture. There's a hint of quiet, feigned pity in each look, which makes me feel more alarmed.

"Car?"

"Yes. The window."

"Window?"

"Yes. The car window."

"Oh! Who was it?"

"Betinho."

"What?"

An invisible dagger slithers down from on high aimed at my breast. I'm as speechless as a stone, I'm terrified. All I can do is sigh and think: Ah, Betinho, my youngest! That car belongs to a rich man. What's going to become of me?

I enter a stage of deep, silent panic. My nerves are buffeted by gusts of anxiety, like some razor-sharp wind. This accident fills me with pain and longing. My Tony, where are you? Why do you leave me all by myself to fill the role of both woman and man in solving everyday problems, when you are out there somewhere?

There are moments in life when a woman feels as isolated and vulnerable as a fleck of dust. Where are you, my one and only Tony, for I hardly ever see you? Where are you, husband of mine, to protect me, where? I'm a respectable woman, a married woman. A deep sense of loathing poisons my way ahead. I feel dizzy. A bitter taste in my mouth. Nausea. Repugnance. Impotence and despair.

Betinho dashes in, hides away in his room awaiting his punishment. I chase after him. My weekend is already ruined, my Sunday

< 10 >

has been overcome by disaster. I need to scream in order to get rid of this bitter taste. I need to give someone hell in order to dispel this pain. I need to mete out some punishment in order to feel I'm alive.

"Betinho!"

I'm unable to scream. The tears glisten like moonlight on Betinho's face. Betinho's sadness is overflowing with innocence. Betinho's sobbing is as sweet as a baby bird chirping. His tremor shakes his whole body like flowers on a bush swaying in the breeze. I sniff the smell of urine.

"Betinho, a man doesn't wet himself with fear."

"It was the mango, mom."

"Mango?"

"Yes, that ripe one, high up there in the tree."

I look up at the mango tree. The mango is swaying serenely in the breeze. It looks a tasty mango, yes sir. Round. Youthful. And Betinho was trying to halt its flight when it was in life's first flush, when it was still very green.

"Oh! Betinho, what have you done to me?"

"Punish me, Mom."

Betinho's voice ripples in my ears like the gentle rustle of pines and my rage melts away into pity. This son of mine is beautiful.

< 11 >

Instead of forgiveness he asks for punishment. I have a just man here. I grow tender. Enchanted. My anger subsides. I feel a mother's pride.

From the bedroom window, I am aware of comments wafting up from the street. The words I hear drive me to despair. I feel their flaming tongues licking the inside of my bones. I boil. My eyes grow moist with tears. If Tony were here, he would berate his son as a father and a man. If he were here now, he would resolve the problem of the broken window with the owner of the car, men understand each other. Oh, if only Tony were around!

But where is my dear Tony, whom I haven't seen since Friday? Where is that man of mine who leaves me to look after the children and the house, and gives me no inkling of where he is? A husband at home means security, protection. Thieves keep away if a husband is present. Men respect each other. Women neighbors don't wander in just like that to ask for salt, sugar, much less to bad-mouth the other neighbor. In a husband's presence, a home is more of a home, there's comfort and status.

I leave Betinho alone and go out into the street. The owner of the car is seething with fury. I thought he would hit me, but not a word. He's one of those men who are classy in the way they talk and don't assault women. I go up to him and apologize on my son's behalf.

I tell him my husband, Tony, a police chief, will settle the matter with him. He agrees, but I get the feeling he doesn't believe me. What respectable man believes the word of a woman in despair?

A whole procession of women comes to meet me. They console me. Children are like that, Rami. They talk about children and the broken window. And they talk about absent husbands who don't look after their children either.

"There's no order because there's a man missing in this house," I burst out. "This is all Tony's fault. He's never here. First he was away for a night, then it was another, and then another. It's become a habit. He tells me he's on duty at night. That he has to supervise the work of all the police officers because night is when thieves are on the attack. I pretend to believe him. But men leave a snail's slime behind them, they can't hide. I know very well what he's up to.

"You're not the only one, Rami. My husband, for instance, left me years ago," a neighbor says, "and ran after a young fourteen-year-old girl because he wanted to start all over again. An old man became a child."

"Mine has those concubines you all know about, with children and everything," says another. "Do you think I care?"

I look at them all. Tired, used women. Beautiful women, ugly women. Young women, old women. Women defeated in the battle for love. Outwardly alive, but dead within, forever inhabiting the shadows. But why have our husbands gone away, why have they abandoned us after so many years living together? Why have they cast us aside like unwanted baggage, like weary loads, in order to pursue new lives and loves? Why, when they are already approaching old age, are their appetites renewed? Who told old men that mature women don't need affection? Oh, Tony, my love! If only you were here. Bring me springtime again. Where are you that you can't hear me?

My neighbors comfort me with astonishing stories. They are mothers. In order to alleviate my pain, they tell me stories of their own unhappiness and suffering.

Our minds wander in nostalgic murmurs. In the eyes of each of us, there are images of a husband who has gone and will never come back. Quelling our anguish has become our daily struggle. In my street, most women have been abandoned, their husbands decided to get out almost at the same time. I'm the only one who

< 14 >

still sees her man's face from time to time – but only when he comes home to eat or change his clothes. There are no men left in this area, it's the women who are the head of their families, but when night falls, lots of men can be seen entering and leaving some of the houses surreptitiously, like thieves. They are married men, for sure, and from these relationships here, children will be born, many of whom will die without knowing their father.

Love. Such a tiny word. A beautiful, precious word. A powerful, elusive sentiment. Just four letters, giving birth to all the emotions in the world. Women talk of love. Men talk of love. Love that comes, love that goes, that flees, that hides, that is sought, that is found, that is cherished, that is scorned, that causes hatred and unleashes endless wars. In matters of love, women are a defeated army, they have nothing left to do but weep. Lay down their arms and accept their solitude. Write poems and sing to the wind in order to chase away their pain. Love is as fleeting as a drop of water in the palm of one's hand.

Dreams dwell in the dead of night. Sometimes they have bright colors, like flowers. Other times, they are black birds dancing,

< 15 >

ghostlike, in the shadows. My God, night is falling, and I am terrified of a cold bed. I lay my head on the pillow and count the number of times I've died. I fight back. I can't accept the idea of being rejected. Me, Rami, a beautiful woman. Me, an intelligent woman. I have been loved. I was a target for rivalry among the young men of my generation. I was the cause of burning passion. Of all those who wooed me, I chose Tony, the worst of the lot, because at the time, I thought he was the best. I enjoyed only two years of complete happiness in more than twenty years of marriage.

I close my eyes and scale the mountain within me. I look for myself. I can't find me. In each corner of my being, all I can find is his image. I let out a sigh, and all I can utter is his name. I sink into the very depths of my heart and what do I find? Only him. My love for him is pure and perfect, can he not see that?

No one can understand men. How can Tony despise me like this if there is nothing wrong with me? When it came to obeying, I always obeyed him. I always did what he wanted. I always looked after him. I even put up with his craziness. Twenty years is a record in modern-day marriages. Modesty apart, I'm the most perfect woman in the world. I made him into the man he is now.

I gave him love, I gave him children so he could gain the esteem of others in life. I sacrificed my dreams for his. I gave him my youth, my life. That's why I say, and say it again, that there's no other woman like me in his life! In spite of this, I'm the unhappiest woman in the world. Ever since he was promoted to chief of police and money began to fill his pockets, unhappiness has wormed its way into this house. His old flirtations were like fine rain falling on an umbrella, they didn't affect me. Now I dance alone on a deserted stage. I'm losing him. He spends his time in the company of the most beautiful women in Maputo, who fall at his feet like diamonds.

I go to the mirror to try to find out what's wrong with me. I see dark rings under my eyes, my God, huge rings! I've cried so much these last few days, I've even overdone it. I examine my face. With this sad mask I look like a ghost, this person here just isn't me. I sputter the words of an old song, one of those that brings tears to the eyes. When it comes to singing, I know my roots. I'm from people who sing. Where I come from, we sing of happiness and of pain. Life is one big song. I sing and I weep. I savor the tears that flow and taste of salt, and I feel the greatest pleasure in the world. Ah, how this crying makes me feel free!

I stop crying and go to the mirror again. The eyes reflected there gleam like diamonds. It's the face of a happy woman. The lips reflected there convey a message of happiness, no, they can't be mine, I don't smile, I weep. My God, my mirror has been taken over by an intruder who's laughing at my misfortune. Can it be that this intruder is inside me? I rub my eyes, I think I've gone mad. I think of seeking refuge from the image in the comfort of my bedsheets. I take two steps back. The image imitates me. I take two steps forward, and we come face-to-face. The image there is a source of light, and I am a deep pit of sadness. I'm fat, heavy, and she is slender and well kept. The color of her skin is similar to mine. Whose image is it that hypnotizes and bewitches me?

"Who are you?" I ask.

"Don't you recognize me? Look closely at me."

"I'm looking. But who are you?"

"You're blind, dear twin."

"Twin? I'm nobody's twin. Of my mother's five children, there are no twins. I'm in front of my mirror. What are you doing there?"

"You're blind, dear twin. Why are you crying?"

I release a whole torrent of complaints. I recount all my unhappiness and tell her that the women of this world are stealing my husband from me.

"Can a living person be stolen, least of all a police chief?"

"In this place, a husband can be stolen."

"Don't be a child, dear twin. He got tired of you and left."

"You're lying!"

I start panicking. The image dances as I sob. I stop crying and remain silent in order to listen to the magical song to which she is dancing. It's my silence I'm listening to. My silence is dancing, making my jealousy, my solitude, my pain, dance as well. My head joins the dance, I feel dizzy. Am I going mad?

"Why are you dancing, dear mirror?"

"I am celebrating love and life. I dance upon life and death. I dance upon sadness and loneliness. I stamp into the ground all the misfortunes that torture me. Dancing frees the mind from life's passing concerns. Dancing is praying. When I dance, I celebrate life while awaiting death. Why don't you dance?"

To dance. To dance to the defeat of my adversary. Dance at my birthday party. Dance upon my enemy's courage. Dance at the funeral of my loved one. Dance round the fire on the eve of a great battle. To dance is to pray. I also want to dance. Life is one big dance.

I attempt to take my companion's hand in mine so that we can dance. She offers me her hand as well, but can't lead me out. Between us there is a cold, icy, glassy barrier. I am heartbroken, and look closely at her. Those cheerful eyes possess my traits. The contours of her body remind me of my own. That inner strength reminds me of the strength I once had and lost. The image isn't of me, but of what I was and want to be again. The image is me, that's true, but in another dimension.

I try to kiss her face. I can't reach it. So I kiss her lips, and the lips taste of ice and glass. Ah, the mirror is my confidante. Ah, my strange mirror. My revealing mirror. We have lived together ever since I got married. Why are you only now revealing your power?

2

I awaken in the vain hope of receiving a little nugget of affection, but the sun has abandoned me and gone on its way. My beloved is as fleeting as the sun's shade. I'm a vanquished woman, my wings are broken. Vanquished? No. I have never fought a battle. I laid down my arms long before I could brandish them. I have always placed myself in life's hands. Given in to fate. I've never lifted so much as a finger to make things go according to my wishes. But have I ever wished for anything?

My life is a dead river. The waters of my river have stopped in time and wait for destiny to bring them the strength of the wind. In my river, the ancestors don't dance to the beat of the drum on moonlit nights. I'm a river without a soul, I don't know whether I have lost it or whether I ever had one. I am lost, imprisoned in mortal solitude.

God, help me to discover the soul and strength of my river. So that the waters may flow, the mill wheels turn, nature pulsate. So as to bring to my bed the light of all the stars in the firmament and allow the rainbow to immerse me in all its vastness.

I'm a river. Rivers find a way around all obstacles. I want to release the pent-up rage of all these years of silence. I want to explode with the wind and restore the fire to my bed. Today I want to exist.

I wake up inspired. Today I want to change my world. Today I want to do what all the women in this land do. Isn't it true that love must be fought for? Well, today I want to fight for mine. I shall wield all my weapons and face the enemy, in defense of my love. I want to touch the soul of all the stones that lie in my path. I want to kiss the sand, grain by grain, that binds the fertile soil where my bed lies. I close my ears to the world and listen only to the flow of my waters. I listen to the intermittent sound of fine rain falling on the glass.

I think a lot about this woman Julieta, or Juliana. She's a pretty woman, so people say. She's had a lot of children by my husband, Tony, I don't know how many. It's a solid, stable second home. Macabre ideas rush through my mind. I suddenly feel like boiling up a pot of oil and pouring it over the face of this woman Julieta or Juliana, to get rid of her. I feel like resorting to blows, like a fishwife. I pray. I pray with all my heart that this woman will die and go to hell. But she doesn't die, and there's no sign of the romance coming to an end. As long as she's alive, I'll never have my husband to myself, and I don't want to share him with her. A husband isn't a loaf of bread to be cut with a bread knife, a slice for each woman. Only Christ's body can be squeezed into drops the size of the world, in order to satisfy all the believers in their communion of blood.

I have a leisurely bath. I have a good meal to give myself energy. I leave the house and walk along, splashing freely along the rain-soaked streets. I get to 15th Street and stop in front of number 20. I make some initial comparisons. My house is one of the nicest places in the world. Full of open spaces. A fresh, abundant grassy lawn. Flowers for every season of the year. But this house is even better. It was built with my husband's money, which is why it's mine. This woman is imitating me and trying to be better than me. I'm furious as I ring the doorbell.

During the brief moment I wait, I wonder what I'm doing there. Julieta or Juliana appears before me. She tries desperately to hold her nerve. She looks at me, quivering with terror as if she had come face-to-face with a snake. She feels her home has been invaded and there's no way of avoiding this meeting. She is aware it's a settling of scores, that she always knew she'd have to face one day. She invites me to come in, and I do so without ceremony. She's plump, my God – I find this irritating – the bitch is well fed at my husband's expense. While she holds her breath, I mumble some excuse for the visit.

"Do I call you Julieta or Juliana?"

"Julieta. How can I help you?"

"I'm looking for my husband."

I go through the house room by room, I rummage around without asking permission, the house is my husband's and therefore mine, I'm his legal spouse, our contract signed and sealed, and in the registry office. I look everywhere, and I see elegance and luster. This house has wider windows, more beautiful windowpanes that allow the fresh air to circulate. I realize that this house is far better than mine, my God, this house makes me incandescent with anger. What was Tony thinking when he had this house built? What did they think of me when they submitted the plans for this house? And where did the money come from to build and then furnish this house? As far as I can see, the power of forbidden love is in full flower. All this ostentation has an air of falseness for me, as false as the love that built this house. I weigh things up at a glance. I want to find out from Julieta what it is she has that I don't. What makes Tony distance himself from me and fall in love with her. She's really pretty, I can see that, but for God's sake, no matter how pretty she is, she has no right to take my husband away from me.

I look at the wall. A photo hanging there makes me even more furious. It's she and Tony, arm in arm, smiling for all the world to see. Their eyes seem to be staring at me, mocking me. In my house, Tony doesn't like photos on show. A portrait on the wall is for the dead, he says, but he allows this woman to do what is forbidden to me.

"Have you managed to find your husband?"

She addresses me from the topmost tower of her cathedral, given that she is more loved than I am. I suffer, I almost die, as if she were sliding a steel scissor blade into my heart. Do you know what it's like to be addressed so haughtily by the person who has stolen your husband? I'm not going to allow myself to cringe before a weeping thief, I can't do that. She's a woman and so am I. I've got fire in my body, and it's too bad I'm going to give vent to it. I'm going to get to the bottom of things and settle this score by hook or by crook.

"So what about that picture there?" I ask.

"What about it?"

"What's it doing there?"

"What right have you to ask that question?"

I look at my rival in the eye. I see in this woman's face the death of my love, the cause of my pain. It's because of this that I feel so lonely. She bewitched my husband in order to take him away from me. But I'm not going to abandon him to her embrace, oh no. I feel the bile rising from deep inside me. I feel sick. The party's only starting.

First round. There are tempestuous explosions of rage. I hurl all the terms of abuse in the world at her. No one can stand my saber-like tongue. I surprise myself by screaming insults I have never used before. Obscenities pour from my mouth that I was never aware of before. She retaliates and the game begins. *Second round.* I throw a punch at my rival. I jump on her, pull her nose, and she is overwhelmed by the shock. She reacts and defends herself with a superhuman force that comes from some unknown place within her. I up my game and deliver some hearty blows like those you see in kung fu films. My body is heavy and my movements sluggish. My rival is lighter and more agile. She scratches me, rips my clothes off, tears me, bites me, punches me. *Third round.* I defend myself well, I tear her wig off and scratch her face. *Fourth round.* I get the feeling I'm losing the fight. I retreat into the street. My adversary chases after me, knocks me over, and we roll around in the puddles while the rain falls on us. She digs her nails into my neck and almost strangles me. Her children unleash deafening screams of alarm. I begin to panic. I feel as if I'm going to die, I start to scream, begging her to let me go. I manage to break free. *Fifth round.* Help! This woman's killing me! As I'm trying to run away, I'm hit by a bottle in the neck. I see stars in the overcast sky. *Sixth round.* I went to war and lost the fight. I faint.

Women leave their houses and come to the rescue. The neighborhood administrator turns up and separates us. I try to explain myself. I stutter. A large lump appears on my forehead. On my shoulders, there are gaping wounds shedding blood. My whole body is covered in mud. On my lips, the stubborn question:

"Where's my husband?"

"If he's yours, you should know where he is."

I'm in such a pitiful state that I can't go anywhere as I am. Julieta takes me inside. She gives me a warm bath. She dresses my wounds. She chooses her best clothes and dresses me like a princess. She washes and combs my hair. She's got a big heart, this woman.

She leads me to the sitting room and we sit facing each other. I take her in. She has neat, painted nails. Well-kept, uncrimped hair, things I never had. Tony forbids me from wearing any embellishments or artificial adornments. He wants me just as God put me in the world. The clothes she wears were made by a carefully chosen dressmaker while I only wear factory-made or secondhand clothes. I rummage through bundles of used clothes in the market on the corner in order to dress the whole family decently and to save money. She has an audaciously plunging neckline, with her armpits on show, while Tony wants me dressed and buttoned up like a nun. What is forbidden for me, the other woman is allowed. I am offended by this contradiction.

We begin to talk. Coldly. Delicately. My rival opens herself up and tells me her long story. Her bed is as cold as mine. She's even lonelier than I am. She has five children and a sixth on the way.

"How did it all happen?" I ask.

"He wooed me when I was a young girl," she replies without beating about the bush, tears in her eyes. "He told me he was single. It was only when I became pregnant that he told me he had a wife and child. But he immediately made a point of telling me he'd been forced to marry and was waiting for an opportunity

< 28 >

to get a divorce. He made wonderful promises. The years passed. I saw my children born one by one, and each time he would renew his promises of marriage.

I am touched. Remorseful. I pity this woman who did everything to destroy me and ended up abandoned. A woman who fought for love and ended up in pain. Who pointed up into the air and declared that the bird in full flight was hers.

"How long is it since you last saw him?"

"Seven months."

"?!"

"Ever since I became pregnant, seven months ago."

"That means . . ."

"Yes, he only comes here to answer the call of the divine creator. To seed my belly, in order to fill the earth and multiply."

"Ah!"

God fashioned man and woman in one gesture, but the birth of humanity was completed in the same act. In the first stage, man places the shape of the woman's head on her. Then he places in her the shape of her heart, her race, her arms, feet, and over the course of months he completes her body block by block. Poor Julieta! She's got her head in her belly and no longer has anyone to put her ears, mouth, and nose on her. Her poor child will be born a monster, without eyes, hands, or feet.

"Why is he doing this to you?"

"He only comes to leave me money and food. He has a bath, changes clothes, and goes."

My rival descends from her pedestal, closes her eyes, and bows her head. From the depths of her being, tears flow in a cascade like acid rain. Poor Julieta, what did she expect? Did she think she was better than me? Sadly, many of us women act like that. We climb to the top of the mountain and only when we're up there do we realize we don't have wings to fly. We throw ourselves from the heavenly heights and fall into a dark, bottomless well, and our hearts break like a porcelain vase. I pity Julieta, who shakes in violent convulsions to the rhythm of her weeping. I give her a hug. I know the bitterness of such crying and the heat of such fire. I'm moved. I sympathize.

Crying has a miraculous effect, for it sweeps away all trials and tribulations. I say nothing and allow her frantic tears to exercise their miraculous effect. Then I comfort her. I suffer with her. Poor thing, she is more of a victim than a rival. She was pursued and betrayed like me.

"We're together in this tragedy. Me, you, all women. All I want is for you to understand why I was so angry. I know I was wrong to attack you. I transferred all my pains onto you, even though I knew you weren't the guilty party."

"I understand," she tells me, her head bowed.

"But," I ask, "if he's not here, where is he, then?"

"In the arms of a third one, perhaps."

"A third one?"

"Yes, a third woman."

"Is that possible?"

"Younger than both of us. More beautiful, so they say."

"Do you know her?"

"Yes. I've come to blows with her a few times."

"But… Julieta, how can you come to blows over a husband that isn't even yours?"

"So what's the meaning of the word yours, when we're talking about men?"

This produces a moment's pause, which is solemn, profound. We challenge each other, eye to eye. Julieta shows me a truth more bitter than a cup of poison. Possession is one of the many illusions of our existence, because human beings are born and will die empty handed. Everything we think we have, life lends us for only a short time. Your child is yours when he's in your womb. Your child is yours when you suckle him. Even the money we have in the bank, we only touch it for a short time. A kiss is a mere touch and a hug lasts only a minute. The sun is yours, from up there, high above. The sea is yours. Night. The stars. Every being is born alone, on their day, at their time, and comes into the world empty handed. I think about what I have. Nothing, absolutely nothing. My love isn't reciprocated. I feel pain and yearning for a husband who is always away. Anxiety. To have is ephemeral, the never-ending illusion of possessing the intangible. Yours is what you were born with. Yours is your husband when he's inside you.

"We're fighting because we've got things in common, see?" she says.

"No, we don't," I reply. "I have to acknowledge you are younger and prettier. That you've suffered more. For Tony to leave me and to love you, you must really be better than I am."

I am really touched. This woman's anguish is far worse than mine. At least I experienced dreams and was led to the altar. My husband was always by me each time I gave birth to our five children. I even had the pleasure of insulting him and blaming him for all the pains I felt while being delivered of his children. Julieta was deceived from the start. There's nothing worse than eternal frustration.

"That's where you're wrong. Women are different in name and in their physical appearance. But for the rest, they're all the same. Just look. He deceived you and he deceived me. When he's not here, I think he's with you and vice versa. He told you he loved you. He told me he loved me. Here we are like two prisoners fighting over the same man. Lord! He said such wonderful things to me. And what came of it all? He stuffed me full of children and then left."

My conscience weighs like lead. A feeling of sympathy springs from my silence. Through the open window, I see the gray sky and feel dizzy. I quiver with pity, sadness, and shame. All women are twins, solitary, with no prospect of dawn or springtime. We seek our treasure in mines that have already been worked and are exhausted, and we end up ghosts amid the ruins of our dreams.

"Julieta, I ask you to forgive me, to forgive me a thousand times over."

I leave 15th Street in a taxi. I'm full of bandages and swelling, and I'm dressed in my rival's clothes. I creep furtively into my

< 33 >

home like a thief. I have a terrible headache. What happened? My children ask, and I tell them I slipped in the mud, and I hurry to my room to change my clothes. I rush to the mirror and see what a sorry state I'm in. The hiding I got has quelled my anguish. I no longer yearn for Tony. He can stay wherever he is until my wounds have healed. The farther away, the better. The image in the mirror appears again and laughs.

"Mirror, mirror of mine, look what they've done to me!"

"You deserve what they did to you, my friend."

"Do you think what I did was bad?"

"You assaulted the victim and left the villain unharmed. You didn't solve anything."

"Ah!"

I take an aspirin and put a bag of ice on my forehead to lessen the swelling. I sit down carefully in the chair, and take a deep breath. Wow! That was some beating I got! All this turmoil began with that business over Betinho. Shattered glass is a bad omen, so the popular saying goes.

I sing my favorite song to ward off my loneliness. A desire to leave everything behind begins to well up inside me. To get a divorce. Smash this home to smithereens. Maybe find a new love.

But no. I can't let Tony go. If I leave him, other women will sleep in this bed, I'm not getting out of here. If I get a divorce, my husband will marry Julieta or some other woman, there's no point in leaving. If I go, my children will be raised by others, they'll eat the bread made by the devil, I can't leave.

3

Tony is snoring like a toad, I don't know what came over him today to come and sleep here. He's right next to me, but more distant than the clouds on the horizon. He fell asleep without speaking to me. When I ask him something, he mumbles yes or no and says nothing else. He's as impenetrable as a rock, inviolable as a rampart. As far as I am concerned, he has neither soul nor breath, he doesn't talk, he doesn't sigh or show any sign of life at all. When I wake him up to talk, he opens one eye, groans, turns over, and snores. It's like having a corpse in my bed. A heap of flesh. A jellyfish, a sea cucumber, a monster. He's like a pile of jelly, stirring viscously in my bed. I shudder.

A mysterious voice deep within addresses me in all seriousness. It conveys a saturnine, diabolical message: Get your revenge, he's in your hands, as still as a corpse, get your revenge. Knock him over the head with a saucepan. A stone. Give him a punch. Stab him in the . . . ! In despair, I pray. Away with you, bad thought, away! Go to hell where all evil dwells, go, I don't want my hands stained by your violence.

My bad thoughts get the better of me, I can't resist them, I wake him up quickly before disaster strikes.

"Tony. Answer me. Why are you never here?"

"Is that all you woke me up for?"

"Tony, you're betraying me, aren't you?"

"Betraying?"

"Yes."

"Ah!"

I summon up all my courage and tell him everything that's on my mind: I talk about how I miss him, about my anxiety. About his continual absences, which make the household ungovernable because of the lack of a man's firmness. He growls like a dog and puts on an angry face. My nerves get the better of me and I accuse him. I tell him about the fights I've been involved in, the wounds, the treatment at the clinic. I was expecting an angry reaction, shouting, a row, a slap. But he turns over the other way, pulls the blanket over himself, and tries to go back to sleep. He's embarrassed.

"Betrayal is a crime, Tony!"

"Betrayal? Don't make me laugh! Purity is masculine, sin is female. Only women can betray, men are free, Rami."

"What?"

"Please, let me sleep."

"But Tony," I shake him furiously. "Tony, wake up, Tony, Tony, Tony…!"

He's not listening. He's snoring. He's able to sleep peacefully, while I'm left in this quandary. Bastard! Miserable, unfeeling wretch! Tyrant! I get out of bed and sit on the settee, just to watch him. He's smiling. He's dreaming. Where is his mind wandering in his dreams? He looks as if he's deep under the sea. Among the cracks between the coral. In some marine paradise full of love, in a happier world than this one. Is he in the arms of Julieta, or of some other love I know nothing about? I am vexed. My Tony, where do you go when sleep takes you? You travel alone and in silence. Why don't you take me with you? Tony sighs and interrupts my thoughts. I watch him closely. He sighs like someone in love. Then he screeches and shouts, he's calling someone's name. I listen carefully. He's dreaming of a woman. He's sighing over a woman. I look at the clock. It's just past midnight. He awakens confused and speaks as if answering a call from another world. He dresses hurriedly as if he were sleepwalking.

"Tony, where are you going? Tony!"

This recurring dream leaves me frantic. I've consulted witch doctors who've given me extraordinary accounts of love charms made by other women. They told me of other love affairs and other tragedies. I didn't believe any of them. My neighbors tell me of *mudjiwas*, wives or husbands from another world who, in previous lives or incarnations, were our spouses, and have returned to reclaim their rights in the present life. My mother told me about this only once, and my father never spoke a word about it. I begin to panic. Tony, my dear husband, my beautiful man, can it be that you've got a *mudjiwa*? Or am I the one with a *mudjiwa*, and that's why you no longer love me? My dearest Tony, there's a woman who steals you away while you sleep. I am a faithful woman, believe me. I'm a virgin, I'm innocent, you are the only man in my life.

"Tony, what's happening?"

"I'm going somewhere I can sleep in peace."

I want to beg him to stay. Ask him to forgive me for waking him. I want to show him how sorry I am for having offended him in his freedom. I manage to open my mouth and let out a muffled whisper. It's too late. He rushes out of the house, jumps in his car, and disappears into the night.

4

Dear God, save me. Give me your advice. Protect me. Tell me what love is according to your doctrine. Dear God, in this world love doesn't work like mathematics. It doesn't operate in accordance with statistical or even supernatural formulae. Love, like the weather, is whimsical. One day it's cold. The next hot, and the one after that, there's wind and rain. In matters of love, one day's solution is no use the next day. In my case, the advice of friends is of no use at all. My urgent desire to transform this love lures me dangerously toward paths I have never trodden before. I, a married woman for the last twenty-five years, mother of five children, an experienced woman, have been doing the rounds, sounding out all and sundry on the best way to keep my husband. My mother gives me lectures full of lamentation. My aged aunts repeat ancient litanies. Some of my friends tell me about potions made from vegetables. Others, made from animals. Yet others tell me of spiritual activities, with drums, candles, and prayers. Others even tell me of love therapies carried out in churches

< 41 >

specializing in miracles. Others recommend consultations with university-trained psychologists, who provide sessions devoted to love. And yet others tell me of subterfuges. My head is full of advice, revelations, and secrets given me by women of all ages. My next-door neighbor insists on taking me to see her medicine man, but I preferred to enroll in a course run by an exceedingly famous love counselor who lives downtown in a hidden location. I'm going to have my first lesson today.

I have a bath and get ready to go out. I try on a skirt but it won't stay up, and slips to the floor. I go to the wardrobe and try on all my clothes, only to discover that I've grown thin. I won't be able to avoid the gossips who'll say I've lost weight because I'm jealous, all because of a man who doesn't care for me at all. I walk over to the mirror and open my heart.

"Tell me, mirror: Am I by any chance ugly? Am I by any chance more sour than a mandarin lime? Why does my husband leave me here to go and seek other women? What have the others got that I haven't?"

The mirror answers mutely and smiles.

"Come on, answer me, mirror."

My mirror gives me a mischievous reply:

"Ah! My fat friend!"

"No! Don't you think I've slimmed down a bit?"

"Yes, you're thinner."

"Thank God I didn't need special teas or diets."

"See how good your husband is? The heartbreak he's caused has worked wonders, and you've grown slimmer. Let's hope this heartbreak eats away at you for another month. You'll be more graceful than a film star. How good it would be if all fat women had husbands who broke their hearts."

I'm the one laughing now. This mirror's crazy. My life is crazy enough as it is, and along comes this mirror to make me still crazier.

"Oh, mirror of mine, what do you think of me? Do you think I should start all over again?"

"Of course, start over. But before that, get a broom and sweep away all the trash you've got in your heart. Sweep away the madness you've got in your mind, sweep it all away, everything. Free yourself. Only then will you have the happiness you deserve."

"Tell me, dear mirror: Where did I go wrong? Will I one day be happy, with my husband surrounded by all these women?"

"Think carefully, my friend: Are these other women to blame for the situation? Are men innocent?"

I abandon the mirror, which is distracting me with useless thoughts.

"Today, I'm going to the first lesson in love that I've ever had in my life."

I arrive for my class at exactly the right time. My love counselor is waiting for me, seated on a large velvet sofa. She greets me with a proud, self-assured, and sensuous tone of voice from the dizzy height of her throne. Cood borning. Velcome. Tank gyou por choossing dis school. She's from the north, this love counselor is a Makua. I don't laugh, but smile and return her greeting. Good morning and thank you for accepting me as your student.

She invites me to sit down opposite her. We look at each other. We weigh each other up. She's almost my age. Tall. Sturdy. Fat even. Fatter than I am. The flesh of her backside fills the sofa, spilling over like a hoard of treasure. She stretches her arms out along the back of the sofa to give her armpits an airing, completely at ease with herself. In matters of love, she's up there on high. I envy her. She knows all about love. She must have experienced everything, tried it all, and knows all there is to know. She can distinguish between a happy woman and a frustrated woman at a mere glance. She wears a huge, golden yellow tunic. On her head, she wears a turban that has been placed there artistically like a queen's crown. She wears gold, a lot of gold. She looks like the Queen of Sheba – the books reveal a Queen of Sheba that's skinny and without curves, a body in the European taste, but African queens are fat, for they are as well nourished with love as they are with food.

We begin the class with a few trivialities: we talk about the weather, our children, Christmas, which is near. This woman has a magnetic aura about her that I find attractive. She is a monument to triumph over love. She must be one of those women who attract love and kill all men who approach them with desire. And she talks like someone singing. She moves like someone dancing. She breathes like someone sighing, dear God, everything about her is love. I'm prettier than she is, but she has something alluring that I don't have.

Then we begin to focus on the first serious question. She asks me about my problems. I look down and don't answer. It's humiliating to talk to a stranger about intimate things. It's as if I were delivering myself to a priest in the confession box in order for him to absolve me of my sins as if he had none himself. This woman wants to console others in their pain as if she could console herself in her own pain.

"My friend," she convinces me, "if love had a price, I guarantee that each of us would buy it in bulk, to use and to keep in our grain-store. In matters of love, there's no shame. Rich people and poor people seek me out every day. And the richest are those who seek me the most. They're rich in terms of money, but poor in love. Love doesn't have a price."

In spite of her words, I don't answer. So we continue our small talk. We talk about traditions and cultures. And she tells me stories of love from the Makua. Love and wooing in her village. Rites of passage.

"How did you prepare for your marriage?"

"I began my trousseau when I was fifteen," I explain. "I embroidered doilies. I made coverlets and tablecloths in crochet. Tablecloths with embroidery in flower stitch, chicken-foot stitch, cross-stitch, Yugoslavian stitch, chain stitch. I did a course in cookery and knitting."

"I was raised in the country and wasn't acquainted with things like embroidery and trousseaus. Tell me, how did you prepare yourself on the eve of your marriage?"

"I had classes at church with the priests and nuns. I lit a lot of candles and said a lot of prayers."

"And what did your family teach you?"

"They talked to me about obedience, about motherhood."

"And what about sexual love?"

"No one told me anything about that."

"Then you're not a woman," she tells me disdainfully. "You're still a child. How can you be happy in marriage if a life lived together is based on love and sex, and no one ever taught you anything about the subject?"

I look at her in surprise. Suddenly, I recall that famous assertion – *no one is born a woman, you become one.* Where was it that I first heard that pronouncement?

"I went through the first rites of passage from adolescence to young adulthood. I went through the second rites between being betrothed and being married. During the rites of adolescence, they treated my skin with *musiro* paste. During the rites of my betrothal, they treated my skin with honey."

"Honey on your skin?"

"Yes, pure honey without any other mixture. It makes the skin smoother than the shell of an egg. They smothered my body with it a few days before my marriage."

We spend some time comparing the cultural habits of the

north and the south. We talk about the taboos surrounding menstruation that prevent a woman from taking part in public life throughout the country, from north to south. About taboos surrounding eggs, which women cannot eat so that they won't have bald children and so that they won't behave like egg-laying hens as they give birth. About the myths that turn young girls into domestic servants and turn men away from the pestle, the fire, and the kitchen in order not to catch sexual diseases such as sterility and impotence. About the table manners that oblige women to serve their husbands the best pieces of meat, while they make do with the bones, feet, wings, and neck. The myths that blame women for all of nature's disasters. When it doesn't rain, it's their fault. When there are floods, it's their fault. When there are plagues and illnesses, it's the fault of those who sat down on the pestle, or who aborted in secret, who ate an egg or the gizzard of some chicken, who went out into the fields when they were having a period.

Women in the south think those in the north are free and easy, and deceitful. Northern women think those in the south are feeble and frigid. In some regions of the north, the man says: My dear friend, to honor our friendship and to strengthen our ties of kinship, sleep with my wife tonight. In the south, the man says: Woman is my cattle, my fortune. She must be led to pasture with a cane. In the north, women adorn themselves like flowers, make themselves beautiful, look after themselves. In the north, a woman is a source of light and should be the source of the world. In the north, women are light and can fly. Their harmonious voices utter sounds that are sweeter and gentler than birdsong. In the south, women wear sad, gloomy colors. Their expression is forever angry, tired, and they shout when they speak as if they were imitating the crash of thunder. They tie a scarf round their head with neither skill nor beauty, as if they were securing a bundle of firewood. They wear clothes because they can't go around naked. They dress without taste. With no elegance. No skill. Their body is merely for reproduction.

When a man from the south sees a woman from the north, he goes crazy. Because she's beautiful, a *mthiana orera*, polished. Because she knows how to love, she knows how to smile, and to please. When a northern woman sees a man from the south, she goes crazy because he's strong and he's got money. A northern man also loves a southern woman because he's servile. A woman from the south loves a northern man because he's gentler, more sensitive, and doesn't mistreat her physically. A southern woman is a saver, she doesn't spend any money, and buys just one new dress a year. The northern woman spends a lot on lace, cloth, gold, creams, because she needs to be permanently beautiful. It's the story of never-ending envy. The north admiring the south, the south admiring the north. It has a logical explanation. A popular saying claims that one's neighbor's wife is always better than one's own.

"Did you attend rites of initiation?" the counselor asks.

"No," I explain, "my father is an out-and-out Christian, and apart from that the colonial regime was much stronger in the south than in the north."

"So that means no one spoke to you about anything before you came of age?"

"I attended other schools," I explain.

"I'm talking about the schools of love and of life."

"I never attended any of those."

"You really are a child then. You're not yet a woman."

"So what do you learn in those rituals that make you feel more womanly than we do?"

"Many things: We learn about love, seduction, motherhood, society. We teach the basic philosophies of how to live together in harmony. How can you expect to have a happy home if you haven't been given the basic lessons in love and sex? Upon your initiation, you learn to get to know the treasure that lies within you. The purple flower that multiplies into innumerable petals, producing all the beneficial qualities that exist in the universe. The initiation rites enable you to live with a smile. You learn to acquaint yourself with anatomy and all the stars that gravitate within you. You learn the rhythm of all the heartbeats deep inside you."

"People only have one heart."

"Women have two. A main one and a secondary one. Sometimes she has three, when she has a child in her womb."

"Are these rituals really so important?"

"Without them, you're as light as the wind. You're the one who travels far without first traveling deep inside your own self. You can't get married, for no one will accept you. And if he accepts you, he'll abandon you straightaway. You can never attend a funeral, much less approach a dead body, because you are immature. Nor can you be present at a birth. You can't make the arrangements for a wedding. That's because you are impure. Because you're nothing, only an eternal child."

I'm left feeling a little uneasy. This woman says I'm not a woman. What is it she knows that I don't know? I conceal my indignation and speak. I tell her some of Tony's history, his infidelities, his concubines, and all my lonely nights.

The conversation makes me more and more angry, and I begin to talk about all the things that hurt me so that she may understand. I tell her I always fulfilled my role as a wife: I've washed his underpants, darned his socks, stitched the buttons back on his shirts. When he leaves the house all fine and dandy, someone turns up and takes him away, all of him, leaving me with just his underpants to wash. Why can't she take him away completely, once and for all?

"Don't blame the other women for your failure. Just like you, they were conquered and answered their bodily call. A man's desires are God's desires. No one can deny them."

I take a good look at this woman. She's mad. She's a complete charlatan. She's the hook, ready to fish up the money from people like me who are at their wits' end.

"I don't understand."

"The solution is to make him only have eyes for you and not look at others."

"How? Am I supposed to deprive him of his eyesight?"

"Why not? Life is all about sharing. We share a blanket on a cold day. We share our warmth with a dying man in the hour of his peril. Why can't we share a husband? We lend money, food, and clothing. Sometimes we even give our life to save someone. Don't you think it's easier to lend a husband or a wife out than it is to sacrifice one's life?"

Cultures are invisible frontiers constructing the fortress of the world. In some regions of northern Mozambique, love is shared. One shares one's wife with a friend, with a trusted visitor, with one's brother in circumcision. A wife is water that is offered the traveler, the visitor. Making love is a footprint in the ocean's sandy shore that the waves erase. But it leaves its mark. One family alone may be a mosaic of skin colors and races depending on the type of visitors the family receives, because woman represents fertility. That's why in many regions, children receive the mother's family name. In human reproduction, only the mother is a certainty. In the south, the situation is completely different. A husband only gives his wife to his brother in circumcision when he's infertile.

In primitive practices, solidarity is shown by sharing one's bread, blanket, and semen. I'm a modern woman. I prefer to give my life and blood to whoever needs it. I can give everything, but not my man. He's neither bread nor cake. I'm not sharing him, I'm selfish.

I embark on a voyage through time. Harems with two thousand wives. Rulers with forty women. Wives betrothed before they're even born. Social contracts. Alliances. Women bought and sold. Marriages of convenience. Daughters sold to increase their parents' wealth or to pay gambling debts. Sex slaves. Married off at the age of twelve. My memory extends to the beginning of all beginnings. In the Bantu paradise, God created an Adam. Various Eves. And a harem. Whoever wrote the Bible omitted certain facts about the genesis of polygamy. The Bantus should rewrite their Bible.

We talk about male initiation. I tell her my Tony never attended any school for initiation, at which point she declares:

"Your husband is also not a man, but merely a child."

"A child, my Tony? That's not possible. How can you dare dismiss my husband like that?"

She explains the first lesson of male initiation to me:

"The first principle is this: Treat your wife as you do your own mother. The moment you close your eyes and plunge into her flight, she becomes your creator, the true mother of the whole universe. Every woman is the personification of motherhood, whether she's your wife, your concubine, or even a prostitute. Man should thank God for all the color and light woman gives, for without her, life wouldn't exist. A true man doesn't raise his hand to his mother, his goddess, his creator."

"But that's in the north," I remind her. "I'm from here, from the south."

Of all the things I've learned today, I like this lesson the best. Because marriage should be a relationship without any wars. Because I've received many a slap in my life. Because a peaceful home is made without violence. Because a man who beats his wife destroys his own love. I place my hand upon my conscience and am shaken by a thread of remorse: Why did I attack Julieta?

We talk now about colors. She tells me all men are creatures. Butterflies. Insects. They are seduced by the breeze, by a rainbow, by anything from which color and light emanate.

"Red attracts buffaloes, bulls. Ripe fruit attracts the hunger and greed of all birds. Flowers attract the eyes of all human beings.

The secret of seduction lies in color. Imitate nature and dress like a flower in order to attract the gaze of all and stimulate hidden desires.

"Man is a creature susceptible to sounds. In the murmur of the pine trees, he sleeps and dreams. In the rustling of the palms, he finds ecstasy. He finds enchantment in birdsong. In the wafting of a flute, he feels elated. In the hissing of a snake, he is alarmed. Set your sonorous trap. Make your flute play a voice that lulls, softly, whisperingly, slow and melodious. From those pines, take the divine murmur that will help him rest from his fatigue. If you hiss loudly like a snake, you'll scare your prey away.

"Man is an elephant. Majestic. But an elephant is attracted to an ant. A large eye is always charmed by something small. Don't try to be big, be small. Very small, almost microscopic, but astute and aware so as to attack the vital points. Be the bacterium that causes man to sway in the dance of an itchy skin. Be the virus that causes a great man to shiver to the rhythm of a fever. Be yourself. Natural. An adult surrenders enchanted before a child's smile.

"Man is a javelin. The tip of a spear. Man is a line without end, as straight as a die. Man is a bullet that wounds space on its way to conquer the world. Straight lines join the heavens to the ground, extending to the very end of the horizon. Let man be the end, for you are the beginning.

"Woman is a curved line. Curved are the movements of the sun and the moon. Curved is the movement of the wooden spoon in the clay pot. Curved is the position adopted in repose. Have you noticed how all animals curl up when they sleep? We women are a river of deep and shallow curves over each part of our body. Curves move things round in a circle. Man and woman are united in one sole curve in the meanderings of our paths. Curved are our lips and our kisses. The uterus is curved. The egg. The celestial dome. Curves enclose all the secrets of the world.

"Not to have love isn't a question of fate, but a disaster. Learn from this lesson of mine. Love is an investment. It is born, dies, and is reborn just like the sun's cycle. Look here, never say I didn't teach you. Love is a taper that has been lit, and it's up to you to keep the flame going. The rest is all trickery, my pretty one. Techniques. Knacks. Everything in life is mortal, everything comes to an end. If your flame is extinguished, the fault lies in you. Do what I say, and no amount of magic will ever defeat you in life. You are the epitome of bewitchment and you shouldn't seek any other magic. A woman's body is magic. Strength. Weakness. Salvation.

Perdition. The entire universe can be contained in a woman's curves."

My fear of losing Tony is temporarily thwarted. These classes are attuned to my hopes like a velvet blanket. I feel as if a huge veil is falling away from in front of my eyes, while tiny secrets fill my soul like dewdrops. This woman is like the morning star as far as I am concerned. I'm being reborn, I'm growing, rejuvenating. Her voice penetrates me like the gurgling of spring water. She is a refreshing breeze.

"Nature favors us, she's our sister, our confidante. Dress in the colors of the flowers, of the sky, the wind, and the entire firmament. Seek out the soul of precious stones and make a pact with them. Gold, silver, pearls, diamonds, rubies, emeralds, topaz. Learn the secret of their contrasts. A really dark black with very white teeth is a fatal attraction. You are a nice dark black woman. Wear plenty of gold to make your black hue shine. Wear ivory."

I'm completely won over. No one dominates a man better than a seductress in vampish colors. A wild bull is hunted using red. In love, there are neither big issues nor small. The polish on a fingernail can capture a man's heart. An eyelash. A contrasting shadow in the corner of an eye. Smooth skin. A soft voice. One's toes.

We talk of gentle hands in a relaxing caress. Of techniques to soften the skin with the white mask made of *musiro* paste. We pause for a moment to discuss contradictions. In southern culture, it's said that smooth skin is as slippery as a catfish, and men don't like it. It's no coincidence that women of an older generation have thick tattoos on their hips, their belly, their breasts, and their face, to make their skin wrinkled and palatable. We agree: sensuality is a cultural matter.

I was introduced to how eyes express love. The eyes of a cat. A snake. Eyes that draw you in. Sensual eyes. There are no ugly women in the world, according to the counselor. Love is blind. There are only different women.

She insists on the principle of pleasing your man.

"If you want a man, captivate him through the kitchen and in bed," she says. "There are male foods and there are female foods. When it comes to chicken, women eat the feet, the wings, and the neck. Men are served the thighs. And the gizzard."

"Chicken gizzard? In the north as well?" I ask, full of curiosity.

"Yes, in the north too."

"How funny. I would never have imagined it."

"In the north, the business of the gizzard sometimes produces conflict between couples that may end in violence and even divorce."

"Wow! It's like that in the south as well. This tradition must be resisted."

"Challenged? Changed? What for? As far as I'm concerned, I think it should be maintained, because it's a good bit of bait. A man is vanquished through his gluttony. If you want to make some love magic, make it with what they like most. The gizzard."

An ironic smile comes to my lips. In matters of food, there's no north and south. All men are greedy and they only invent myths relating to meat, fish, and eggs. There are no myths about cabbages and lettuces. Occasionally, you get myths involving beans and rice, money-producing crops. Men are all the same. We laugh heartily together.

"When you think about it," the teacher says, "what's in a gizzard? Women can well do without it, even if they can die from it as well."

"Could it be that a gizzard has some aphrodisiac power?"

"Not at all. It's merely a chosen piece. And it's not even tasty. At least, I don't like it."

I attended many classes, fifteen in all. I even went to the most secret classes that focused on themes one can't talk about. While in other parts of Africa they carry out the famous so-called female excision, here genitalia are left to drop. Elsewhere, pleasure is repressed, here it's stimulated. My teacher tells me that preparation for love has no age and I believe her.

These classes are my initiation rites. The church and other systems regarded these practices as heresy, and set out to destroy a field of knowledge that they didn't even possess. I review my life. I was thrown into marriage without any preparation at all. I am bitter. I was made to learn things that are of no use whatsoever. I even went to ballet school – just imagine! I learned all these things from European ladies, things such as how to bake fairy cakes, embroider, be well mannered, all things associated with the drawing room. Anything to do with the bedroom? Nothing! The famous sexual education was limited to the study of the reproductive apparatus, and the various cycles. About living together as a couple? Nothing! The books, which were written by priests, invoked gods in every possible position. On a married couple's positions? Nothing! While in the streets, there were pornographic magazines. Between pornography and saintliness, there was nothing! No one ever explained to me why it is that a man exchanges one woman for another. No one ever told me about the origin of polygamy. Why is it that the church prohibited practices that were so important for harmony within the home? Why is it that the generation that brought us freedom raised their fists and shouted, "Down with initiation rites"? Is it a crime to have a school about love? They said these schools encouraged backwardness. And they do. They say they're conservative. And they are. So is the church. So are the universities and formal schools. Instead of destroying the love schools, why not reform them? The colonized man is blind. He destroys what's his and assimilates what's from outside, without seeing his own navel. So what now? There's much pain and disappointment in our country, women lose their husbands because they lack skill in love. People talk about love and they point straightaway at the heart, and that's all. But love involves the heart, the body, the soul, dreams, and hope. Love is the whole universe and that's why neither anatomy nor cardiology has ever managed to indicate on which side of the heart love lies.

During these last few days I have learned some interesting things. Very interesting. Things that can't be talked about woman to woman, but only among students of the academy of love. I learned that initiation rites are a far more important institution than all the other formal and informal institutions put together, and that their secrets are never divulged. I learned the most intimate secrets. Secrets about love and life. Secrets about love and death. Women evince an air of weakness, but they can sting like bees. They can make a man weep with love like a child, until his soul is drained. They can hold a man's life in the palm of their hand, humiliate him until he surrenders breathless, until he gives himself up body and soul, and becomes their slave. Now I understand that swaying but secure gait that northern women have. Now I understand that singing tone of voice, that dormant, reptilian gaze. More than ever before, I now understand why men from all quarters of the world who migrate to the north of this country never again return to their native land. I don't know how or when I shall be able to apply all this knowledge. I'm going to confess a secret to you: I feel like going out and seeking someone upon whom to try out all the lessons I've learned. In my old exhausted marriage, Tony has known me for long enough and is sick of me. He's going to notice a change in my behavior. Even so, I'm going to give it a try. But what a pity I've only learned all this now!

I think I now have a better understanding of why some husbands in the north are submissive, why they transform their wives into queens, and have them go around in rickshaws so that they don't have to tread on the ground and pick up dust. When they go out for their Sunday stroll, some husbands carry their baby and a bag of diapers, so that their wives won't crease their dress. At the end of the month, husbands spend almost all their earnings to buy cloth and gold just to adorn their queens. These women know a lot. They know all about the body's geography. Where the sun resides. They know how to ignite flames and guide men through unknown caverns. They know how to lull a man, make him small, until he seems to be floating once more in his mother's womb.

In the north, without the rites of initiation, you aren't a person, you're lighter than the wind. You can't get married, no one will accept you, and if they do accept you, they'll abandon you straightaway. You can't attend the funeral of your parents or your own children. You can't approach any dead body because you haven't gained maturity, you are still a child. Any child who is accidentally born before the parents have fulfilled the rituals is considered trash, impure, nonexistent. Initiation rites are like baptism for Christians. Without baptism, a human being is a pagan. He has no right to heaven. In the south, a man who doesn't pay the bride price loses his right to paternity and cannot carry out the funeral of his spouse or children. Because he's an inferior being. Because he's less of a man. Children born in a marriage where the bride price hasn't been paid have no homeland. They can't inherit their father's land, much less that of their mother. The children keep the mother's family name. There are men who pay their wives' bride price after these have died, just so that they can give them a dignified funeral. There are men who have paid the bride price for their children and grandchildren, even when these are grown up, just so that they can leave them their inheritance. A woman who hasn't had her bride price paid has no homeland. She is rejected to such an extent that she isn't allowed to step onto her father's land even after death.

The bride price in the south and initiation rites in the north. Strong, indestructible institutions. They resisted colonialism. Christianity and Islam. They resisted revolutionary tyranny.

< 65 >

They will always survive. Because they are the essence, the soul, of the people. Through them, a people affirms itself before the world and demonstrates its will to live according to its own ways.

I got some really brightly colored clothes made in yellow, red, and orange. I put them on and went over to the mirror. I was magnificent. Everything about me spoke of ripened fruit. Cherries, cashews, apples. I was quite simply a temptress. Along came Tony, and his eyes latched on to me. My heart was pumping, dear God, how right the counselor was! The lessons were paying off. Soon he came over to me. He was going to kiss me. Caress my silky skin, softened by the *musiro*. He was going to lead me to the bedroom, where I would put into practice part two of my special classes. He placed his hand on my shoulder, dear God, how right the counselor was! All of a sudden he let me go, took two steps back, and gave me a mocking smile.

"You're so full of color, you look like a butterfly. You look like saffron. Ripe chili pepper. What inspired you to such gaudy tastes?"

< 66 >

I was crestfallen. Everything was going well. I think I overdid the perfume, it was too much, I reckon. Too much perfume is nauseating, even if it's good perfume. But no, it wasn't the perfume, no. It must have been the image of the other woman – the third one, not the second – who broke the spell. I'm left angry about everything. I want to meet this third woman who has driven my husband out of his wits.

I rush to the mirror and spill it all out.

"I dreamed about this moment so much, everything's gone to pieces, what shall I do now, my dear mirror?"

"Where's your fighting spirit, my friend? You've failed today, but you can try again!"

Thank you, dear mirror. Losing a battle isn't losing the war. Tomorrow's another day.

< 67 >

5

I woke up thinking about the third woman, who is driving my husband crazy. Who has turned me into a married woman with an empty bed. Has made the second woman, Julieta, a rejected spinster with a child in her belly. I would so like to meet this third woman, who has so much honey inside her, not in order to wage war, but to learn from her. I'd like to know what color clothes she wears. The smell of her perfume. The color of her skin. I'd like to know who her tremendous love counselor is. Julieta thought she was so much better than me that she usurped my position, dethroned me, but along came this one, and game over! This third woman was incredible, and avenged my jealousy.

I left home first thing in the morning, spurred on by curiosity to meet this woman, this exceptional artiste. I didn't go seeking her out of malice, as I've already said, but the moment I entered her home, she felt as if she'd been invaded, threatened by my presence, and immediately set about assaulting me physically. We fought. We knocked over everything around us: glasses, dishes, vases, plants, everything was smashed to pieces. I came with good intent, I shouted, alarmed. Get out of my house, she kept saying. You don't own anything, I replied, furious. Everything here is my property, it was bought with the money of my husband, who is mine by right, we were married in both the registry office and the church, and for your information, with full community of property, I replied while suffering the worst hiding of my life. That's where you're wrong, you'll see who's right, screamed my adversary as she dug her nails into my skin, leaving my body with deep scratches. The blows I was suffering were just too much. I decided to get away, I opened the door and ran off down the road. But she chased after me and struck me so many times that I was almost left for dead. Our screaming attracted the neighbors and a lot of onlookers who commented among themselves: Two women fighting in broad daylight? It must be over a man! The men shouted: Sock it to her, punch her, stick one on her. I couldn't understand whether all the shouting was encouragement for me or for her, but she was knocking me about with unusual ferocity.

The police caught us red-handed and took us off to the police station, where we were arrested, charged with causing a public disturbance. We were greeted straightaway at the entrance by a nauseating stench, like some message of welcome. The police had trawled the scum of the earth and got a good catch, the cell was overflowing with outcast women of all types. It was a small cell. Hot. Packed with people. We had to brush against each other's bodies whenever we wanted to move an arm or a leg. Some were robbers. Others had sexually assaulted other women. Others sold drugs, while others still, their consumers, drifted in fantastic dreams. Some had been involved in public disorder, like ourselves. Lying in a corner was a girl who looked about fifteen. She was groaning with pain and fever. She had thrown her newborn baby on the rubbish dump. The heat caused our bodies to stew, showing how putrid human beings are. The place smelled of blood, of childbirth. It smelled of people, of women. Of heat. Those who were menstruating could be smelled from afar like open-air latrines. The place was seething, stinking, nauseating. I prayed to the gods to give me strength to withstand such torture.

As we went in, I took Luísa's hand and trembled. She didn't reject me and also held on to me. We stood there, stuck to each other, paralyzed, while the other women looked at us in surprise. Ours was a private fight and we weren't supposed to end up there. Ah, my love, what paths are you leading me down? My dream of holding on to my husband had thrown me into the hands of the police. Me, Rami, arrested, but who would have thought it? Me, a married woman. A good housewife. Me, an exemplary wife, meek and loving, behind bars. I hadn't even seen to the household chores that day, my children didn't even know where I was, I didn't tell anyone where I was going. All I could think of was how to get out of there and run back to the comfort of my home. While I wept, I shot Luísa a remorseful look.

The officer on duty strolled down the corridor, his shoulders high, like a well-trained policeman. We were desperately awaiting our interrogation that never came, while the sun was reaching its peak. I shouted to the young policeman:

"Officer, come here. Why have I been arrested? Do you know who I am? If my husband finds out you're keeping me prisoner here, there'll be problems, officer. I'm a respectable woman, a married woman."

The policeman looked at me and laughed.

"Married women don't fight in the street."

"I'm a saint, ask anyone who knows me. I never harmed a fly."

"A rowdy saint."

< 72 >

The young policeman answered disdainfully and continued his rounds. When he passed by for a second time, I shouted angrily:

"My husband's your superior, and he'll punish you, just you see."

"Is that so? Who is he, then?"

"My husband is a chief of police and he gives all of you your orders. It's Commander António Tomás. My name is Rosa Maria."

"What?"

The invocation of his superior's name left him perturbed. He gave me a long, suspicious stare from head to foot; prisoners always lie to try to escape justice.

"And so what were you doing in the street?"

"You must understand, my good young man. I got tired of being betrayed, humiliated, scorned. I got tired of going to bed alone. I got tired of being insulted by younger women."

"Is that so?"

"They steal my man and keep him as if he belonged to them."

The young man scrutinized me and seemed to be pondering on something serious. Maybe he was thinking about his job, if I were indeed the person I said I was.

"If your husband leaves you, then it must be that you are embittered and frigid. A man is a man, and has every right to go and seek what he can't get at home."

"Ah, officer!"

"And what are you doing here? A police chief with a wife like you?"

"It happens. That's life."

"I'm going to let you out and you can come and tell me your story while I check your identity. If you're lying, you'll pay double for making false declarations."

The policeman unlocked the cell door and pulled me out. I looked at my rival and felt remorse, given that I had caused the fight. I told the policeman: "This woman is with me."

"Who is she?"

"My husband's other woman."

I felt a huge resentment as I uttered these words, but I had to save her because I had caused this disaster after all.

He looked at us both and laughed.

"Now I understand everything!" He pulled Luísa out of the cell. "Get out of here immediately, but don't go home yet."

He led us down a narrow corridor and stopped outside a door.

< 74 >

"Now, stay in this room and come to a civilized agreement between yourselves, while I go and check your identity."

The room was cool, so much so that the metal chairs froze one's backside. I sat down opposite my rival. There was an initial silence to placate our fury. Then a sigh. Another sigh. A word. Two words, and the dialogue began to resume timidly. There was a release of tension and she threw me a challenging look. I uttered the first words of reconciliation.

"Forgive me for what happened. I didn't mean to ..."

"You treated me like a thief, as if a man like that could be stolen."

Her voice was gentle, and she had a smile like the moon. Her hair was straight, like all black women of a certain social status. Her nails were painted tomato red. She wore a silk dress the color of saffron and crushed red pepper, the color worn by northern women. She must be a *xingondo*, one of those northern bumpkins. Her skin had the perfume of cashew or of the water berry. She moved her lips as sweetly as if she were giving a kiss. Her voice was like a flute on the breeze, the song of a skylark. Her gestures were smooth, like the movement of a cat. How beautiful she was, dear God, how graceful. A man, the weak sex in matters of the flesh, would lose himself when faced by such beauty. My Tony could never have resisted, that was for sure.

"Tony's my husband," I told her, "get a man just for yourself, you're a pretty woman. Leave my husband alone, because apart from the fact that he's already got two women, he's showing signs of being tired. He's growing old, my Tony. I don't want to attack you. I'm just trying to defend my home."

"He's mine as well."

"Do you know what it means to be the mistress of a married man? It's the same as making children in the other woman's shadow. It's not being socially acknowledged as a spouse. It's about running the risk of being abandoned at a moment's notice, being used, being exchanged. What future do you expect?"

"And what about you, what present do you have? Fighting your rivals in the street, being locked up in a cell, was this the future you expected?"

"But you're not institutionally married, while I am. You're the concubine and I'm the spouse. You're secret and I'm acknowledged. I've got security, the right to inherit, and you don't have a right to anything. I've got a marriage certificate and a wedding ring on my finger."

< 76 >

"But I'm the one who's got all the pleasure, I receive all your husband's love and his salary. I experience the joy of living. Do you consider that so unimportant?"

Tension was threatening to rise again. With an iron resolution, I stopped myself, and didn't respond. I felt as if I were swallowing poisoned communion wafers, needles, broken glass. I made every effort to keep calm. I examined her. A woman with no name. No shadow. No house, no husband, no job. But who had a lover who visited her whenever he could. Who didn't care about being a parasite in someone else's shadow, or about causing me emotional pain.

"Didn't you know he was married?"

"Yes, I did. But he loves me. I love him. He visits me whenever he can. We have two children."

"What kind of home do you expect to make with a married man?"

"I have no illusions. Whether a wife or a lover, a woman is a shirt that a man wears and then takes off. She's a paper handkerchief that gets torn and can't be mended. She's a shoe that comes unstuck and ends up in the trash."

I was struck by this woman's honesty. That she accepted being used and discarded like sugarcane trash. Who lived the moment of love as if it were eternal. Who spoke about bitterness with sweetness. She didn't beat about the bush. I listened to her. The woman astonished me. Her frankness impressed me.

"You were used and stripped bare. I'm on the crest of a wave, but I'm bound to become obsolete like so many other women. That's why I live for the moment while the tide's in my favor."

"There was no need to attack me physically when I visited your house, Luísa."

"It's my unlucky week. Yesterday, Julieta, the second woman, was there and attacked me. When you arrived, I went on the attack. It was to defend myself. I couldn't guess your intentions."

"I just wanted to get to know you."

"Why? What's the point of knowing a rival? Apart from anything else, your man only visits me occasionally!"

"I want to know who you are, where you're from."

"I'm from far away, from Zambézia," she told me. "I come from a region where young men emigrate and never come back. In my home village, there are only old people and children. I've got eight brothers, each one by a different father. My mother never managed to have a husband just for herself. I only ever heard about my father. From an early age, I learned that man is bread, the communion wafer, a fire surrounded by women who are dying of cold. In my village, polygamy is the same as sharing scarce resources, for leaving other women without any cover is a crime that not even God forgives."

This discourse is typical of the women of my region, where man is king, lord of life and of the world. A world in which woman is leather. The soft, well-dressed leather from the skin of a bull. A world where woman is the twin of a drum, for both unleash spiritual sounds when loosened up and beaten by vigorous, rustic hands.

I took a deep breath to refresh my lungs and to calm the anguish I felt. I raised my eyes in search of the blue of the sky and they met the high ceiling, where a solitary, motionless lightbulb hung on the end of a flex. I blocked my ears, for my rival's voice was rich and abundant, a fountain of bitter words. All of a sudden, she lost her calm demeanor. She put her weight on the accusatory lever and chastised me:

"You southern women, you're the ones who steal our menfolk."

I was thunderstruck and began to shake slightly. This woman was mad. I glared at her angrily, ready for a fight. I clenched my fists and prepared myself for war.

"They left the villages and are concentrated here in the capital. There are also lots of foreigners here. Thousands of businessmen of all races go back and forth across our borders every day. It's full of men here everywhere you go, men that are only for you southern women. That's why when we northern woman catch a man, we don't let him go, we make up for our loneliness and absence of love or tenderness. When we catch a southern man, we don't let go of him, ever."

"If, as you say, there are so many men, why didn't you get one all for yourself?"

"Yes, there are lots of men, but there aren't many with money."

The conversation flowed like a shooting star. We opened up our hearts and swept our hurt away. We exchanged hatefulness, anger, jealous feelings. For we were rivals, enemies. Two starving lionesses competing for the same prey. Two bitches gnawing the same bone. My anger passed and I managed to ask her:

"Luísa, do you feel you're Tony's legitimate wife?"

"As long as he provides me with support, yes. We northern

women are practical. We don't waste much time with bride prices, marriages, and other unnecessary confusion. It's enough for a man to spend the night with me for him to be my husband. And when a relationship like this produces a child, a marriage is consolidated for good. As long as Tony gives me food and lodging, sustenance, then, yes, I'm a legitimate spouse."

"And when he stops supporting you?"

"That's another matter."

"Has he given you regular support?"

"He's been forgetful lately, because of that woman Saly."

"Who's Saly?"

"A highly strung Makonde woman who lives downtown."

"So what do you do when your support doesn't come?"

"I get by. I take on any jobs I can."

This woman excited me. She was provocative, she destroyed my sanity. She stole my husband and, to make matters worse, beat me, then insulted me and accused me of goodness knows what. My Tony's from the south, he's Shangaan through and through. He was acquainted with the north but only in military operations and never lived there for very long.

Dear God, this woman was right in so many ways. God, who

is father of the world, made many women and few men. He gave some greatness and others he humiliated. I entered this war and this cell for lack of a man. I was being shoved around by a rival because of a man. It's all God's fault, not Luísa's. Once again, I tried to identify all the things she had and that I lacked. She had smooth skin while mine was wrinkled. She had abundant, uncrimped hair while mine was sparse and frizzy. Once again, I admired my rival. She had fire in every vein. She exuded strength with every breath she took. She had a shooting star in each thread of hair, my God, how resplendent she was. Her eyes were as gentle as moonlight, that mouth of hers must be as sweet as honey. Why was I showing her such sympathy, why, why, why?

This woman's face was familiar to me, very familiar. Where had I seen her before? In the street, at the market, on the bus? In this time dimension? In another? In this world or in some other incarnation? What was it that attracted me to her? The gentle look? The smile? The lines on her face?

I thought about it so hard that in the end I discovered why. Many things about her reflected the image of what I had been and no longer was. She had all the charm I had lost. My sympathy for her stemmed from her appearance. This woman looked like

< 82 >

me. Tony sought new love in an old body, and found my image in that of another woman. Maybe he had even gone back in search of his own self so as to live the illusion of perpetual youth, for men also grew old.

The young policeman came back and released us. He declared in tones that chided us:

"It's shameful, two wives of such an important person descending to such a level. If this happens again, the person who will personally resolve it will be Commander António Tomás himself. So stop staining the image of such a dignified, illustrious man. Behave in keeping with that most worthy husband you managed to catch, ladies."

I embarked on a series of frantic searches. I wanted to know all about my Tony's loves. I went and met Saly, the Makonde woman. She passed me on to Mauá. Mauá Salé, a charming young Makua girl.

My Tony's heart is a five-pointed constellation. It's a pentagon. I, Rami, am the first lady, the queen mother. Then comes Julieta, the woman deceived, who occupies the position of second lady.

< 83 >

She's followed by Luísa, the woman desired, the third lady. Saly, the woman fancied, is fourth. Finally, Mauá Salé, the woman loved, the youngest and most recently acquired. Our home is a six-pointed polygon. It's polygamous. It's a loving hexagon.

6

I feel my body heavy, pummeled by so many defensive blows from my rivals, who felt their territory invaded. Everything hurts. I've got a swollen shoulder, I can't move my arm or my neck. I applied a miracle balm to it, but it didn't work. There's nothing else for it but to see a doctor right away. I go to the hospital, and sit down on a bench to await my turn. From the end of the corridor an elderly couple appear. The husband is lying on a trolley pushed by the old woman, who advances with anxious steps. All the waiting patients step aside to allow the old people through. The two are placed by the door to the doctor's surgery, right in front of me. In the figures of this aged couple, there are the signs of life's cycle, as clear as water. Barefoot, thin, and in rags. Clay pots already broken into pieces. In their wrinkled skin, secret messages of a life that flourished only for time to consume. They have come seeking treatment in order to secure a life that is slipping away from the palms of their hands. The doctor receives them with a smile and asks them what the problem is. Wanting to help her companion, the wife tells him all that she knows. Suddenly, the old man raises himself from the trolley and growls angrily:

"Keep quiet, woman. Since when have you been good enough to address a doctor? I never gave you permission to talk to any man. You're behaving like a whore."

The old man's words awaken hidden rage in the woman. All her bitterness surfaces like a hurricane, this woman's suffering has been constant over time. She reacts and shouts at the doctor:

"What a peevish old moaner! I've put up with him for my whole life. If he doesn't want me to speak, then let him die!"

The old woman abandons her companion stretched out on the trolley. She walks away. She rushes down the corridor as if answering the call of freedom. Her old husband shouts after her angrily, calling her back, but she doesn't turn. He passes out. The doctor is left with the painful task of awakening that sleeping soul, without knowing the causes of his slumber.

The scene fascinates, shocks, amazes me. The old man's body falls like a rotten fruit, but his vanity soars into the air like a balloon on its way to the stars. He is merely burning straw on its final flame. Ah, male arrogance!

< 86 >

7

For days on end I try to listen to the voice of my conscience. I try to find a solution to my problem, which gets more complicated by the day. My emotional counseling has failed. The wars with my rivals have only brought health problems and annoyance. I decide to try magic, there's no other alternative.

I go looking for a dealer in fortunes. I tell him my problem in a nice low voice so that the wind can't hear my lamentations. He reaches his diagnosis and prescribes the cure. He makes promises. He says my life will know moments that are loftier than the clouds. That my husband will love me like no one else. He says it's easier to secure and hold on to a husband than it is to fetch water from the fountain.

"I can bottle your man for you if you wish. I have the power to transform the world into a huge bottle."

It seems this man doesn't know much about the body's limits. A human being lives on air and light. If he's bottled, he'll die of asphyxiation. This is one of those prophets who create myths that

< 87 >

perturb the whole world. His virtue is to distract attention from the problems of the moment.

"If the world is transformed into a huge bottle, I'll be inside it too. He'll go on betraying me, and it won't solve anything."

"Yes, it will. You will hold the key." And he continues: "I shall make you into a dragon with flaming wings that can fly aloft and set fire to its rivals. You will be powerful. Trust me and you'll see."

"Is that true?"

"I can give you more than you think. Many women who are now happy have passed through here, through my hands."

He gives me the recipe for love: Prepare Tony's favorite soup, to which should be added enough cobwebs, two threads of my hair, three threads from his underpants, four drops of sweat from both me and him, two castor seeds, four white lizard feet, enough fat from a mole, mix it all up and serve it to him. The moment he drinks this, all my problems will be solved.

I feel sick. My flesh creeps. I regret this. I'm not going to allow myself to fall into the grip of a madman. Unfortunately, there are a lot of folk who believe in this type of thing. A mole's fat? What would such a soup taste like? This town's full of these fortune peddlers whose stories hold the balance between what's real and what's fantasy. They put incredible beliefs into people's heads that are then the cause of misunderstanding between friends, family, and even colleagues at work. Some of these individuals reduce people to penury. They want money. Money from the outset to greet the spirits and read one's fate. Money for a chicken to be sacrificed, money for sacred cloth and roots. Money to pay for their services. Money again to ask the spirit if the work has been carried out well or if it will deliver success. Money here, money there, money everywhere. These days, there are even Christians who give priests money by way of payment for divine miracles. This medicine man won't be getting any money from me.

I close my eyes. Memories of some good times begin to take shape in my mind. I hear my Tony's voice singing love ballads just for me. My arms weaving caresses, his lips moistening each cell of my body. The two of us, hand in hand, strolling through mountainous ravines. I open my eyes, and I am faced with the bitterness of reality. Silences. Memories. Yearnings for a body whose soul has left for other universes. I see myself at the dead of night, feeling the walls, the sheets, empty, my lips humid from so many tears kissing the air that meanders through the shadows of the night. Convulsions, the ashes of a love that has become extinguished and can no longer be ignited.

I think. I've run out of chances, I can no longer hold on to my husband with food, affection, fantasies. He's a shrewd butterfly. Beyond capture. My case requires magic. Only magic can save my marriage.

There are miracles in this world, to be sure. I once witnessed an extraordinary case. A thief entered a shop. He robbed it. When he was about to leave, he suddenly grew fat and couldn't get through the door. When he drew away from the door, he grew thin, when he drew near, he grew fat. In despair, he smashed the huge display window, which was about three meters wide. He tried to get through it, but he grew even fatter than the shop window. All of a sudden, he went crazy and cried like a child, until the shop owner came to free him. This is a true story, I saw it. What I didn't see was the man growing fat. I saw the thief in fetters, the broken display window, and the bag of stolen goods.

I can accept magic, but not the mole soup. If he eats it, he'll come and kiss my lips with that frightful smell. Without having eaten, I'll end up eating through the kiss. And what if he forces me to eat from his dish? What if he gives a bit to the children?

No, I don't want anything to do with this witchcraft, I prefer tattoos.

The seer's wife does me a tattoo in a secret place, and for a good price. She cuts my skin with a brand-new razor blade – to avoid the possibility of HIV – and then rubs me with a pomade that burns like pepper but that has the appearance of cow dung. I'm scared: What if I pick up tetanus?

For days after that, I ask God not to let Tony appear before my tattoo has dried up. The damned tattoo has given me a fever, it's got infected and is bleeding. I panic and go back to the wizard's house. He gives me a potion designed to produce a scar. I take it and it produces more bleeding that just won't stop.

Then my Tony turns up. And he's in a good mood, dear God! He wants to stay, inspired by love. I feel tense. The tattoo still hasn't scarred. While Tony speaks sweet nothings, my tongue turns into a sword, a dagger. I realize I'm shouting hysterically. He has no alternative but to go to the bedroom, get his hat and coat, and disappear into the night.

Oh, Lord! This wizard has wrecked my one chance. His cursed tattoo has scared my prey off. How unlucky I am! What a disastrous, ill-fated woman I am! Oh, how I want to die!

8

I'm that woman who has a mirror for company in her cold bed-room. Who dreams about what isn't there. Who tries to hold on to time and the wind. All I have to smile about is the past, the present is for weeping. I'm no use to anyone. People look at me as if I were a failed woman. What future can I hope for? My husband has become a tourist in his own home. Changes occur quickly in this home. The women increase. Children are born. A monogamous family has become polygamous. Unity has been smashed into a thousand pieces, Tony has multiplied. My friends ask after Tony only to tease me. The more fatalistic among them try to convince me that love has had its time.

I've been to the furthest horizon in search of my lost love. I've done all I could. I've spent sleepless days, despairing nights, while my love gets ever more remote. I began to secretly frequent a sect devoted to miracles. I had myself baptized in the River Jordan – which was in fact the beach of the Costa do Sol, near Maputo. In this sect's miracles, even the sea can be turned into a river.

I bathed in corn flour. In popcorn. In the blood of magic chickens. I released white doves to bring me back my lost love from the four corners of the world. Nothing! I became a member of the congregation of John Malanga, a miraculous prophet born in the Shona lands of Mozambique or Zimbabwe, I'm not quite sure which, but he was famous for miracles to restore health, wealth, and love. I fulfilled the sect's commandments, not to eat duck, or rabbit, or pork, or any other palmipede. Once again, I had myself baptized in the River Jordan – this time it really was a river, the River Matola – my body was immersed in the waters of the river, while milk was poured over my head – cow's milk, which they called the milk of the holy lamb of God – in the name of the Father, the Son, and the Holy Ghost. I dressed correctly, wearing the sacred colors of red and white for more than six months. I rummaged around for ghosts. I followed my man's tracks, which was easy, because with each step he took, he produced a child. I went looking for Julieta, his second woman, and found a wild animal who gave me a princely beating and sank her talons in my neck. She did to me what an animal of the wild does to its prey: I was easy meat. I calmed her display of hysterics. She took it out on me for all her sleepless nights. She's got five kids and is expecting a sixth. She's given my Tony many more children than I have, his wife in name. I went to see Luísa. She defended herself with all the valor of an ancient gladiator, and we got ourselves locked up like a pair of lionesses in a police cell. He's trapped her in his roots. She's got two children he occasionally supports when he's in the mood. She has to use a lot of initiative to feed her children, to conjure up flour to bake her bread. This woman hasn't got a job. I went to see Saly, the fourth woman. She also gave me a beating and told me: Yours is what you carry with you, in your belly, in your stomach. Yours is what you've eaten. This man gives me what is his. As long as he remains with me, he's mine, while he's with you, he's yours. And she told me: I'm poor. No father, no job, no money, no husband. If I hadn't stolen your husband, I'd have neither children nor any life whatsoever. My existence would be barren like a desert. The love he gives me is almost nothing, but it's enough to make me blossom. He's given me these two little ones. He's given me a few moments of happiness that I've stored in the archive of my memory. I tell everyone I'm married and have a husband on one day a month. And I'm happy. There are women who don't even have one day of love during their whole lives. I went to see the fifth woman, Mauá. She's still a child.

A wildflower born in the gardens of the north of my country. She's the woman Tony loves the most. Was I jealous of her? No. I can't be jealous of a flower, or of a butterfly on the wind. The girl can't be more than nineteen. How could I settle scores with a creature the same age as my third daughter? I've been involved in brawls, scandalous acts, witchcraft, schools for seduction. What is it that I've gained from love? Nothing! Only problems, just problems. And while I get all hot and bothered, my husband just goes on behaving in the same old way. He's like an eel in muddied waters, I'll never be able to get my hands on him.

What do women want, hanging around just one man? We all fear solitude and that's why we put up with what is intolerable. It's said that there are many women – according to the statistics and men themselves – and few men. To tell you the truth – and paraphrasing Lu, the third woman – there are enough men. Men with power and money, these are the ones that are few. In the history of our country, no woman died a virgin for lack of men. For all these women, Tony is a job, a source of income.

The world thinks women are self-seeking. And aren't men, as well? Any man demands one basic attribute of a woman: beauty.

Women demand another attribute of men: money. What's the difference? Are men the only ones who have a right to make demands and women not?

Out in the countryside, the only man to attract a pretty woman is one who has a powerful transistor radio, so that he can play her sweet music to lull them on the nights they make love. The one with the guile to possess a bicycle can have all the women in the world. It must be romantic to ride round the world on a bicycle, a prince and princess on their princely mount, traveling the world on their majestic steed.

Even in the Bible, woman is no good. The saints, in their time-honored preaching, say woman is worth nothing, woman is an animal who feeds on evil, she is the butt of all arguments, quarrels, and injustice. It's true. If we can be exchanged, sold, tortured, killed, enslaved, corralled into harems like cattle, it's because we're not needed. But if we're not needed, why is it that God put us in the world? And this God, if he exists, why does he allow us to suffer in such a way? The worst of it is that God doesn't appear to have any wife. If he was married, the goddess, his wife, would intercede on our behalf. Through her, we would ask to be blessed with a life based on harmony. But the goddess must exist, I keep thinking. She must be as invisible as all of us. No doubt her space is limited to the celestial kitchen.

If she did exist, we would have someone to whom we could direct our prayers, so we would say: Our Mother who art in Heaven, blessed be thy name. Give us thy kingdom – of women, of course – give us thy benevolence, we don't want any more violence. Let our prayers be answered, on Earth as it is in Heaven. Give us our daily peace and forgive us our trespasses – gossip, malice, busybodying, vanity, envy – as we forgive our husbands, lovers, boyfriends, companions and other relations I can't name, that trespass against us with their tyranny, betrayals, immorality, drunkenness, insults… Lead us not into temptation to imitate their madness – drinking, mistreating, stealing, expelling, marrying and divorcing, raping, enslaving, buying, using, abusing, and let us not die at the hands of these tyrants – but deliver us from evil, amen. We could surely use a heavenly mother, without a doubt.

I have just learned life's lesson. The story of one sole love, an everlasting love? Nonsense! That's a song for poets. Love is unleashed from the breast and runs out of control like a rock rolling toward a precipice. To have only one love in life? Baloney! Only women, forever stupid, swallow that story. Men love every day. Every time the sun comes up, off they go in search of new passions, new emotions, while we wait forever more for a love that's gone old and feeble. All men are polygamous. Man is a species of human with various hearts, one for every woman.

I'm not giving up this fight. I shall pursue my Tony to the furthest reaches of eternity. I shall pursue him as far as where time dwells. One day, I'll find him again, I swear. I'll catch him even if it's my last act in life.

9

I'm going to visit Aunt Maria, and she'll tell me stories of polygamy. She first married when she was ten. Her marriage had been arranged before she was even born. Her father had a debt, he couldn't pay his taxes, and so he told the tax collector: My wife is pregnant, if she gives birth to a girl, I'll give her to you as payment. And that's how it was. At the age of ten, she became the twenty-fifth wife of a king. She had a prince in her belly. A royal guard fell madly in love with her, and she had two children by him. As if that wasn't enough, she's now got two husbands, both of whom live under one roof.

"How did you manage to live in a home with twenty-five wives, Aunty?"

The old woman offers me a look of infinite tenderness.

"My girl, life is a never-ending process of sharing. We share the air and the sun, we share the rain and the wind. We share the hoe, the sickle, the seeds. We share peace and the pipe. To share a man isn't a crime. Occasionally, it's necessary to share a woman,

< 101 >

when a husband is sterile and needs to harvest the semen of a brother.

"Were you happy, Aunty?"

"I was still a young shoot, my eyes still reflected the sun and the moon. I hadn't yet learned the meaning of bitterness. We were a huge flock of women waiting to be covered. We gave birth to babies who flew over the grass like fireflies, loose stars lighting up the darkness of the savannah. I met the king in fact when I was thirteen."

"A queen in a harem, Aunty?" I ask, horrified, imagining the harems from the *Tales of the Arabian Nights*, with all their restrictions, their eunuchs and suchlike.

"In our world there were no harems," she explained. "They were true families, where there was social equality and democracy. Each wife had her house, her children, and her property. We had our organ of government – the assembly of the king's wives – where we would discuss the division of chores, decide who would cook the sovereign's morning pap, who would prepare his baths and rub his feet, cut his nails, massage his back, shave him, comb him, and provide other cares. We would take part in drawing up His Majesty's matrimonial rotation, which consisted of a night for each wife, but everything conducted on a strictly equal basis. And he fulfilled this duty to the letter. He had to give proof of statesmanship, be a good model for the family. If the king was imprudent enough to favor one wife in particular, he had to face criticism at meetings with his advisers and elders. As for me, the king had me whenever he wanted, but no one ever mentioned the matter. My status was never questioned. All the wives surrendered to my charm. I was a great lady, you know?"

I note great pride and vanity in her tone of voice. I can't understand the reason for such happiness, in a home with more than twenty spouses, without any rights or freedom whatsoever.

"Were you all happy there?"

"We were free. We had a lot of freedom. The ladies didn't lack for anything at all. They didn't even lack affection. No one ate vegetables in that house: only meat. We didn't drink water: only milk. Women grew fat like elephants. The earth was our mother, and not such a stepmother as it is today."

"Even so, why so many wives and so many children?"

Aunt Maria looks at me and smiles.

"Every age has its history," she says. "Prosperity is measured by the number of properties. Virility by the number of wives and children. A great patriarch must have various heads under his command. When one holds power, one needs somewhere to exercise it, isn't that so? Abraham, Isaac, Jacob, were polygamous, weren't they? Our old kings also were, and still are. What harm does that do? In the Bible, only Adam wasn't polygamous. In our house, the ladies produced children and gave the kingdom an image of prosperity. If the king had difficulties, he would resort to conjugal and reproductive assistants, who were recruited among the most handsome, robust, and intelligent men in the kingdom. A king has to display the air of virility, he has to be a man over all men.

I laugh out loud. A kingdom is the center of human reproduction, and the king is the reproductive commander-in-chief.

"How many times a year did a king get married?"

"As many times as he needed to. Two, three, four."

"He spent his time in wedding celebrations."

"Not at all," she explains, "the king didn't have time for such trivialities. The people who organized everything were his ministers, governors, advisers, who would choose the bride, negotiate the marriage, pay the bride price, and see to all those types of things. The new bride's reception in the royal palace was arranged by his previous ladies. I was received by his twenty-fourth wife, as

I was the twenty-fifth and last. That day, the king was sitting in a corner, having a beer and playing cards with his friends. He didn't even look at me. All these marriages were contracts, political alliances between the different ethnic groups within the kingdom, except in my case, as I was given to him to pay my father's debts. I never felt married to that man, who was old enough to be my grandfather.

"Ah, but Aunty! Kings shared their spouses with their assistants."

"No. A wife who was passed over to an assistant never again returned to the royal bed, which was good because she regained her freedom and could go off gallivanting. She could even bring any children she bore into the royal domains. In a polygamous home, there are no illegitimate children. Those born to the assistants couldn't inherit the throne. The first lady, the *nkosikazi*, she was sacrosanct. No man could touch her under pain of death. She was the only wife who could guarantee the royal lineage. When I got married, the king was already a granddad."

"What was the king's bed like?"

"The bed? No one entered the king's bedroom except for his first lady. Like a doctor, the king made house calls."

< 105 >

"Aunty, if you were never in the king's bed, then you were never queen."

"I was a queen, my dear, I was a queen! Wherever I walked, all the other women would make way for me. There aren't many women in the world who could boast of such merit."

"Aunty, what was the king like?"

"The king?" She talks with passion. "He was a man like no other. Tall. Lean. A white beard. Intelligent. He was powerful. Very powerful. He was venerated like a god. He ate green vegetables and drank milk. He was an affable person but he was also stern. Once he had one of his wives put to death because she had tried to poison him. The queen, the first lady, was a kind of commander of all the womenfolk. She was very beautiful and distinguished, the first lady! Proud and distant. An embittered woman, and gossips speculated that she was skinny because she was jealous. She was like that, no curves in front, no curves at the back, as flat as a board, which made her the target of scorn in the eyes of any Bantu man, who loves to let his hands wander into the undulating labyrinths of a well-endowed woman. She was like a little bird inside a cage, I remember. She seemed more prisoner than prima donna. The king held her in great respect.

< 106 >

Nowadays, I think her deep sadness came from the lack of love shown her. It's painful sleeping alone when you know your husband is out there!"

"What an awful system!"

"Polygamy has its advantages."

"Advantages?"

"Yes. When the wives agree with one another, the man can't abuse them."

"You've got two husbands now, Aunty. Is that to make up for those polygamous times?"

"One is the father of my children. The other helped me to raise them."

"Both of them in the same house and the same bed?"

"Not at all."

"I don't understand."

"I left the royal house when the king died, and then married Marcos, the father of my two little girls. He left me and set off along the byways of this world. He carried sacks, slept on the quay, he was the lowest of the low, and then finally, he worked in the gold mines of South Africa. He was left with gilded lungs from so much dust, and this turned his saliva into blood. The doctors

< 107 >

told him it was silicosis. He was deported. He had no home and no food. All he had were these two daughters that Tomás, my new husband, helped me bring up. Tomás took Marcos in out of charity. They became close, like twin brothers. Now they are inseparable.

"But then, how does the relationship work?"

"What relationship, my dear? What are you talking about?"

"Aunty, I've heard some strange things."

"What?"

"Oh, come on, Aunty! You know what I'm talking about."

"I've also heard things. That dissolute, Marcos, is known to like men."

"But...!"

"Let's not talk about this anymore, my dear. In the eyes of the world, I'm the shameless one with two husbands in the same bed."

"So, don't you do anything about it, Aunty?"

"What for? Let people say what they will."

10

I drink a glass of wine. Happy birthday to you.

Children's voices float through the air like kites in the wind. Luísa's son is two years old today. My ears are filled with gentle sounds like flowers falling on a tomb. Crowded round a cream-filled cake, the children try out their voices to see what tones they can reach. Then they take a deep breath and draw in pure, clean air. Their sounds are stronger than the wind and touch the most sensitive points of the sky's navel. For them, life is a soapy bubble, swept along on the crest of a wave, all is lightness. They don't know that all that is born dies. That all that grows ripens. They don't yet know that life offers more thorns than it does flowers. How I wish I could be a child again.

I drink another glass of wine.

I like this birthday boy. He's handsome, like my husband, Tony. He reminds me of my little boy, Betinho, when he was a baby. It's as if both had come out of the same mold. They're alike. Identical.

I drink another glass.

< 109 >

I observe everything around me. The curtains have become unfastened in one corner. In the hall, a lamp bulb has blown. The sofa I'm sitting on has a broken leg, and perches on a brick. This house needs a man's hand. My Tony spends most of his time over here. Between these four walls, he produced two children with this woman. Why doesn't he use his strength as a man to carry out some repairs on this house? Luísa's women friends and neighbors wander wherever they want here, talk out loud and say anything they like, pry into everything without asking. It's a house without any order to it. A woman's house. A man is needed here to impose respect on this house.

Another glass of wine.

This Luísa's a bit crazy. Didn't she phone to invite me to her son's birthday party? I said no, not in a month of Sundays. It just doesn't make sense to go to the party of the son of a rival. But here I am. I don't know what spell, what piece of wizardry, dragged me here. I passed a shop and bought the little boy a toy car as a present. But I don't regret it, I'm having fun. I'm getting to know new people, and socializing. I'm showing these rivals that I'm better than them and don't harbor resentment or grudges. It was a good opportunity to get to know this Luísa up close, the world she lives in, her circle of friends, and even something of the spell she has managed to cast on my husband.

Night is falling and the party comes to an end. The children disappear like a flock of birds returning to their nests at sunset. I pour myself another glass of wine. The last one.

The doorbell rings, and the door is opened to let in another guest. A man. But who is this marvelous man who is holding a bouquet of flowers like a bride? Who is this man who has followed the twisting streets to reach this little hideaway, under the romantic cover of dusk? Who are these beautiful flowers for, if the birthday party is for a two-year-old baby who's only interested in a toy, a chocolate, a cream cake? He must be a thief. A beautiful thief. A stolen kiss is given and received in the darkness of dusk.

The man's presence transmits the energy to me that I need in order to live. Those flowers bring the perfume to my sense of smell that I need in order to breathe. The man wears a smile on his lips that makes me excited. I invite the man to sit down next to me. He plays hard to get and I insist. He obeys me.

"Handsome man, I've never seen you before. Who are you? What are you doing here?"

< III >

Luísa is awkward and whispers something in the guest's ear. She does the introductions. She stammers.

"You're Luísa's lover, aren't you?" I take him to task. "Yes, you are. You should know, my good man, that Luísa is a woman with commitments. She stole my husband from me and they had two children together. But then who is the man who wouldn't let himself be stolen by this beautiful thief, my good sir?"

The man prevaricates, but stumbles at every step, and I conclude: He really is her lover. I'm furious. This Luísa, apart from being a betrayer, is a hussy. Barely is her husband away and she jumps over the fence as fast as she can. Adulterer! Suddenly, I feel like screaming and causing a huge explosion. Then I think for a bit: What for? I'm here at this children's party to enjoy myself and not to defend the conjugal interests of another adulterer. And apart from that, this woman doesn't have any formal property rights, she's not registered anywhere, she's free. Beautiful as she is, sensual as she must be, why shouldn't she make the most of life?

I drain my glass of wine.

"Do you know my husband, sir? He's Luísa's husband. A handsome man who allowed himself to be stolen away by this thief's charms. But I'm not angry, I feel no resentment. Although she's a rival, she avenged my jealousy. Do you know Julieta, my good sir? She's got a pretty face, but she's all dried up, all skin and bone. Bone without any marrow, bones that wouldn't make a stew or a soup. I'm an abandoned woman. A bitch without an owner, my good sir. All because of Julieta and Luísa. But Luísa's pretty, don't you think?"

The man doesn't answer, he just looks at me. With pity and tenderness. A tenderness that makes me want to fly. He smiles. A smile that bathes me in mad thoughts. I'm struck by a thousand sensations. Heat. Cold. Hunger. Fire. Thirst.

Dear God, my body is being knocked sideways by a rush of blood. I feel desire rising in my heart. I fidget desperately this way and that, the chair can no longer hold me. My skirt makes me feel an inner heat, I feel like taking it off. Maybe it's the wine. I didn't have much wine, but I'm drinking large quantities of aphrodisiac springing from this stranger's sultry eyes. I forget all the rules of good manners and sink fast. I'm a rushing river, flowing toward the cascades, I'm plunging over a precipice. Where will I come to a stop, dear God? I'm in the abyss, I'm sinking. Shame, my own shame, don't leave me alone, adrift in this life. Where are you going, shame, leaving me all alone like this? I can't control myself. Shame is forsaking me, leaving me defenseless. I struggle with all my strength against the madness that is destroying me. In vain. My God, what is this change that has overcome me? Prior to this, no other man ever seduced me. Only Tony. My Tony. Where is my Tony, who has left me to journey alone in this perilous world?

Luísa drags me to her room. She undresses me. She lays me down. I won't be going back home today, I'm sorry. The bedroom is simple and the bed a modest one. A woman's bed. It needs a man's touch here to give it the consistency of a love nest. In this bedroom, in this bed, Tony made two children. Why doesn't he lend his man's strength to make this room more comfortable?

I ask for another glass of wine. Luísa refuses me. So I then raise my tearful voice in a prayer, and ask God to give me this ultimate comfort; like a woman condemned to death, I'm hanging on a cross at the top of a hill.

This man is God, he answers my prayer and comes to me. My arms open like flowers bursting into bloom as they are caressed by the sun. All the stars in the Milky Way spread over my bed and I dance to the sound of my silence. I close my eyes and soar into flight. This man has the infinite power to make me live. And die.

< 114 >

And make me escape to other planets while my body remains on Earth. I fall asleep on the moon.

The sun has risen. I open my eyes with difficulty. I can hear distant humming, and there's a hammering in my head. I look at everything around me. This room isn't mine, nor is the bed, nor the clothes I'm wearing. Can it be that I'm on the moon?

Then I remember. It was all my fault. My whole body shakes like an earthquake. From fear. From shame. I slept with Lu's lover! That parched woman was me, in the middle of the desert, chasing a raindrop. That depraved woman was me, drinking wine, glass after glass, like a whore. Like some tramp, I gave myself to a stranger. Could it be that Luísa set this trap? Who is Luísa? Who is the stranger? I was as firm as a rock. Incorruptible. I always lived on a higher plain than other women because I was someone who stood for all the virtues. I have tainted my fidelity, a breach has been opened up, a wound that will never heal. I've pulled down the pillars that held my values in place, I couldn't resist the temptation. I wish I had some detergent to rub this stain away. A deep cavern in which to hide the weapon used in the crime, but the weapon is my body, ah, my body, my enemy! How could I resist your appeals? Cursed flesh, what have you done to my soul? It's hard to remain faithful when one's body is on fire. This forced abstinence is hard, dear God, it's hard being a woman.

A voice of wisdom gives me counsel: Never say I'll be back in a minute, I'm just going to the end of the street. Because a journey has no length. You take a step and are involved in a fatal accident. You meet a mugger. You tread on a thorn. You experience sadness and pain. You take another step and you find a flower. A great treasure. You make a lifelong friend. You meet the great love of your life. A journey is as mysterious as all the fissures of fate. That's why they always advise you: Woman, always take your *capulana* with you, to cover you if there's sun. To be your shroud if you die. To cover your bed if you find love. To cover your face if you are ashamed. To cover your naked body if you lose your clothes, and hide your shame from the eyes of the world. I came for a humble birthday party and ended up succumbing to forbidden love. I didn't bring my *capulana*. How am I going to wipe away these tears of shame?

Luísa appears, smiling, in the doorway. Carrying a tray, she looks like a servant. She's bringing me hot coffee. She's like a mother with a bib in her hand, fussing over her little child.

< 116 >

"Did you sleep well, Rami, sister?"

I manage to get up with difficulty, my arms shaking. I swallow the coffee at one go, and feel more lively.

"Luísa, how did this happen to me of all people?"

"Oh, Rami! That man isn't a child. You are a woman in need, neglected, abandoned, it's obvious. He helped you. There's nothing wrong in that."

"What happened was rape. I was raped."

"Do you think so?"

"Yes. I was unconscious, drunk, the man took advantage of my weakness."

"Is that so?"

"I invaded your space."

"I'm not possessive. I come from a region where solidarity knows no borders. I come from a place where one lends one's husband to a best friend to have a baby as easily as one lends someone a wooden spoon. In my part of the world, a husband lends his wife to his best friend or to a respected visitor. In my village, love is solemnly shared in common as if it were communion bread. Sex is a glass of water to slake one's thirst, everyday

< 117 >

sustenance, necessary and indispensable like the air we breathe. If we already share a husband, sharing a lover is all the easier. So we're quits, Rami, aren't we?"

"I feel so ashamed!"

"Look, Rami, you haven't committed a crime."

"This was adultery."

"Adultery? How long have you been waiting for someone who never comes? You southern women waste your time with such stories and prejudices. You renounce life, and may we know why? What's all this fidelity if he's already left you? Even widows get some relief at some point. And you're not a widow, Tony's alive, he's happy, going about his business somewhere out there."

I want to tell her no, that I won't agree to all this, that I'm a decent woman and all the other adjectives women like to use when describing themselves. But I can't. Her arguments are stronger than mine.

"I know I'll never be Tony's real wife," she says, "which is why I live every day as it comes. A bit of love here, a smile there, little by little the hen fills her belly. When you can't have a downpour, a bit of drizzle will do. In the absence of drizzle, a watering can is enough to moisten the earth. Have you ever been hungry, Rami?

If you don't have any green vegetables, you eat thistles, cacti, roots. Has no one ever told you that if you don't have any water, your urine will keep you alive if you drink it? Those women who sell their bodies are people just like us, Rami."

"No, I'm not like them, I can't be like them."

"Yes, you are. You suffer just like they do. You suffer more than they do. You're a wife only on paper, you're in fact the greatest spinster of us all. That's why I lent you my lover."

"I'm a married woman, Lu. Even you shouldn't betray him. You have a commitment to him, don't you?"

"Big deal! This Tony we're fighting over, what do I get out of him, Rami? I ended up accepting my humiliation at being his third wife, without any legal right or status, just in order to get a few crumbs, just crumbs. There are lots of men in this city. But what men? Was I to go and get me a countryman, a truck driver from my home village? I want a house with electricity, a television and telephone. I want my children to have a good name and opportunities that I never had. I want a different future for my descendants."

I envied Luísa. A practical, down-to-earth woman, fulfilling the laws of nature. She was born in a straw crib, but she has a dream and sweeps the stones from in front of her with an iron fist.

< 119 >

I drink another coffee and am more light-headed. I take a cold shower and feel refreshed. I go back to bed and close my eyes to reflect on things. I dream. In vain, I try to visualize the man who made me fly. I don't even recall the shape of his face. Or his name. Much less where he was from. What I do recall is his voice, singing a lullaby in my ear. I imagine beautiful fantasies about him and journey as far as the stars. I hear a voice calling for my body and I open my eyes. Dear God, am I suffering some sort of acoustic mirage? They say alcohol produces buzzing sounds, voices, hallucinations, I must still be drunk. Within me, I feel those signs of madness that psychiatrists love to interpret. Lord, is it possible to go on being drunk after a night's rest?

I glance around me and once again fall to the bottom of the well. The beautiful stranger stands before me. I flutter like a dry leaf, the heat in my body shows me no mercy, it devours me. I crackle, hiss, burn. I still try to summon up the strength of my shame, but I see no sign of it returning. I'm an ant imprisoned in a tower of honey, nothing can hold me back.

"Rami, good morning!"

The stranger greets me. I am pleased. That young head with a few wisps of white hair pleases me. That manly voice and that

< 120 >

smile please me. I am even more pleased by the heat of this latest embrace. I close my eyes. I retain that little piece of air, the delicious mystery of his breath, in my lungs. I travel through space. Drops of rain fall from the abundant sky onto my body, and douse the flames that devour me. My feelings of solitude, anguish, rejection, float like jetsam in the torrent of honey. Once again, I am a river. I listen in silence to the gentle murmur of waves in my blood. I travel on high, I'm a star, I'm light, I shine. I'm a rainbow, I contain all the colors of sensuality, I am floating in space, I'm on the moon. My voice unleashes sweet, light tones like honeyed breath. I look down on the world from above. The Earth is a planet of thorns, and a stolen kiss is its most precious relic. There are no beautiful or ugly women when they make love in the dark, nor frigid women when fire exists.

I awaken with my body in ashes. I think about justifying my attitude. What for? It would be a monotonous ditty, a litany of wild lamentations and expressions of regret over my shameless behavior. He makes conversation. He encourages me.

"I like you," he says. "I like Lu as well. I like both of you. You are wonderful, Rami. How can a man despise someone like you? You are beautiful, and you are young. You're at the stage of your

< 121 >

life when you need to experience the most passionate emotions, and there you are weeping like a widow."

"You're just saying that to please me."

"You're a true lady, a mother. How I wish I had a wife like you."

I'm annoyed and sulky. Men are all shameless and this one abused me in my fragile state.

"You took advantage of the fact that I was drunk."

"You cried for me like a child. You called me, and Lu persuaded me to go to you."

"But…!"

"You were sending out all the signals, I could see it in your eyes. You were the perfect example of a dried-up flower in the desert. The way you sat down, your smile, your gestures, all closely reflected the absence of affection in your life. It's not fair what your husband is doing to you."

I look at the man with some irritation. Why is he telling me all this? What's he trying to say? Lovers take advantage of the weakness of couples and destroy the homes of their mistresses. Is that the case? I don't know why, but I sense some truth in his words.

"How can you say you admire me?"

"I know a lot of things about you. I admire your courage. You're a rare example. I think all women should unite with each other against the tyranny of men. If I were a woman, I'd do that. And that's where your strength lies. Instead of waging war, you're here side by side with your rival. You've got spunk, woman."

"But it isn't easy."

"You're not replacing one tyranny with another. Don't treat these women badly. Like you, they're shattered and searching for life. They deserve your support and your forgiveness. What's more, they're younger and even more star-crossed than you. Teach them to love and to forgive."

"What are your feelings for Lu? Love?"

"No, of course not. I just feel sympathy for her. She's a good girl. I admire her."

"Are you married?"

"I was married and I lost my wife because of my own madness. She left, in the arms of another man."

"So what part does Luísa play in your life?"

He tells me. He met her on a cold, rainy night.

"I was coming from a nightclub when I saw a woman in her nightdress in the cold night air," he tells me. "I slowed down. I stopped and looked. The poor thing was barefoot and disheveled,

< 123 >

and her belly was huge, that of a woman in an advanced stage of pregnancy. At first, I thought she was one of those many mentally ill people one sees wandering along the street. I opened the door of my car and invited her in. Then, I saw that her arms and face were covered in wounds, and that she was bleeding. I asked her why she was in such a state. She didn't answer. She cried. It was obvious she had been beaten up and banished from home by her husband at that late hour and in that state. I asked her where she wanted to go. She said she had nowhere to go. I took her to a guesthouse and paid for a room where she spent the night. The next day, I went to see how she was. They told me she had gone to the maternity hospital. She gave birth prematurely, because of the beating she had suffered, the shock and the anguish. I helped with her child's delivery, Rami. His name is Victor. Lu insisted on giving him my name as a way of thanking me. If I hadn't helped her at that moment, the child would have been born out on that road, in the cold of the night."

"That can't be. My Tony would never do something like that."

"Ask Lu. She'll tell you how your troglodyte of a husband would get drunk, beat her up when she was pregnant, and shut her away in a room and deprive her of food. And she never did anything to upset things because she depended on him to eat, to exist."

"He never did that to me! I can't believe it."

"You are the queen, the first wife! There are things a man does to his mistresses that he never does to his spouse. I'm sorry, Rami, but that husband of yours is nothing more than a son of a bitch . . . He's got that grandiose title of chief of police, but he's no more than a common criminal. A man who doesn't respect his own child in its mother's womb doesn't deserve to be called anything else. You people should give him a good kick in the pants to feel better. Instead of correcting his behavior, you submit yourselves, take it all on the chin, and what's more, fight each other to the death because of him."

"Why did you help Lu?"

"Because of the strength of my own remorse. I was also a tyrant for most of my life. I beat my wife during the last month of her pregnancy. She was rushed to the maternity clinic and lost her son, the only son she would ever give me. We already had two little girls. I yearned for a boy and I lost him. I killed him. Because of my own stupidity. Dear God, how I regret it! Hardly had she come out of the hospital than she went back to her parents' home and never came back to me, and quite rightly so. She married another man and is happy, to make my punishment even worse. I'm on my own, I haven't settled down again, but one day I shall marry again. I love Lu so much, I'm so fond of her, but she prefers Tony, who has made her his third-class concubine."

"What? How can she dismiss a man like you? I would have expected everything but that."

"Help me. You can help me because she listens to you. Convince her to come to me. You'll have one rival less, Rami. And she will have a man to herself, who will look after her."

"How does she justify rejecting you?"

"She doesn't want to give her own children a stepfather. She says that we southern men are very prejudiced, and that we consider a wife with previous children junk, a secondhand wife. I sense that she loves me, but she's elusive, and prefers being a polygamist's mistress to suffering the humiliation of being a secondhand wife."

"What do you feel for me?"

"I don't know what to say. All of a sudden, I saw you as an ally I could count on. But all I want is to marry Lu."

"If I had this girl Lu's luck, I wouldn't look twice, I'd say yes right away. If what you say is true, I'll try to help you, both of you. Poor Lu. What happiness can she expect from Tony?"

We said goodbye as friends. We exchanged kisses to seal our pact. I wake up to the truth. What happened wasn't the result of alcohol. Nor was it an accident. It was fatal attraction, love at first sight. He looks at me steadily and I avert my gaze downward, concealing a feeling of madness that overwhelms me, and that I can't even interpret.

Lu escorts me home. I walk along with a fluid, watery meander, while the sun today is dressed all in fresh blue hues. My soul soars aloft, lifted by invisible wings. The morning breeze whispers love songs in my ears. I arrive home. As I go in, I smell the marvelous scent of all the flowers. The rosebushes in my front garden have put out new shoots. I feel like rolling around like a child, my lawn is a lustrous green. My children jump into my arms. They have been celebrating.

"At last, Mother," they shouted, "you've left your widow's retreat, you've gone out into the street to live life, refresh yourself, fill your lungs with oxygen, reinvigorate yourself. You always lived indoors like a prisoner, Mother. Why?"

I'm happy. I'm sad. They can't even imagine that their mother,

< 127 >

who left for a birthday party, isn't the same person who came back from it. Ah, how this journey has transformed me!

I begin to spend time at Lu's house. We share secrets. Vito starts being the mysterious shadow that pursues my own. The moon that gleams through the crack in my window. An excellent polygamous lover, distributing stolen love between us, on a fair, egalitarian scale. I find the situation embarrassing, sometimes sickening. My conscience censures me, but my body is there at the agreed time, utterly dependent on those secret encounters like a heroin addict. Sometimes, I'm afflicted by the fear of being discovered. When Tony finds me, the cover of fidelity will have been gnawed away down to its last thread. Morality is a coin. On one side of it is sin, on the other virtue. Silence and secrets united to keep the world in harmony.

< 128 >

11

I need somewhere for my spirit to repose. I need a piece of homeland. But where is my homeland? Where my husband comes from? No, I'm not from there. He tells me I'm not from there, and if his family's spirits don't want me there, he can banish me. My umbilical cord was buried where I was born, but tradition has it that I'm not from there either. In my husband's land, I'm a foreigner. In my parents' land, I'm merely passing through. I'm from nowhere at all. I'm registered nowhere on the map of life, and I have no name. I use this name given me at my marriage, and that can be taken away from me at any time. I've borrowed it. I used my father's name, but this was taken away. I had borrowed it. My soul is my dwelling. But where does my soul live? A woman alone is a speck of dust in space that the wind blows here and there as it busies itself with purifying the world. A shadow with no sun, or soil, or name.

No, I'm nothing. I don't exist anywhere.

Do you think I should embrace polygamy and start shouting hallelujah and praise be the Lord just so I can hang on to

< 129 >

a borrowed name? Do you think I should say yes to polygamy just so I can keep this tiny patch of ground under my feet? No, I refuse, my arms are tied too tightly to applaud, and my throat too dry to shout. No, I can't. I don't know. I just have no desire to do so.

Polygamy is a fishing net that has been cast into the sea. In order to catch women of all types. I've already been caught. My rivals, my sisters, all of us have been caught. Should we sharpen our teeth, gnaw the net through and escape, or wait for the net to be hauled in, and catch the fisherman? What's the best solution?

Polygamy is a solitary howl under the full moon. Living through the early hours of the morning in a state of anxiety or forgetfulness. It is to open one's breast with one's hands and cut out one's heart. To drain it until it becomes as solid and dry as a stone, so you can kill your love and draw out the pain when your husband sleeps with another woman, even while lying next to you. Polygamy is a whole procession of wives, each one bearing a little snack with which to feed the lord. While he tastes each dish, he says: This one's very salty, this is watery, this one's no good, this one's sour, I don't like this one, because there's one woman who knows how to cook what he likes. It's them calling you ugly when you're beautiful, because there's always one that's more beautiful than you. It's being beaten every day for what you've done badly, or what you haven't done, or what you thought about doing, or what you're going to think of doing one day.

Polygamy is an army of children, lots of half brothers and sisters growing up happy, innocent, future reproducers of the ideals of polygamy. Although I don't accept it, my reality is this. I'm already living in a state of polygamy.

Polygamy is being a woman and suffering until the cycle of violence begins. Growing old and becoming a mother-in-law, mistreating your daughters-in-law, hiding the mistresses and bastard children of your polygamous sons in your own home, in order to avenge all the bad treatment you suffered at the hands of your own mother-in-law.

To live in polygamy is to be bewitched by greedy women, who want your husband only for themselves. In the polygamous home, there's a lot of rivalry, casting of spells, gossip, even poisoning. Living in polygamy involves using subterfuge, techniques of seduction, wizardry, intrigue, competing your whole life with other more beautiful women, wasting your whole life for a little shred of love.

Polygamy has been the fate of so many women in this world since time immemorial. I know of one people where polygamy wasn't a tradition: the Makua. These people abandoned their roots and adopted polygamy through the influence of religion. They became Islamic. The menfolk seized their chance and converted immediately. Because polygamy is power, because it's good to be a patriarch and dominate others. I know one people where there was a tradition of polygamy: mine, in the south of the country. Under the influence of the pope, priests, and saints, it turned its back on polygamy. It became Christian. It vowed to abandon its barbaric custom of marrying many women to become monogamous and celibate. It had the power to do so and renounced it. Practice, however, demonstrated that you can't become a great patriarch with only one wife. That's why the men of this group now reclaim their lost status and want to return to their roots. They practice a type of illegal polygamy, an informal arrangement whereby they don't follow the time-honored rules. One day, they say no to their customs, and yes to Christianity and the law. The next day, they say no where they had said yes before, and yes where they had previously said no. They contradict themselves, but it's easy to understand why. Polygamy endows them with privileges.

To be lord of one's home is good: a woman to cook, another to wash your feet, one to go for a walk with, another to go to bed with. To keep reproducers for future workers, to tend pastures and cattle, the grain fields, everything, all with the minimum of effort, for the simple reason that one has been born a man.

At political rallies, we applauded the speeches: Down with polygamy! Down with it! Down with the rites of initiation! Down with them! Down with the culture of backwardness! Down with it! Long live the revolution and the New Man! Viva! After the rally, the leader who made all the popular speeches to the shouts of "Viva" and "Down with" would go and have lunch and put his feet up at the home of a second wife.

The whole problem stems from our ancestors' weakness. They allowed the invaders to establish their own models of purity and sanctity. Where there was no polygamy, they introduced it. Where there was, they banned it. They created havoc, the hapless wretches!

Men always repeat the same story: I'm a man, I'll marry as many women as I want. And they force women to accept this whim. Okay then. When you think about it, whose fault is all this? Men defend the soil and crops. Women merely preserve

< 133 >

them. In the past, men allowed themselves to be defeated by the invaders who imposed their cultures, religions, and systems however they wished. Now they want women to rectify man's weakness. In the Christian doctrine, women are educated to respect one sole king, one god, one love, one family, why are we expected to accept what even they can't deny? To deny something doesn't involve screaming: it's a question of looking at the law, changing it, challenging religion and introducing changes, saying no to the philosophy of others, reimposing order and reeducating society to return to the time that has passed. I'm talking too much. I'm trying to say that women are orphans. They have a father but don't have a mother. They have a god but they don't have a goddess. They're alone in the world surrounded by fire. Ah, if only we had a goddess in heaven!

If polygamy is nature and destiny, then I beg of you, God, order a new Moses to write another Bible, with an Adam and as many Eves as there are stars in the sky. Order some Eves to take turns in grinding the corn, scrubbing, cooking, and massaging and washing Adam's feet. There's no point in writing anything about love and sin. In this polygamous world, women are forbidden to be jealous. If jealousy is love, then they are prohibited from loving. Original sin, when they commit it, isn't in order to feel any pleasure, but only for the purpose of reproduction. It can speak of punishment, pain, suffering, because women understand that type of language only too well. Don't mention the apple, because it doesn't exist here. Speak of the banana instead, which makes more sense for this story. Or of the cashew, if you can't talk about bananas. We've got plenty of snakes, except that the ones in our tropical Eden don't speak. And to you, God, we ask one thing: Free the goddess – if she exists – so that she can show her face even if it's only for a second. She must be tired of preparing so much sacramental wine, so much communion bread up there in the heavenly kitchen ever since the world began. If there is no goddess – forgive me, God – but with so many women in the world, why don't you keep a few dozen for yourself?

What a pleasant system polygamy is! For a man to get married again, the previous spouse has to give her consent and help him choose. What a pity Tony acted on his own and informally, without following the accepted norms, because if he had, I would only have agreed to him marrying women who were uglier and more disaster-prone than myself. Polygamy isn't about substituting any woman, it's about having one more. It's not a question of waiting for one to grow old and then exchanging her for another. It's not about waiting for one to produce wealth to then pass it on to another. Polygamy doesn't depend on wealth or poverty. It's a system, a program. It's one family with various wives and one man, so it's a self-contained unit. In Tony's case, it's various families scattered around with only one man. It's not polygamy by any stretch of the imagination, but a grotesque imitation of a system that's almost out of control. Polygamy is about sharing love equally, an equality that's calculated with mathematical precision. It substitutes the male for an assistant in the event of incapacity: a blood brother, a friend, a brother in circumcision. Tony was certainly circumcised. Does he have a brother in circumcision? I don't know, I've never heard him mention one.

Life is an endless process of metamorphosis. Just take my case. My Christian home became polygamous. I was a faithful spouse who became an adulteress. Adulteress? No, I merely resorted to an informal brand of conjugal assistance, just as this household's polygamy is informal.

With regard to women, there are already five of us. There are sixteen children, including those that are still in their mothers' wombs. Another four and there'll be twenty. Despite my forty

< 136 >

years, I'm going to have another child by way of revenge. The concubines can't have more children than I, who am the first wife and lady. No concubine in this world is going to steal my status from me, I swear. I'm not entirely sure about this last affirmation. Tony breathes fertility and germinates like pumpkin seeds, multiplying by the dozen like a nest full of mice. If things go on as they are now, Tony will end up having fifty children, with so many beautiful young women being born every day.

< 137 >

12

I decide to prepare a little conspiracy against Tony, with my family's support. I want him to know that where I come from, I've got someone who will defend me. I shall first speak to my father and ask him to summon my brothers and my fat aunts. My white-haired uncles must be present to give an aura of wisdom and gravitas to the meeting that will discuss my situation. My priest uncle will be there with his cassock, my doctor brother and my sister, who is a director, my godfather, who is a minister, will also have to be present. I want Tony to feel the weight of my status, at least once in his life. He's going to know me, he must know the real me. He must be convinced that I'm not just any old woman. Together, we'll pin him to the wall. He'll be obliged to give up his concubines or lose me. And if he loses me, I guarantee this: He'll never find anyone in the world better than me. I am his real wife, before God and men.

I go to visit my parents. My father's appearance is sad and ghostly. He lives in his world of solitude and silence. I look at him and see that he bears the burden of life on his shoulders. He lives with his eyes closed as if he doesn't want to look at the world. Things must be very gloomy inside that soul. There must be many a wound in that heart of his. Scars. Cancers. There must be disappointments and frustrations the size of the world. There must be a burning passion for the death that won't come. I greet him. He answers me with his slow, moribund, uninterested voice. Everything about him is a harbinger of death. I begin by telling him about trivial things and then deeper questions. I tell him about the children and my husband. I tell him about all that is happening. I complain. His lifeless eyes widen and he accuses me:

"If your husband doesn't respond to you, the fault lies in you."

"What fault, Father?"

His tone of voice is harsh and corrosive, like poison spread on the wind. He speaks scornfully, like someone saying: Look, girl, don't bring me more problems. I've had so many in my life. And he continues his speech:

"Women nowadays talk a lot about this thing called emancipation. You talk too much, Daughter. In my day, women weren't like that."

I find it hard to accept what I'm hearing. My hopes have died, I'm a lost cause. How ashamed I feel. I'm desperately seeking help and I get a macho reaction by way of response. The problems of a woman are stored in the archive under the heading of trivia, whims, incapacities. That's what parents are like. Always educating their sons to be tyrants and their daughters to accept tyranny as the natural order of the universe. It's said that a father represents security. What security? My father doesn't want me disturbing his never-ending meditation. I'm the gall he's trying to expel from his heart. A thorn to remove, to cast aside, to whittle away. A daughter's feelings are no more than grains of sand. Mere dust. Insignificant. Look, Father, I'm going, I tell him. God save me from having to spend another minute in front of this old man. I look for my mother to convey the secrets of my heart to her. I approach her.

"You're as pretty as a flower, girl."

"Yes, a flower," I complain. "A cactus flower. A flower buffeted by a storm. A flower brutally pulled up by mischievous hands."

"Why are you so sad, girl."

I lose control and tell her everything.

"I'm so sad, Tony doesn't love me anymore, he doesn't pay me any attention. He doesn't sleep at home, he's got other women, Mother. Tell me, Mother, I'm not ugly, am I? I know I've got a great butt, good enough to charm any Bantu man. Julieta, the other woman, has a lighter skin than me, Tony must despise me because I'm dark. He's even gone looking for Makonde women. He's got this woman called Saly, and I don't know what sweetness she's got because she's far uglier than me. He's got a little Makua girl, Mother, who's pretty and as light as a little bird. She's called Mauá, Mauá Salé. She sings when she speaks, and her walk is like some graceful dance. He's got a Sena woman, Luísa, who's caused me some sleepless nights. Her breasts are larger than mine, Mother, why did you give me such small ones? This Luísa has got silky hair while I've just got hair like straw, but that's not so bad. I'll get myself some extensions at the beauty salon, Mother, that's an easy problem to sort out. What do you think of my weight, Mother? Should I slim down like Julieta? That's easy enough too, I can improve my body with massages and by doing some aerobics. But I'm scared of growing thin. Black men like chubby women, cushioned out both back and front, like me. It's true, Mother, these women have all got a grip on Tony using magic spells that I don't have. Why didn't you make me prettier than them, Mother? Why didn't you give me lessons in love, lessons to live without pain, dear Mother? These northern hussies have already given Tony children. One of these days it'll be white girls bringing mulattoes home to my family, Mother."

My mother answers me with a triumphant smile that sets my nerves at rest. She stretches out her hand and caresses my face gently.

"That handsome husband of yours is just grazing in other pastures, but he'll come back. There are many women out there looking to be chewed by that old goat's teeth. Hold on to your husband with both hands. A man has to be held on to, girl."

She's reproducing the same old litany and intoning the hymn to chastity.

"A husband is like a billy goat. He likes to graze far away, but he always comes home. Don't be scared, hold him by the horns."

"But how?"

"You understood what I said. Hold him."

They all talk about holding. Always holding. To hold is to defend. To defend oneself. Holding on to the ball in a game and holding one's course. Holding on to life. Holding on to love by one's fingernails. Holding on to a rose and its thorns until one's fingers bleed from the pain of it. How good it would be to hold love in a clenched fist. But love is a fistful of water escaping through the cracks in one's hand. One of these days, they'll ask me to hold the world by its reins. To hold the sun by its rays. Hold the wind by its gusts. The only advice women always get is: Hold, close, cover, conceal. For men, it's: Let go, fly, open, show – can anyone understand this world's contradictions?

I look at my mother. Dear God, how she's weeping. Can it be that my story has inspired such sadness?

"What's wrong, Mother?"

"Your voice reminds me of my sister, the one who died."

"Which one, Mother?"

"The eldest. You never knew her. She died before you were born."

"You've told me about her. What did she die of?"

"She died because of a chicken gizzard."

"What?"

"The gizzard is for husbands, for sons-in-law, you know that." She tells me the whole story.

"It was Sunday and my sister cooked dinner. It was chicken.

< 144 >

She carefully prepared the gizzard and put it aside in a dish. The cat came and ate it. Her husband came home and asked: What about the gizzard? She explained. It was useless. The man felt he'd been treated without respect, and beat her furiously. Go back home to your mother to be reeducated, he shouted. Now! She was so distressed that she lost all notion of danger and set off in the dead of night. Her parents' home was about ten kilometers away. She was killed by a leopard out on the savannah. She died in the flower of her youth over a piece of senseless stupidity. She died and the cat survived."

My mother's tears glisten in the sunlight like crystal, and reflect the colors of the rainbow. In my mother's heart, there's a silver dagger stained with blood. An eternal volcano. All because of a chicken gizzard, a mere sump for collecting grains of sand. An insignificant muscle inside a bird. That doesn't even fill the palm of one's hand. That doesn't even satisfy the hunger of a cat. The story penetrates me as if it were my own, for I'm a woman too, so help me God! I recall my love counselor and understand the incredible message about tyranny concealed inside a chicken's gizzard. No woman has a home in this land. A woman is a passing phenomenon, she doesn't merit any land. A woman is a piece of

< 145 >

coconut fiber thrown on the trash heap. A woman is her own enemy, she invents problems that kill her. It's a woman's fault, she turns the universe upside down, and that's why she may die because of a chicken gizzard.

"Mother, why didn't you tell me this story before?"

"I wanted your world to be full of color. So that you wouldn't have nightmares."

The story has a therapeutic effect on me, my pain becomes insignificant. One rancor erasing another. One love curing the pain of another love. Oh, Mother! Thank you for telling me this story! Now I can see I'm not the only woman to suffer, and that there are far graver problems in the world than mine.

"Mother, how did the womenfolk react to this incident?"

"The only strategy we had in our existence was to obey all the whims of the menfolk to the letter."

"So what was Father like?"

"Don't you know him? Didn't you hear his answer to your problems?"

Mothers, women. Invisible but present. A puff of silence giving birth to the world. Stars glittering in the sky, smothered by loathsome clouds. Souls suffering in the sky's shadow. The sealed trunk,

< 146 >

hidden in this old heart of mine, has been opened today to reveal the mantra of past generations. Women of yesterday, today, and tomorrow, intoning the same symphony, without hope of change.

< 147 >

13

I went from house to house, from one person to the next. I tried to gauge what people thought of my story. I asked women: What do you think of polygamy? They reacted like gasoline set off by a spark. Explosions, flames, tears, wounds, scars. Polygamy is a cross to bear. A Calvary, a hell. A burning brazier. And each one told me her tragic, moving, incredible story. I asked men: What do you think of polygamy? I had to listen to laughter, as steady as water bubbling from a fountain. I saw smiles stretching their lips from ear to ear. Their salivary glands went into overdrive as if I were serving them some delicious tidbit. They applauded. Polygamy is nature, destiny, our culture, they said. There are ten women for every man in the country, polygamy must continue. Polygamy is necessary, there are lots of women.

Once again I asked women for their views on my story. Some of them said: That's awful! If I were you, I'd kill all the concubines. I'd boil a pot of oil and put them in it one by one like the story of Ali Baba and the forty thieves. Others said: Ignore those women and their children, and pretend you know nothing. Keep your status as a married woman, and just make sure your man doesn't run away so that you can get your share of love, even if it's only once a month. Yet others said: Make friends with them because that's the only way you'll get the better of them without resorting to blows and curses. They're not the ones at fault, it's men who are worthless rogues. Men said: It's your obligation to accept all that your husband decides. These women are your sisters, and their children are also yours.

It was hard for me to take a stance in this forest of different opinions. The issue was more than my intelligence could take. What point was there in being drawn into wars and quarrels? Why ruin my already precarious state of health? Why try to erect walls of straw when the man holds his lance up and spreads like a bamboo root wherever he goes? I might shout and bluster all I liked, I'd never erase the lines that had already been drawn. That was why I decided to follow the time-honored formula: to make the pumpkin vine attractive because of its pumpkins. Aunt Maria said that when women agree with each other, men don't abuse them.

I investigated Tony's life. He wasn't as loving as they said. He didn't provide support as he should have done. He would turn up, take a plunge, and go on his way. He spent most of his time with Mauá. I pitied those women who sold love in order to buy bread and soap. When the charms they put up for sale grow thin, that's when poverty will knock at their door. What future awaited them, without a job or any security? And what would become of their children, with neither name nor protection? There was no doubt that all they could expect was the shelter of the street. Hunger, disease, life's dregs, that's what awaited them.

I assembled Tony's wives at a secret meeting. It was difficult, but I managed it. Mauá didn't attend. She was in love and living her moment of romance. She was the chosen one, the queen of our man's heart. Besides, the meeting was for the women who had been rejected, and not for sweethearts. Apart from this, that little Makua girl might betray our plan. I began the meeting by asking them all what they thought of life, the future, and whether they were happy.

"Ah, Tony, a honeyed tongue, a heart of gall," said Julieta. "He's responsible for my despair. He tricked me and left me in this sorry state."

"As far as I'm concerned," said Luísa, "it's not all bad. He gave me wonderful kids. He pays me attention whenever he can."

Suddenly, I felt happy. Fulfilled. It was a good feeling for me to be chairing this meeting when I'd never chaired anything in my life before. I felt I was the first spouse, the principal, senior wife, queen of all the others, a true first lady. But this term, first lady, doesn't it conceal vestiges of traditional polygamy? There's no first or second lady. The kings had a queen just for show, and smothered themselves in the pleasures provided by the beauties in their court, by their harems, concubines, and other similar categories of women. Who invented this term and first used it?

"Family?" asked Saly, furious. "A nest of birds, that's what it is. Running around out of control. Eggs left unprotected. Eggs dropping out of the nest. Rotten, abandoned eggs. What future can we expect for these children of ours? They don't know their aunts, grandparents, living as they do, hidden away like moles, their father never there, lacking any points of reference. Just people growing up to fill the world."

I put my finger on the wounds of their souls and extracted their sorrows from them. Discontent. Angry outbursts. These women personified the world's suffering. I imbibed their pain, their emotions. They wore a flower in their heart and gave themselves out of love. They opened up their bodies, that magical labyrinth, and allowed other flowers to germinate without nurture or hope. I suffer for these children. The situation of these concubines is far worse than mine. They have no legal or family protection. The houses they live in are the man's property, it's he who pays the rent at the end of every month. He can expel them when he wishes, he can cast them out into abject poverty. If he dies, they won't have a right to anything, because they're not an integral part of his family, they are mere satellites of the main family. The order of things needs to be inverted. But how? I brought together all the sentiments voiced by each of them and carried out a detailed diagnosis of love.

"Julieta, my dear Ju, you were deceived. You were torn from adolescence straight into old age, and enjoyed nothing in between. Your life is a never-ending summer. And you, Luísa, my dear Lu, will be the object of desire as long as you have fire in that beautiful body. Life is a never-ending process of change, one day is hot, next day is cold. What will become of you when winter arrives? Saly, you are the one who is used during quiet moments, you're a snack, a light meal, an intermediate stage to break the monotony of his love menu. Mauá is the one he loves most, but only for the moment. Tony's loves are ephemeral, we already know this."

This conclusion churned up a torrent of hidden emotions. I saw tears flowing, frustrations swelling to bursting point, uncertainties reflected in the silence, a tenuous hope flickering on the horizons of this world.

"We are lost mares galloping across life, being fed crumbs, enduring vicissitudes, waging war on each other. Time is passing, and one day we'll be forgotten. Each one of us is a loose branch, a dead leaf, at the mercy of the wind," I explained. "There are five of us. Let us unite, and together form one hand. Each one of us will be a finger, and the great lines of our hand will be life, heart, luck, destiny, and love. We won't feel so unprotected, and we'll be able to steer our course through life and choose our destiny."

They all looked at me in surprise, as if they hadn't understood what I was saying. But they did understand. I'd thrown my dice. I had joined the women and children together to construct the patriarch's family. I had gathered together the pieces and sculpted a monument held together with tears, and polished it with a luster that could reflect the rays of all the suns in the universe.

< 154 >

14

Tony's fiftieth birthday was approaching. I prepared everything for a really big party, it was going to have to be a proper
celebration.

The great day arrived. The wider family had already assembled.
There were ministers who were godfathers to us and our children,
and ministers who were friends of Tony's. Our priest uncle was
there to bless the party. There were many families, important
families, conservative, Catholic folk. There were gossipmongers
who frequent parties hunting for scandal that will then feed the
coming week's tittle-tattle. The cream of society was assembled
there. The room contained only perfume and silk. Good wine,
good food, all top-notch of the finest quality available. My Tony
was radiant, I'd never seen him look so happy. He hugged me.
Kissed me. Showed the whole world how great our love was.

I was the mistress of ceremonies. I started off by saying a
few light, hypnotic words. I spoke with an elegance that left
me moved. I even shed a tear or two. I was thinking about my

< 155 >

plan and my heart was throbbing. I began to tremble and could scarcely disguise my discomfort. It was the emotion of it all, forgive me, when one's companion celebrates his fiftieth birthday, things get highly emotional.

A woman guest walked in. Ju entered timidly with a cortege of five children and with a baby in her arms. She was dressed exactly as I had instructed. I went over to greet her and took her baby in my arms as if it were a present. I offered her a place next to mine and tried to make space for her children. At this point, Lu arrived with her kids and I entrusted her to Ju to look after. Saly made her entry like a hurricane, a warrior amazon, ready to win any battle that came her way. Finally, Mauá Salé arrived, gentle as winter sunshine, a star casting its light upon the world. We were all dressed alike, just as a polygamist's wives were supposed to present themselves. The children were also dressed the same, sheep from the same flock. And we chatted to each other in lively fashion, like sisters. I looked after them and their children to ensure that they had all they needed. I made all the appropriate introductions and played my role as first lady with distinction.

Thank you, dear God, for ensuring my plan went well. They all came in as treacherous as snakes. As softly as the music of the soul. As elegant as true ladies. They claimed their own space with smiles. They waged war with perfume and flowers. They were the rain watering the soil so that new life should spring from it. Together, these women defeated prejudice, advanced with confidence, and exposed the charade.

Tony's face revealed surprise, shame, tears, and rage. We stripped him of his sheep's clothing in front of his executioners and riddled his skinned body with a salvo of bullets. He took a deep breath and staggered to his feet. He attempted to make a speech.

"I hope you understand . . . we are African . . . our culture . . . you know . . . women . . ."

The guests whispered to one another, the case merited it. His old uncle was thunderstruck. He was silent for a few minutes and then objected:

"We are Bantu in body and soul. Passionate men. In questions of virility, even whites respect us. But, son, don't you think this is a bit of an exaggeration?"

I offered Tony my hand of stone. I was the first lady, his support in all awkward moments.

"I didn't want this great family to remain invisible on this day. On this, of all days, I wanted you all to bear witness to how this

< 157 >

man's heart is as fertile as loam. Tony is a man who loves life, and for this reason he multiplies. He is no coward, but has drawn his sword to affirm himself through five women and sixteen children."

When I'd finished my speech, the priest uncle crossed himself, sighed, said a prayer, gave his blessing, and fled that den of sin. Tony, his nephew, was a Christian who'd been led astray, a lost sheep. Tony helped himself to a double whiskey on the rocks. The godfather minister gave a diplomatic speech. He spoke about culture, acculturation, enculturation, miscegenation, idiosyncrasy, cosmogony, concomitance, the black renaissance, and a whole list of other long words no one understood. He took his wife's hand, bade his farewells, and left. Tony helped himself to another whiskey. His professional acquaintances, police officers, and ministers all congratulated him and wished him well, had another little drink, and then dragged their wives off home, telling him they had other commitments, so as not to expose their womenfolk to any further iniquity, so shielding them from being inspired by such vengeful examples, given that they too were guilty of the same thing. Tony had another whiskey on the rocks. All that remained were the neighbors, the scandalmongers, and my sister-in-law to control the explosion if it occurred. They gossiped.

They whispered among themselves and giggled teasingly. They ate, drank, and danced. They were intent on being present at the final act, and seeing the curtain come down on the stage. Tony knocked back another whiskey on the rocks.

I invited Tony for a private conversation with all his ladies. He came, mumbling something incomprehensible, and sat down next to us fearfully. I never thought a man could be such a coward when faced with his wives. I embarked on another speech.

"Dearest Tony, happy birthday. Today, we, your wives, decided to organize this surprise for you. As proof of the love we have for you, we decided to come together so that you could feel our hearts pulsating. We decided to bring your five wives together as one. We are aware of what you suffer by loving us: one day here, another day there. So we decided to honor you with our presence all together and of one voice on your big day."

I was all for going on with my speech, but he interrupted me and said:

"I'll be back in a minute. I've got to give the minister some documents he left behind."

He opened the door, got in his car, and left. We waited for hours on end, but he never came back. He'd fled.

< 159 >

"Girls! Rest assured once and for all. Now we've taken this step, there's no turning back. We've destroyed the mantle of invisibility, so let's celebrate. We've forced Tony to acknowledge publicly what he did in secret. Girls, why are you so scared? Have you ever attended Tony's birthday party before? Have your children ever sat on their uncles' and aunts' laps, surrounded by love, like full members of the family? Don't be scared of Tony. The king's gone, but it doesn't mean it's all over. Let's eat our fill and drink to our heart's content."

We had great fun. Lu and Saly told stories and we howled with laughter. Ju and Mauá listened and smiled. The children played, screamed, and ran all over the house. The party went on into the early hours of the morning.

I retired to my room. I went over to the mirror to look at my face and the mirror gave me an accusing look in return: You drunkard, you brazen woman, you killjoy! I tried to get to sleep, but couldn't. I went back and had a stiff drink to try to forget. I'm a bit of a strange one. The more I drink, the more lucid I become, the more I remember. I closed my eyes and saw a multitude of startled faces, booing poor Tony in his despair, his tail between his legs like some stray dog.

< 160 >

I reviewed the day. Bringing these women here was an act of inspiration, of courage, an instant triumph in the game of love. Tony mistreated me and I paid him back in kind, using the same tactics as he had used. Will the world understand or condemn me? Who has won this war? Who was the loser? Maybe we all won. Maybe we both lost. What future have I opened up today with my madness? I don't even know, I'm certainly crazy, and crazy is what people call me. I now begin to realize that I've gone too far. Where's my poor husband at such a late hour? At Mauá's house? I have a fit of remorse and start crying inconsolably. This isn't what I wanted for myself or for my home. This isn't what I wanted for my husband.

Why did Tony run away from us? Can a husband be such a coward in front of his wives? We five decided to come together as one, as we explained to him. Men like to conquer. Then they can't keep it up. Eventually, they arrange subterfuges, intrigues, in order to escape. This love of mine is a turbulent affair. A love doomed to fail from the start. If a man's time in life is shared between work, rest, socializing, a good polygamist is a love machine, who doesn't work, doesn't socialize, but just produces love by the ton, to be distributed as appropriate among his wives, mistresses, and concubines.

< 161 >

My rivals have all gained paradise. They certainly have. From being marginalized, they have begun to gravitate within the family circle. From being ignored and invisible, they have become recognized and visible. From now on, they can greet the uncles and grandparents of their children, without fear. As for me, what have I gained from this comedy?

15

My mother-in-law gave me an urgent summons at six in the morning. I rushed to meet her. I thought she must be ill. What she had wasn't a physical illness, but a deep bout of depression. Her eyes were red from lack of sleep and from crying, maybe she'd been dreaming of her dead husband. Hardly had she seen me than she started screaming. She said I was a murderer, that I'd tried to kill her son, that I was evil, stupid, irresponsible, and didn't appreciate the quality of the man I had. She went on and on. I was astonished. My old mother-in-law is strict, but kind. She always did talk for the sake of talking, and I'd switch off and stop listening. A daughter-in-law, as far as her mother-in-law is concerned, is an eternal child, who must know how to listen, to suffer in silence, always having to accept being addressed in vicious terms, inherited from a tradition where differences in rank were marked. I asked her what the problem was and she told me. Tony had spent the night there. He'd arrived sad, crestfallen, as if carrying the weight of the world on his shoulders. And he was

< 163 >

crying like a child. He asked for something to eat, and his mother served him what little she had. It was an insipid plate of food. He was burning with fever and raving: I've been poisoned, Mother, I've been poisoned.

I felt faint and my throat was dry. I told her my version of the facts. I told her about my war of love and jealousy, a war without victors that saw Tony fall at the first hurdle. A war of treachery that can end in death. I explained that I'd turned my rivals into allies, had poisoned my javelins in the battle of love. I spoke of the vanquished man who fled his wives and children to hide away at his mother's home. Of the man who abandoned mouthwatering delicacies to eat his sick mother's insipid food.

"It's true there was a moment of shame. Collective shame. Shame is poisonous. It crushes," I explained to my mother-in-law.

The old woman listened to me attentively and collapsed in tears. I'd been violent, I realized. I'd told her everything, without any concern for her feelings. I'd given her a bizarre image of her son, whom she had thought a saint. She fell silent, withdrawn. An icy, agonizing silence. The lady must have been deeply hurt. Like me, she must have felt betrayed, for she was also against polygamy

< 164 >

and its damaging effect on the Christian family. Then, suddenly, I detected a light in her old face.

"Is it true you brought all the women together for everyone to see?"

"Yes."

"Thank God! That wasn't only your wish, Rami, but it was mine, too. The ancestors guided you to organize a great family reunion on an important day. You're a great woman."

"Do you think so?" I replied, astonished.

The old woman's voice lost its hard edge, and its rhythm increased gradually, sweet and melodious. Her shoulders straightened. I was witnessing life being reborn, triumph over death. The extended family is a living, mobile collection of assets. It's a form of social security and a guarantee of food in times of need.

"Praise be to God! I didn't know I had such a large family. That's good. Of these seventeen grandchildren, some will give me joy and others sadness. Some will give me my last glass of water, others my funeral shroud. It's good to have a large family, Rami."

"But all these children are illegitimate, isn't that so?"

"Illegitimate for you, who are bound by laws and command-

< 165 >

ments. Illegitimate because they're the children of your rivals. For me, they are merely grandchildren, the continuation of my lineage."

She was rapturous, I had brought her comfort in her sadness. She now condemned her son. She said he was mischievous, bad mannered, selfish, that he'd turned her whole night upside down inventing nonexistent monsters. All this because he'd been scared to live a clean, honest, worthy, transparent life, without having to hide away. She said a man's greatness is proved by the number of children he has. That polygamy is in man's nature: although we may condemn it, it's not a crime, and doesn't do anyone any harm. That a man worthy of respect must have at least three women. That her own husband had never been polygamous, because he was a poor workingman, but Tony had a profession and was rich, which was why he had to have someone on whom to spend his wealth. Now she wanted to know all about her four daughters-in-law. I told her how marvelous they were. I invented stories to sweeten her and she was delighted.

"Ah! Rami, why did you never tell me this? Why did you people go around postponing my happiness? I've got this huge garden, and the children can come and run and play here. I've got

< 166 >

these trees loaded with fruit that goes rotten and falls because there's no one to eat it, and here I am with so many grandchildren! Where do they live? When will they come and visit me?"

She was in a hurry to hug all these hidden grandchildren.

"That doesn't depend on me."

"Please have a word with Tony. Tell him I need to see him urgently, and that we need to bring these children over here."

Now that her solitude was coming to an end, the old woman began to think of human warmth. She was delighted at the prospect of a house full of children to enliven her sad world. In this war, my mother-in-law and my rivals came out winners, while I, Rami, lost the battle.

Sweet little Mauá was inseparable from our Tony. But he wasn't happy according to our personal detectives. He looked like a ghost. Did anyone know what he was thinking? No one. He lived in silence, he'd go upstairs, come down, eat, go out. Had anyone asked him anything? No, no one. We didn't have the courage. We were at a complete loss from fear, and so was he. He had become nervous, trying, shouting at those under his command. And he'd lost weight. He smoked a lot and drank more than he should. Tony was in need of therapy. Therapy of the type polygamous love could provide and not hospital appointments. But why is a polygamist happy when his women are at war with each other, and unhappy when they get along together?

< 168 >

16

One day, I told my rivals: Come, come and demand food when you don't have enough, come and wake Tony up if by any chance he's here, when your children are ill, or when they are at school and the teacher wants to see whoever is responsible for their education. Come and queue up to see him, he's usually here at lunchtime. You are his wives and your children are my children's brothers and sisters.

A procession of mothers and children began to arrive. Tony couldn't take it anymore, and ran away. Rami, you see to this riff-raff. I did what I could for them, until eventually I said: Things are like this because you don't work. Every day you have to beg for a few crumbs. If each of us had a source of income, a job, we'd be free of this problem. It's humiliating for a grown woman to have to ask for money for salt and coal. Saly said she had a business but it went bust because she used all her money to pay for medicine when her son was ill. Lu said she'd like to have a fashion boutique, which had always been her dream. Ju said she liked children. She

< 169 >

said that the day she looked for a job it would be to work with children. Mauá said she didn't have a talent for anything. She'd been brought up to be a wife and to care for people. She couldn't imagine herself working and didn't want to become involved in such a plan.

"We've got to work," Lu said, "we've still got a bit of bread because Tony is still alive. What happens when he dies? From a period of mourning up until the time we manage to find new partners, that's a lot of hunger to put up with. We must think of the future."

"What are we going to do?" said Mauá. "I don't even have any qualifications or skills to do anything at all."

"Ah! Mauá!" said Saly. "All those people selling things on the street corner are women just like us. If someone were to lend me a bit of money, I'd set up my own business."

"I would too," said Lu. "I'd sell clothes, even if it was second-hand. I've always dreamed of having a clothes shop."

I grabbed some money I'd put aside and lent it to Saly. She bought whole sacks of cereal and sold them by the cupful in markets out in the suburbs. Two months later, she paid me back with interest and gave me a present. Some cloth for a *capulana*, a silk scarf, and a red rose bought on the corner. Lu said: I'm inspired. If Saly has managed to make a go of her business, I can as well. Rami, can you lend me some money? I passed Saly's returns across to her. And she began to sell secondhand clothes. And she began to put on weight, her tone of voice became gentler, and her smile broadened as the money began to flow. Three weeks later, she returned the money to me with more interest, a little hug, and a bunch of roses. Ju and Mauá protested.

"Rami, why don't you give us the same treatment?" Mauá asked. We're poor women too, like Lu and Saly. You helped them. Why don't you help us as well?"

I transferred Lu's money to Mauá and gave Ju a bit of money Tony had once entrusted to me to look after. Mauá set up as a hairdresser, straightening hair, which is something she knows all about. She began on the veranda of her house. She managed to build up a clientele. Work increased and she took on two assistants. The veranda got too small and she moved her salon into the garage of her house. Now Mauá has a whole host of customers.

Ju goes to the warehouses, where she buys crates of drink and sells it retail. She makes a lot in the way of profit. In this country, people drink like fish. She's begun to smile more and gained more

< 171 >

self-confidence. Tony has reacted badly to our initiatives, but we don't listen to him and get on with our lives.

I decided to accompany Lu in her clothes-selling enterprise. We sold them in the market on the corner of the street where there are plenty of customers. The market is full of women, all of them talking at the tops of their voices, touting for customers. When business slackens, the women sit in a circle, eat their day's meal, and talk about love. A love transformed into hatred, anger, despair, trauma. I was raped by my stepfather when I was eight, said one. That was better than what happened to me. I was raped by my real father when I was ten. I got an infection and lost my womb. I haven't got any children. I can't have any. I got married, said another. I was happy and had three children. One day, my husband left the country in search of work and never came back. I had to put up with a lot of beating, said another. He'd lock me in the room with my children and sleep with other women in the next room. I was raped by five men during the civil war, said another. This handsome son I'm carrying on my back, I don't know who the father is. Every time I look at this poor little creature, I remember that horrible moment when I thought I was going to die. My mother died in my arms, said

< 172 >

another. She was brutally beaten by my father and died on her way to the hospital. From that time on, I couldn't face men. Nor do I want to bring children into the world for them to suffer life's torments. My husband drinks, said another, he drinks so much that he can't even work anymore. At the end of the day, all we have in our house is violence. He wants my money so that he can go and drink, but I won't give him any. One of them said she'd been married for twelve years and was happy. She'd never had any problems and sells in the market to help her husband, who doesn't earn much. Another said her husband was a good man. She'd betrayed him. She'd been caught red-handed with another man.

I told them my husband is a professional man and they were all astonished. The wife of a man with a profession doesn't sell old clothes on the street corner, they argued. But we're five wives, I explained. The salary of a professional isn't enough for seventeen children. I've got my diploma for secondary school, I could get a job, but salaries are low, and selling at the market pays better. I explained to them all that this business of liking women isn't limited to age, race, or social class. I told them Lu is my rival and no one believed me. You call her sister and she does too. You look

< 173 >

alike, we thought you really were sisters. We're sisters in love, the same man's wives, I retorted.

Then we went on to talk about men, our favorite topic of conversation. I told them I go through all my business accounts with my husband. I told them how much I earn and how much I spend. Our colleagues laughed. One should never provide men with the exact details of our earnings. Men were made to control, and women to work.

None of these women gave their companions exact details of what they earned. Instead, they told them hard-luck stories: They didn't make any money that day, there's a lot of competition in the market, there are thieves on the street, and all my goods were stolen, I didn't make any money.

This was when I began to see things. My rivals were making progress in their businesses while I wasn't. Don't tell him the truth, Rami, they advised me, tell him lies. Never tell him the whole truth. Keep your money hidden away in a corner. Money in a man's pocket is for all his women. In a woman's hands, it's bread and food. The money you make is safer with you than it is with him.

We talked about love, and they whispered a few secrets in my ear. Get yourself a fisherman lover if your business is fish. A baker if your business is bread. A customs officer if you're in the import-export business. A dockworker if your line of business is loading and unloading. I stifled a laugh and exclaimed:

"Can I give myself to anyone just for love?"

"So what's love except for an agreement to defend one's interests?"

"If I ever get myself a lover, I'll find a man with a degree, like my Tony, who can talk about life," I answered.

"Educated men? They talk a lot about philosophy. They can say things like: The lower orifice of the digestive canal responsible for expelling human excreta. So many words to describe an asshole. They offer you flowers, dinners, lights, music, poems, just so that they can get to that place a few millimeters away. They waste a lot of time on trivia. They get in the way of business."

"How unfair you are! Listen, a lover who's a minister improves your status and can solve lots of problems."

"That's where you're wrong… ministers, politicians, directors, and all that race of refined folk are damaging for business. They make you dress expensively to be in their company. They eat well and talk pretty. They frequent palatial houses and are profligate. They sign documents with a gold pen. They glitter on the surface, but they're no good at managing money. They're poor."

"You people are exaggerating!"

"Where's the exaggeration? You have to make an appointment with them to discuss a problem, and when they agree to help, they flash their credit card or write a check. It's better to be the lover of the black marketeer on the corner of the street because at least he's got money in his pocket and is always available."

I died laughing at the secrets more experienced women passed on to me.

"Rami, use *xitique*, our own credit and savings system. Join *xitique*. You'll see how quickly your life improves."

I joined *xitique* under pressure from my market women friends. And, my God, did it make things better! *Xitique* is a form of compulsory savings. It's a traditional credit system that has operated for centuries, and is far better than bank credit.

We sold used clothes for six months. We built up some capital. Then Lu and I each opened a little shop for selling new clothes, and business began to blossom. Saly built a shop. She sells drink in bulk. She's got a café and tearoom. Ju managed to get herself a small warehouse and sells drink wholesale. Mauá opened a downtown hairdressing salon, but still does some work out of her garage. She's got countless customers.

We've managed to get ourselves a minimum amount of security to buy bread, salt, and soap without having to put up with the humiliation of begging for crumbs. My rivals are ecstatic, and regret the way they once gave me a beating, but I tell them: It doesn't matter. That's how things were done in those days. What did you expect?

< 177 >

17

My mother-in-law has been dashing between houses and along different routes. She visits her new daughters-in-law, her grandchildren, showering them with candy and chocolates. She has been winning them over. She visits brothers, sons, their families. She seeks alliances and treaties. She spreads news by word of mouth. She seeks votes of confidence. She embarks on a campaign in favor of the extended family, her daughters-in-law should be subject to a bride price. I'm not speaking for myself, she told me. She speaks on behalf of those children who grow up abandoned, ignorant of their origins. She speaks in the name of those women caught in the desert of life, and who produce souls that enhance our family but who live outside the shadow that is rightfully theirs. They are called single mothers, confused with divorcées and adulteresses because they live far from the shadow of their man. She shouts "down with monogamy," that inhuman system that marginalizes some women while privileging others, that gives a roof, love, and sense of belonging to some children, while others are rejected and left to run around in the streets. She shouts "down with" the new custom of having a spouse for all to see, and various concubines, with children hidden away. My grandchildren, marginalized by the law, are clamoring for recognition. The blood of the enlarged family should be reunited in the shade of our ancestors' great tree. My son is beautiful, she said. Women cannot resist his charms. My son's blood is strong, every time he makes love, he produces a child. My son is a spreading root. He's bamboo. He spreads through fields, creeping over the ground, multiplying himself. My son is destined to be a king, a patriarch. His father only had three children, but God has given us Tony to regain our family's fertility and extend our great name to the four corners of the world. She went and confronted her priest brother. Because of your doctrine our African families are no more than isolated mountaintops floating in the clouds. You, Father, are a product of polygamy, the son of a third wife. How can you condemn polygamy, which brought you into the world? Keep your bad influences away from my son. Leave him in peace with his wives and children, we Africans are happy like that. All those women should have their bride price paid.

< 180 >

My mother-in-law turned herself into an arrow. She projected herself against good Christian family customs and became a spokesperson for the return to roots. She met no resistance.

The bride-price cycle began with Ju. It was paid in money rather than cattle. The mother was paid a lot of money in a bride price wedding ceremony. The children were legally recognized, but hadn't been presented to the family spirits. They needed to be brought from their mother's house into the protection of the patriarch's shadow in an act of bride-price profiling, a way of giving them legitimacy given that they'd been born outside the rules of the game for a polygamous family. After this, Lu had her bride price paid and her children were acknowledged. The northern women were astounded. This bride-price story was new to them. They wanted to say no to it given that it was against their cultural norms. But it involved a large amount of money. Money for their parents, money for them, and money for their children. Money that was needed to be able to eat, live, and invest. When it's a question of a lucky break, any culture will do. They forgot matriarchy and said yes to the patriarchal tradition. We spent three months going from one party to another. It was important

< 181 >

to get the bride-price payments out of the way in one fell swoop before Tony changed his mind. In all the bride-price ceremonies, we introduced a novelty feature: the bride-price certificate, including all the contractual clauses but without the bit that talks about conjugal assistants in the event of the husband's incapacity. That would look a bit immoral, don't you think? All on officially stamped foolscap paper, typed and signed by all parties present at the ceremonies. With so many signatures, it looked like more than just a certificate, and more like a petition. Well, we're in the age of the written word, aren't we?

I was left depressed. My husband had been cut up into little pieces and shared around. All my assets had been shared around, our social security, our retirement savings, our comfort that was being tossed to the ground like a handful of salt into a saucepan of water. I share bread and wine in communion. I share my husband among five, while Lu and I share a lover. Ah, how deep love is! It cuts up my heart and destroys me with each breath. Life, you force me to accept a few crumbs of love that belong to me alone. You make me die little by little, cell by cell, and you bleed me dry, one drop at a time. Farewell, my only complete husband, my love and intimacy. Ah, life! You make me wear this muzzle just to keep

Tony near me. If I were to refuse this muddled state of affairs, my love would be scared off and run away.

We had our first formal meeting of the conjugal parliament, summoned by my mother-in-law and the old aunties in order to give us lessons and to tell us everything we might wish to know about polygamous love.

"By formally marrying five wives, my Tony has reached the top of the mountain," my mother-in-law declares. "He is the star that shines on high, and should be treated as such. And you, Rami, are the first wife. You are the pillar of this family. All these women revolve around you and owe you allegiance. Give them orders. Punish them if necessary. You are the keeper of the throne and the scepter. Exercise your power over them, submit them to your command. You are the queen of this household."

I felt I had been promoted within the hierarchy of this tyranny. I've been given a whip they call a scepter, to beat any unfortunate women who cross my path. But I'm not going to whip anyone. I'm going to lock this piece of insignia in a trunk and chuck it into the sea where it's nice and deep.

"To start with, you should plan a conjugal rota. Your husband should stay with each of you for one week at a time on a rotational basis. Whoever is menstruating when it's their turn should inform him immediately. You mustn't soil Tony's body with the impurities of your menstrual blood. This could make him fall ill with the type of illness that causes a man's testicles to swell to the size of pumpkins."

Those old ladies have nightingales in their throat, but twitter morbidly like slave women. Their toothless old mouths have been sucked dry by all the blows they've received in life. Their lips have never known kisses, only lamentations.

"You must serve your husband on your knees, as the law demands. Never serve him from the pot, but only on dishes. He can't touch china or go into the kitchen. When you serve him chicken, don't forget the rules. Men should be served the best pieces: the thighs, breast, and gizzard. When you serve beef, the best steaks are for him, the biggest bones full of marrow. You need to invest in him, not only with your love but with his food. His dish should be the fullest and most brimming with food, so that he may have the strength to produce healthy children, for without him, the family doesn't exist."

We didn't burst out laughing, but we certainly felt like it. Faced

< 184 >

with this litany that has sent women to sleep down the ages, we kept our silence.

"You modern women are in the habit of feeding men any old way. You keep food in the fridge for days on end. A man should be fed fresh food. The stove needs to be lit every day. Don't give them potatoes that have been cooked the previous day, because this swells men's testicles, especially those of growing boys. Never eat a fish head, or that of a cow or of a goat, because that is man's food. The head of an animal represents the head of the family. The head of the family is the man."

"In the father's absence, the eldest male child takes command of the family, even if he's a baby, he's a leader, he's the head of the family by substitution."

"Organize a conjugal rota. One week in each house is enough for living life together. It's healthy to go to sleep and wake up in the same place. The man shouldn't have to travel around the city each day, because it's tiring and can lead to an early death. There are many advantages to this system: in times of affliction, you will all know where to find him."

Their voices are like salt on the breeze, gradually gnawing away at us like niter. They only know about what pain has taught them. They know of no other world except that of darkness itself. And they see darkness in front of them as the only source of their wisdom.

Ah, Tony! I'm not the only one on your trail now. There are five of us. Let's see if you can escape us now, you cunning little rat!

18

The weeks pass. We nourish our bodies with dreams and memories of loves that only last a week. Good things don't fill our belly, what's good doesn't last long. Polygamy is precisely this. Filling our soul with a tiny grain of love. Holding back our body's fire with hands of straw. Proffering our lips to the passing breeze and harvesting kisses from the dust-laden wind. Waiting. Listening to your man's sighs in another woman's arms and hiding your jealous feelings. Feeling you miss him while not suffering. Feeling pain without crying.

We draw up the conjugal rota just as we were taught, and we've even become experts in the matter. Tony has been with Mauá, but the end of his stay with her has arrived. Here we are together to take delivery of the baton. Passing the man from one set of hands to the next with the care of people carrying an egg. I, as the first lady, always ask some questions as part of the handover ritual.

"Mauá," I ask, "how is Tony?"

"In terms of health, he's been good, he ate well."

< 187 >

"And how did you serve him?"

"On my knees."

"Did you make chicken?"

"Yes."

"What bits did you give him?"

"The thighs, the breast, and the gizzard."

"Excellent. Now tell us about the other matter."

"He was all right, he sang and whistled while he was having his bath, as if he were completely happy, but when the time came for it, all he did was sleep! And how he slept! He'd snore like a trumpeter at the gates of paradise, and that would be that."

"Nothing more?"

"Nothing!"

Mauá's face has lost its recent sheen and her words tumble loosely like leaves when winter announces its arrival. Her eyes are misty. A couple of teardrops fall. Love's like that. One day it sets you soaring as high as a church steeple, the next it sends you plummeting to the ground, making you wallow like a worm in the fetid waters of a bog.

"They say this sort of thing sometimes happens," Ju explains, "it's probably due to stress, too much work, depression, whatever!"

< 188 >

"I also thought it might be that and tried everything. I put aphrodisiacs in his soup, his stew, his curry, his tea. Nothing worked!"

"Nothing?"

"That's right. At first I thought he was ill. But one day, I found a thread of hair in his clothes. A long, thick hair, not one of those artificial hairs. I got suspicious, I got on his trail and found him out. He's got another woman."

"Another?"

"Yes, another."

She speaks of betrayal and her pained words spill out like javelins. She sobs convulsively like a kettle on the boil. On her moistened face, the different colors of her makeup mingle to form black, blue, red tears, and she turns into a multihued smudge.

"I'd just like to meet this woman who's been capable of competing with me, Mauá Salé. I'd like to see the face of this woman who has affronted me. I've wasted my time preparing Makua love potions so that he can live it up with some other woman."

Love's thorns open up wounds, gashes, cancers, and no one knows the cure, for if we did, we would certainly administer it to Mauá to heal her pain. She's like a poisoned flower, fading, dying.

"Why are you crying?" Ju asks in an ironic tone, taking advantage

< 189 >

of the moment to wash her dirty laundry. "What you're feeling, we've all felt, Mauá. We've suffered betrayals, one after the other. You chose a polygamist, so what are you complaining about?"

"Are you hurt?" Saly asks sarcastically. "Weren't you aware this is how things are? Are you sad? Who told you Tony was only for you? Did he by any chance tell you that you were his be-all and end-all? Oh dear, Mauá! For a man who's had five women, you might as well add a zero and call it fifty. Tony will have fifty, you'll see. When it comes to polygamy, passion has no limits, Mauá."

The other three take the opportunity to get even. Any woman who's been rejected gets some consolation from another woman's misfortune. The cowards gang up together to hurl stones at Mauá – beating the shadow without touching the tree.

I'm the only one not to say a word. What for? I've got four massive betrayals on my conjugal curriculum. One more, one less, what difference does it make? Polygamy is man's destiny and chastity is that of women. A man kills to save his honor and is applauded. A woman expresses her jealousy and she's condemned. In this thing of creating man in his own likeness, God failed in one aspect of the formula: He's still a bachelor and men are polygamous.

To be honest, I've no bone to pick with polygamy. I've already explained my problem: If I complain too much, I lose my husband completely. If I play his game, I remain quietly in my own little corner in the knowledge that he's not straying too far. For the rest, in our traditions, polygamy depends on each man's power. The king of our land possessed the power to have more than twenty women, and Aunt Maria was the twenty-fifth. Ministers, governors, and all the nobility had sufficient power for between five and ten women. The poor, with few assets, were limited to three. In fact, three is the ideal number. A man with one wife is a kind of senior bachelor, the chief of the bachelors, he's insignificant, he can't elect or be elected because he belongs to the class of those who lack experience. A man with two wives is almost a man. He can give an opinion but doesn't have the power of decision. He can't be a king or a regent or a local ruler. A man with three wives is a true man, he can mediate in disputes, and conduct the affairs of his family. In our traditions, women don't have a right to vote; apart from this, there's no voting among the aristocracy, but women acquire some status. A woman only gains status if she agrees to share her husband, if she overcomes her jealousy, if she preserves the values enshrined in tradition, and carries out all that the law prescribes. The wife who suggests to her husband he should marry again and who helps him choose a new wife gains a considerable amount of prestige.

If only it had been so with me. I would never have chosen or approved of such a lusty rival as Lu. Saly, yes, she's an ideal rival. She's very impulsive and resorts to her fists to resolve problems. Tony would spend his time quarreling with her, and would end up weeping in my arms and sleeping in my bed. I wouldn't choose that lazybones Mauá, who spends her life combing her hair, filing her nails, and preparing *musiro* to soften her skin. I'd choose unrefined women, good for scrubbing the floor and making the tiles shine like a mirror. I don't really have a view when it comes to Ju, poor soul. A pretty face. But she's disillusioned, embittered, humiliated. Tony consumed her completely and then cast her aside. She's a figure of sadness. She's like a living phantom.

Ah, how I wish I had the privilege to choose my successors. I'd choose women uglier than myself. If he chose a pretty one, I'd invent some convincing story, and he'd end up agreeing with me. Oh God! What a fate! It's been bad right from the start. Woman is cursed even before she's born, and the curse doesn't disappear

< 192 >

even after her holy baptism. What's the point of baptizing woman if she can't free herself from perdition?

"Stop crying because the world isn't going to stop for us," Ju shouts in a tone of utter scorn. "It's obvious you've never experienced this before. Betrayal is a bitterly hurtful thing, Mauá."

Lu decides to elaborate on the subject.

"Who does this Tony think he is? Just any old bachelor? Doesn't he understand his responsibilities have just increased fivefold?"

"We've really got to do something," chips in Saly. "Polygamy gives us some rights, so let's make the most of them. A polygamist can have lovers, and should have them on occasions when his wives are in a period of confinement."

"You're right," Lu adds. "None of us has aborted, nor are we lactating."

"I wasn't even having my period, I was pure, completely pure," Mauá says disconsolately. "He had no reason to do what he did to me."

"This is serious," Saly remarks, "a person spends four weeks waiting just to watch the man sleeping like a cherub? A polyga-

< 193 >

mist must inform his wives and explain the reasons for any new conquest. Have any of you received such an explanation?"

They all confirm they haven't.

"Mauá, tell us the whole story. In every detail. What's she like? Is she pretty?"

"She's no better than I am. Compared to me, she's older, fatter, even ugly. Why does he like her better? Because she's a mulatto woman?"

Our enthusiasm vanishes. A *mulata* is a serious rival. Black men are obsessed with lighter skin, just as white men are obsessed with blondes. But the truth is that dark-skinned women are hotter, they know that only too well.

"A *mulata*?" Ju asks, showing some curiosity. "I don't like mulatto women. They're our men's perdition."

"Must be a third-class *mulata*," scoffs Lu. "She's probably the daughter of a horny-handed white, a slum shopkeeper, out there in the suburbs."

"Why all this racism?" I ask crossly. "Isn't a *mulata* a woman?"

"*Mulatas* are women and much more: They're specialists in love magic. They're temptation in the heart of paradise. You'll see, we're going to lose Tony. Tell us, Mauá, is she prettier than we are?"

"I've already said, she's no better than us," Mauá snorts by way of reply. "And she's older. Fatter, ugly. But she dresses well and she's got a good car."

"Is she married or single, Mauá?"

"Oh, it's hard to tell from a distance."

"Polygamy is for black women, it's certainly not for *mulatas*." I allay their fears. "The woman only wants to have some fun at our expense, steal Tony for a bit, gobble up his money, and then let him go when she's had enough."

"Poor *mulatas* are blacks and don't mind polygamy," Lu argues, "what they're looking for is somewhere to perch, so that the world will say: She's got a husband. It's important we know whether she's single or not. If she's married, there's no danger at all. If she's single, she's probably up to no good, a spinster with a polygamist can only be after a husband or she's a gold digger. She'll soon get pregnant and then demand recognition. And then we'll be six. If she's a widow, she'll have inherited from her late man and is only after a bit of love. Divorced? You never know what a divorcée is thinking, whether she wants to pass the time, get her hands on his money, or just enjoy life to the full."

Man has wings, and flies. From perch to perch, kiss to kiss, enjoying the fun this life offers. And we women sow love, one grain at a time over every inch of soil, and when it germinates, along come other beaks to reap our harvest, leaving us with a hunger the size of the world.

"But what does our Tony want with this woman?" Lu asks with interest. "Isn't it enough for us to have to put up with this rota, all this horrible waiting? If she joins us, we'll have to wait six weeks instead of five. We must avoid such a disaster."

I give the matter some quick thought. Five is the ideal number for a conjugal parliament. It's an uneven number and therefore there's no danger of a split vote. Six confuses things. We have to do something.

"Mauá, this is your problem," I say, "you're the one who must solve it. You've got to find out more about this woman, get all her details: name, civil status, bank account, her aims in pursuing a relationship with our Tony."

"It's no good asking," says Saly, "she needs to be caught unawares. Take a photo of a furtive kiss and bring us a picture of this woman."

"What for?"

"We'll know when we get it."

< 196 >

We drew up our plan. We organized things between us. The following day, Mauá and Lu set off in search of a photo opportunity, which wasn't hard. Knowing Tony's tastes and his favorite places made the work easier. Mauá and Lu got a good shot of them in flagrante and brought photos of the wrongdoing. They paid for all the information they could get on her and came back with a full report.

We had another urgent meeting. We studied the photos closely. God, the *mulata* looked superb. She had the beauty of a film star. Jealousy apart, she was much prettier than Mauá, she looked like one those goddesses that light one's path. Her smile was one of love and total surrender. A smile of triumph over solitude. The photo was taken with such a magical eye that it even revealed the lovers' souls. Tony's smile was a daggerlike betrayal that made our hearts bleed with pain. Mauá couldn't take it anymore. She wept like a widow. I wish the earth would swallow me up, she yelled, I want to die.

But the reality of love is this. To love and be loved is a man's thing. For a woman, the love she gets lasts a mere puff of air, a camera flash, the bat of an eyelid. For a woman, to love is to be exchanged like a piece of old cloth for another younger, more

< 197 >

beautiful one – just as I was. It's to be buried alive when meno-
pause arrives: "She's dried up, exhausted, sterile, she can produce
neither children nor pleasure, and she no longer blossoms once
a month," men say.

The image of this new Eve threw us all off course for a minute.
A thousand questions arose in our minds. Might Tony wish to
take that relationship to its uttermost term? What place would
this woman command in his life, what gap would she plug that
the five of us were unable to satisfy? What words did he whisper
in her ear to produce that divine smile on her face? Did he say
he loved her? Did he tell her she was the most perfect woman in
the world? That he was single or only married to one woman?

We needed to act quickly, my rivals concluded, we needed to
wreck this love affair before the *mulata* usurped our places. We
tried to discover the reasons that might lead Tony to seek another
woman, and Mauá was submitted to a barrage of accusations.
You didn't take good enough care of Tony, you didn't hold on
to him. You fell asleep when you were supposed to be vigilant,
and he went and hooked the other woman. But who were we
to condemn Mauá, if we were all incompetent when it came to
holding on to Tony?

< 198 >

"Tony's a catfish," Mauá defended herself, "he's slippery. He slithers out of your hands, you can't hold on to him. He's faster than the wind."

"Ever since you entered our lives, we've lost space, status, our voice, everything," Saly burst out. "We've been in the grip of a marital crisis. Tony didn't even want to know about us. Now you're the one crying. It comes to us all eventually, Mauá."

"The new rival is separated," Lu explained. "She was a politician's wife but was cast aside because she's sterile."

"Sterile? Ah! Poor soul!" We all sighed and fell silent for a minute.

We were swept by a momentary feeling of pity. A sterile woman is condemned to solitude and bitterness. What life does a sterile woman have? Being marginalized and forgotten. What feelings does she have? Pain and silence. What dreams does she have? Never-ending anxiety and despair. A sterile woman feels lifeless deep within her, that she is condemned to disappear without putting down the roots of existence in the soil. A creature who exists without existing. Deformed without being so. A woman who is expelled from everywhere, endlessly looking for a position, in a society where a woman is only considered as such if she can

< 199 >

give birth. And who is it that makes her feel this way? Society, men, and women themselves, especially the mothers-in-law who decide the number of children who may be born in a household.

"I was getting ready to give her the biggest slap ever seen," said Saly. "But I pity her. She may have all the treasures this world can offer. But a woman without children, where's the joy in that?"

"You may feel sorry for her," Lu argued, "but it's a fact that polygamous men like to have a barren woman. It's convenient. She doesn't smell of milk. In the arms of a barren woman, a husband is a son, while when we hold him, he's a father, a husband. A barren woman is always young and beautiful. A good polygamist always has a barren woman in his flock. While we divide our affections between our children and our husband, all she thinks about is her man. That's why Tony sought her out. He must be tired of making children everywhere he goes. This woman is dangerous. Mauá, it's your turn to do something to try to put a brake on this relationship."

"What else have you discovered?"

"The woman's got money and power. She's got status. She's a boss in her job. She tells men what to do. And she drives a flashy car."

"Did she buy it with her own money? Our Tony didn't give her a hand, did he?"

"It doesn't look like it. It was probably bought with her old husband's money. Or hers. But if she's got so much money, why's she getting involved with a poor devil like Tony?"

"What shall we do now, girls?"

We decided on a protest that would fall short of a sex strike, but a corrective measure, a demonstration of passive love that might help Tony get in touch with his own conscience.

A polygamist's first wife is this. She sits on a coveted throne. She wears a disputed crown. She controls the repressed desires of other wives when they feel horny, angry, dissatisfied. These women talk about their anguish and can't even imagine the pain I feel because of all this.

< 201 >

19

We invited Tony for a family dinner. We explained that it's good to be all together once in a while. He liked the idea and agreed. We dressed up to the nines and got ready for battle. We met together at Saly's place in the early evening. Tony was sitting in the lounge reading the day's papers. My little doves, he greeted us with the most candid smile imaginable, a breeder reviewing his females assembled together in the corral. He addressed us in honeyed tones, his words sweeter than sugar candy. The dinner was good, the atmosphere pleasant. We got him to drink enough to unlock his tongue.

"Tony, we've always wanted to know why you like us so much. Pretend you're our mirror and tell us: what do you see in us?"

"Do you want to know?"

"Yes, of course!"

"You won't get angry or be offended?"

"Of course not!"

Tony starts off by talking about the youngest one.

< 203 >

"Mauá's my little bantam," he said, "she attended a school of love, and she's the sweetest thing. Saly's a good cook. Sometimes, I wake up in the morning with a yearning for her tasty snacks. But she's also feisty, which is good for calming my nerves. On days when work goes badly and I feel like screaming, I seek her out just to have a row. We argue. And I shout good and loud to fill my lungs with oxygen and get rid of my tension. Lu has a good body and is very tasteful in the way she adorns herself. She radiates such magnetism that it's a pleasure to walk down the road with her. Her company does me good. Ju is my monument to error and forgiveness. She's the woman I deceived the most. I promised I would marry her, I changed the course of her life, I filled her with kids. She was a good student and had a promising future. She's the prettiest of you all, and she could have had a good marriage. What of Rami? I won't even comment. She's my first lady. Through her, I asserted myself as a man before the world. She's my mother, my queen, my rock, my pillar."

"Tony," Ju burst out somewhat bitterly, "each one of us has a function. For you, women are objects to be used, a bit like toilet paper."

"That's not quite true, Ju. I've got a lot of respect for women,

< 204 >

a lot! Jesus, the son of God, was born from a woman's womb. I've got great respect for all the women in the world."

He stumbled around between insult and gallantry like some Don Juan. He was unaware of the injuries he was causing. The idea of an insult never occurred to him, because he wasn't in any danger. Danger of what? The women were his. They'd had their bride price paid. They'd been bought. They were in love. They'd given birth to children. They were safe, landed in the net. A caught fish is prepared, seasoned, cooked, and eaten. He could say whatever was on his mind without running any risk. The conversation was taking a rocky path and our faces were twisted with anguish.

"You do feel fulfilled with us, don't you, Tony?" Lu asked, her voice shaking.

"Very much so!"

"So why have you got yourself another woman?"

"Another what?"

"We're talking about Eve, the mulatto woman."

He looked as if he's been caught in a mousetrap, but he quickly regained his calm, and raising his voice he answered without batting an eyelid.

< 205 >

"A desire for variety, girls. A wish to touch some lighter skin. You're all dark, a bunch of black women."

"You filthy worm," shouted Mauá.

"It's my business, don't stick your noses in."

"We're your wives and we need some explanations," Saly replied.

"Let's take a look at your behavior recently," Lu protested. "You make less effort as each day passes. Instead of putting right what's bad, you go and get yet another woman. You're good at getting women to fall for you, but you can't seem to handle us. What do you want another one for?"

Tony's eyes revealed surprise, anger, arrogance. He answered with a rude remark and humiliated us with his usual macho talk. We were already expecting it.

"Who do you think you are? I'm your husband, but that doesn't give you any right to meddle in my life."

For the first time, we confronted him without fear and told him a few home truths. We told him why we were offended. We went wild. We're tired of your love affairs, scratching around here and there, pecking away, letting go and hightailing it like some bird of prey. We're full of children and deprived of any affec-

< 206 >

tion. In each of our houses, there are children shouting in chorus, where's Daddy, when's Daddy coming, where's Daddy gone, I want Daddy. We want to make ourselves pretty. But who for, if we don't have anyone to see us, to take us to the movies, out dancing, or out to dinner? We want to improve our cooking. But why if we just eat alone? You're no better than a bee, a kiss here, a kiss there, so that you can produce your honey, spreading disease from one to the other, so that one day we'll die from some incurable illness. You've got a heart the size of a truck, to carry so many women at the same time. We've kept quiet for the last four weeks waiting for this to end. We've made sure we've been faithful to you. But listen carefully: This is going to end badly. No day is the same. Nature has other flowers, other perfumes, different honey. You are our star, but planets shine too, they have their own source of light and cause happiness as well.

"Since when have you earned the right to insult me?"

"From today, now, and that's how it's going to be."

"And what right have you got to do this?"

"The right that polygamy confers on us. We could even summon a family meeting to declare your incapacity and request the freedom to have a conjugal assistant, are you aware of that?"

"You are my wives."

"What wives, Tony?" Ju chipped in sadly. "We're no one's women, lone women with a cross to bear."

"What do you mean by this?"

"Merely that we love your company, but solitude might be even better."

"I can abandon you to misery under any bridge, you should know that."

"Is that so?" Lu screamed. "Are we by any chance entered in any register of marriages as your possessions? Leave us if you want. We won't weep over you, you're not dead."

"I did you a great favor, get that into your heads. I gave you status. I made decent women of you, can't you understand? You're five fewer women selling your body and begging for love along life's highways and byways. Each of you has a home and your dignity, thanks to me. And now you want to control me?"

Dear God! For these men, to love a woman is to do her a favor. To lead her up the altar steps is to give her status. Oh, what a generous distributor of statuses my Tony has become!

No one answered, in order not to sour the atmosphere even further. We looked at him with hurt expressions on our faces, but

< 208 >

we forgave him for the cruelty of his words. He spoke until he was foaming at the mouth. Then he threw us a deadened glance, like a tired old bull chewing the cud. But why was he getting so worked up? In polygamy, the wives cater for their master's sentimental life. They give their opinion. They defend the interests of the household. A new wife must contribute prosperity and harmony, and not conflict or differences, which is why the opinion of the other wives is considered important. On this occasion, Mauá, the latest wife, must provide the defining view.

"Mauá, you're the latest wife: what have you got to say about this relationship?"

"I don't accept it. I'm very young and I've got a lot to give: love, children, joy. And wealth too. My business is going really well. I've managed to attract good-quality clients. Ministers' wives, Makua deputies and their friends, businesswomen, all come and have their hair done in my salon. You don't need another woman, Tony."

Saly was perspiring. She stared at Tony, and then threw us a conspiratorial glance. Suddenly, she got to her feet, bolted the doors, and hid the keys. She's a woman of action, not words. She called Lu and together they went into the bedroom. We could

< 209 >

hear furniture being moved around. Maybe they were looking for something. They reemerged. Saly issued her invitation.

"Let's not prolong this conversation. It's bedtime. You're all invited to sleep here."

It wasn't in our plans to sleep there. What was Saly up to? Tony was taken by surprise.

"All of you sleep here?"

"Today, Tony, you're going to show us what you're worth," said Saly, fuming. "If each one of us gives you a bit of satisfaction some of the time, then get your satisfaction in one go with all of us, if you are able."

Tony didn't know what to do. We were five against one. Five weaknesses together become a force to be reckoned with. Unloved women are more deadly than black mambas. Saly opened the bedroom door. The bed had been dismantled and the floor covered with sleeping mats. We thought it an awesome idea and got into the spirit of it. Tony needed to be shown what five women together can do. We went into the room, pulling along Tony, who resisted us like a billy goat. We got undressed as if doing a striptease. He looked at us. His knees began to tremble slightly.

< 210 >

It was very hot in the room, but the windows were open. There was a cool breeze, but the room was hot, where was all this heat coming from? Ah, it was the heat of perspiration. It was the flame of anger leaping from the human body. I looked at my stark naked sisters. All of them were well endowed. The floor would surely cave under such weight. I looked around and got a shock. My God, there was a lot of backside, a lot of bosom here. All this for one man alone?

Tony raised his hands to his head and then to his face to shield his eyes, and then he shouted:

"My God! Please, stop this, for the love of God, what torment are you trying to heap on me now?"

He gave us a frightened look. None of us could possibly imagine the sensations, the complications, and the confusion generated by what we'd done. He held his breath, pretending to smile. He tried hard to convey the superiority of a cowboy before his herd. Saly undressed him. He lay down in the middle of the five of us. He quivered. What can a man do with five women?

A hostile silence descended upon him. The world had just fallen on his shoulders. A woman's nudity is a bad omen even if it's only one wife's expression of anger. It's the ultimate protest, the protest to beat all protests. It's worse than passing a famished lion in the remote savannah. It's worse than the conflagration of an atomic bomb. It brings bad luck. It provokes blindness. It paralyzes. It kills.

I examined the room. The walls painted blue. The light shining on the ceiling like a sun keeping the night away. The floor without a mattress as hard as stone. Skirts, blouses, panties in little heaps here and there. Surrounding Tony, five bodies covered by white sheets, like corpses in a morgue. He moved his arm to turn to his left. He bumped into a human rampart, there was no room to maneuver his body. He said a polite excuse me, and then got up, his face covered in tears. His bravado had been broken.

"Can it be my mother's going to die?" he raved. "Can it be I'm going to lose my job? Am I going to have some accident? Am I going to lose one of my children? What disaster is coming my way, dear God? Not even my grandfather, who was the most polygamous of all polygamists, went through a marital experience like this. You've lost your senses. You could have shown your displeasure in some other way. And you, Rami? You're siding with these sluts in their conspiracy? You're not like these other women I picked up on the street corners of life. You've got value. Dignity.

< 212 >

You're of good birth and morals. Ju as well. You've changed a lot, Rami!"

"You're the one who's changed, my love. You left me and preferred other women, Tony. I'm just following in your footsteps. I'm obeying you. I'm satisfying your desires, a slave of every moment."

"You're my real wife. You shouldn't get involved in this type of thing, Rami."

"Tony, look at the field you cultivated. Is the love you sowed growing or not? Are the wounds you caused in each of our hearts healing or not? Why are you accusing me?"

He looked at me intensely. In his startled expression, he seemed to be asking for help. He shuddered violently and revealed the terror embedded in his soul. We remained motionless, surprised, awaiting the outcome of his madness. We were all completely astonished as we contemplated this new, unknown image of a blubbing husband. He said his throat was dry. He went to the kitchen and drank a little whiskey, but derived no pleasure from it. It wasn't that type of pleasure he sought. He was trying to get from alcohol the strength he didn't have. Our attitude pointed to a war he couldn't win. He decided to confess everything.

"Eve is just a friend, she's not what you think she is."

He told us the whole story. She wasn't illiterate, he explained, but had studied to an advanced level, she was a graduate. She was the director of a firm, she was rich. She doesn't take anything from me, on the contrary, she gives. But she's an unhappy woman. Because she doesn't have a husband. Because she has no children. Unhappy, her soul adrift in the sea of life. Anchorless. No father or mother. All she has is money, lots of money, and that's why I gave her a bit of my company.

"Sometimes, we offer our friendship out of generosity," he commented. "As women, you will never understand that."

In our eyes, he was no longer a man. He was a superman, a legendary hero, a defender of lost souls, who gives of his oxygen so that the plants don't die. We listened, hovering between truth and lies. His version of Eve's story might well have been true. But it might have been untrue. Men are specialists in covering up their extramarital deviations. It was because we believed his lies that we eventually fell into this trap. But all women like a good lie. You're the most beautiful, the best, they tell us. And we believe them. I'll give you the sky. And the sun. We close our eyes and open our arms and our heart to receive the sun and the sky, which will be given to us as a present. You are the only one. We open our mouth, and swallow the bait and behave like the only ones, carried along in the ritual dance of coupling, until the illusion is lost.

We were all there, five women, five heads, five judgments, accusing him, demanding from him, punishing him. We were the fertile soil left untended, devoid of fertilizers or irrigation, where the sower had once cast his seed before abandoning it in search of new conquests. When one can't have a man to oneself, then it's better to share him than lose him completely. Oh, my good Lord Jesus, you who performed the miracle of multiplying the loaves of bread, come back again and multiply men as well. Multiply Tony too, by five, one for each of us. Scientists of the world, clone my Tony so that he's no longer just a divided portion, shared out like a crust of bread.

Tony began to despair. He lay down on his back. The moment inspired him to feelings of light-headedness. The moonlight must be lovely outside. It must be a beautiful night outside. The air must be cool outside. Ah! It must be nice outside. He got up again and went to the kitchen. He downed half a bottle of whiskey in one go. He came back to the room and shouted:

"Rami, let's go home."

I hoisted the heavy burden onto my shoulders. We left. We arrived. Suddenly, I was overcome by a huge sense of pleasure. How good it was to arrive home with my husband next to me, even if he was drunk. The lights were on in the bedrooms, the children were studying, listening to music, relaxing. I made him a strong coffee. He drank it. He was sick. I took him to have a cold bath. He felt refreshed. I put him to bed and he pretended to be sleeping quietly, hugging his pillow as if his mother had left him an orphan. I could see his heart beating strongly under the sheets. I could see the flames devouring his soul, terrified at the prospect of the reverses that morning would bring. His disproportionate greed had caused a love blockage in his tiny stomach. Poor mite! He thought he could herd his wives to pasture without any trouble or sacrifice.

I looked through the window. The night was dense and cold, the moonlight had gone. I thought. I suffered. But what was so extraordinary about nudity? It was beyond comprehension, dear God, beyond understanding. Tony trembling with fear at his wives' nudity, filling his dreams with phantoms. I lulled him in my arms. Sleep well, my husband, my frightened little boy, let your little soul rise and be purged, let it soar courageously!

Nudity. Wicked nudity, sacred nudity. Nudity that kills, nudity that delights. Miniskirt. Striptease. Nude carnival. Carnival buttocks, fatal attraction. Mermaid's nudity, in the aquaria of the finest brothels. Pornography in films, in vaudeville, in peep shows. Pornography perambulating down the city streets as night falls. Nudity inspiring wondrous flights and apocalyptic disasters.

A friend of mine once dreamed of a nude woman. That woman was me. He was so disturbed that he summoned his whole family to share his misfortune. He invoked all the spirits and carried out rituals to protect himself. He spent a fortune having spells cast on my shadow and on my luck, because he thought I was bewitching him. He was so desperate that as he drove his car around a bend on the marine boulevard, he crashed through the wall and plunged into the sea. He escaped by the skin of his teeth. He later confessed to me: I dreamed of you naked because I desired you so much and you, quite simply, took no notice of me.

A woman's nudity is a blessing, a curse, a protection. There are many stories of nude women accompanying warriors in times of war. They say that during the civil war, fierce commandos, armed to the teeth, always had a nude woman at the head of the platoon, with only a string of beads round her waist. She would advance, fearless and brazen. On seeing her, the enemy would lose all courage. They would become demoralized, because the sight of a nude woman before a great battle meant defeat and death. The end of the world. In their advance, the *naparamas*, or suicide squads, always have a nude woman at their head, to serve as their protective shield.

A woman is a curse even when dressed. Hunters stalking wild beasts halt their advance toward their prized prey when they're unfortunate enough to pass a woman on her way to work. But a woman may be a blessing as well. A great xylophone player can only receive inspiration and transmigrate over to the other side when a woman sits down beside him, like a goddess, like an inspirational muse. Many footballers receive their blessing from a naked woman before they leave for an important match. Women dance naked in a hidden place on the day of a funeral in order to reject death. The *mbelele* is danced by naked women to bring rain. Dancing naked next to someone dying attracts death.

African people, naked people. People dressed in loincloths, in poverty. Humble people at one with nature. In Africa, heat comes from the sun and from the soul. That's why women strip and cool off in the rivers when they wash clothes. Out in the fields, they work, their breasts loose, while they sow, reap, and hoe. Oh, Mother Africa! Naked mother! How can your daughters' nudity be more shocking than your own, Mother Africa?

There was once an African king. A despot. A tyrant. Men tried to resist him. The rebellion was crushed and the men flattened like fleas. The women wept for their misfortune and conspired together. They marched to demonstrate their discontent before the king. The king answered them with high-flown words. They turned their backs on him, bent over, lifted their skirts, showed His Majesty their backsides, and beat a retreat before he had finished his malevolent tirade. The king couldn't take such an insult. He had a heart attack and died that same day. The target that the warriors' bullets couldn't hit was brought down by a whole multitude of backsides.

A naked wife only in the dark or half-light, because she's the center of life, the point where it all started. It's just a short step back to paradise. Man and woman lived naked before they sinned.

What an insomniac I am! I crossed myself and begged God to bless me with some sleep. God didn't pay me the slightest attention and let me wallow in my despair. I went to the lounge and drank a glass of wine to make me merry. And to make my merriment complete, I needed to break the silence. What I decided to do was listen to some nice music, to the grave, masculine voice of a good ballad singer. But no. Then I felt like listening to the gentle, aureate voice of Rosália Mboa. But before that, I needed to take a bath to cleanse my body and my soul. I went to the bathroom. I submerged myself in the white froth of my bath salts. I washed my hair with cold water. The shampoo smelled good, it smelled of orange blossom.

I had a terrible fear of presenting myself in front of my mirror, but I went. I needed to. I wanted to see my body in all its nudity. Would I get a shock? I also wanted to see my soul in all its nudity. I glanced at the mirror, which looked back at me disapprovingly: Can it be that you've got to this point purely for the sake of love? And what type of love is it that robs you of your dignity and decorum to the point of displaying your bare body in front of your rivals?

I shielded my eyes from the mirror's glare. This love was smothering me in unseemliness, to the point where I let myself be persuaded to commit shameless acts. What sort of woman am I, so lacking in self-esteem? What sort of a person am I who tramples on her sense of decency and her jealousy and turns her body into

< 220 >

a weapon of revenge? My God, save me from this charade, this hypocrisy, this veiled malevolence!

I returned to the bedroom and lay down next to my husband. He turned over in bed. He must have been having a nightmare. In his dream, there must have been a whole throng of naked women, continuously multiplying. Maybe his dream was identical to the one that African king had had. There must have been a whole succession of misfortunes, accidents, terrors, mysteries. He was tossing and turning under the sheets like a snake. I thought of my own story. I thought of the millions of women imprisoned in the seraglios of this world, and asked God for forgiveness for the evil that life does them.

< 221 >

20

Tony has summoned a family meeting to complain about our bad behavior, and makes a great fuss as if this was a huge problem. He needs this meeting in order to gauge ideas. To gain witnesses to his misfortunes and so alleviate his conscience. He's trying to gain allies in order to keep a better grip on his flock, which is slipping from his control. He has summoned fathers, mothers, uncles, who have all turned up with scrupulous punctuality. My father refused the invitation, but my old mother has come. All these strangers have crowded into my lounge, invading my privacy. Violating me.

"Welcome," Tony addresses those present, "please be seated and listen carefully to the ingratitude of these women. Their malevolence. Their witchcraft. They have united and have conspired against me, they have brought me bad luck, and things aren't going well in my life."

My mother reacts angrily:

"For twenty years, there was never a family meeting in this house, because you only had my Rami, who is a woman of sound

< 223 >

principles. Everything went well. You decided to become a polygamist and you've brought these problems upon yourself, so now take it, accept it, the spell's on the other foot and you're the one who's the witch doctor, Tony!"

I feel dizzy. I have a tight feeling in my throat, but I resist the strong temptation to open my mouth for fear of letting fly all the insults I've been forced to swallow throughout my life. My angry breath is a dragon's fire, and I feel capable of setting everything alight. All I want to do is cry.

"They don't respect me, they won't stay in their place, they don't obey me, but confront me, they don't treat me as they should."

He speaks, but doesn't get to the crux of the matter. He's very tense. Then he falls silent and is unable to utter any more words. An angry aunt fires a salvo of questions at us:

"Have you cooked his food for him?"

"Yes," we reply in unison.

"How do you serve it?"

"On our knees."

"Do you prepare the chicken?"

"Yes, we do."

"What bits do you serve him?"

< 224 >

"The thighs, the breast, the gizzard."

"Can you confirm this, Tony?"

"Yes, I can. But I don't remember ever having eaten a gizzard."

Murmurs of censure and disapproval can be heard. They're used to eating the good bits of meat, while the women eat bones, feet, the neck, and wings. They are disgusted by the fact that their male descendants are losing their privileges, and try desperately to erect a barrier against time. But traditions are born and die, like life.

People prepare for a pitched battle. On one side, there's the man's family, on the other the women's. Our enemies hurl javelins against us, shout insults at us, and even humiliate the men in our family. They think they're winning, because we're not retaliating in kind. They want to destroy us, while we want to build, which is why we fight with our weapons laid down. Mighty fighters can be defeated with silence.

"Tony," Saly defends herself, "I serve gizzards. I go to the market and buy a kilo, and prepare peanut curry using chicken gizzards at least once a week. We all eat it, and in fact there's some left over. What are you saying, Tony? Don't we have a little dish of gizzards when we eat out at a restaurant?"

"That's where the big problem lies," an old man says. "You talk of gizzards. I'm talking about one gizzard. You need to understand the difference between gizzards and gizzard."

"What's the difference?"

"Gizzards from a chicken farm are one thing. The gizzard from that chicken that's been lovingly plucked and dotingly roasted for your husband is something else. That's the gizzard we're talking about. Were you never educated by your mothers? Madam," the old man addressed my mother, "you haven't educated your daughter. As the first wife, she is the one largely responsible for this anarchy. You've got to show her again that the gizzard is sacrosanct. The gizzard and not gizzards."

My mother cries silently. Her weeping is a song about absence, pain, yearning. About the sister who was killed out on the remote savannah by a leopard because of a chicken gizzard. About the humiliation we have both suffered, two different generations following the same path. I am disgusted. I feel like opening my mouth and letting the whole cat out of the bag, setting everything ablaze and avenging the honor of my mother, who has been so outrageously insulted without any consideration for her age. Suddenly, I glimpse the message of peace in my mother's eyes. She doesn't want me to say out loud what has been kept silent.

"These slaughterhouses are an attack on our customs," another old woman screeches. "Civilization is against our culture. Selling gizzards by the kilo, and to anyone, who ever heard of such a thing? So children eat them, women eat them, that's why there's no longer any hierarchy or respect within families, because we're all eating the same thing."

We wives look at each other. These people brought us here to humiliate us. To make us bow our heads. But to look down at the ground is to look at the cultivated soil where the cornstalks carry the ears of corn on their backs like infant children. It's to look at the green rice plantation lighting up the soil with its golden carpets of grain. The ground contains the fields of peanut, of lilies, thistles, violets. The ground contains the ocean, the rivers, and the fields of sugarcane. Pigeons alight upon the ground to conduct their mating ritual. Men walk with their heads raised to the sky, but the earth is the cradle and the sky merely the Milky Way, in eternal flux.

We keep our mouths and our souls closed. Do we by any chance have a right to speak? And no matter how much right we might

< 227 >

have, what difference would it make? A woman's voice is good for lulling children to sleep as night falls. A woman's word isn't given any credit. Here in the south, young men who have gone through their initiation learn one lesson: If you confide in a woman, you sell your soul. A woman has a long tongue, a serpent's tongue. A woman should listen, comply, obey.

Mauá can't stop herself, she opens her mouth, protests, seizes the word without having been given permission, and says everything that's on her mind. She comes from a society where women speak in front of men and are heeded. Where women are loved, respected, and where they are queens.

"Have you called us together here just to talk about chicken gizzards? What crime have we committed? As a united family, all we wanted was to offer our man an orgy of love. These are purely matters for the bedroom, and of no interest to the whole family. If we squabbled with each other, we would be upbraided for being jealous. Now that we have come together, why are you criticizing us?"

Mauá's protest brings the problem back out into the open. Tony has to recount the whole story – very much in his style, and we are mortified, crushed by the shame of it all. He says we

< 228 >

insulted him, stark naked as we were. He says we were responsible for negative forces being created against him. Ah, Tony, my love, I've lost you. Now you're my firebrand of a husband, my gorilla, my orangutan husband, who declares his love by hurling rocks and uttering cusswords. The voice you're cradling my soul with is a whiplash of raucous notes dressed up as a musical score. My feelings die away. I have allowed myself to be shut away because of love inside this iron cage. Eagles hovering above, lend me your wings so that I can fly away and seek a refuge in the horizon's highest branches. The council of the elders listens to the story of the aborted orgy, it quivers with astonishment and shrieks its disapproval. Ooh! Ah! You are the most shameful women in our land! The very thought of it! They howl as if one, like a chorus of famished wolves baying at the full moon.

"I'm an old man! I'm the most polygamous of all polygamists! I've never had an experience like that. I've never seen such wickedness before. Son, you're right, you're absolutely right!"

"But... have you had any bad luck?" Mauá's uncle asks.

"No, we haven't noted anything yet," Tony's aunt replies, "but it's bound to happen, one of these days."

< 229 >

Tony's nervousness is miraculously quelled. For everyone supports his claims and expresses their future condolences for the succession of misfortunes that is still to befall him. He throws us a mocking but triumphant glance while he wipes the sweat from his face. He feels vindicated. Loved. Ah, Beelzebub! Lend me your fork and your dog's face to give this crowd a fright, this throng spewing out its superstitions and uttering its profanities!

The women join the chorus of recriminations, of advice, and of all those things they think they know about. And without a second thought, they start talking about a life they hardly know. They grind us firmly into the soil, like ripe papayas under their feet. They tell us about love as if they'd ever received any in life. They abandon the enemy, turn their guns on their allies, and play the men's game. Ah, what a wretched life! When will women feel solidarity with one another? Generous mothers, they pass on all they have. Crowns of bile and thorns are their legacy as they become dowager queens, as they enthrone a new generation. They crown us the queens of obedience. Miss Submissive, mistresses of fearfulness.

"It's all your fault, Rami," one of the aunts says. "You are a bad example to the younger wives. You're their mother, you should teach them."

"What are you accusing me of? I've always swept his rubbish under the carpet. I've kept all his sins to myself. Ask Tony, ask him if I've ever been negligent in my care for him. I look after his physical well-being. Not even his feet smell. Do you want proof? Smell them! Ask Tony's four wives here whether they've ever seen a hole or a tear in Tony's underpants, ask them!"

For obvious but also unknown reasons, I begin to sob convulsively. All the gloom of the heavens has been contained within me. My weeping represents the unveiling of a mystery. I weep freely, because weeping is a woman's destiny. The tears that fall wash the heavens, wash the moon. They also wash my teeth, my eyes, and my smile. I feel so light and so free!

"I have no complaints about the housework." Tony comes to my defense. "They look after me and the kids very well. I've never heard of any of them being unfaithful, I'm sure of that. But they're wicked."

In one thing, Tony is right: We are obedient machines. Perfect. Complete. If we weren't, we'd be out on the streets, in the moon, enjoying all the pleasures of life. We're obedient, yes sir, we surely are. That's why we're here, gravitating, like satellites, around the sun king.

"Don't be like Vuyazi," says one of Tony's aunts.

"Vuyazi?" we ask, curious.

"Yes, Vuyazi, the non-submissive princess whose face appears on the moon."

" … ?!"

"There was once a princess. She was born into the nobility, but she had a poverty-stricken heart. Women had always been obliged to obey men. That is nature. But this princess disobeyed her father and her husband, and did only what she wanted. When her husband reprimanded her, she would answer back. When he hit her, she would reply in kind. When she cooked chicken, she would eat the gizzard and the thighs, and serve her husband whatever she felt like. When her first daughter was a year old, her husband said: Let's stop nursing the little girl, and make another child. She refused. She wanted her daughter to be nursed for two years just like the boys were, so that she would grow strong like her. She refused to serve him on bended knee and to clip his pubic hair. Her husband, sick of her disobedience, appealed to the king's justice, the king being her father. Heavyhearted, the king ordered the dragon to punish her. On a thundery day, the dragon took her up into the sky and stamped her into the moon, and so made her

< 232 >

punishment an example for the whole world. When the moon waxes and is full, there's a woman one can see in the middle of it, a bundle on her head and a baby on her back. It's Vuyazi, the disobedient princess stamped into the moon. It's Vuyazi, a statue of salt, calcified high up in the heavens in an inferno of ice. That's why, every month, the bodies of the world's women putrefy into open wounds and become impure, weeping tears of blood, in punishment for Vuyazi's insubordination.

"We are obedient women, you don't need to stamp us into the moon," I say peevishly.

Are we obedient? I'm lying! We have our ways of seeking revenge in tiny, inadmissible ways. The polygamist isn't a superman, occasionally his fire goes out and we go looking for a spark from the bonfire of a godfather, a male friend, the man who lives next door.

"Love one another just as your husband loves thee," says Tony's uncle, striking a pastoral pose. "Give thanks to the Lord who lit up your road ahead, for otherwise you would be single mothers like so many out there in the world. Men are rare. Having a husband is a lucky state in this day and age. This nephew of mine is a pearl in the middle of the desert."

< 233 >

Mauá's uncle would like to say something to defend his niece. He assesses the situation and decides to keep his mouth shut. This man's pockets are still a bottomless pit. When marriage comes to resemble paid employment, it's better to put up with an irritable husband's bellyaches in order to guarantee one's salary at the end of the month.

"Thank you for coming," Tony says, already smiling. "If I die, you should know then that it was these women who brought disaster upon me."

The litany of complaints ceases, and there's silence at last. Now I understand why, in women's souls, there is only death, the rustle of leaves falling, the babbling of invisible rivers flowing underground, bits of trash bobbing aimlessly in muddy waters. We were beaten down by other women as part of a conspiracy. As a source of strength, we were annihilated by the weakness of other women. No one asked what we felt, what we ate, how we lived. They threw us over a cliff, and we fell headlong and were crushed. They wrapped our bodies in shrouds of bile and vomit. But deep within us there are hearts pulsating in the tropical snow, whose flakes fall from a freezer powered by panels of solar energy.

< 234 >

Why did God make me a woman? If I wasn't a woman, what would I be? A man? Why be a man? In order to corral women like cattle? To draw up a polygamist's rota and spend my time going from one bedroom to another? To feel as if I'm lord of the universe when I don't even have wings to fly? I'm nothing, but that's fine by me. I'm a sad, embittered creature, but don't trouble me about it. My God, I'm a woman, I'm a flower, a rose, and my home is surrounded by thorns!

With the meeting over, those present make a dive for the food like goats in front of a pile of hay. They chew the meat and potatoes like industrial crushing machines. I serve them wine from Portugal, and they drink like camels. They get drunk and their voices gain the unpleasantly festive pitch heard in nightclubs.

I gaze at Tony, my firebrand of a husband, my twenty-first-century polygamist. Who will die prematurely, on the road, between one house and another, always hurrying here and there, managing his love affairs. Who eats food prepared by various hands and who will eventually die from poisoning, without ever knowing who is killing him. Who dives into any nook and cranny, like someone fishing for fatal diseases or tilling the soil of his own death. Whose body is always on show like cattle in the pleasure fair.

While the others eat and drink, we go back over the meeting. We deliver our comments on the nightmare. The outcome of the meeting was to attribute even more powers to our man. No one pointed a finger at him or charged him. He was a king. Our prince. He was an emperor emerging from the waters, pristine and resplendent like a sun. He was the gold on high, so mighty and brilliant that even our parents turned against us on the battlefield. I tell them: Girls, we were over the mark! But our revenge wasn't too wide of the mark, on the contrary, it surpassed our expectations. We made a fascinating discovery that revealed secrets we could never have imagined. It was wonderful to discover a weak Tony, a crazy Tony, who cries like a child and, when frightened by the bogeyman, seeks help from the family. We have, after all, discovered our most potent secret weapon. We can use our nudity to scare him, torture him, make him quiver to his marrow, and in accordance with the degree of his wickedness. We laugh. Mauá gives a sigh of amusement:

"Ah! You southerners!"

I go into a sulk. I always do this when Mauá speaks to me like this. But then I think how right she is. This rabble is a whole dung heap of superstitions.

"We overdid it, don't you think?" I repeat.

"Not at all!" Mauá says. "That day, I stripped to the rhythm of the drumbeats of my homeland and I was getting my spirit ready to dance the *niketche*."

"*Niketche*?"

"It's one of our dances, a dance of the Makua," Mauá explains, "a dance of love that newly initiated girls do in front of everyone, in order to proclaim: We are women. We are ripened like fruit. We are ready for life!"

Niketche. The dance of the sun and the moon, the dance of the wind and the rain, the dance of creation. A dance that moves and shakes, that heats you up. That makes the body stand still and the soul fly. The girls appear wearing loincloths and beads. They move their bodies with skill, welcoming the awakening of all springtimes. At the first beat of the drum, each one smiles, celebrating the mystery of life as expressed within the *niketche*. The old recall the love that has passed, the passion that was lived and lost. Unloved women encounter once again, within the space of the dance, the enchanted prince with whom they gallop away hand in hand on the moon's back. In the young, the urgency for love is awakened, for the *niketche* is pure sensuality, the queen of all sensuality. When the dance ends, one can hear the sighs of those who have seen it, as if they were stirring from a pleasant dream.

"Tony should celebrate rather than cry. Five wives dancing the *niketche* for him alone," Mauá says. "What greater proof of love could he hope for?"

We all smile sadly. We ask each other what the purpose of the meeting was. It was merely to give us a fright. To create more opportunities for him to have affairs, men like variety, we conclude. But we already are a variety, in terms of language, habits, and culture. We're a sample from north to south, the whole country in one man's hands. When it comes to love, Tony symbolizes national unity.

We wash the dishes. We talk while also washing our worries. Memory unearths histories of days long gone, histories of life's cycle. Ju relates events from her childhood. The birth of a girl child is heralded with three drumbeats, that of a boy with five. The birth of a girl is celebrated with a chicken, that of a boy with a cow or a goat. The birth rites of a boy are carried out inside the home, or under the tree of the ancestors, those of a girl are carried out in the open air as the night mist falls. A boy child suckles for two years, a girl for one. Girls learn to use the pestle and to cook, the boys study. A man marries, a woman is married. A man sleeps, a woman is slept. A woman is left a widow, a man is left with one fewer wife.

Lu tells us stories about her village. She says that she learned from other women that a woman lives to please. To please until she dies. When talking about love, it's important to use a verb of possession: to have. I have a polygamous, drunken, shameless, mad husband. But I have one. The verb "to have" is magical. It infuses the soul with power and strength. If I say I haven't, my strength is sapped and my soul emptied. Despair comes. It's the end. That's why I please, merely in order to be able to use the verb "to have."

Everything I've done in life has been to please my Tony. What have I gained from it? Solitude. Solitude in love is like being a loose grain of sand that produces no shade. It's to sleep on a mattress of stars gathered by my own hands. It's to live in the world's margin and walk forward on one's own because one is an uneven number. Like Eve. I've never emerged a winner in this struggle, only a loser. But I'm sturdy, hard, I've got nerves of steel. I weep not out of weakness but out of rage. I'm going to roll

< 239 >

up my sleeves and embark on another fight. I'm going to attack Tony with his own weapon: women. One can't sleep with all the women in the world, we know that. But I'm going to urge him to have all the women on the planet. All of them! There are already a few strands of white hair on my temples. A sign of maturity and wisdom. That is experience. These four women before me are my weapons and the others yet to come will be my bullets. We'll see who the winner is!

21

My husband isn't dead, but he's become an apparition seen from afar in an erotic film. A shadow that comes, a shadow that goes, that one imagines, dreams of, but that one can never touch. My God, he has turned me into an imaginary widow. I'm nailed to a windblown cross, hung up there on high, I have open wounds on my arms, my breast, in the oven that heats and grows cold without ever cooking anything. Why do I need a husband like this? Why don't I leave him once and for all?

Leave him? On every street corner, there's a woman pining for a man. Leave him for whom?

We need a man to give us money. For us to exist. To gain status. To give millions of women let loose in the world some prospects. For many of us, marriage is a job, but without a salary. It's security. During the days of Operation Production, all the women who had no husband were arrested and deported to reeducation camps, accused of being prostitutes, vagrants, criminals.

< 241 >

Everywhere you look there's sexual harassment of the men who are most well endowed, whether in body or wallet.

Men also harass women. So as to keep them at home to wash their clothes. Obey them. Lay the table and take out the china. Bear children and fill the house. They say a strong man doesn't weep when his wife leaves him. A solitary man sets off along his path, takes two steps and feels a pain in his knees, and so abandons his journey because it's too long. He makes an excuse, saying that there's no life, only stones beyond the horizon. And so he finds consolation and companionship in alcohol, solitude provides bad counsel. A man without a woman is as substantial as the wind. He's seen as irresponsible, women reject him because they don't consider him manly. A solitary woman says the world is a dunghill, that no one understands her. She's bitter. She rants at everything and at nothing. And she says that flowers are weeds. That all the glint of sunshine does is cause you injury. That darkness and night are better. She seeks death in life. She's a walking corpse.

I'm lying in my bed and I hear the bedroom door creak. Someone opening it and coming in. My God, I'm going to die, it's Tony on the warpath. What does he want here, if this is Saly's week?

< 242 >

I wasn't expecting him at this hour. He's not supposed to be here now. He wants to make me get up and prepare a coffee and a whiskey for him, today of all days when I'm feeling so tired. I've been all day on my feet, I had a lot of clients to attend to. Too bad for him, I'm not going to get up, I'm not in the mood for putting up with anyone today. I look at him. The expression on his face is very serious but it doesn't suggest any anguish. Something very serious has brought him here. I know that look, that smile, those gestures. Something's not right in that heart of his, I can sense it.

"Rami!"

"Yes?"

"I've come to a decision. Let's get a divorce."

"What?"

Tony's decision strikes me like an earthquake. I feel as if the huge mirror within me has been shattered by a stone. My tears flow, dripping to the floor, shards of broken glass. Ah! These eyes of mine are a limitless source of weeping that never run dry. A divorce never appears suddenly. There's always a ritual to its appearance, with angry quarrels, aggression, insults. I accepted and even surpassed the limits of violence to avoid such a step being taken. The ground is shaking under my feet, making me

< 243 >

utterly dizzy. I lie down. Ah! The ground is solid after all, it's my knees that are shaking.

"Why a divorce now?"

"I want to assure you of one thing: It's not for lack of love. It's a punishment. Pure revenge. I want to place you on the same level as the other women. Your recent behavior has been unworthy of a spouse. Just because you are registered on my documents, you think you're some sort of a queen. Instead of educating the other wives, you encourage them to adopt malicious attitudes. I've got to put an end to this. I've organized everything: It'll be divorce by mutual consent. You'll sign the papers, and my lawyer will come and see you in a few days.

He goes on and on. I'm not listening. I'm in the future, I'm on the moon. I'm in the world that awaits me when my divorce goes through. I shall be a muddy stain on the immaculate white sheet of my mother's family. I shall be a spot of absolutely indelible cashew juice on my father's white shirt. Society will look at me with scorn, pity, malice, like birds that scavenge at night. I shall be flogged with sticks and stones, like a snake greedy for sex, flesh, blood, and forbidden pleasures. I shall live between the earth and the moon. Between the dross and the street. An outcast.

< 244 >

Old friends will take me to the bar, but not to dinner. The bar is on the street corner, dinner is with the family, and people go out to dinner as couples. I shall live in places where mice hide, so as not to be chased by cats, because a divorced woman is flesh for any dog. A divorced woman is a witch, she makes love potions in order to attract rich gentlemen and steal their cash. She's a murderer, she kills the wives of her lovers so as to take their place. She's a thief, she steals husbands, she uses and abuses. She's a cannibal, she devours men and other people's loves.

"But Tony!"

"You're meddling too much in my life. Your zeal is too much and is damaging me. I've been angry with you ever since my birthday and the whole rigmarole that led to me having to take on the commitments of a polygamist, which I didn't even want. The orgy of revenge was the last straw. I've had enough, let's get divorced."

"I'm not going to sign the divorce papers."

"Yes, you are. And in doing so, maybe you'll lose your superior airs."

"Superior?"

Superior, me? I've never felt superior to anyone else just because I wear this band of gilded wire on my ring finger. I'm on

< 245 >

the side of those women who fight, who win, women who lose, who hesitate, who fall. I'm just another woman who hugs the air in the kiss of clouds and laughs as sweetly as doves cooing as she greets the sun on each new day. I'm a woman like the rest.

"Rami, my life was good. I did whatever I wished. I visited women when I felt like it. I would take money out of my pocket and pay them when they deserved it. Now that you people have got these business ventures, you think you're ladies, but you're no better than whores. You think you've carved yourselves some space, but you're no more than a hole. You think you've got rights and a voice, but you're no more than dumb ducks."

"We're earning money to improve our lives, Tony."

"That's why you're insulting me, because you've got money. That's why you abuse me, because you've got businesses. That's why you lack respect for me, because you think you're ladies. But I'm a rooster, I've got my head held high, I crow, I've got a talent for crowing loud. So you'd better be aware that your fate is to cluck, lay eggs, hatch them, and keep your eyes on the ground while you scratch around to catch the odd worm or grain husk. No matter how much power you may get, you won't be any better than a race of clucking hens forever begging the protection of a rooster like me in order to gain some recognition in life. You're bats in the night twittering sadly, and your voices, perpetual lamentations."

Oh, God! We women, beggars for love, for embraces and kisses, we beseech you, pour your blessing into our hearts. Give us a little justice, we who plant corn, reap wheat, who fill the planet with life, with bread and light. Give us too a stone stair that we may step up from the ground, contemplate the heavens, and breathe in the pure air of the stars. Give us the strength to advance in step with sister nature, dressed in our uniform of sweat and calluses in the never-ending struggle for bread, for life, and for justice.

He wants to divorce me to marry who? Only women divorce to be alone. Men divorce in order to marry someone else. I've always been obedient. Fulfilled my duties. Today, I'm going to disobey for the first time. There's not going to be any divorce. He wants a divorce? Over my dead body! I close my eyes as if they were dikes to stem the flow of tears that is turning into a cascade. I can't stop myself from weeping. I'm a good person. I'm pure in spirit. I'm the one who always dreamed of a world in blossom. Even my rivals I treat with love. I had opportunities to be another, independent woman. I rejected them. I chose marriage as a profession. In her matrimonial career, a woman never rises through the ranks. She sinks. I'm of an age to mount the throne and devote my life to being queen, and here they are trying to take my royal seat away from me. What will become of me? If Tony chases me out of here, where will I go and live with my children? Seek a new husband? With so many children?

22

One fine morning, a dapper-looking man knocks on my door. He's plump. He's carrying a black briefcase and his shoes are well polished. He wears a white shirt of good quality material, a tie with golden swirls and bright red dots. The well-fed sort, who drives around in a car and doesn't need to ask any favors. I open the door.

"Are you Rosa Maria, madam?"

"Yes."

"Please sign here."

"Sign what?"

"I'm the lawyer dealing with your case."

"What lawyer?"

"Dealing with your case."

"Look, with all due respect, I must tell you that we don't need an intermediary to deal with my problems. I suggest you leave."

"Madam, as a lawyer, I must advise you to sign these documents and settle the matter peacefully. Otherwise you'll have to go through a painful, litigious divorce process. You should be aware that your husband accuses you of moral abuse, mistreatment, and psychological violence. The poor man has been made profoundly unhappy because of you."

"Do you know he's polygamous?"

"That's not the issue. The fact is that you, madam, are the main party responsible for this situation. Because you didn't look after him appropriately. You didn't enable him to fulfill himself. You didn't satisfy him. You didn't complement him. You didn't please him enough. It's your fault and you should account for your crimes. You didn't know how to hold on to your husband and what's worse, you offended him."

"Me?"

The man's voice is like dagger thrusts of fire in my chest. I feel as if my whole body's ablaze. This man's extraordinarily haughty. Arrogant. I allow Tony to walk all over me with his leathery feet, but not just any man.

"Madam, you are Tony's only legally recognized wife, have you forgotten?"

"Look, sir, don't oblige me to give you a piece of my mind. I think you'd better get out of here."

"Madam, it's only a signature. It's very easy."

"Get out of here and don't come back."

"You are going to sign this, madam."

This lawyer's an unpleasant character. Repulsive. I'm not a piece of cattle, I'm a woman. I'm not made of stone, I've got feelings. When people attack me, I fight back. I raise my hand and it comes crashing down on the lawyer's face like a hammer. This fight gives me special pleasure, and I give his chubby cheek a good scratch. He takes two steps back, for he hasn't realized what's happening. He never imagined being slapped by a woman. He passes his hand over his sore cheek, where his black skin is slightly flushed. I advance. I'm a wild beast. A cannibal. I feel like chewing his tongue off so that he'll never again utter an ugly word or insult a woman. Help, the man shouts, while calling for his mommy. I want to eat him alive. Although he's fat, he'd fit nicely inside my stomach.

The lawyer plunges deep into the sofa. He spends quite some time silently caressing his injured face. He throws me an irate look.

"You're going to pay for this, lady!"

"Yes, of course. I pay a good price. I pay well, and I'm going to pay you right away!"

"I'm a man of justice."

"What justice? Go on, tell Tony I'll kill him, and I'll kill you as well, if you two continue to molest me. A man of justice, what justice? Go on, tell Tony I'm waiting for him with a dagger in my hand. Let him come!"

I give him another scratch. If he returns my aggression, there'll be trouble, I promise. His head and his job will be on the line. He soon realizes the trouble he's got himself into. He gathers his papers and leaves in a hurry.

God help me! Forgive my madness. It's the first time I've done something like this, I swear. But I must admit I enjoyed it. How wonderful! I feel light, as if I weren't myself. My whole life has been spent avoiding blows or running away from blows. This is the first time I've raised my hand against a man, and a man of the law at that, something that gives me even greater pleasure. How good it was!

I think about the divorce, and I have a rush of blood that causes me to faint and then come round, my heart thumping. The heat rising. I get the shivers and feel cold. I've got the summer in my body and winter in my soul.

23

I'm on the edge of a precipice. One step and I'm gone. Ah, my heedless love. I accepted everything from you, put up with it all: illnesses, desires, problems, complaints, shame, dirty tricks, squabbling. Now you're breaking free, getting rid of me, exchanging me, humiliating me, in favor of other, younger, more beautiful women. I wish you happiness, my love.

I go to my bedroom and engage my mirror in conversation.

"Mirror, oh, mirror, what's going to become of me?"

The mirror rewards me with an image of tenderness and the clearest answer it has ever provided.

"You won't be the first woman to get a divorce, nor the last. Divorces happen every day, like births and deaths, but relax. There's a big difference between the will of man and the will of God. What God proposes, man doesn't dispose."

"And what is God's will, dear mirror?"

"And what is your will, dear twin?"

If men and women had been made to die together, they would

< 253 >

have been born together, from the same womb and at the same time. But each one of us is born on our day and at our own hour. Only love has the strength to bring people to union. Tony and I, two rivers, two parallel lines, become one during the course of our journey. Now, we've arrived at the estuary, and our paths have divided. Once again, we are two, each one flowing freely toward the ocean's deep waters.

"Dear mirror, I'm an earthenware basin with a crack in the middle and I can't retain water anymore. I'm a shoe with a sole worn through that's no longer any good for walking. I'm a failure. I'm defeated. I'm a woman abandoned because of conjugal incompetence. An old woman. Dross. Worthless."

"But the world doesn't begin with you, my dear twin. Nor does it end with you. There are women suffering much more than you in this world. If the divorce goes ahead, it'll be because it was written in the book of life that you and Tony were not to die together."

The image I see is my certainty, my subconscious mind, reclaiming sayings and knowledge hidden away in my memory.

Within me there's a deep sense of emptiness. An endless ache.

I go back to my bedroom and lie down for a bit. In this bed I had dreams, I bore children, I wept over the long absences, the

< 254 >

jealousy, the disappointments. The end of it all has arrived and the bed will be no more than a stretcher, on which to rest from my weariness. Me and no one else. The bed has now grown in size and seems different. There's a cool breeze and I close my eyes. The doorbell rings.

I open the door. It's my four rivals. The news of our divorce has left them in a state of complete shock, as if it were some seismic shift. They come with a whole list of questions. I answer them.

"It wasn't I who took the decision to seek a divorce. I'm leaving the road ahead clear, my post vacant. I've been thrown out."

Ju places her hand on my shoulder. Her embrace has the feel of despair. The strength of her despair. Her body is cold, her arms are shaking.

"What's happened for him to act like this?"

"I'm damned if I know, I ..."

"You can't accept it, Rami!"

"Don't come here asking me to put up any resistance. I'm not the one who left, it's him. You'd do better to tell him to come back. I'm the victim. I loved so much, I got trodden on, I want to get out of this prison cell. Love is a cancer. The more they reject you, the more it grows."

"Rami, are you going to accept the divorce just like that, without contesting it or anything?" Saly asks with a concerned air.

"He's closed the door," I answer. "He hasn't left me with any hope whatsoever. There's no point in prolonging this suffering."

"Rami," Lu says, "if Tony leaves you, he'll leave us sooner or later as well."

"Women aren't all the same, each one has her luck or fate." I try to reassure my rivals. "Each one was born on her day and has her own destiny."

"So what's going to happen now?"

"Wherever I may be, God will be there as well. I won't have the arms of a man to give me affection, but the wind will be there to refresh my soul. I shall drink the early morning dew just like the grasses of the savannah. This love of mine drove me mad, punished me, perverted me, consumed me, ravaged my whole life. I left the field of combat with nothing to show for it, I lost my weapon, I lost my lance, I lost my strength, I lost hope. Ah, dear God! I lost myself."

"Rami, you are my security." Ju fell into a delirious fit. "If you leave this group, it's the end of me. My children were mushrooms

< 256 >

that the wind caused to grow. They were orphans, born out of loveless sex. My children only knew bread, they never knew love. They knew their father from the photos and the fleeting visits that always took place at night, when he would come and fertilize my womb. They knew their father from behind the wheel of his car out on the road, and they would show him to their friends: See that blue car? The gentleman behind the wheel is my father. And when their friends asked which blue car, my children would reply: Oh, what a pity, but he's gone now, our father and his blue car. With the rota system we set up, I managed to have him for a whole week. I felt the joy of washing his clothes. Laying the table for him. Having lunch with him. My eldest children were surprised, for they'd never, since the day they were born, sat down at the table with their father."

From Ju's inner being, a river of tears flows, weeping in the desert for the drop of dew that has disappeared in the direction of the noonday sun. Ah, Tony, devourer of hearts, slayer of dreams. Tony, a catfish, slipping through his captors' hands. Tyrannical, inaccessible king. Poor, deceived, wounded, vanquished Ju. Her smile made to light up the world, extinguished under a snot-laden

< 257 >

crust of leprous slime. Her body made to enchant the catwalks of the world, now covered in scars and rags. That heart of honey turned into one of vinegar and bile.

"How did you get as far as producing six children without any pleasure, with a man who never loved you?" Asked Mauá, with pity in her voice.

"I never stopped hoping to keep him with me. But instead of keeping him, I tore myself to pieces, procreating."

"This southern culture never ceases to amaze me!" Mauá concludes. "For us, love and pleasure are extremely important. When one of these elements is absent, we change partners. Why suffer?"

"I wanted to have more children. I did all I could to avoid joining different family names in one womb. I was scared of being called a prostitute. A poor wretch. A witch. A stealer of husbands. Our society doesn't accept a woman with children from different fathers, and different surnames."

"Ah, you southern women!" Saly says, smiling sarcastically. "It's not a weakness to have children by different fathers. On the contrary, a woman in that position has given and received a lot of love. She's experienced. She was lucky enough to be desired by

< 258 >

many men, and life is made up of trial and error. You fail here, but get things right there, what's the big deal?"

"It's a moral issue, Saly."

"Moral!" Lu exclaims harshly. "A morality that obliges you to hatch a viper's eggs. Just look at what morality did to you. You're a ghost. Your life is a living hell. The man turned you into nothing more than a machine for reproduction, and you accepted the pact. Your situation is really serious. In your place, I would have abandoned this man long ago."

"No, that's out of the question."

"Our society in the north is more humane," Mauá explains. A woman has a right to happiness and to life. We live with a man as long as he makes us happy. If we're here, it's because a state of harmony still exists. If our love comes to an end one day, we leave in search of other worlds, with the same freedom that men enjoy."

The northern women are unanimous in their criticism. In the south, society is full of women yearning for the past. Insane. Ghosts. In the south, women are exiled in their own world, doomed to die without knowing what love and life are. In the south, women are downcast, more enslaved. They walk with their heads bowed. Unsure of themselves. They know nothing of the delights of living. They don't look after themselves physically, they don't have massages or paint themselves to make their faces more joyful. We are happier up in the north. We dress extravagantly, in bright colors. We paint ourselves, we look after ourselves, we adorn ourselves. We tread the ground confidently. The men give us presents, woe betide them if they don't have a present to give us. When it's time to get married, the man comes to make his home in the wife's house, and when love is over, it's he who leaves. In the north, women are more beautiful. In the north, no one enslaves anyone else, because all men and women are children of the same God. But be careful, in the north, man is God as well. Not an oppressive god but a friendly god, a god you can confide in, a god who is a companion.

"Tony lost his vigor," Lu says accusingly. "He wore you down, made you grow old, and now he wants a change of scenery? He can't leave you like this. You managed to hold on to him. Thanks to you, we learned how to share and we succeeded in controlling his movements. We made progress. We invested our efforts in useful, productive things. We even managed to start businesses, and now we live well. Think of us, Rami."

"I can foresee a life of dispute, conflict, and intrigue," Saly confesses. "We're going to spend our time running from hole to hole, trying to catch the same mouse. Then there'll be confrontations and tears."

"Rami, think carefully," Lu shouts. "Divorce is for adolescents, young people."

"You're going to sign your divorce papers after twenty years of marriage just to satisfy Tony's whim? Or because of us? This home is yours, we're the ones who invaded it. Do you want to hand us the victory? We're not your friends at all, what each of us wants is to take your place. Are you going to risk losing everything just for us? Do something, Rami!" Ju warns me.

Lu has well and truly touched a sore point. I'm speechless. I cry. Men are like that. They change women as if they were changing shirts. I've had twenty years of love and struggle just to end up like grains of salt being dissolved.

"I've used up all my weapons, I've lost the battle. Give me some suggestions. Tell me what I can do to get around this problem."

"Tell me something, Rami," Lu asks, "what do you do to hold on to Tony?"

"What do I do? Nothing!"

< 261 >

"Oh, I don't understand you."

"I'm the one who doesn't understand."

"Rami, you know very well what I'm talking about. Have you never made him a little love potion or something?"

"No, never."

"I can't believe it. I sometimes season his food with ground salamander or cobwebs. I choose those potions that make the body more ardent. He can't resist me, you all know this only too well."

"I rub my sexual parts with mosses, rues, and nettles that grow next to gravestones in the cemeteries," Saly says. "I know he doesn't care for me so much now, but when he remembers me, he gets so excited he can't sleep and comes rushing over to see me even in the middle of the night."

"I've got magic throughout my body," Mauá fires back. "When we make love, I wrap myself round him, hold him tight, cover him, and he sleeps like a child. I started having lessons in love when I was eight. Of all of you, Eve's my only true rival. We were initiated in the same school. We've got the same skills in love. It's a struggle between equals, with the same weapons. None of you counts for anything, you lie at my feet.

"I never did any of that," Ju confesses, "never! It's not in my nature."

"It's a pity," the others say, "love is an art, a job, a business. In any business, you have to make investments. How do you expect to be loved if you don't invest in it? And you, Rami? What investment have you made to make your love work?"

"I," Saly chips in again, "light a cheroot at midnight and fill the house with smoke. Then I grab a broom and start sweeping the house. As I sweep, I invoke Tony's name. I enter the world of dreams. Wherever he is, he answers me with a sigh. He shouts out my name. And he dashes off to find me. You can say whether I'm lying or not. How many times has he woken up from his nightmares in your beds, shouting Saly, Saly, how many times?"

Saly's confession brings me back to reality. I remember. Countless times, Tony would wake up and vanish from the house in a flash, defying all the dangers of darkness, as if he were responding to a summons by the devil. I'd never for once imagined that this was the effect of some love spell. Oh, how sad! The idea of holding a man by means of magic is delightful. But can these women be happy knowing that the love they receive is the result of magic?

< 263 >

What taste can love induced by magic possibly have? Does it taste of honey or of falseness? I once tried witchcraft. Nothing happened and just as well. I'm one of those who believe in pure love, true love, everlasting love.

"Rami," Lu confesses, "do you remember the times Tony was with you and couldn't do anything? It was I who was closing him up. I put a cork in him. I bottled him. I occupied his entire memory. Whether he was with you or with Ju, when the time came, he couldn't get it up. He would back away. Grow cold. He'd abandon you and hurry over to me, where he would get his satisfaction."

There was no doubt that she was telling the truth. Her confession was utterly malicious and filled me with loathing, with anger. I began to understand everything. Tony's escapes, his betrayals, his lies. He wasn't acting of his own free will, he was the victim of a carefully prepared trap.

"You northern women only think about sex," I say, my voice laden with resentment.

"Who doesn't think about sex in this world?" Lu says. "When a child is born, it's down there we look, and we shout: It's a boy. Thank you, God, for this gift. Or we mumble: It's a girl. Another one, my God, how unlucky I am! Only after this do we look at the face and the rest of the body."

Back comes Mauá: "You southerners don't worry about important things. You make love in the European manner. You focus all your energy on kissing the mouth, as if a kiss were worth anything. You say we only think about sex? How many southern men have left their homes for good? You call us backward. All you have in your heads are books. You've got money and glitter. But you haven't got spirit. You've got good schools, jobs, luxury houses. What's the point of all that if you don't know the color of love? What's the point of traveling to the moon if you've never traveled inside yourself? Have you ever made a journey inside you, Rami? Never, it's obvious from the pain you have in your face. Paradise is within us, Rami. Happiness lies within us. You southerners aren't yet women, you're children. Reproductive creatures, that's all. That's why men abandon you left, right, and center. Your married lives together are devoid of magic. That's why, no sooner had you declared independence, you shouted: Down with the initiation rites. What did you think you were doing?"

In this group, the unpretentious women are myself and Ju. There's no artifice in either of us. We are just as life brought us into

< 265 >

the world. That's why we're despised. I didn't know that everything was played for when it came to matters of love. I always thought that love resided only in one's heart. Now I understand. Love is a major enterprise. I always believed in natural love. Platonic love. But in questions of love, all manner of tactics are valued. The men who pass through these schools know how to love. Know how to please. Know how to sail a boat deep into their own interior.

"Rami, you should send your daughters to a school to prepare them for initiation."

"No, never."

"Why?"

"I want to preserve my daughters' virginity."

"Oh, Rami, virginity is a primitive state. A state of childhood. Man doesn't need virginity, but perfect love. Teach your girls the good things they have. Prepare them so that no man will despise them."

"I don't have the courage."

"You northerners should abolish these schools," Ju bursts out.

"Abolish them?" Mauá objects. "No, never! What is a woman who has never been through sexual initiation? A child, who knows nothing of life's contours and curves."

< 266 >

"Rami, you have a good heart," Saly challenges me. "But your body is still a child's. You're a virgin in spite of your five children. But there's still time for you to get to know the world."

"What would you advise, then?"

"Get what we call your squid, your labia, elongated. That's a good start. It's a practice that many people criticize out of ignorance, and it produces more solutions than problems."

"At my age?"

"It can be done at any age. You can't go on like this. You can't resign yourself to living and dying without knowing love."

"I've loved, I still love, I was loved long before you came into being."

"To love involves embarking on a journey into your inner being, and you've never done that. Rami, who doesn't like sleeping on a foam mattress? Who doesn't like to lie down on a satin bedspread or a fine linen sheet? If you don't get your labia fixed, the ground is hard. It's the same as sleeping on a mat, on a camp bed, without the least bit of comfort."

My God, it must be true. My northern neighbor's daughters go to a school for sexual initiation. They like it.

"It's not your fault," Saly remarks. "You people in the south allowed yourselves to be colonized by those folk from Europe and their priests who were hostile to our practices. But what's that kiss worth compared to what we have inside us? Then they brought in pornography and all its silliness just to deceive the inept and entertain imbeciles."

I surrender to these countrywomen, who are such experts in sex, and who view the twists and turns of life in sexual terms.

"Any man is a child in our arms. He transmigrates. He forgets life and death, because a woman's body is eternity."

"Don't exaggerate, Mauá," I shout to try to shut her up.

"Ask Tony, if you want it confirmed. I sometimes tell him: If you don't bring me what I want, I'll go on strike when it comes to sex. You'll have to go hungry. I'll close my doors for your journey in time. He gets flustered and does everything to please me. Rami, you've got to believe it. Any man is a slave in the hands of a woman who knows how to love."

"If I was a man, I wouldn't be a witness to all this adversity. I curse the time God made me a woman," I burst out.

"I bless the hour God made me a woman," Mauá says. "Women were made for love and not to suffer. I can eat without working, because Tony gives me everything I want, because he's my slave."

I find this revelation painful. My husband is sucked dry by women amphibians. Women with scales. Squid women. Octopus women. They came from the sea and live on dry land, my God, they've destroyed me, wrecked my marriage. They've defeated me. I'm done for. Now I understand why initiation rituals were fought against, but then maintained in secret, they survived for centuries as secret societies. A man who goes through this type of education knows how to love. A woman who is schooled in this enchants, bedazzles, is vibrant in the way she lives.

"You southern women are big. Strong. Good for work," Mauá concludes almost insultingly. "You've got a big pelvic area and huge hips, ideal for childbearing. Your hands are good for chopping firewood and scrubbing the floor. But when it comes to being companions in bed, you're not so good. You break the bed frame, crush the mattress springs, you sweat a lot and ruin the sheets. We northern women, we're refined, petite, good for love and for bed. That's why we're queens, and men are our slaves."

"For these same reasons, I'm going to follow my own path."

"Rami, please, put up a fight!"

"I'm too old for such things. You appeared during the course

< 269 >

of my journey to throw flowers in my path. Goodbye, look after my dear Tony."

"Don't say goodbye, Rami."

"Fight, Rami. Fight for your love."

"I'm tired."

Oh, Rami! You'll only hold on to a man if you've got claws. Your body's as smooth as a catfish. You don't even have a tattoo. Your body doesn't graze. It doesn't scrape. It doesn't rub. It doesn't leave any marks. That's why men leave you."

"Are you saying I should go and have my body tattooed?"

"Tattoos are sticky, they glue, they hold," Lu admits.

"We've got tattoos on the most important bits of our bodies. Look, mine are so big, they're the size of nuts. I've got them in places where he puts his hands. By the oven door. On top of the oven. Internal tattoos to thicken the corrugations inside the oven. A man who gets as far as these never forgets," Saly explains.

"Do some tattoos, Rami, just one or two little ones, at least in those places where he's going to put his arms or rest his head," Mauá advises.

"You can even get your squid seen to," Lu suggests.

"I'm old."

< 270 >

"Love has no age. It's very easy. It'll just hurt on the first day, and after that you'll feel a pleasure to beat all pleasures. Use stones to clean the waters and reduce the internal dimensions. Use herbs, teas, salts. Use manioc seed oil to elongate and give your body shape. I'll give you an acid solution to use in small quantities. Castor oil. Almond oil."

I cover my face with my hands to hide my tears. All I want is to get out of there and not to have to listen to any more of this strange conversation. I want to send them all packing and be alone. But I can't. It's the first time each of them has spoken so openly about their stratagems in love. I want to hear more. I want to know everything to better understand this cancer that's killing me.

"In life's story, only men don't grow old," I say to contribute some light relief to this painful conversation. "Man is the tree of life. We are the leaves. We fall so that others may be born. The time has come for me to fall, goodbye, my friends."

"We are friends for always," Lu says, her eyes brimming with tears. "We four are the reason for the pain you are now feeling."

"If it wasn't you bringing me down, it would be others. Women's lives are a hellish cycle."

< 271 >

"What a pity!" Ju speaks tearfully. "The five of us managed to mold this clay to make its sculpture more solid every day. You're going to withdraw your support. What will become of us when we're alone?"

I go to the bathroom and feel myself underneath. No scales. No squid. No octopus tentacles. Only a broken shell where the wind passes, songless and without echo. An insipid shell, with a taste of water that doesn't quench one's thirst. Through here five heads passed, three sons and two daughters, and through them, I've affirmed myself in the history of the world, but for northerners I'm still a child, I've never embarked on a journey into myself. Mauá boasts she's got a bunch of labia capable of wrapping themselves around a man like a diaper. Mad! She and her magic can go to hell.

24

I go out into the street humming a tune of disappointment. Women are a world of magic and silence. People say they talk a lot. That may be true. They say they talk too much. Maybe. But they speak of futile, insignificant things. They know how to preserve their true world deep within themselves. Women are a world of silence and secrecy.

The language of the belly is the most expressive, because it can be read in the multiplication of life. The language of hands and arms is also visible. When you hold a newborn baby. When you hold a bouquet of flowers on the day you get married. When you hold a wreath of arum lilies at the funeral of your loved one. And the language of the heart? An invisible diamond rampart. The silence of the grave. An impenetrable absence.

And the language of…? If it… could be spoken, what message would it give us? It would surely intone beautiful poems of pain and yearning. It would sing songs of love and desertion. Of violence. Of violation. Of castration. Of manipulation. It would tell us why it sheds tears of blood in every cycle of life. It would tell us the story of its first time. In the marital bed. In the bush. Under the cashew trees. On the backseat of a car. In the director's office. On the beach. In the most incredible places on the planet.

Ah! If these languages... could be spoken! They'd tell us extraordinary tales of the *licaho*, the chastity knife. What would... medieval women who experienced the chastity belt tell us? What would the women who'd been circumcised tell us? What would those who participate in the orgies of the Makonde, the Sena, and the Nyanja tell us? The women who defied the *licaho* have been reduced to silence, they've died along with their secrets. The Ronga and the Shangaan have astonishing tales to tell about the debaucheries surrounding the drinking of the juice of the marula, aphrodisiac of the gods, during fertility celebrations.

Today, I feel like tearing the veil of ignorance from my eyes. I want to update all my knowledge about these... women. I sit down on a bench at the corner of the street. I want to listen to their silence as they whisper in my ear. Today, I want to listen to secrets. From afar, I manage to engage in a mute dialogue with each woman who passes by.

Pretty woman, where are you going? I ask. They give me broad grins by way of reply, conveying happiness, bitterness, yearning, loss of hope, anxiety, expectation. I ask those who pass: Do you believe in platonic love? They all laugh and ask me whether I've gone mad. They want to know what planet I'm living on. Platonic love only happens on the moon.

I ask them whether they're happy with their lives. Each one of them tells me endless tales of love spells using witchcraft, salts, herbs, homemade remedies, tobacco smoke, cannabis, brooms, bottles, menthol, all just to make a man fall for her, lock, stock, and barrel. Make him think just of her when looking at other women. To ensure his passions aren't raised with other women and that he will only sleep with her. To sharpen his sensations. Create a better impression. Make him stick. Hold him. Suck him dry. Make a man abandon his body and follow the route of the stars.

I listen to this woman's story, and then another. They all say the same thing. Women are all the same, aren't they?

The same? No, we're not, they cry. I'm shaped like a squid. And I'm a half-moon. An octopus. As flat as a plank. A broken conch. A turkey's beak. A clamshell. A cannibal. An anthropophagite.

A deadly throat. The devil's tunnel. A cavern full of silence and mystery. And I'm dangerous, whoever touches me dies.

So then I ask: You, broken conch, who dwells hidden away in the middle of the world, have you ever seen the sun? Have you seen the moon? Do you know what a star is? Are you aware the sky is blue?

Ah, she replies, I'm the one who blossoms in each cycle because I am the moon. I am much more than the sun because I offer the whole world a luminous, romantic glow. I am the most wonderful star in the firmament. Without me, there's no beauty in the world.

Presumptuous! Pretentious! Vain! Liar! Men say you taste of water after giving birth to so many children, and that's why they discard you and go after much younger women!

Oh, they're the ones who are lying. I'm linked to water by fate because I belong to the ocean. My body, more than any other, is the one that dives into the water when it awakens, when it lies down, in the noonday sun. I contain the humidity of the shores and the banks of rivers. I'm a piece of the sea that can't survive without taking a dip in its tepid waters.

And you, my dear cannibal, have you had enough meat to eat? There's hunger in the subterranean depths! There are tears, screams, lamentations. The earth is angry, it's becoming a desert. Some species of animal are becoming extinct. There are few men left in the cities, in the forests, in the savannahs. They are being destroyed by wars, by bombs, by machines, and by the explosive devices that they sowed out in the bush when they were waging war for ideals that only they understood. There are few left to feed our cannibal appetites. That's why we fight over them and the winner is the one with the sharpest claws. We who are less courageous in combat live in self-denial and abstinence, and suffer the martyrdom of sleeplessness.

But the fault is all yours, strange, unfathomable appetite, I censure her, because you're capricious, greedy, and because you vomit all that you eat.

I go through years of abstinence, another one says. My companion is a miner in South Africa. He only gives me a sixty-day ration every other year. He comes home on holiday just in order to get me pregnant and then he's off again. I feel I'm going to grow old without having lived. I console her, no, don't despair, because your hunger makes you suffer but it doesn't kill you. Let us light lots of candles and say a prayer so that God may bless you and let you have more bread.

< 277 >

I've been tricked, despised, forgotten, another woman confides in me. I don't know whether it's because of the cold. I don't know whether it's the smell. I'm an uncultivated field abandoned to the sorrel. I hate this life. I'd rather die than live in this misery. I tell her in reply that suicide doesn't solve anything, go to war and kill the beast, lamentations are for the elderly.

And you, unrelenting octopus, where do you find so much prey?

I'm an octopus, can't you see? I suck up everything. I've got an endless pot of honey. My supplies are infinite, I give all wayfarers something to drink. I'm your ambushed enemy who provokes fires, explosions, sleeplessness, nightmares, and drives men mad.

I look at her, and lowering my gaze, I say: You give all and sundry a drink, and in exchange for what? Be warned that your supplies are the sanctuary of life, and holy places should be kept pure. That little corner that is all yours is an altar that God created to demonstrate all his love. Don't sully it. But if it makes you happy, then thanks very much! . . .

I am obedient. I've always been faithful and have never sinned, not even in my thoughts. I always wait for my lord and master to give me the orders. I'm scared of the *licaho*, the chastity knife.

< 278 >

You don't believe me? Have you never heard of the *licaho*? Yes, it's true, it really exists. It's a magic jackknife. When an intruder breaks into another person's premises, the jackknife snaps shut by magic and at that precise moment, the two lovers are stuck to each other, unable to move, and that's how they remain for days on end, until death comes for them. Have you never heard it said that a man died on top of a woman or a woman under a man? It's the *licaho*, my friend, it's the *licaho*.

I don't answer, I merely sorrow: the poor dear woman! I grow sad and weep. This woman lives in a hermetically sealed compartment, where she can admire neither sunrise nor sunset. She can't cry because there's not enough air. She can't scream because there's no echo. She doesn't know the breeze, or the blue of the sky, or the stars. She learned to say yes, but never to say no. She learned to say thank you, to say sorry, and to live humiliated. When her executioner says: Maria, come here, she replies, yes, master. Now lie down. Yes, master. Now open. Yes, master. Now eat. Yes, master. Thank you, master. Now get up, you've eaten too much today. Sorry, master.

And you, squid, you, turkey beak, do you feel at ease with your image? I've heard it said that a Russian doctor cut off a woman's

< 279 >

squid when she was giving birth. The poor doctor had never seen anything like that and thought it was some malignant, foreign body that was entwined round the baby's neck and placing the life of the child and of the mother in danger. When the mother learned of this accidental amputation, she committed suicide because she no longer felt a woman. Aren't you afraid something similar could happen to you? Aren't you scared of showing these anatomical alterations to a foreign gynecologist? Don't you feel bad?

What is there to be ashamed of? Of that which gives us pleasure? We explain everything before any type of procedure. Doctors are astonished, but they understand. It's good to have a pair of squid. They protect us. Men invented the *licaho*, and we invented the squid. When there's any risk of rape, we tuck the flaps of our squid inside and we shut the door against any ill intention, and nothing can get through, not even a needle. We are inviolable. We might get killed, but we'll never get raped.

Hello there!... You're well dressed. Pretty. You drive around in good cars and you must enjoy the most refined food in the world. You're the image of someone who's living life to the full and doesn't need to ask any favors.

Ah! How mistaken you are! You're right in one thing though. I've got lace, silk, perfumes. My companion is well spoken and generous with his money. But... he's an intellectual.

So what?

Educated men spend their time sitting on the sofa, their computer on along with the air conditioning. They eat yogurt, mashed potato, tinned food, and are as flabby as battery-reared chicken. When it comes to body-to-body activity, they're feeble and lose the fight. They're no use. My gentleman is like that. I began to ask for a light here, a light there, to make up for my privations. I specialized in responding to begging requests for love, and now there's no holding me back.

You hussy, you double-crosser. It's because of... like you that men despise us, and tell us we're worthless, I accuse her.

Men lie. Oh, how they lie! They tell us we're worth nothing? That we're no use for anything? Poppycock! There's nothing more miraculous than us in the whole human community. That's why they hate us, fear us, mutilate us, rape us, torture us, seek us out, hurt us. But it's for us they yearn their whole lives through. It's us they seek, night and day, from the day they're born to the day they die.

< 281 >

I smile. This woman's fantastic. She speaks all the languages in the world without speaking any of them. She's a sacred altar. A sanctuary. She's the nirvana where the just can repose from all of life's tribulations. She's magic, a miracle maker, tenderness. She's the sky and the earth within people. She's ecstasy, perdition, surrender. Ah, my friend, you're my treasure. Today, I'm proud of being a woman. Only today have I learned that you reside within me, that you are the beating heart of the world. Why have I ignored you all this time? And why have I only learned this lesson today?

< 282 >

25

I have an intense desire to talk to someone who understands me. Who loves me and listens to me. My mother. I'm going to savor that fresh smile that placates me. I want to listen to a bedtime story. I want to bathe in the reflection of the few sad eyes that have the color of moonlight.

I find my mother pounding grain in the pestle. She sings. She smiles. My father is talking with two friends in the shade of the mango tree.

"How are you, girl? You've got your sad look. What's happened?"

I tell her. I tell her everything and start crying. I talk about the divorce he wants and doesn't want. About my rivals. About my endless afflictions.

"There's no man without a woman. Nor is there a woman without a man. There isn't one without the other."

"I doubt myself, Mother. Everything I do in life is wrong. I don't know how to cook as I should. I don't have any pleasing words to say. I've lost all my appeal, Mother. He criticizes me for everything

< 283 >

and for nothing at all. Everything about me that he used to like no longer pleases him. I'm a disaster. A disappointment. His eyes have turned to other landscapes, I no longer mean anything to him."

"Ah, my beautiful girl!"

"Just look at my body, Mother. My breasts were round like massala fruit, but now they're like papayas. My backside was as smooth as an orange, but now it's like a pumpkin. Look at my legs, Mother. Full of varicose veins, crinkled with cellulite that looks like cauliflower."

"My daughter! Motherhood has transformed you and made a woman of you. Do you dislike your body? Was growing ever a crime? Your body sports the signs of time, the signs of maturity and wisdom."

"He's leaving me because of the spells put on him by the other women, Mother. Each one of them does everything in order to get rid of me so they can take my throne. The number of spells they tell me about, Mother, if you could only hear them."

"Lift your head up high and smile, my dear girl. You're the one with the spell, in that heart of yours. You were a sweetheart, you had your bride price paid, you were married in accordance with the rules. You're the one who can cast spells: you were a virgin

< 284 >

when married and stained the sheets on your wedding night. These other women, what are they?"

I gaze at her, astonished. It's any woman's dream to be led up to the altar. I fulfilled that dream. That man who is now abandoning me was once the most coveted of men. I conquered him. I had him. I consumed him. He gave me five children. I affirmed myself. I am protected by the law, and the other women have nothing. I'm certainly luckier than them.

"Why did you never tell me about love spells, Mother?"

"It was religion, girl. It was the city. Your father's a man of the city and didn't have any time for traditions. He had his principles and only spoke Portuguese."

"Teach me some secrets, Mother."

She starts to weep silently. Tears of moonlight and silk, that touch me, injure and inspire me. A vision of light opens in front of me like a mirror, in which my image is reflected. I see the sadness of this woman who stands before me. A sad woman like myself. My daughters will bear this sadness, just as we women of all generations and the whole universe do.

I stop talking to spare her old heart further pain, and embark on a silent dialogue with her.

I feel like telling you, Mother, that your problem is less burdensome than mine. You've got a brute for a husband. I've got a brute and a polygamist. A polygamist who said I was his darling and dragged me into perdition. He told me I was the only one, and now tells me that women are in abundant supply. I've got rivals, Mother, who get undressed before my very eyes and show off their honey sweet bodies to me, eat at my table and boast of their sexual pleasures with my husband. I know you've got tattoos, I'm familiar with all of them, the ones on your back and on your belly. I feel like asking: Do you also have those marine specialties on your body, Mother? Did you suffer some subterranean hunger? Father only had you, but see what I have to put up with. Suffering unhappiness that not even my own mother experienced. I understand the meaning of your tears, Mother. That's why I'm not saying anything to you so as not to increase the burden of your pain, Mother. But, Mother, if you knew that life was like this, why did you bring me into the world? Could it be for the same reason that you never told me the reason why your dear sister died, Mother?

26

I leave home and set out for work. I go on foot, Tony never took me in his car. I walk. I sing. *As I journeyed along I found love, I dreamed of treasure, but...*

An ambulance siren interrupts my song and I look left. There's a river of red flowing across the asphalt, someone has been run over and killed by a truck. The man's blood, released from his veins, has soaked the road, setting the ground ablaze with its scarlet flame. The passersby stand silently, bidding farewell to the soul that is crossing the frontiers of this life in flight. There are sighs. Bewailing, murmurs. When human life is struck down, all the living hold their breath. Even the stones are alarmed. Even the waters of the river offer a minute's silence.

He was an adult, strong, the appearance of a man of about fifty years of age. I sigh as well. In this inanimate bundle, I imagine a whole heap of commitments that have been interrupted and many bright hopes snuffed out. For him, all the channels for fulfilling his dreams and hopes have been closed. All his conquests,

< 287 >

love affairs, his goodness and his malice, are over and done with. It's the end of love. Of tyranny. Polygamy. Disharmony. Let his blood fertilize this unloving ground. Let the earth provide his final resting place.

This time last year, at precisely this hour of the day, another man was run over here – some onlookers comment. This place is cursed, there's a malign spirit at large on this stretch of road. Poor family. A wife is probably cooking lunch for her husband who will never come home. Children awaiting their father who is late. I stop for a moment, I look at the dead man, and I continue on my way, comforted by my own song until I get to my shop.

I'm stalked by depression for the rest of the day, but my work goes well. Hardly do I begin to sing my song again than the image of the dead man returns to me. I go home exhausted after the day's events and go straight to sleep. In the early hours, the phone rings. Saly wakes me up, alarmed.

"Saly, what's wrong?"

"Tony. I don't know what's become of him. He left home at about eight in the morning, saying he was going to buy some cigarettes, he didn't come home for lunch or dinner, and he still hasn't come back. It's two in the morning."

< 288 >

"Is that so?"

"Yes. I was just calling to see whether he was over there with you."

"No, he isn't."

"I'm really worried. He's not with any of his wives."

"I'll be over in a minute."

I get out of bed and start thinking. I get irritated. So much fuss over a good-for-nothing? I dress quickly and leave for Saly's house in spite of the late hour, determined to put her mind at rest. When your husband's a womanizer, you live in a permanent state of tension. We imagine him dead, murdered, the victim of an accident, arrested, when the simple truth is that he decided to hide away in a honey trap. When I get to Saly's house, the other wives and Tony's two brothers are already there. I involve myself in the search only to alleviate my conscience. We divide ourselves up to follow different possible routes. First, we go to places he often frequents. We search high and low, mountains and vales. We turn whole worlds upside down. We rummage through the underworld. When you lose a goat, you look for him on the topmost peak of the mountain range. On the conical roof of the grass hut. At the top of the tree. In the curve of the sun. In the flight of the clouds. There's no sign of him.

"Saly, what makes you think Tony's got lost?"

< 289 >

"He went out in his shorts and slippers. He left the car and his documents. He went out for a few minutes."

"But you know what Tony's like. Here we are getting worried and maybe he's sitting with his feet up in the home of some new conquest of his."

"That might well be the case, but I don't think so. Something must have happened."

By now, it's six in the morning. I go back home and sleep for a bit.

27

Seven o'clock. I hear someone beating on my front door. I wake up and go to open it. My house is invaded by my sisters-in-law and my husband's aunts, who burst in wailing and screaming.

"Congratulations, Rami," one of the women shouts at me. "You're free, you've got what you wanted. You're not going to have to endure any humiliation. There's no risk of a divorce now. You're a widow!"

"A widow? Me?"

"You've got rid of a heavy burden. You're free. You killed our brother so that you could get his inheritance."

While they're shouting at me, they start taking the chairs and tables from the living room and tell me to sit in a corner. Why am I being confined to this corner as if I were a prisoner? I shout back and ask: How did Tony die and where, who killed him, who found him, how was he identified? The women answer me: Behave like a dignified widow. I don't know what's happening, but I know that a respectable widow isn't supposed to understand anything, or ask questions, or make any suggestions, in order not to be labeled a bawdy, merry widow.

I'm horrified by the speed with which they've come to the conclusion he's dead and by the urgency with which they've started calling me a widow. I was looking for the Tony they're talking about all through the night, and so far he hasn't been found anywhere. They enter my bedroom and dismantle the furniture to create space and cover all the furniture with white sheets. They drag me into a corner, shave my head with a razor and dress me in black. I've stopped having any power over my body and my own home. I begin to regret things: Why didn't I sign those wretched divorce papers? I had an opportunity to break free from all this oppression and I didn't take it. Once again I ask:

"How did my Tony die? When? Where?"

"Women are witches. You ate our brother, Rami. You Ronga women are like that. You kill your husbands so you can live it up on the dead man's assets."

People turn up from various directions like lines of ants. Within a minute or two my house is full. Nowadays, greater value is given to death than to life, and death is more important than birth. Women like funeral wakes. At wakes, they can wail away all their pains like wolves at night, they can purge their embittered bodies through their copious tears. When their throats become dry and their strength wanes, they recharge their batteries with sweet tea and bread and butter paid for by the family of the deceased. Men like wakes because they can relax, play chess, checkers, cards, and they can chat about politics, soccer, and women. A wake is a good opportunity to unload slanderous comments, exorcize ghosts, have a dig at enemies, meet up with relatives and old friends, and receive some assets. In death, everyone comes together to weep, but in life, man is left to fight on his own.

They take me to my bedroom like a bunch of green bananas being dragged to the hothouse. Like an obstinate goat being led to the corral. They do what they like with me. I don't belong to myself anymore. They place a veil on my head. Some folk hug me and weep, but I still don't see why. I need to understand, to accept things, to see in order to believe. No one gives me time. I tremble with terror and alarm. My whole being is invaded by a feeling of emptiness. What's going to become of my life without Tony? I live through hours of rage, peevishness, and bile.

"Tony was run over yesterday morning at about eight, on the bridge."

I take a deep breath. I saw the dead man on the bridge. But it had nothing to do with Tony. How have they arrived at the conclusion it was him if we, his wives, haven't yet identified the body?

A whole crowd of women sit down around me. I'm in a prison cell made out of thick walls of people. The air becomes a lethal gas. There's heavy breathing. All the bodies together form one sheet, one current, one heat, and the pores of our skin become communication ducts. It's snug. The women's voices buzz in my ears like the lowing of cows about to be milked. There are prayers, litanies, dirges. I am the queen bee in this hive of lamentations. A widow with any feelings should produce tears by the bucketful, and everyone assesses the volume of my weeping. Men's hands distribute candles like flowers, in the bedroom, the living room, the veranda, all over the place. Their little yellow flames sway like sunflowers to the rhythm of the breeze. There's a smell of death, a smell of tears, a smell of wax. Everyone is crying over Tony, who has left for the great beyond, except for me, who weeps because Tony left me for the arms of another woman. We all weep with devotion. We weep lovingly.

The other four wives have arrived and we shut ourselves away in one of the rooms for a chat. To exchange impressions and feelings. I wanted to share my doubts, my frustrations with them. We try to agree on a common strategy in the face of all this mourning.

"Rami, why are they in such a hurry to declare him dead? In little more than an instant, they've obtained the death certificate and fixed a date for the funeral. Why are they doing this, Rami?" Saly's voice is like a hoarse gust of air, originating in the most secret corner of herself.

"Why have we been excluded from the process of identifying the dead man?" Ju explodes, seriously disgusted. "Who knows the man's body better than we do? Are we not his wives? Why don't they organize a detailed examination of the body? Tony's a policeman. The police have got appropriate technical methods and systems for things like this."

"Tony's colleagues and superiors have been here," I explain, "and have offered their services. They were shooed away like flies. These perverse people invoked religion, tradition, and a whole host of superstitions I'd never heard of before."

"This whole story smacks of treachery," Lu bursts out, "someone wants to poison us, I can feel it. Someone is spitting in our face. Someone's sharpening his claws for a major act of plunder. Get ready, girls. There's going to be a bloodbath very soon.

Someone's sniffing around whatever inheritance this death is going to produce."

"The bloodbath's already started. They've already called us witches, gold diggers, whores, self-seekers," Saly vociferates, "one of Tony's brothers keeps looking at us as if he were measuring us up, planning something. He's got the look of a butcher about him."

"Death sometimes comes without warning," says Mauá, who has so far been silent. "But before someone dies, there's always some slight forewarning. A bad dream, an eyelid twitching, a snake crossing one's path, a black cat meowing at night, a bat screeching, the wind swirling and lifting the leaves skyward, something like that. But there was nothing, absolutely nothing!"

"I've got pigeons in my yard," Ju explains, "pigeons can sense death from afar, without fail. When there's a death in the household, they all land together on the ground and start cooing really loudly, and then they take off again and don't come back. But the pigeons in my yard are cooing merrily. Something's not right, Rami, and I don't know what it is."

I sense a smell of bile invading my body. A smell of heat, a smell of pain. My rivals are expecting me to say something, but my throat is a closed door. I have my doubts and my certainties, but the ill omens I feel prevent me from sharing my apprehensions. I'm scared of bringing about unforeseen events. It's better to let the ship sink and the fruit fall to the ground once rotten.

"Ah! You southerners!" Lu remarks in an accusing tone of voice. "I'm a Sena. Among us Senas, death is a private affair. As private as a kiss, as love, as birth. Death concerns just a small nucleus of people. Relatives and friends drop by to express their condolences, but don't stay in order not to be contaminated by the sight of death. Here in the south, death is a celebration, it's a party. A good opportunity to eat without having to pay. With such high levels of mortality, I know folk who go from funeral to funeral, singing, weeping, eating and getting fat without spending anything whatsoever. Tell me one thing, all of you. Who's going to fill the bellies of all this rabble?"

Late afternoon and Tony's brothers take us to the morgue. At the entrance to the morgue, the people working there put white coats on us, and white masks. We go in. Everything is white. White walls, white corridors, cupboards and huge drawers also white, white tiles, white washbasins, white bricks, white stretchers. Workers dressed in white. Here, immobile bodies sleep like

< 297 >

sawn tree trunks, covered in white sheets on icy waves. Death is white. On the ceiling invisible souls hover, and they must be white and freezing cold too. I shudder at the thought of it.

The body of our dead husband is awaiting its abode. The body is disfigured, difficult to identify. He was crushed, misshapen, like a jelly spread out on the ground. The eyes are outside the orbits and expressionless. A man dressed in white shows us the corpse of the man they say is ours. I take a close look behind his right ear. The scar from one of our old squabbles is missing. I whacked him over the head with a bottle, which produced a huge gash and he was stitched up like a piece of lace in the surgery. A scar doesn't disappear because of an accident. This dead man is definitely not my Tony because the evidence of my crime is missing.

My mother-in-law is standing in front of the body. She doesn't open her eyes. She keeps them closed. A mother doesn't need to look. She feels. She must be recalling the good times when her son lived in her belly, in her arms, in her world.

I approach my mother-in-law and whisper in her ear: Mother, this is not Tony. She gives me a sad smile and answers tearfully: My poor girl. It's hard accepting reality. It's always like this, and always was, I know. Courage, my little girl. The old woman isn't taking me seriously. She swaddles me in a look of tenderness, hugs me, embraces me, stifles me. I'm in despair. Oh, you blind, deaf, stupid people! Don't I have the right to be listened to at least once in my life? I'm tired of being a woman. Of having to put up with every whim. Of being an outsider in my own home. I'm tired of being a shadow. A silhouette. If you don't want to listen to me, then my revenge will be my silence. I won't share my doubts. I'm going to let this dead man be buried.

It's taken a long time for me to understand why they were in such a hurry to resolve such a delicate matter. It was all nothing more than an act of hatred and vengeance. They hated us. They hated Tony's prosperity. They were seeking recompense for all that they wanted for themselves, and that life had denied them: titles, women, houses, cars, properties. I'm going to join in this game out of a need for revenge as well. Let's see what happens. I have a feeling I'm going to have a lot of fun. I'm not going to deny these people the pleasure of having an appropriate funeral. They feel a need to cry. So let them cry.

The blindness of these people is the product of their superstition. Of the naked women who bring bad luck. It comes from their time-honored belief in the language of seashells and bones

< 299 >

that speak greater truths than women do. It comes from the mathematics of hatred and envy, in which two plus two equals five. It comes from their belief in the evil and witchcraft incubated in the bellies of women. He asked me for a divorce. I refused. It's well known that being a widow brings in more money than being divorced. In the superstitious thinking of some people, I ordered his death through magic arts, to avoid divorce and get my hands on his assets. On that bridge where the man was killed, there's a mystery. Last year, in that exact spot, at the same hour of the morning, a man was killed as he was leaving the house of one wife and heading for the house of another. That spot lies between Saly's house and Ju's. In that spot, there's a powerful, terrifying, malign spirit, a spirit that devours polygamous men.

< 300 >

28

Late afternoon. Mauá's family arrive to demand her rights as a widow in accordance with Makua tradition. Among the Makua, the woman is mother, queen, and creator of the universe. A Makua widow is the recipient of love, affection, and help. They have come to claim her part of the inheritance as a widow. And the Makua have turned up in numbers. They wait in the living room, and talk in that language of theirs that we can't understand. Before the meeting begins, Saly's family arrives. They are Makonde, and their intentions are the same. Makua and Makonde come together in strength to defend the interests of nieces. Night falls. The electric light illuminates their perspiring bodies, making them look like jacaranda wood sculptures.

The spokesman for the two families begins his speech in a sonorous, elegant tone. He explains the problem and sets out their claims.

Tony's eldest brother is the spokesman for the family. In his reply, he starts by describing the status of each of Tony's wives.

He says that polygamy is a system that has its own rules, and in this matter, the south differs from the north. Each new wife is the product of a need, and not merely of hidden pleasures. In polygamy, the woman is taken from her family's home, she is pure, a virgin like all betrothed women. He says that the true widows are myself and Ju. Even Ju isn't a perfect widow, he explains, because her entry into the home took place without the knowledge of the family counsel, and without the agreement of his first wife. The other women are mere concubines, simply adventurers Tony encountered during his life's journey. They latched on to Tony when he had already achieved a professional position, he had good houses and good cars. True polygamy doesn't stem from self-interest.

This retort offends the Makua and the Makonde, it raises hackles and the tone of the voices escalates.

"We were aware of the bad treatment that was being meted out to Dona Rami," Mauá's uncle says. "We wish to make it clear that the Makua and the Makonde aren't cattle to be mistreated. We have come to warn you that you mustn't lay a finger on our girls. We don't want anything to do with your rituals involving cutting hair, and purifying them with your vaccinations."

"You are from the north, and you should deal with your things where you come from, but we in the south have our traditions," Tony's brother replies. "Don't come and give us orders, because you Makua aren't men. Where you come from, it's the women that give orders. Who's ever heard of a man getting married and going to live with his wife's family? Who's ever heard of a man working his whole life only to leave the product of all his hard work to her when he dies or when they separate?"

"Women are flowers, they should be treated with care. Women are weak, they should be protected. Who better than the mother's family to give warmth and protection? When the husband dies, the house goes to her and their children. After all, it was built for them."

"You northerners are slaves to your women. You work your whole lives just for them. Even the children carry their mother's surname. What sort of men are you?"

"And you southerners are brutes, you treat women like animals. Does anyone in this world know who the real father of a wife's children is? You, sir, who insult us so much, are you sure that the children you say are yours, are in fact yours? Where we come from, it's true that the children have their mother's family name.

That's because the father is always a doubt, whereas the woman is certainty. A rooster never hatches eggs. It's better to give to Caesar what is Caesar's.

Arms thrash around in the air like fish in the sea. The debate gets heated and all inhibitions are swept away. All traces of pride are erased and viciousness surfaces. Death is forgotten, mourning is abandoned. Prayers stop, along with the weeping and the dirges.

"Stupid, backward northerners! Tattoo-covered Makonde! Mind your own business and leave us alone!"

"You Shangaan are inhuman, barbaric, vulgar brutes. You're not human, you murder your women. You don't respect your own mothers."

"All this is Tony's fault. With so many pretty southern women, why did he have to go and get these crazy, mixed-up northern girls?"

"The only pretty women are those from the north, you Shangaan idiots! Northern women are dainty and free. Northern women are beautiful. Your women are heavy, dumpy, they've got big backsides from eating too many peanuts!"

The menfolk are hurling insults at each other like rocks. Their bodies are taut and tense. Their voices are loud like howls on a moonlit night. They take off their jackets and ties, the war is fierce. What a pity there isn't enough room to improvise a ring. Otherwise, we could have a really good boxing match, Shangaan against northerners, or vice versa. This scene is just too good to miss. What a pity Tony isn't here to see for himself the confusion he's caused.

"Go to hell, you stupid northerners with your idle women. You spend your time painting yourselves. Combing your hair. And you men, their slaves, always putting up with these women's caprices, always buying gold, cloth, new clothes. You're nothing. You've got no power at all and you can't even give the orders in your own home."

"That's where you're wrong. Our women work hard. They look after the house, sweep the yard, wash the clothes, distil good liquor for us, their husbands, fetch water from the well and prepare our bath, they're good in the kitchen and in bed as well. We invest in their beauty. We invest in their repose and everyone is delighted with the women of our locality. Ask the Arabs, who were the first to reach the land of the Makua, anchored their ships, and stayed for good. Ask the Portuguese, who passed through there and fell mortally in love with the most beautiful black women on the surface of the earth. Ask the French who are there, and were so dazzled, so maddened and besotted by the beauty of our Makua women, that they forgot how to get home. Ask the priests who abandoned their cassocks and fell in love with the Makua women of our island. Ask your Tony, who abandoned his family and became infatuated with our Mauá's charms. Our women are educated for life and for love. They are the breeze, the flower, perfect love."

"That's all rubbish, you wretched northerners. You invest in women? What sort of investment?"

"Of course we do. Because the woman is earth. Without fertilizer or irrigation, she doesn't produce. While you beat them, stamp on them, we adorn them, we love and care for them like plants in the most beautiful garden."

Mauá and Saly are shaking with fear. They come over to me and ask for help.

"Rami, we've got to do something. They're going to kill each other."

"Calm down, Mauá, they're not going to kill each other."

"This argument is getting really violent."

"You only hit what you are making. A hammer hits a nail. Metal against stone. A spade against the sand. Don't be scared."

"This argument is going too far," Saly complains.

"All the better. Far is the horizon, the frontier beyond which we cannot see. Every pilgrim wants to travel far. We also want to travel far, isn't that so, Saly? This is a fight among roosters, with winners and losers, but no one is going to die."

My brother-in-law's power of argument is beginning to wane. He starts lamenting. He says it's the fault of that shameless Tony, whose lust for love takes no notice of the north or the south. That he loves women from all parts of the country as if he could be a true husband of the nation. He says Tony's loves know no boundaries, no races, no ethnic groups or region, much less religion.

There's a skirmish between north and south, south versus north, in which a fistful of sand is thrown at the problems of the moment. In the fields, the corn has been burned by the sun and children are crying from hunger. The father has lost his job. The eldest son has got AIDS and is falling to pieces, a strip at a time, like a centipede's body. The youngest daughter has taken up with a white foreigner, was made pregnant, and the white has left for home. Up in the north, the River Zambezi has overflowed, killing lizards, grass, ants, and people. It dragged crocodiles with it from its riverbed, and these lie hidden in the pestilence of mud, feeding on children. Here in the south, the young use drugs, don't attend school, rape women, and steal cars. Some of the rabid men in this room were soldiers who helped liberate the whole country but have no home, much less a piece of land on which to build one. They live under a tree and make liquor, which they drink in order to forget, while they trade their daughters for sex and sell marijuana.

Whether from the north or the south, each one wants to reach higher and be the first to touch the sky's navel. Each one wants to be a heron, a falcon, or an albatross, in order to reach the top of the hill more quickly, where they'll still find a bunch of bananas hanging and a chicken roasting on the world's brazier.

< 308 >

29

Ju and I are summoned to a new family meeting. The northerners are left out. Everyone turns on me to unleash their fury.

"Rami, you have to take responsibility for what happened with Tony. It was your fault that he lost his life."

I say yes.

"He began to get himself other women and ended up a polygamist because you didn't satisfy him. Because you never had his food ready and your bed was always cold. Because you're haughty and unfeeling. Because you didn't know how to love or to get on with someone."

I say yes.

"You're the one who's the witch, Rami. If it weren't for your obsession with bringing the wives together, none of this would have happened. The five of you joined forces and produced negative vibrations in this house."

I say yes.

"The spell was yours. You killed him to avoid a divorce, and so you could inherit the dead man's assets."

I say yes.

"You killed our brother like a cat and seasoned him with garlic."

I say yes.

"We went to a medicine man, a good one. He blames you. He says you went looking for revenge, without being aware that it was death you were buying."

I say yes.

It's the women who do the talking. And how they talk! They spit out their pain, their barbs, their resentment, their frustrations. I don't swallow the torrent of dirt they serve me in their chalices of fire. I take a swig of mineral water and spit it out in their faces. I get a slap on the cheek. I turn the other poisoned cheek, whoever slaps this one will die.

They tell me that all the traditions of death must be fulfilled to the letter. We must return to our roots. They want to turn back the clock, and they flounder around as if blindfolded, for they don't know the way back. Time merely returns to me, whom they cut up into slices like a cream cake at a birthday party.

Now they are talking about *kutchinga*, the tradition whereby a widow has sex with her husband's brother for the purpose of sexual purification. My brothers-in-law, the candidates for this sacred act, look at me with eyes that gleam like crystal. There's a whiff of eroticism in the air. Growing expectation. Who will be the lucky one? Who will inherit all Tony's wives? I'm startled. Disgusted. My skin is covered in sweat and fear. My heart beats with endless surprise. *Kutchinga!* I shall be allotted to any one of them. And all of them are readying themselves to have me. The wall is hard and cold. It supports me. The surface of the ground is hard, it provides security. It supports me. But these people are so mischievous, so cruel… I ask any God for any help He can provide. No one comes to my aid, neither God nor the saints.

Kutchinga is all about cleansing one's grief with kisses of honey. It's about launching a widow into her new life little more than a week after the death. *Kutchinga* is a stamp, the sign of ownership. A woman's bride price is paid in money and cattle. She's property. Whoever invests in her expects something in return, the investment needs to pay. All of a sudden, I ask myself a crazy question: Does a woman ever groan with pleasure during the act of *kutchinga*? But not everything is bad. Something positive has emerged out of this disaster. With the shortage of men that we are all told about, it's good to know that my widowhood guarantees me someone else, even if only occasionally. It's comforting to know that there's some shoulder to lean on without my having to walk the streets selling my steadily waning attractions. Incest? No, it's not incest, just *kutchinga*. It's only incest if the same blood flows through our veins.

30

Eve has come to pay me a visit. She introduced herself and pulled me into a corner. Her conversation doesn't have anything to do with deaths or mourning. I'm surprised. I take the opportunity to find out what it is that got my Tony so hooked. I look at her appreciatively. Her mouth is a fresh cashew fruit, ripe and crimson, plucked from the divine cashew plantation. Her smile is more sparkling than a diamond. Her voice is like birdsong, it releases white doves, pearls, droplets of gold into the air. Her skin is smoother than polished glass. How beautiful she is, my God! I feel a wave of sisterhood for her, such a magical attraction that it's like love at first sight. We exchange confidentialities like old friends, like twin sisters.

"I'm Eve, you don't know me. I'm a friend of Tony's. Who told you Tony had died? And how did he die? Who identified him?"

Her questions are incisive, like a scalpel incision during an operation. I tremble. I look down and don't reply. I don't know what to answer, I don't have anything to give her by way of a reply.

"Forgive me, Rami, but I don't believe one single bit of this story. This dead man they're about to bury died in the morning. On the evening of that same day, Tony left for Paris on vacation. I took him to the airport myself. He didn't say goodbye to you for reasons that shouldn't concern us right now. I did the check-in for him. I saw him board the plane. He arrived and phoned me the following morning. Can someone be both dead and alive at the same time?"

I take a deep breath. Her revelation has the effect of extracting the fatal bullet that has lodged in my breast. She takes my hand. She transmits the heat of her body to me. In her gesture, she holds my entire soul together. I relax.

"I don't want to get involved in this story, Rami, but the truth is that I can't ignore it completely."

In Eve's eyes, there is the suggestion of a couple of tears, threatening to break through the dam and flow freely down her light-skinned face. If they fall, they'll wreck her makeup, she'll become all smudged, ugly, dear God, do something to stop such a disaster.

"Why this interest? Tell me."

"I've got my reasons. First of all, it was I who suggested to Tony he should go on this journey, in order to see a doctor about that problem he has with his knee. I saw to everything, from his flight bookings to his hotels, and his appointments with a specialist. When we were all set, along he comes with another woman in his luggage for a honeymoon trip. A woman called Gaby. Second, I wasn't aware he had so many women. I only knew Mauá, who he convinced me was his only legitimate spouse. I found out he was lying. I was really hurt."

More tears run down my cheeks from their limitless source. She tries to dry my flowing river with her bare hands. Those hands feel so smooth on my skin, like flakes of cotton. Those hands transmit warmth like the wings of a hen covering her chicks. An ocean of tenderness washes over me. She places her dainty arm round my shoulders. She gives me a hug. I smell her perfume. Tony is right to be head over heels in love with her. Lord, how nice she is!

Now she's telling me about my rivals. After being insulted at the family meeting, Lu, Saly, and Mauá had turned up on her doorstep, furious, to tell her of Tony's death and to make demands. They told her: The man you once loved was ours. It's not fair that we should be alone in having to grieve. They demanded that she should join them in mourning. As she'd been taken by surprise, she didn't know what to say. They gave her a list of options, and she chose what seemed the most reasonable: to cover the catering needs of those folk who have come to eat and weep.

"I've brought a basket full of food. You southerners make the most of your grief to fill your bellies."

"Forgive them. They left here having been treated like dirt, chased away like chickens, and went to your house to let off steam. And where are you from, Eve?"

"I'm from Palma, up in the northern tip of the country, on the coast, a place no one talks about. I'm Makonde."

"Ah!"

"I want to emphasize that Tony and I were just friends. There were no commitments."

"Thank you!"

"Rami, I've brought travel documents that prove what really happened. You've got all the proof you need. You can tell them to cease their madness."

"I need to think."

"Come on, call the police. If you want, I'll hire a lawyer to put an end to this farce."

"It won't help. Tony's chief of police, you know that only too well. I suggested to my brothers-in-law that there should be a more serious, more technical investigation and identification. They invoked tradition and religious practice, and told me to shut up. They want to do everything their way. Just look at what they did to me."

I take off my headscarf and show her my shaven head.

"They did this because I'm a widow. Because it's tradition. They bathed me in a variety of oils and grease that smell like shit. They shut me in a room full of incense and other strange smells that made my sinusitis even worse. They cut my skin with razors and rubbed peppery pomades into my wounds, to what effect I have no idea."

"They've shaved your head, Rami. There's worse to come."

"Let them get on with it."

"These Shangaan traditionally banish a widow and her children from her home."

"Let them banish me. Besides, I'm not a widow."

"They'll do this thing they call *kutchinga* on you."

"Let them do it. In fact, I'm really in need of a bit of love. I even know who it's going to be with."

"Who?"

"Look at the men sitting over there. Do you see the one with the distinguished air about him?"

"The one with the blue shirt?"

"That's the one."

"My God!"

"Has he scared you?"

"Quite the opposite, he's inspired me. He's a jewel of a man, that one. If all that beauty were translated into shares on the stock market, I'd buy them all, I swear. If he was being auctioned, I'd put in the highest bid, just to have him to myself for a night of love. If I could, I'd even buy the ground he trod. You'll have a good time, congratulations, Rami!"

"Well, that Adonis is going to be mine for the *kutchinga* ceremony. It won't be for long, but he'll be mine. I can't wait. The day can't come fast enough!"

I hide my face behind my veil to conceal my laugh. I pretend to moan and weep. Eve imitates me.

"So how will Tony react to this whole story?"

I tell her all the bitterness of my marriage, the conjugal rota, the orgy of vengeance, the request for a divorce that never happened, and she can't believe what she's hearing.

"Tony's a madman," Eve bursts out.

"He deserves to be well punished."

"I agree. He's got to learn the biggest lesson of his life."

"It's a good opportunity."

"I'm on your side. This lunatic must be taught a lesson."

Eve says goodbye and leaves me alone with my sadness. I follow her with my gaze. Eve, my lovely rival. Who brought me the dawn in the petal of a flower, who killed my pain, who, in the palm of her cupped hand, brought me the truth surrounding this whole ridiculous story. I return to my post as widow to assume the proper role of a woman. A woman is a solitary being in the crowd's great surge forward. A woman is the collective pain covering the world. She is past, present, and future, the security of a place and the great unknown joined by the same scream. Every step you take there's a woman prepared to give herself, to give life to life. In every instant there's a woman spreading herself like the wind, fertilizing the fields in order to transform the planet into a lacy bassinet.

I think about my situation. This is the price paid for so many years of dedication. I'm a good woman. I was always good as a girl. Good girls are the ones who are most hunted, married, and shut away in their homes like treasure. They live in a box, without light or air, between love and submission. Bad girls are rejected and left free. They fly anywhere they feel like going, like butterflies. They lend nature the color of their wings and breathe the fresh air of the fields, between love and freedom. There are no half-measures in a woman's life: treasure and submission, or butterfly and freedom.

31

The day of the funeral has arrived. The other four widows are here with me. They're all dressed in black. But their clothes are lighter than mine. These perverse people have hurled all the black colors in the world against my body. Black satin and lace gloves – just imagine that in all this heat – black stockings, black earrings and necklace, a long black dress with long sleeves, a black headscarf, a black shawl, black shoes. All that remained for them to do was to paint my body really black, to complete the black of my race. The clothes I'm wearing I had made by the best dressmaker in the city, and I'm extraordinarily beautiful in my mourning outfit, really beautiful. All I want is for everybody to remember me when they recall this day.

The funeral cortege reminds me of a wedding procession. There's a priest, the scent of perfumes, flowers, veils, hymns. I'm the bride, the presiding queen at this party. The line of people resembles a procession of ants transporting crumbs of bread into the ground. The crowd tramples the surface of the earth like galloping horses.

< 321 >

The whole performance is better than I had expected. There are a lot of women weeping. There are only five of us widows. Who are these wailing women bursting my eardrums with their wild screeching? Tony's girlfriends or mistresses? A cemetery is a place where no pain of any description lies hidden, and they scream as loud as they like, to release the pain from their own bodies. A cemetery is the final home. A happy home. I also weep, elegantly and in silence. I weep for those who weep for the loss that doesn't exist.

It's late, the sun takes its leave, smiling. I'm lost among shadows. Shadows that rise and fall to the sun's rhythm each day. The fatal hour has arrived. The coffin is lowered into the bowels of the earth, this fisher of bodies with invisible tentacles. Neither words nor prayers can stop the final flight. There's a pact between pain and silence. Between murmurs and tears. The image of the deceased reflects one's destiny, one's fate. We are all mortal. Death is the ripened fruit freeing itself from the tree to follow its own path. I think about true widowhood. In this life, all is transient. Love. Kisses. A melodious voice speaking of passion. The strong arms rocking one like no one else. The fights. The repressed desires. The misunderstandings. That dead man who is being lowered into the ground liberates me from deep anguish. I don't want to know about anything else in this life. A blanket of bitter memories invades my mind like a swarm of fireflies. I feel the vastness of night embracing my soul and I lean my body against the horizon's walls. Tony's now dead, in the body of this stranger. I never want to see him again, it's all over as far as I'm concerned. He destroyed all that I saw and admired in him. He didn't accept the limits on his freedom. In the name of love, he mixed pleasure and pain. Like a lot of men, he didn't understand that love is an enterprise that requires competent management and maintenance. It's an enterprise with losses that are difficult to absorb, such as this misunderstanding, these tears, these heartaches, this grief. The whole world will view him according to the portrait he has fashioned of himself. A man full of life who turned himself into a corpse. Dear God, have mercy on my Tony. Have mercy on all men who commit the most heinous crimes in the name of a tradition or a culture, such as my mother's brother-in-law, who sent his wife to her death because of a chicken gizzard. Dear God, forgive that tyrannical king who condemned Princess Vuyazi to the inferno of the skies, far from the warmth of the dead in this earthly paradise, round the fire of her ancestors. Amen!

The crowd projects their loud cries toward the heavens. It's an ocean of despair. Whoever the dead man is, he's had a worthy funeral, with tears that weren't for him. I remain serene, I shed just one solitary tear in order not to spoil my image. I look over at Levy with hungry eyes. He is going to be my sexual purifier, the decision was taken and he grabbed the chance with delight. Not long now, and I'll be in his arms for the *kutchinga* ceremony. I'll be a widow for just one week. I'm a bit older than him, but I get the feeling he's going to give me a lot of love, because in spite of my age and girth, I'm very sweet and charming. In a week's time, I shall undress. I shall dance the *niketche* for his eyes alone, while his legitimate spouse stands outside, consumed by jealousy. I shall ask Mauá to teach me the steps for this dance. Ah, I can't wait! I hope to God Tony only comes home after the act has been consummated.

Our tradition is far better than Christian mourning. Why so many tears, so many candles, so many flowers, fasting, abstinence, if the dead person is dead, and life goes on? You can call me shameless. Call me all the ugly words you like. I'm a woman, and that's it. I'm carrying out to the letter the tradition dictated by my husband's family.

After the funeral comes the dividing up of assets. They take whatever they can away with them: iceboxes, beds, crockery, furniture, curtains. They even fight over Tony's socks and underpants. They've taken pictures, bathroom mats. They've left me with the walls and the ceiling, and have given me thirty days to leave the house. They've pillaged me, only me. They haven't taken anything from the other wives. They tell the most incredible stories about them. They say they're not true widows. They say they're from the north and have a different culture. Northerners are united, and if you provoke one, you provoke the lot. The spirits of these Sena, Makua, and Makonde, apart from being powerful, are dangerous. To benefit from the status of being a widow, do you have to be stripped bare, without a penny to your name?

< 325 >

32

I can hear the buzz of voices out in my backyard. It's Friday. The ceremony for the week after the funeral is being prepared. A group of women are making a huge fire. They're putting green leaves into a huge pot. What are these witches doing here, don't they ever sleep? It's cold. Judging by the sky, it's still early morning. Ever since the man died, these hags haven't slept and never seem to get tired of whatever it is they're up to. I return to my sleeping mat and go back to sleep.

One of Tony's aunts comes and pulls the sheet and blanket off me. I'm angry. Unprotected. Vulnerable.

"What's happened?"

She doesn't answer. She grabs my wrist and drags me up forcefully. I put on my bathrobe and rush to the bathroom. I sit on the toilet and have a pee. My nerves are getting the better of me. I go to the mirror to seek some comfort. They pull me out of there.

"Where are you taking me?"

< 327 >

No one answers me. They bring a huge pot containing an infusion, with thousands of leaves bobbing around in it.

"What's this for?"

They ignore me. They pull my clothes off, almost ripping them. They cover me with a rough cotton blanket and submit me to a steam bath. I sweat. I burn. Oh God, they're trying to flay me. My God, they're going to disembowel me. They rub my whole body with herbs, as if I were a saucepan covered in soot. They've completed my bath.

"Where are my clothes?"

Silence. They cover me with a white sheet and haul me over to the bedroom next door. On the walls, there are green-colored drapes. There's the whiff of incense. On the floor, there's a carpet of fresh leaves, as if all the leaves in the world had fallen there. They tear the sheet off me, exit the room, and leave me there alone, in my birthday suit. Lord, what do they want from me? What harm have I done them? From deep inside me bursts a thunderous, explosive cry. With my hands cupped, I shield myself from the cold and shame.

I raise my eyes, seeking the heavens. I pray. Dear God, watch over me. I'm a grain of sand on the sole of my Lord's foot. Dear

God, why did you put me here? Why are you indifferent to my suffering? I live in hope of a miracle from you, but you have never favored me with one, why? Think about it, dear God, I've never shamed you. I've never disobeyed you. What sort of punishment is this that has no end?

My fate contains a myriad of supposed surprises that dance in front of my eyes like whimsical visions. I console myself. I'm not the only one. All the widows in this family have been through this.

I feel something hot touch my shoulder. It's a hand. An arm. I sense the smell of a man. A rope squeezes my waist. It's the other arm embracing me, seizing me. The time for *kutchinga* has arrived, and tradition delivers me into the arms of the inheritor. Why didn't they tell me it was today? Why all this secret, this surprise? I have no control over my existence. I have no desire, no shadow. If I refuse this act, they'll take everything away, even my children, and I'll be left empty-handed. Nothing in this world is mine and I don't even belong to myself.

He gives me a little kiss. A soft little kiss that ignites my whole body with its flame. His soft hands play the drum of my skin. I'm your drum, Levy, touch my soul, touch it. Oh! My God! I feel my body lighten. I feel a river of honey flowing through my mouth.

My God! Paradise is inside my body. The fire is lit in my oven, I'm burning, I'm going crazy, I'm sinking. We plunge deep into the weightless waves. A sparkling shower of starfish falls over us. Flying fish lend us their wings and we fly into the very depths of the ocean. The land is a sad, distant place. I feel I'm about to die in this man's arms. I want to die in this man's arms.

A fleeting moment of love? So be it! It's better to be loved for a moment than to be despised for one's whole life.

33

Tony comes home like a man defeated, a contrite deserter, a prodigal son. A wreck, a dead man. He looks around the empty house. With quick strides, he takes in all the rooms. He goes around several times. He is beset by the feeling that he is stepping through some unknown place, and not his home. The rooms seem to him like indoor football fields. In the other bedroom, he sees his children sitting on a sleeping mat like prisoners in a cell.

"Rami, what's happened here?"

"Sit down," I tell him, "so that the shock of it doesn't knock you over."

"Where are all the chairs, the furniture, the beds?"

I go to the yard and fetch an empty beer crate. I offer it to him.

"Here's a chair. Take a seat."

He sits on the crate, while I sit on the floor. We talk. I tell him all I can. Anxious, he wants to know everything. But I'm unable to tell such a long story all in one go. I skip some chapters of the story as I recall how things happened. He sits in silence for a long time, and there's a hint of tears in his eyes. My God, today we're going to witness a miracle, Tony's going to cry on my shoulder for the very first time. But the tears recede, his eyes dry. Only his arms fall like petals separated by the wind. His body's strength evaporates and flies invisibly up into the blue atmosphere. He crosses his arms over his waist like a safety belt for his plummeting body. It's as if some magical hand were undressing him and a catheter were draining his blood, the air in his body, his soul, everything. He abandons his seat and sits down on the floor like an empty sack. One doesn't need a sense of smell or even touch to gauge his affliction. It is cruelly visible.

"I witnessed your death and went to your funeral," I fulminate. "I wore heavy mourning clothes. Those cursed relatives of yours even shaved my head. I even had to go through the *kutchinga*, that sexual purification ceremony."

"What?"

"It's the absolute truth."

"When?"

"A few hours ago, early this morning. I've been done, I'm newly purified."

< 332 >

He glances at his watch. It's ten in the morning.

"And who did it?"

"It was Levy."

"Didn't you react, or resist?"

"How was I to do that? It's our tradition, isn't it? He didn't mistreat me, don't worry. In fact, he was very sweet and gentle. He's a true gentleman, that brother of yours."

It gives me such pleasure to say this, and he feels the pain of a betrayed husband. There's a burst of applause in my heart. I'm surprised at myself. I feel I've hardened in my attitudes. My desire for vengeance is stronger than anything else in this world.

"You're a strong woman, Rami. A woman of principles. You could have accepted everything short of *kutchinga*."

"You taught me to be obedient and submissive. I always obeyed you and your folks. Why should I be disobedient now? I couldn't betray your memory."

"So what now?"

"Ah, Tony! I'm thin, disfigured, finished. I'm bald. They shaved my head with a barber's razor, as if I were a recluse. They stripped me of everything as if I were a criminal. On my shaved head they placed a crown of thorns. They sat me on a throne of thorns. A scepter of thorns. They cleared everything from the house and left me this mat of thorns."

At first, his voice was strong and contained a dragon's flame. Fiery. Now his voice has lost its ring and he speaks in an undertone. He can't seem to get his head around what this terrible world has offered him.

"Rami, you knew it wasn't me, you knew it."

"Yes, I knew. But who was going to listen to me? Has my voice ever been heard in this house? Did you ever once give me any authority to make a decision on even the most insignificant things in our life? What did you want me to do?"

The man's heart is shattering into a thousand pieces. Honor, dignity, vanity, are huge waves, among which he is foundering. He's on the edge of a precipice. His soul is plunging into a deep ocean. He doesn't know how to swim. He looks up at the sky, maybe seeking God. He turns his gaze to the horizon, riding the clouds like gulls in late springtime. The horizon is a distant rampart, where everything ends and everything begins. In the horizon he sees his own sad reflection. He becomes stiff and dry, like a dead man. There's no movement, no gesture, there are no words. It's a short flight when one's wings are broken. For us mortals, the ground is the surest place, just as the sea is for fish. Life changes in a flash, just as death can take you in a trice. He shuts his eyes against the life that is causing him so many troubles, and waits for his energy to be reborn within him. He is both volcano and lava. An explosion. He is both ice and death. Arid soil. He is ashes, straw, dust. He is nothing.

"And the other women?"

"They're completely bewildered, poor things. They're beautiful young widows. They're probably planning new love affairs. I've got Levy. Your brothers keep visiting them to offer their condolences. But they were luckier than I was and managed to keep what was theirs. The expropriation, the pillage, and all the other acts of barbarism, they were just for me."

My language is harder than a gust of hailstones. It whips. I speak without mincing my words. I want him to have a taste of his own poison once and for all. I want him to get a whiff of his own shit, and to recognize at long last the evil that envelops him.

"Why on earth didn't they leave things to the police? The police have very efficient means to identify people. Why didn't they make use of them?"

"I tried to alert your superiors, God knows how. They forbade me, they curtailed my movements, because it's not well seen for a widow to be walking around out there."

"What they did to you was inhuman. What a murderous culture!"

He becomes delirious. He says he never knew life was that bad, nor could he have imagined how much women suffered. He had always thought the social structure was harmonious and that traditions were good, but he now understood the cruelties of the system.

"What future would you have had if I really had died? And what would have become of my children and their studies? I worked for so many years to build all this, and now I see it all destroyed because of a mistake. They could have taken everything, Rami, but they might at least have left a mattress for my children."

"Don't condemn tradition, Tony."

"Rami, I've already been murdered by tradition. That's why I'm going to assume the risk of challenging the world of men. I've just proved that within the human race, you women aren't people, you're mere exiles from life, condemned to live in the world's margins."

Suffering carves out behavior patterns in proportion to its degree. It provides short flights and profound insights. It tears down pedestals, pulls people's shoes off and forces them to tread on the dirt of the earth. It plucks out the peacock's plumage and makes its body roll around in the mud and dust. Tony has donned the suit of his suffering and is crying like a child. His throat has shrunk, he speaks like the birds, imitating the sound of a flute. Ah, but how this voice and its song comfort me! I feel as if I'm falling in love all over again.

He comes over to me for a hug. Furtively.

"I'm a widow, Tony. And you are beyond the grave. I can't be certain you are really you. You must be some evil shadow, a ghost, leave me alone, Tony."

Before, it was I who sought affection. And he would deny me. Now I'm the one refusing him, this love of ours is crazy, a game of cat and mouse. I wasted my whole life seeking this one instant, to have him nestling in my arms. Here he is before me. Defenseless. Mistreated. In need. I don't want him anymore, I don't want anything anymore, everything has died for me. He refuses to accept things. He pleads with me, grabs me, shakes me, takes me by force like a rapist in a deserted forest. I resist. I was getting prepared for a divorce, and now I'm a widow by mistake. He doesn't give up. Now he's talking to me of love. He reminds me of the moments of happiness we spent together. He talks of the problems we always had and for which I managed to forgive him. To love is to allow one's heart to beat at the same rhythm as the other's – that's what I say. To advance together at the same speed. To view the horizon from the same perspective. Love is the two pans on a set of scales, each one lifting the other until the divine equilibrium is achieved.

"You could have avoided this tragedy, my dear Rami!"

"Tony, your voice always dictated what I should do. What I should think. You planned my present and my future. You gradually built me, grain by grain, my divine creator. But the walls you placed round me are made of straw, and the wind, the cold, and the rain pierce them. You built me up on foundations of sand that have crumbled away at the first serious test. You covered me with a roof of wind, of air, porous, permeable, defenseless. Now that you've been given up for dead, see for yourself what's left of you.

The birds swarm upward from a falling tree. The startled monkeys fall screaming. The snakes faint and then come round. The fruit is released and dispersed. The wind howls during death's storm. After the alarm, silence follows. A mere minute of silence.

The next stage is to gather up one's belongings and leave for new patches of shade.

"A man can be measured by the solid work he leaves behind, when death summons him. Look around you: What do you see? Ruins, desolation, sadness. You built your castle in the sands of the ocean, and it was destroyed by the tide, by the wind, by cats and mice, you're a weak man, Tony darling, a wretched man."

Night falls and we stick to our own corners. Tony sits ruminating on his beer crate. The children and I sleep on sheets of newspaper, while the other wives sleep comfortably on their soft mattresses bought with my husband's sweat. They sleep safe and sound whereas my children and I don't even know how we're going to have our tea when the sun comes up, without any cups, a stove, or a table. From the height of his cross Jesus of Nazareth forgave the world, wearing a crown of thorns. I'm at the top of the hill with my own crown of thorns, and I forgive all these miserable wretches for their malevolence toward me.

He sits there quietly, as if he no longer wanted anything to do with this world. He suddenly looks tired, terribly tired. He has a drink. It revives him. All he wants to do is sleep. But he hasn't got a bed. Not even a mattress. He thinks about buying one, but it's too late. Ah, furniture shops should open at night to help in these emergencies. He gets up from his seat and puts his hands in his pockets. I look at him. He looks like a monument to impotence.

I wake up early in the morning. The road is silent, for today is Saturday. I go to the living room to turn on the radio and listen to the day's news. How angry I feel. The radio's been pilfered as well. Tony sleeps like a cat, curled up on himself. He awakens. We look at each other. This morning, his trousers look loose, he's lost weight. He's got sunken eyes. He hasn't slept, he's been suffering. It pains him that he's lost everything, but I know that the *kutchinga* pains him even more. He's been replaced in every way. A murdered life. Trodden on. Hurt. Turned to pulp like that unknown man killed on the road. He greets me with the gentlest of voices and says his headache is worse than being hit with a hammer.

"I've ordered all those people who took part in this pillage to be arrested, including my own mother. They'll have to answer in court for the acts of vandalism committed in my absence, Rami."

< 340 >

"And who's going to arrest you? Morally, you are the instigator of this whole sequence of events."

"Me? How?"

"The sun only leaves its marks on things that already exist. There's no shade without an object. You were the main subject of this whole story."

"How can you accuse me like that?"

"Ah, Tony, darling. You're always adrift like a dinghy in a choppy sea. Every day you travel round the city. You sleep anywhere when the night comes, a woman here, a woman there, sowing babies wherever you go."

"You said you agreed with polygamy, Rami."

"In true polygamy, it's not the man who imposes his desire to take another woman but the wives themselves who suggest a new marriage. The women aren't raped and they live near one another. Marriages are prearranged, planned."

"I've made mistakes all my life. I tried to do things my way. I was looking for life, and got lost."

I go back to the bedroom and pack the few possessions we still have. I rouse my children and we all take our leave of Tony in a line.

"Where are you going at this hour of the day?"

"To Levy's house. He's the husband widowhood has conferred on me. I slept with him and enjoyed it."

"You're not going anywhere."

"Yes, I am."

"You'll go to that tyrant's house over my dead body. If you were going to your mother's house, now that I could allow."

"They gave us thirty days to leave this house, what do you want me to do?"

"Rami!"

"You're a dead man, Tony, can't you see?"

"I'm going to get everything back, Rami, right down to the last speck of dust. I'm going to get back to work. I'm going to look after you. There's no need for you to wander through the world like a lost soul, certainly not."

"I'm not interested in anything, and that includes you, the house, everything. In each room, I see the image of your death. I don't want to return to this life. I'm going to start all over again. My hair's gone white, but my spirit is strong. I'm going to start again."

"Forgive me."

"Don't ask me for forgiveness. Ask God and yourself. I'm nothing. I want you to get on well with your wives, lovers, concubines. I wish you all the women in the world, except me. I wish you happiness!"

He blocks my way to stop me leaving. I push him. If it weren't for the fact I'm so tired and weak, I'd give him a good thrashing, and make him pay for everything, an eye for an eye, a tooth for a tooth. Even so, I manage to slap him good and hard. He doesn't react. I grab my bags, ready to go. He seizes my bags, and tries to tear them from my hands. We fight over them.

"You're not going anywhere."

"I am."

We wage a tempestuous war, and whirl around in the dance of our fury. Our eldest son hears our cries and comes to help me. We stop fighting. He doesn't say anything, just looks at us. He looks at us and weeps.

The doorbell rings.

34

A man's presence changes the course of everything. A man's birth has greater value than that of a woman. Tony has come back, bearing a handful of thorns by way of a gift.

My rivals arrive, one by one. They've come to see for themselves this man who constructs in order to destroy. Who sows flowers in order to kill them later. They attempt to put their pain behind them, they have taken off their mourning clothes and have donned flowery colors. They are all wearing fresh, brightly colored clothes from Lu's shop. Their dresses, with hemline slits on the side and daring necklines, freshen their bodies like open windows. Their hair has been carefully coiffured, and their perfume and makeup are from Mauá's shop. They all smell nice, all of them except for me, burning hotly inside these black clothes of mine. They each choose somewhere to sit down on the floor, and we form a circle as if we were having a picnic. Tony sits, perched on his crate, in the midst of the women who surround him, as if he's a birthday cake. He's shaking, he feels awkward. One can see the anguish he

< 345 >

feels at his return, stamped all over his physique. Why is he suffering? Is it for himself or for us? What does he have to say to us?

"Welcome home, Tony," says Saly, to break the silence.

He hides his head, his facial expression full of shame.

"Did you have a good journey?"

Tony attempts a word of greeting. He pauses and then sobs as if he had a frog stuck in his throat.

"Ah, darling Tony, fisherman of love," I burst out, "this time you cast your net into the sea of grisly love. You ended up caught yourself, fished up on the devil's fishhook. Over on this side, you were in the earth's mouth, while over there, you were in that woman Gaby's mouth."

Lu reacts nervously.

"So you didn't die after all, Tony? Where were you, who were you with? Tony, tell us the truth. Tell us whether we're in control of our senses. Tell us we're not going mad. Tony, can we pinch you and make you cry to prove you're real?"

Lu, Mauá, and Saly get up, approach Tony, and carry out the antiphantom test. They pinch him until he says ouch and sheds one or two tears, upon which they exclaim: It's really him, he's got flesh and bones, he even felt pain, groaned and wept.

"I want to ask you for forgiveness," he says hoarsely and in between his tears. "I don't know how all this happened. Men make mistakes too. Making mistakes is human."

"He who loves doesn't make mistakes. If you do something for love, you make sure it's done well," Lu says.

"Forgive me for all the suffering I've caused you, forgive me."

"You're asking for forgiveness?" Mauá asks in a tired voice. "Oh, Tony! You left a fuse in a pile of hay. Your passion burned the world to a cinder with its blazing fire. We are the remains of this, we are ashes, the ruins left behind by your passionate love."

The atmosphere is dense. There's expectation. He's unable to utter any grand words, but feels the intense pain from his gaping wound. I feel very sorry for him at this moment. He makes a supreme effort and gets rid of everything that's on his mind. What he says is wonderful.

"I scaled the heights of forbidden paradises and was assumed dead. I stamped my face on the world's shame."

He doesn't speak. He murmurs and his voice sounds sweet and melodic like the rustling of the pines. He explains himself, justifies himself, with truths, lies, and promises. He scatters into the air perfumed words that flutter like petals.

< 347 >

"I ask for your forgiveness, my dear wives, forgive me."

Tony kneels at our feet in humiliation. We are five queens on thrones of sand. Life has placed me above the ground.

"I want everything to return to how it was before. I'll never betray you again, I promise. I shall observe the weekly rota strictly."

"Tony, shut that mouth of yours," Saly orders, furiously. "You were the cause of all the suffering we went through. Why did you come back? Why didn't you stay dead, there where your family wanted to keep you? Why didn't you stay in your European paradise, with that saint who fired up your heart with love, who made you forget everything and took you with her to the stars? And now you want us to forgive you? Shut up, Tony, go to hell, you're dead. Don't come and talk to us about love, because all your life was about falseness, malice, and the very antithesis of love."

"Your family did what it liked with us, because we don't exist," I shout.

"We were rocks, walls, thin air. They cast us into the fire and banished us from our homes as if they were chasing away demons. And while this was going on, you were all smiles with that Gaby woman, on your honeymoon," Lu says.

< 348 >

"In the hands of your sacred family, we were cashew nuts on the charcoal brazier, we were grilled fish, with vinegar and pepper. And while this was happening, you were enjoying springtime in France with that woman Gaby," exclaims Mauá.

"Rami was tattooed with a red-hot iron. Branded like a slave. Expelled from her home with fire and incense, as if she were a demon. While that was going on, you were all smiles on your honeymoon with that Gaby," Saly screams.

"Rami went through *kutchinga*, my God, she was well and truly kutchingered, did she tell you? She was like a sheep being sacrificed. She endured *kutchinga* like a little orphan girl, lost in the middle of the world. It was painful, wasn't it, Rami?"

I lower my head, embarrassed. It wasn't painful, it was delicious. I was kutchingered, but at the same time I was loved. The man responsible violated my body, but left the trace of a caress in my heart. It was necessary for Tony to be given up for dead for me to discover that love has other hues and other tastes. I prayed a lot, I prayed Tony wouldn't return from the dead, because I'm getting my share of love. Now, at this very moment, I renew my prayer. Ah, dear God, why does bitterness fill life's entire path, while the good things don't even fill a spoon?

"They gave us food for widows. Badly boiled greens with no salt. They fed us little so as to increase our pain and hunger, a kind of fast and flagellation especially for widows. A widow who fills her belly falls asleep and doesn't cry as she should," Lu explains. "While this was happening, you were talking away in French, in a French restaurant, drinking French wine and eating French cheese with that Gaby."

"We went through every type of tribulation and were labeled widowed witches. While you were visiting the Arc de Triomphe, the Eiffel Tower, the Louvre, Notre-Dame, next to that Gaby woman," I pitch in.

"We were given vinegar, thorns, dagger thrusts, insults, fires, while you offered that Gaby French flowers," Mauá says in a tragic tone of voice.

"You made us bathe in a pool full of shit. And while this was happening, you were bathing in a French spa, with French soap, French perfume, with that Gaby woman," Lu chips in once more.

We have said everything. We have screamed everything. We've spat out all the resentment borne in our hearts, until our voices became hoarse. He listens in silence and replies with two tears. And he waits, impassive, while we bellow at the wind to extinguish the flames that burn our souls, sorcerers of our own selves. But he isn't frightened and doesn't quiver at the violence of our shouts, because women's voices don't reach the skies. He gazes at the horizon. He seeks inspiration. And he feels he's growing eagle's wings to fly into the loftiest branches of the horizon. He reassumes his perch and issues his command.

"Don't be like this, girls, life's blanket is woven with threads of love and forgiveness. Here I am, I'm at your mercy. Crucify me on a cross of stone, tattoo my back with whiplashes and branding irons, girls, come, please avenge yourselves, but please, I beg you: forgive me."

Tony is making a strategic withdrawal. He's hoisting the white flag, like a man laying down his arms and appealing for clemency. He personifies Samson succumbing fearfully before the power of a thousand angry Delilahs. His performance is masterly. He speaks in a low voice, but with a gentle fever. And he asks forgiveness for all his sins. He holds out his hand and volunteers for a session lashed to the whipping post.

"Before all this, I had a divorce hanging over me," I remind him. "I want to sign the papers now."

"But you told me you didn't want one, Rami."

"I want it now!"

"Forgive me, Rami. Wipe away the hurt."

"I went through *kutchinga*, remember?"

"As your husband, I've wiped away that hurt just as the waves wash away footprints by the seashore. As far as I'm concerned, nothing happened. Do the same as me, Rami."

"I want a divorce!"

Ju smiles every time I mention divorce. She's the ideal woman. She's as quiet as the tomb and says yes to everything in bold letters. She welcomes fire and brimstone without so much as a yell. She's waiting for me to die so she can be led to the altar and say yes to my Tony. What she doesn't know is that I'll die long after she does. She'll be able to marry Tony in some other life, but not this one. If there is such a thing as marriage in another life, I'd rather marry another man rather than this numb-skinned creature.

"Tony, tell us the truth: Who were those beauties who were crying more than we, your widows, on the day of the funeral, and who then deposited the most beautiful flowers in the world on your grave?" Mauá asks.

"How should I know if I wasn't even there?"

"Of all of them, one stood out, dressed in gorgeous black satin and lace, and crying so much she fainted. Who was it, Tony?"

"I've already said, I don't know."

"We'll find out, never you mind."

"Ah, Tony, my living-dead one, how you were mourned, dear God! The messages of grief read by your graveside were so beautiful. Every one of them had extraordinary things to say. They all spoke of the work you left behind, as if you'd done any. They all praised you incredibly, and all your stupidity was forgotten."

There's a new pause. Bits of evidence emerge one by one. Tony doesn't have an answer for everything, he's like a mouse caught in a trap. He replies here and there, like a sieve trying to block out the sunlight. Truth and untruth are extracted from his heart like hairs yanked out by two fingers. There's a smell of blood in the air. There's a smell of lies and hypocrisy. There's a smell of anguish. There's a smell of salt-laden tears.

"Tony, what would have become of us if you'd really died?" Lu asks in a distressed voice. "Have you seen what your sacred family did to us?"

"You people from the south are tyrants," Mauá says, "you strip widows of everything like hyenas. You flaunt your political power right there at the funeral. The dead man can't be lowered into the earth until the relative who's a minister arrives."

"They're worse than tyrants. They're murderers," Saly complains, "I had to defend the welfare of my children by hook and by crook against those assailants with their invocations to tradition. They invaded my house as if I were a thief. But I gave as good as I got. I gave one of your aunts such a violent punch that she'll feel the effects for the rest of her life. If she ever tries to lay a hand on me again, it'll be the end of her."

"That family of yours is all theater," Lu declares. "First, they pray and sing. Then they start howling and weeping hideously, and do some high kicks to work up an appetite. After that, they eat toast and butter, black tea with white sugar and condensed milk, roast chicken and salad, and then they drink beer."

"Their stomachs are garbage bags, Tony," says Mauá, returning to the fray, "their mouths are chewing machines. I now understand why these southern women have such big butts. They eat too much! Who paid for all this? We did! And to cap it all, they insulted us and bitched at us. Tony, give us back all the money we spent to feed that rabble that spent its time sobbing and eating."

"Up in the north, things aren't like that," Saly concludes. "For us, death is a dignified affair. Death is solemn and serious. Unfortunately, you southerners are spreading your curse through the whole country, and there are now northerners who make a point of displaying their economic and political power every time there's a death. They carry with them all the symbols of their power to funerals: military uniform, flags, medals of rank, bottles of mineral water, cell phones, academic diplomas, luxury cars."

In this war of love and hatred, we're not on an equal footing. A woman is inferior, lower, her pride can be shattered with a mere puff of breath. In this game, we're five against one, but he's strong, he's got power and money. That's why he's saying he's sorry, but he also dictates the rules of the game. He asks for forgiveness only in order to calm the waters and reassume control. Our only recourse is complaint. If you don't cry, you don't reap.

"We have no protection. There was nothing left except for the little business concerns, which were all Rami's ideas. And these were bound to go under because they ran the risk of being confiscated. Your seventeen children would have been condemned to living in penury, Tony."

< 355 >

He's scared stiff of losing everything and dying again. He makes concessions.

"I'm going to pay all the bills and put everything back in order. I'm going to leave a written will. This type of shameful situation will never happen again."

"We closed our businesses for a week," Lu returns to battle. "We had expenses, we lost money. Who's going to pay for all this?"

"Go back to work immediately," he says, half nervously. "Make up for all the time you've lost and let's put an end to this sad episode."

The distance between a man and a woman is considerable. A woman bears the burden of thorns because she's weak. A man flies airily aloft, free of thorns and pain, because he's strong. Here, in this room, strength and weakness are breaking through their borders and revealing themselves, hand in hand, in the circle of sunlight and shadow.

"Shall we go back to our conjugal rota again? Where should I begin? Rami, you always administered these things. Tell me anything you like, and I'll comply."

"Before we start on all that," says Saly in a threatening tone, "return everything to Rami, everything! But it's all got to be new.

There's no question of bringing back the furniture that's now been sullied by your murderous relatives. Return everything to her within a week."

"Yes, of course, I promise. Rami, go to the shops and buy whatever you need and like."

"And there's another thing," Lu promises, "if you don't stick to your word, we'll cut off your nose and one of that woman Gaby's ears."

"Tony, don't come looking for me before you've put Rami's house back in order," Mauá fires.

Tony is now appealing for unity. We are drifting between nightmare and reality. What we feel can't be expressed in mere words.

"Tony, I'm willing to organize your rota," I explain, "but in your new rota, there are two missing: Eve and Gaby."

"Ah! Not them. They're just friends. There's nothing between us. I don't want them included."

I'm suddenly overcome by a sadness without bounds. What is a woman in this life unless she's just a blanket to keep his feet warm on cold nights? What's woman's fate unless it's to bear children, pains, and fears? Who is Eve to Tony in his life? A mere fruit for a bird to peck at as it flies through the skies. And Gaby? A freshly caught fish. After she's been salted, baked, and consumed, she'll be in an even worse predicament than we are.

"Ah, my precious Tony, you've got a real gift for rooting out fantastic women. Where did you get Eve?" I ask. "During the week of the funeral preparations, Eve's help was invaluable. The dead man's coffin was bought with her money. Your people stuffed themselves with the food she brought us. Grief drew us together, Tony. For someone who already has five wives, what difference does one more make? As for Gaby, morally, she's the author of this whole complicated story. And now that things are as they are, why do you say you don't want anything to do with them? Have you come back in order to start deceiving us again?"

"Please understand, Rami, it was just a fling, nothing more."

"You love Gaby."

"No, I don't love her."

"Yes, you do. It was your love for her that got you lost out there on life's trails. It was love that raised you up into the clouds to the point where you were presumed to be dead, because only the dead reach the lofty heavens."

Women, women, women. Women of your salvation, women of your perdition. It was because of women that Tony embarked on this deceit. It's because there are too many women that he choked on his own greed. He turned love into a suicide mission, like a samurai, a kamikaze, a *naparama*. Ever since he was small, he's been taught that a man flies, without wings, but flies nevertheless. Ever since he was small, he's been told he's mighty, he's the boss, he's the master. But the moment he breaks a feather, he comes running back to his mother's embrace.

"Rami, I'll spend this week here, I'll be with you. You've gone through a lot with this whole business."

"I'm going to Levy's house."

"No, you're not."

"Yes, I am."

"Over my dead body."

"You've already been a dead body, what's the difference?"

"You're not going, I've already told you."

"I'm going to my mother's."

Deep inside, I'm all confused, I don't know whether I'm alive or dead, or whether I've just lost consciousness. My life is endless suicide. Always ready to die for some space in a home riven with lies and shame. I find solitude intimidating and I can't see any road toward a new dawn opening up on the horizon. I gave birth to five little rabbits. In order to feed them, I need our daily carrot. I don't have a vegetable garden. I've got women's businesses, businesses as restricted as those selling chickens and ducks in the market on the corner. For these reasons, I've struck through my dreams with a red pen. I can't leave here and wander at will at the mercy of lions on the prowl along the road. So I'm better off staying here, protected by this cracked roof. I'm better off under a roof with a gaping hole in it than having the sky as my ceiling.

"Rami, get this straight, I'm not going to leave you."

"I'm the one who's going to leave you."

That's exactly what marriage is all about. Agreeing to snuff out your candle, so as to use your companion's torch, while he decides the amount of light you should have, and at what time and on what occasions. In marriage, women's hands are shells open on the sand of the seashore, begging for love, bread, salt, and soap. Marriage means mounting a throne of firewood and waiting for the fire to be lit. Marriage is romantic. For men, it produces honey and sweetness. It produces happiness and tenderness. For women, it produces tears, anguish, exile, and death. It produces a world of delusion like the one I'm experiencing at the moment.

"Very well, Tony, I'll stay. But you've got to resolve the issue with Eve. As first wife, I want and insist that she should be your sixth wife. She's got to be rewarded in some way. I don't know what you think, girls."

"Eve deserves her place, she proved herself to be a good companion in difficult times," Mauá says. "She suffered the torment of a false widowhood along with the rest of us. She gave proof of the love she feels for you. And how she cried at your funeral!"

"But how did she get involved in this business?"

"We paid her a visit to demand our rights. It was the five of us who pampered and groomed you, so that she could appreciate you. It was the five of us who cooked you energy-giving dishes and potions so that she could enjoy the pleasure of your company. So that's why we went and insisted she pay her quota as a widow. She paid, my God, how she paid!"

"I don't believe what I'm hearing."

"She used you. It's only fair that she should share in any losses. That's why we are of the opinion that she should be your new wife."

"Never. Even if I asked, she'd never accept."

"Have you ever proposed to her?"

"No."

"Why?"

"I haven't got the courage."

"We understand why you're shy. We'll organize a delegation and see to everything."

"Please, no."

"Tony, Eve is a serious woman. An adult woman. A cultured woman. A woman who would be worthy of being your sixth wife. We've all been witness to this woman's generosity. Oh, what she went through on account of us, poor soul! We don't want to see her cast aside, we just can't have that. If she accepts, she's going to be your wife whether you like it or not. We'll take care of everything."

"Have pity on me!"

I feel terribly uncomfortable and my bones ache. It's weariness. Sleepless nights spent lying on the hard ground of widowhood. I leave the meeting and go to the bathroom, where I sit on the toilet, my only piece of furniture. Outside, I hear the squeak of gates opening. Who is it? I get up and peep outside. It's my rivals leaving, some of them disappointed, others more animated, but all of them astonished. They drag their feet as they walk, overcome by surprise.

I feel very hot and take my headscarf off. I go to the mirror to see if there's any sign of change in my baldness. I shut my eyes, scared of seeing my awful image. I open them again. They are completely tear-soaked. My flat mirror suddenly turns into a crystal ball, reflecting images, reflecting secrets. It predicts the future and reveals unseemly secrets. It asks me:

"Who are you? I don't recognize you."

I reply tearfully.

"I'm the one who dreamed of being loved and ended up being despised. The one who dreamed of being protected and ended up being exchanged. It's me, a married woman, who was violated as soon as her husband looked like being absent. I'm Rami."

"You're not Rami. You're the monster that society created."

I lean my face against the mirror and cry disconsolately. I regain my self-control and look in the mirror once again. The image in the mirror smiles. It sways and floats as light as foam. As light as a jaguar's feline gait through the forests of the world. It's my spirit unencumbered by social inhibitions. It's my childhood dream, it's my dream of being a woman. It's me, in my inner world, running freely along life's path.

I gain courage and ask.

"Dearest mirror, what do you think of me?"

"Be at peace with yourself. There's no woman in this world more beautiful than you."

"Dearest mirror, is there a woman in this world sadder than I?"

"Yes. There are millions and millions throughout the world."

"Tell me, dear mirror. Is there a woman in this world more betrayed than I?"

"All women are. Every single one! In love, all men are betrayers."

< 364 >

35

I leave work and head toward the restaurant very near my shop. This week, I'm on my own, as Tony has left for other embraces. That's why I've invited Lu for lunch, just the two of us. I want to get down to resuming a conversation we had previously, and which was interrupted. I'm the first to arrive at the restaurant and I choose a table for two. While I wait, I sip a glass of iced water.

I look through the window. I see a woman parking an expensive-looking car. The woman takes off her sunglasses and I see it's Lu, my God, it's Lu. Whose car could it be?

She comes in and sits down. She's graceful as only she knows how.

"You at the wheel of a car, Lu?"

"I wanted to give you a surprise. My new car. It's secondhand, but it's my first car."

"It's an emotional moment. We hug. We laugh. We cry. I can't believe what my eyes are seeing. Lu's making real financial strides.

< 365 >

"Congratulations, Lu!" I say while we toast each other with glasses of water.

"I've just got it. You'll be the first to go for a drive with me."

We smile. We eat. We drink to each other's health. I get to the point and begin the conversation.

"My dear Lu, the reason I asked you to have lunch with me is an old conversation we had, before we became friends. After all the unpleasantness we've been through together, I ask myself sometimes: Why are you still here?"

"I don't understand."

"Vito."

"What about him?"

"He loves you very much."

"So what?"

"He wants to lead you to the altar and make you his wife. You turn your back on that bit of luck in order to wallow about in the filth of polygamy. What do you gain by being Tony's third wife?"

"Do you want me to marry him so that I can be like you?"

"Like me?"

"Yes, like you. Married, mistreated, a widow with a husband who's still alive."

"I don't understand you, Lu."

"Let me explain: For men, the first wife is the wife for duties, the second wife is for pleasure. The first wife is the one that's given thorns, the second gets flowers. If a woman's fate is to live in polygamy, I'll never be the first. I want to be what I am now: the third. Pleasure and flowers."

"That's why you entered my home as a parasite, isn't it, Lu? To be a flower in my garden and cause the thorn to grow inside me? Tell me, Lu, why did you invade my home?"

"It wasn't I who invented the world. I only know that that's how things are. When I entered your home, I wasn't aware of who I was injuring. If you only knew the sleepless, remorseful nights I spent after I got to know you, if you only knew! Rami, you didn't deserve such suffering. How could Tony cause a woman like you, Rami, so much anguish?"

"You're being unfair, Lu. And ungrateful."

"When you think about it, you suffer, I smile. You sowed the seeds, I reaped the harvest. I never knew what conjugal hardship was like. You bathe your husband, make him smell nice, while we second and third wives receive him all clean and perfumed. You maintain him and we use him and wear him out. Tony only comes to my arms to find happiness, and when the time comes, off he goes without leaving any problems in his wake. And he leaves you with all the chores: taking your mother-in-law for her doctor's appointment, visiting his sick brother, attending all the social events in the name of the family, representing him at funerals, and so on, while I, the third wife, am free of everything, I look after my house and my body, and the only thing I have to prepare for is love."

I wasn't expecting to hear this. Her words stir up old wounds and hurt like spurs. I fall into an epileptic fit and feel as if I've been struck down in the middle of some dance of death. Good God, she's not lying. She's my mirror showing me my portrait as a submissive woman in the cruelest possible way. I scold myself: Why did I provoke this conversation? Why didn't I stick to my corner, hidden away in the peace and quiet of my silence?

"Don't assume I'm just trying to get rid of one more rival. Far from it. Lu, you are an elegant, extraordinary woman, how can you put up with this pigsty? You're a classy lady worthy of a classy gentleman. You have such a man at your feet, but you prefer to make him your lover. Why?"

We both remain silent, like two buffaloes during a pause in

< 368 >

their fight. I drink a mouthful of water to calm me down. She rotates her glass on the table nervously. I look at her as she lowers her head. She is breathing deeply. I'd really like to get out of there, but I'm not going, because I want to get to the bottom of this story and follow it through to the end. I pluck up courage and go on the attack once more.

"Answer me, Lu."

"Vito is like Tony, they're both from the south, two Shangaan barbarians. I'd marry him and on the day he died, they'd shave my head, make me go through *kutchinga*, and pillage everything we had built up over the years. I really love Vito, but I swore to myself: I'll never become the legal wife of a southern man."

I detect a flash of apprehension in Lu's eyes. She leads her life along concealed paths in order to avoid pain. I understand her. It's difficult to face the sea if you don't have fins to help you fly through it. A woman is a mutilated fish in the depths of the oceans. I envy her ability to say no to pain and avoid the need for sacrifice.

"Marrying Vito would mean having new rivals, who could be far worse than the ones I already have."

"I don't understand."

"I have a husband for one week in four. While I wait, there's always Vito to keep me company to relieve my boredom. You must understand that I'm made of flesh and can't just eat rice."

"What are your feelings for them both?"

"Tony looks after me, I respect him. Vito pleases me, I love him. They both complete me. If I was married to Vito, I would have lots of pleasure, love, and new rivals."

"Men aren't all the same, Lu."

"Neither are women."

"You surprise me."

"Rami, we share a husband and a lover. Everything's fine. What's your problem? I feel part of this system. Why go looking for more pain?"

I begin to admire this woman. The practical way she resolves life's problems. Her sincerity. Her courage. She doesn't worry about the scandalmongers. She's mistress of her own destiny and does what she wants. She resists. Fights. Decides. Chooses. And she carves a bit of space for herself out of life. It may be a barren bit of space, but it's hers. She knows how to choose the fertile soil where flowers will grow, perfumed and devoid of thorns. And she chooses the delicate hands that will go out and gather them: those that give pleasure and those that give care.

"You're a hard woman."

"A woman is trained to be as sensitive as a porcelain doll that shatters at the slightest fall. We are prepared for grace and delicacy, but men caress us with hands as hard as iron and break us with the slightest touch. They want us to be as soft and meek as threads of hair. But men cut them with the icy snip of steel scissors."

I'm astonished by the way she faces up to me, without fear of hurting me. I'm captivated by the way she fights for a bit of air. I fire a salvo of questions at her.

"Lu, where did you learn to be so rebellious, where do you get that strength that enables you to defy the world? Where do you get that happiness that never dies? Those tears that are held back and never flow? Where does the heart of your strength lie, Lu?"

"I obey God's tenth commandment: Love your neighbor as you love yourself."

"Eh?"

"Men are taught to love themselves first and only afterward

their neighbor. Women are taught to love their neighbor but never to love themselves. I love myself and after that, others, just like men do."

"But you're a woman, Lu."

"A woman and one of God's daughters. With a right to happiness."

"You're supposed to be obedient!"

"You've observed the rules of obedience your whole life. And what have you gained from it? A crown of thorns on your widow's throne. You were a lamb, burned as a sacrifice. Rami, you were a butterfly in flight, a piece of honey whose purpose was to sweeten life. You never harmed anyone, Rami, how can they harm you?"

"Forget the past, Lu."

Lu's words are magical. They shred my clothes, item by item. They're caustic. They shred my skin, cell by cell, until they penetrate my breast. Instead of a heart, they find a blackened tunnel. They light a candle and extract from it the causes of my pain: knives, stones, barbs. Poisons. Harmful herbs. As if they were a shaman, they remove the syringe I use to inject myself with the denial of my own existence. I close my eyes, from where tears flow, with a sudden burst of relief. I sigh.

"Rami, you are a mother, you are life's center, you are existence itself. How do men dare to torture the womb of their own mother?"

I answer without words. I've had enough. The world is topsy-turvy, everything has been inverted. The creator made man and woman to live together in one single bundle, neither one of them worth anything without the other. Two sides of the same face. Bread and tidbits for the same meal. Where sky and earth kiss on the horizon. Sun and moon at the same tender moment. Fire and water at the same boiling point. We need to regain our innocence and become children again. To be limpid like the waters along the shore. We need to reflect each other like faces in the mirror. We need to jump the ring of fire, to be once again sperm and ovum, to invade the fertile womb and embark on creation's dance.

"Ah, Rami, you have the hands of an enchantress. Everything you touch turns to gold."

"I don't understand."

"You gave me supreme love. You forgave me my misdemeanors. You gave a slice of your man, whom we share like sisters. You generated love where there was only hatred, Rami, your strength is endless, you can transform the world."

I imagine the world, the universe. The landscape on Mars, the moon, and Venus. Saturn's rings. I imagine all its horrors and all its wonders.

"Ah, Lu, you're a dreamer. The world is a colossal ball traveling through the cosmos. The world is a creator. One single creature cannot transform its creator. The world is far bigger than me."

"With your own hands you transformed our world, Rami, isn't that so? You tamed the wild animals that dwelt in our souls. Before you came along, the war was a fierce one. We were bitches let loose in the dump waging war on each other over that old bone, Tony. We were wandering, characterless stars. You gave us our sparkle back when you bathed us with the breath of your soul. You forsook a bit of your flame in order to light our candles. We are the wives of a polygamist, we are socially acknowledged, no one looks at us as if we were single mothers, in spite of all our sorrows. Our children have the right to a father and an identity. As for ourselves, we have business concerns, our own lives, dreams, and a roof over our heads. We don't have to stretch out our hand to beg for salt and soap. We have security, even if our ex–dead man were to die."

Now I understand. The world is this piece of ground upon

which my feet tread. It's this chair where I sit down. It's the affection I give, it's the flower I'm given. The world is my mirror, my bedroom, my dream. The world is my womb. The world is me. The world is within me.

"There are marvelous things in what you have built, Rami. Tony is a collector of women, but you are a collector of anguished souls, a collector of sentiments. You've gathered around you women who have been loved and who have been scorned. You're brave, Rami. You've sown love where hatred reigned before. You're a limitless source of power. You've transformed the world. Our world."

I slowly savor breaths of air and surprise. Memories of torture flow through my mind while night dissolves into fragments of light. I begin to dream. Lu's words are bitter but restorative. Women should be better friends with each other, show more solidarity. We are the majority, we've got strength on our side. If we join hands, we can transform the world. Wars to conquer a love that is finished consume our time and the best of our energy. We naively seek to conquer a world that has already been conquered by the terrible forces of destruction.

"Rami, in this world, whoever is good ends up in hell. I'm bad, Rami, and I live in heaven."

"You're not bad, Lu!"

"Yes, I am. I think first and foremost of myself. I defend my interests, without weapons, but I still defend them."

I think about myself. My male children get to eat first at mealtimes. Like their father. They eat the best bits of the chicken, and their sisters are left with the wings and feet.

"I understand, Lu. But you haven't yet said anything about Vito."

"I don't know, Rami."

"Lu, fight these fears of yours and go and seek out the love that's waiting for you. Say yes to love and allow your deeper scars to heal, my dear Lu!"

"I'm not scared of love, I'm scared of suffering."

"You'd rather drift through the night so as not to be dazzled by the morning light. You'd rather be a firefly out on the savannah than be whipped by the endless rustling of the waves. You fear love because of the pain."

I give the matter some thought. I teach the boys to have self-esteem, I've never said anything about loving their neighbor. I teach my daughters about loving one's neighbor, but don't have much to say to them about self-esteem. I transmit the culture of

< 376 >

resignation and silence to the women, just as I learned it from my mother. And my mother learned it from her mother. It has always been like this since time immemorial. How could I ever imagine I was paralyzing the flight of the girls from the time they were born, blindfolding them before they'd even known life's hues?

"Think of life and forget the past. Get married. And conjugate the verb 'to love' in capital letters. You'll have more prestige and better status in society."

"I had my bride price paid, I've been given recognition. What more do I need?"

"The law is stronger than tradition."

"I'm fine as I am."

"You're not at all fine. When you think about it, what are you, the four of you? Why put up with these ridiculous meetings with the other wives when you can have your own space? After your week of conjugal bliss, solitude when he's gone."

"Ah, Rami."

"I'm protected by the law, I can use it. And what about the concubine? And the third wife? Marriage has its benefits, Lu."

"I'm not interested in marriage."

"You're afraid of a failed marriage, like mine."

"Rami, in my family, no woman was ever led to the altar. It's our fate."

"Don't you think it was God who sent this man to compensate for the loneliness of all the men in your family? With Vito, you'll have the father you never knew. The emigrant brother who is far away. The love you always dreamed of and a companion for all the hours of the day."

I see two serene tears on Lu's face. She gazes absently for a moment. There's a window opening in her subconscious. She must be thinking of the village she left behind. Of the harrowing childhood she suffered. Of the world that awaits her, of the love she has and doesn't want to give. The window opens and her words are uttered with some difficulty.

"When I was little, I was raped by soldiers in the bush. I didn't become pregnant, thank God. Some years afterward, my mother gave me away as a wife to an old man in our area, in exchange for a cotton blanket to cover my brothers, as it was very cold at the time. The old man was good, he was like the father I never had. But his old wives treated me badly, and lumbered me with all the heaviest tasks: fetching water from the river, for a family of seventeen people, grinding corn, looking for firewood out on the savannah, making charcoal. I ran away from the old man, I wandered through the bush, living on wild fruits, until I reached the city of Beira. I sold myself for sex on street corners when I was fourteen. I was treated badly by society, by clients, by the police, who locked me up in a cell more times than I can remember. I came to the capital by hitching a ride on a truck. I met Tony on a street corner in town. We had a child together and then another one. Ah, Rami, I'm a wild plant educated by the wind and the four seasons."

I've heard many tales of hardship down at the market on the corner of the street, but Lu hadn't yet told me hers. Any woman who has passed by the gates of hell weaves herself a suit of armor to protect her against life's claws, and wraps her heart in a layer of ice. A song of comfort wells up from my heart: Look at love as it smiles. Shed your armor, let the sun melt the ice that tortures your heart.

"My dear Lu. Birds build their nests on top of trees. Women marry in order to build a home. Anchor your roots in the deepest part of the ground. Stretch your branches to reach out to other nests in the shade of your tree, Lu, get married."

"I promise to give the matter some thought. Tomorrow."

"Your past is only the shores of a raging river. Tomorrow only exists in the dreams of those obsessed by the future. When tomorrow arrives, it turns into today. Time is a game of light and shadow, and eternity is the present moment."

"I understand."

"You're going to be happy, Lu. Vito is a special man, affable and sincere. And he loves you. Get married and love for real."

"I don't know, Rami, but I'll think about it."

I think about my Tony with some emotion. Not everything he did was wrong. He was a Samaritan. A good Samaritan. He came across a woman selling her body on the street. He bought himself a portion, tasted it, and enjoyed it. So he bought the whole thing, guaranteeing her board and lodging for a few more days. Women are poor. That's why well-fed old men point their rotten beaks toward the forest of temptation and peck away at the girls, ready for harvesting on their stalks, letting a few crumbs of bread fall to the ground. God passes by and sees what's happening, but has nothing to say about the misery experienced by these creatures he has made.

< 380 >

36

My house has become a place where everyone comes to vent their frustrations. My children don't like this, but I don't mind. They put up with my whims in silence. Hardly have the womenfolk arrived than my kids go out. This state of affairs must be very painful for them.

It's Friday today. They're all arriving for yet another conjugal parliament. Tonight, Tony is switching to Ju's house. They all turn up punctually, because I don't allow late arrivals.

The meeting starts on the dot, English style. Saly's the one handing over and gives the same details as always. Tony's well, he's slept well, doesn't need to take any medication, I always rubbed the ointment into his knees at the right time, etc., etc., etc.

"How did you serve him his food?" I ask.

"On my knees, of course."

"That's good. It's on one's knees that one gives thanks to God. It's on one's knees that one serves kings. It's on one's knees that one should give thanks to husbands."

< 381 >

They laugh.

"I've learned to be submissive like Shangaan women. Kneel down to give him a glass of water, kneel down to invite him to the dinner table, kneel down to serve him his coffee, kneel down to receive a member of his family, kneel down at his beck and call, kneel, always on your knees."

"Saly, now tell us about the gentleman's behavior. Was he well behaved? What time did he go out and what time did he get home? Did he eat all you gave him?"

"I gave him everything a man could desire. I gave him food he could eat with a spoon and he swallowed the lot: okra, dried fish, mealie pap, and all the northern spices you can get in the markets down here. If he didn't eat with pleasure, at least he did it to please me."

"Bravo," I reply.

"Not everything went as well as it seems, Saly," Lu criticizes her. "He turned up at my house without warning at nine o'clock at night. I don't like surprises and I like to receive my husband at the appropriate hour. You forgot to phone the others to tell us he'd left the house. I could have been busy in some meeting over work. I could have been busy with something else, just as I could also have been away. Oh, Saly!"

I throw Lu a knowing look. While the king is tied up, we're more free for the occasional frolic. Only Lu knows her secrets, although she's shared some of them with me. But is it only Lu who has secrets? I don't think so. We all phone each other when he runs off. It's a sign. The lion's at large on the streets and no one knows where he'll end up. He needs to be kept under control. Bound and gagged. With him under wraps, we're the ones who are free.

"So how was the weekend? Did you go dancing?" Mauá asks.

"No, we didn't. He was tired and I took pity. Apart from that, you know I'm not too keen on dancing."

"Pity?" Ju complains, suddenly aroused. "The man's strong, Saly, he doesn't need your woman's compassion."

"Aren't you people human? Haven't you got the tiniest bit of consideration? Can't you see what a polygamous man has to go through?"

"He doesn't have to go through anything, Saly, the man's strong," Lu says.

"Listen, he's no spring chicken. He's over fifty."

"The man isn't growing old, Saly, he's still young," Mauá replies.

"Think hard, girls, just think. Have you seen the energy he uses up on us?"

"The man doesn't use up anything, Saly, he renews his strength," Lu chips in again.

"I didn't go dancing because I wanted to spare him the trouble."

"Did you skip dancing just to spare him?" Mauá asks with bitterness. "There's no point in sparing a horse. While you spare him and look after him, some smart dame will come and steal your mount. A man is strong, he's made of iron, he's tough, he doesn't grow old. While he's yours, use him."

I find Mauá's words deeply offensive, as if they were addressed to me. I looked after, I nurtured, I spared my poor Tony. I washed the horse. I put up with the smell of his shit. I groomed him. I respected him. He had such a shiny coat as he trotted along that he ended up luring these bloodsuckers who, as they mounted him for their romantic little ride, unseated me. I was the stupid one. A good little woman. So daft that I ended up in these shareholders' meetings just to get a weekly slice of all that was mine.

"Very well. Next time, I'll go dancing, if that's what you want."

Tony fulfills his role as passionate lover of us all, doing his best to please us with all the stamina that his male faculties allow. He spends his weekends rushing from one disco to another, from one dance to another. With Saly and Mauá, he frequents clubs specializing in rock, zouks, rap, and raggy music. They're of the younger generation and they dance this type of thing. With me and Ju, he goes to slow dances, soul music, pop, blues, and jazz. We're of the older generation from the time when folk danced hugging each other, cheek to cheek, sweatily, in the tropical breeze. Rock was also popular in our time, but we didn't dance to it. We're fat and busted. Lu is somewhere between the two generations of dancers. She doesn't mind going to either. But what she really likes is to sit al fresco at a steakhouse, with her double martini, watching couples gliding across the dance floor. It's we who pay for our weekend expenses as our business concerns make enough money for that.

We besiege him closely and surround him with affection. We suffocate the man with love. With food. With dances each weekend. The swelling on his knee increases and subsides with ointments,

< 385 >

tablets, massages. We plunge him in baths, in oils, in soft clothes and perfumes, and he never tires of praising his wonderful spouses. We feed him his daily bread, day after day, each day anew. We give him the care and attention worthy of a king. He is our Balthazar, our magus. He no longer reads the newspaper, he doesn't have time as he's always busy in his ladies' quarters. His eyes and ears are full of lights and images that make him feel dizzy. Sometimes he wakes up not knowing in whose bedroom he is. He confuses his wives' names. He says Ju when he wants to call Lu. He says Saly when he wants to call Rami. With Mauá, though, he never makes a mistake.

"Don't forget to take him to the hairdresser's on Wednesday, Ju. The ointment is important, don't forget to apply it after he's had his bath. At half past six."

Ju scratches her nose and looks away.

"Ju, it's you I'm talking to," Saly insists. "Aren't you the one receiving your husband this week?"

"Couldn't you keep him another week?"

"He's been with me for three weeks already."

"He's not leaving your house because you don't dance. He likes being shut away there because he can relax with massages, little

< 386 >

treats, and have a fuss made of him. I don't have time for all that anymore," says Ju, to everyone's surprise.

"What are you accusing me of now? I'm very fond of him and feel sorry for him. He's got to take care of his work, service his wives, almost all of them young, and pay attention to the kids from time to time. Don't you think that's a lot of work for one man alone?"

"Don't you want to keep him all for yourself?" Ju asks, to everybody's astonishment.

For us women, a man isn't a trifle, he's a burden. A husband isn't a companion, he's your owner, your boss. He doesn't give you freedom, but ties you to him. He doesn't help, but makes things difficult. He doesn't give tenderness, only hardship. He gives you a spoonful of pleasure and a whole ocean of distress.

Ju's question surprises most of us.

"You want him to move out?"

"It just doesn't suit me. I don't have time to give him any attention. The volume of work has increased for me and I've been busy right through until late at night."

"So who hasn't got commitments, Ju? None of us wants to take care of Tony just like that, without any forewarning."

"A man in the house represents double the work," says Mauá, "there's no time. We need to follow through business deals and earn money where we can."

"Don't any of you love Tony anymore?" Saly yells. "What's wrong? He's been in my house for more than a fortnight without me being able to get rid of him, and you people complain. Didn't we agree to share, a week here, a week there? I need some time as well. I want to look after my business interests, earn money to raise this son of mine, and plan for my future. If none of you want him, I swear, I'll chase him away in a hail of stones. I can't live with him forever and a day."

"Calm down, Saly," says Ju. "I'll take him, but I'm warning you right from the start. Looking after him has become too much trouble. Cooking his lunch and dinner. Laying the table, clearing the table. Putting up with his whims that you people seem to have got used to, that's something I'm not going to do anymore."

I think about Lu's words. Changing the world. The world is in a permanent process of change. It changes silently. Only Tony hasn't noticed the change. He's still dancing the man's dance, in which everything is permitted. There's mischief in the air that tastes like nectar. There's a poison-bearing flower in every kiss.

Torture carried out with sweetness, drip by drip, falling on the hardened stone. He hasn't yet noticed my silent vengeance, nor does he see the lionesses who devour him with delight. Ah, dearest Tony. You live for women, you'll die at their hands.

< 389 >

37

Night is falling. The doorbell rings. Who's come to see me at this hour? I open the door. Ah, it's the beloved Mauá, with her sensuous walk, like lilies swaying as the breeze blows across the fields. She's dressed in yellow, green, and red. She's done herself up in all the colors of spring. Her yellow headscarf looks as good as a queen's crown on her. She smiles at me. But in her soul, she carries that black sheet which she throws over me so that I am totally invisible to the man I love. She has come to dazzle my night. She has come to give me yet more nightmares. It's she who wears that smile of triumph over my anguish. She has the power to outshine my existence with the light of her presence. She is the mysterious mermaid who enchants men with her marine bewitchment. Suddenly, I feel besieged by this aggression. Her smiles drip onto my face like snot.

The doorbell rings again. I tell Mauá to answer it. It's Saly. His leisure time tidbit. She comes bearing the gift of her mocking demeanor. She perches on my sofa and offers me a smile with lips moistened by my Tony's kisses. Soon afterward, there's yet another knock on the door. It's Ju, the betrayed one. A bag of bones. A ship wrecked in darkened waters. A black tide advancing haphazardly, blown by the wind. A bilious smile. Harsh. Luster-less. A sour fruit grown in rocky soil. There's a lot of fire concealed in her, for sure. She's got a malign spirit that doesn't allow the honey that flows through her veins to manifest itself. She's a malign spirit according to my Tony as well. Her kisses lack salt and sugar. He says her bed lacks everything: things to hold on to, fish-scale tattoos, passion. Without anything back or front, she's a dried-up wooden plank. All she has for me is a beating heart, he says. An exceptionally beautiful woman, but without any magic. Her voice lacks melody, with its manifestations of sorrow and anger. Her eyes lack a gleam, only tears abound. Ah, she's a tiresome woman, this Ju. If it weren't for the kids we've had together, I'd leave her, he repeats.

He always said things like this to me. He used ploys to avoid my kisses. He used to tell me: You smell of onions. Your mouth smells of garlic. You like garlic too much. You're ruining the kids with this taste of yours for garlic. And he would dodge past me without a kiss for me. And I would ask him: Is that why you're moving away from me? He would say yes. That I should smell of the scent of lemon. Sometimes he would come and tell me I smelled of menstruation. That I smelled of childbirth. That I smelled of milk and baby's wee. My body only smelled of things that made him feel sick: raw meat, fish, onions, and beans.

Lu is missing from this meeting.

"To what do I owe the pleasure of this evening visit, girls?"

"Sister Rami, it was Tony who summoned us. Do you know why?"

"Me?"

"I'm surprised. It's the first time he's called us. Something must be going badly."

"I don't see any reason for surprise," I say.

"Yes, there is a reason," Saly says. "At first, it's the men who seek out the women. The moment we're safely in the pot, it's the opposite. This man Tony's a man with a wandering eye."

"Lu's missing," Ju says, "can it be she's not coming?"

My rivals are anxious and come out with a torrent of questions. I don't answer their anxieties. I'm the only one who knows the reason for this encounter, but I'm not saying anything. Deep inside me, I feel the glee of anticipation because I'm privy to information that the others don't have.

We make small talk while we wait. Conversations continue at length, while others come to an end. We talk about the fevers the children get as the weather changes. We talk about how some of them are naughty. Others are successful. The boys are rebellious. They have a lot of girlfriends and don't study enough. They've taken after their father. The girls are diligent, loving, delicate, harder working at school. They've taken after us, their mothers. We talk about putting on weight and going on diets. We throw carefully sifted words backward and forward to each other. We've got money. We're becoming refined. Big headed. We pay each other compliments. Pink suits you. Thank you. High heels enhance the elegant way you walk. Thank you. Your skin, your perfume, your makeup, aquamarine on a burnt sienna base. Thank you. Your nail polish matches the color of your skirt perfectly. Thank you.

I'm dressed in blue. I like blue. I was wearing blue when Tony first met me and fell in love with me. I like my hairstyle, which is like that of the Beatles' backup singers. I always leave a fine lock of hair falling scantily over my brow, almost hiding my eyes. It was at the time of the Beatles that I met Tony. I also like those

< 394 >

tight-fitting clothes and short skirts that are back in fashion again now, except that at my age and with my weight I can't wear them anymore of course. But in my youth, I would walk along the seafront, showing plenty of leg, hand in hand with my Tony.

I think to myself. Whoever invented women's fashion must have been a man. He invented high-heeled shoes so that a woman couldn't run and escape his grip. If he'd thought of her, he would have invented boots and moccasins, flat-heeled shoes so that she could walk, run, and hunt for her victuals, like the amazons. He invented clinging skirts to force a woman to keep her legs tightly closed. If he'd thought of her, he would have invented some nice wide skirts, so she could walk in a relaxed fashion and her underparts enjoy a bit of cool on summer days. Instead of all this, he invented tight, audacious clothes, so that he could delight in contemplating the undulating curves of any woman and climax with a mere look.

Here in the twenty-first century men dress us in armor plating from the era of Don Quixote and tell us we're beautiful. Panties. Girdle. Bra. Nylon stockings. Short skirt. Slip. Full skirt, blouse, a light coat to accentuate your ladylike air. Headscarf, scarf, necklaces, earrings, bracelets. Rings. Hair in buns. Rollers. Hairpins, hairgrips, hairbands, and a wildflower behind the ear. A love charm. And men? Just a pair of shorts, pants and a shirt. Free to jump, run, and hunt. Lord, what a difference!

I feel like telling all women: Beauty doesn't lie in the color of your clothes. Or in the softness of your hair. Much less in the harmonious contours of your body. You feel beauty with your eyes closed, when you migrate to the moon in the serpent's flight.

Tony arrives, hot and flustered. He doesn't greet us, and seems angry. He lights a cigarette and smokes furiously, flooding the room with tobacco smoke. We remain cool and silent like the sea just before a storm. He takes an envelope from his pocket and passes it to me to read. I open it. I read. It's a short letter of farewell. A short, beautiful letter. And it contains an invitation to a wedding, signed by Vito and Lu, who are getting married this weekend. I put the letter back in its envelope and hand it back to Tony, who returns it to his pocket. A quiet growl brings us back to reality. We look at him. His expression is solemn and impenetrable, like that of a wild animal.

"What have you got to say about this?"

No one replies. What answer can we give? The inevitable ensues, the news is like a dam bursting. He accuses us and pursues

< 396 >

his line of questioning as if we were the real authors of what had happened. Fear rules. We exchange alarmed looks.

"You all knew about this. You knew and didn't warn me. In your weekly meetings, you laughed at me behind my back. You made your plans to escape and betray me. You plotted against me, you killed me little by little without my being aware, I was blind, blind, blind!"

He lets out a sigh, and then another sigh. His confident tone of voice is transformed into a moribund murmur, assailed by the pain of loss. His eyes half closed, he listens to the voice that comes from deep inside him. The departure of the woman he desires is a tragedy, a roll of thunder, death, a tempest.

"You've betrayed me!"

We exchange looks of alarm.

"You knew about this all along!"

No one answers. His eyes sweep over us, looking for proof of our complicity.

"Come on, girls, talk!"

There's dismay. There are many women. Shoals of them. Tons of them. In each man's hand, they explode like stars in a firework display. There are millions of them. If one dies, another is born.

< 397 >

With so many others waiting for a little piece of Tony's heart, what's the reason for so much hurt?

"But there are so many, Tony!" Mauá says by way of consolation.

"You are mine, I conquered you. I bought you like cattle. I domesticated you. I molded you according to my desires, I don't want to lose any of you. And you, Rami, should be at my side in the management of my cattle, because that's why you're first wife. You should guide the others in the steps they take. Ensure the conjugal fidelity of each one. But you stood there with your arms folded and allowed everything to pass. You were against me, me who led you to the altar steps and gave you the status of queen over my womenfolk. In your women's meetings, only your own interests seem to count."

Tony talks a mile a minute. There's a hint of foam at the corners of his mouth. Tears are welling up inside him. Deceived by one, deceived by all. Putting up with one woman's impulses is deadly, putting up with five is hell. A horse whinnies with joy when free of its load. A good Samaritan appeared and wants to relieve him of his hell. Why does he react like this? These men are difficult to understand.

"Who's going to be the next one to deceive me? Is it you, Rami? Is it you, Saly? Is it you, Ju? Ah, Ju, I know you're faithful to me. You

< 398 >

always wanted me as your husband, certificate in hand, in front of an altar and wearing a veil. You who deviated from your own life's path for my sake, are you going to betray me as well? I have no doubts at all about Mauá. You are beautiful, Mauá. You're a Makua and a mermaid from the island of perdition. When you pass by, everyone marvels. You'll leave me, I know."

Mauá opens her mouth to say something but then remains silent, observing the magic formula for dealing with alarming situations: Keep quiet, don't speak, don't raise your eyes to see.

"Lu's fiancé has the same name as my youngest son. Is that a coincidence? Or was her romance going on before the child was born? Is it mine?"

A volley of poisoned arrows has been aimed at our chests. And our blood is flowing, thick and black, along the pathways of this world. We are all huddled together like ostriches. With our heads tucked under our wings. The day has arrived for us to free the roots of the baobab tree from the soil. The tree with the good fruit will remain. There are more than enough fruit trees whose fruit are as sour as lemons. But why are we so sour, dear God, why? Women are gentle shade when well watered. When the soil is damp, women offer the world a green that is softer than velvet.

Than silk. But in this home, all we have is salt and sourness. All we have is pain and thorns. This soil is a desert. This home is torment.

"And the other children, are they mine? The ones from Rami may well be, at least the first ones. From Ju, all of them probably are. This poor woman doesn't have eyes for any other man in life except for me. From Mauá, I don't know. From Saly, I also don't know. Even with Rami, maybe none of them are mine. A woman who allows herself to be kutchingered when her husband's still alive isn't worthy of trust. Any trust at all!"

I feel like abandoning this home, right now! Traveling through this life, directionless. Seeking out new terrain. But they say badly kept trees die when they're transplanted. My wings are broken, I'm scared of flight.

He gazes at his right hand. He turns it over and over, as if he were in front of a palm reader.

"I've lost my middle finger. My hand is no longer the same. It's lost its shape. Lu was my middle finger. I'm not the same person anymore."

"But we're still here," Saly exclaims. "We're here. Are four women enough for you?"

< 400 >

"Yes, they're enough. But what will everyone say? All the men will laugh at me. Everyone will doubt my virility and I'll be a laughingstock. They'll say I've entered the andropause. That I'm losing my potency. That I left the cage door open through incompetence."

I begin to get worried. His anger is going to find an outlet against me, I know. I'm the one who's going to have to put up with all the raving that's bound to come, it has always been like that. He'll come to my arms and sing his age-old song. Rami, it's your fault. You were here, but you allowed me to fall in love with the others. You didn't keep a grip on me. You let me travel through other pleasures and I got lost. You allowed me to taste other charms, and I ended up becoming a polygamist. Why didn't you bewitch me, Rami? You allowed me to fall under other spells. Why didn't you put a spell on me, Rami, why didn't you bewitch me? Oh, what a wretched fate. If I'd bewitched him, what would his family have done to me?

"Rami?"

"Yes, Tony!"

"It's all your fault."

"I already knew that."

The air I breathe has become acrimonious. The string always breaks at its weakest point. It's the cycle of subordination. The white man says to the black man: It's your fault. The rich man says to the poor man: It's your fault. The man says to the woman: It's your fault. The woman says to her son: It's your fault. The son says to the dog: It's your fault. The dog barks furiously and bites the white man, and the white man once again angrily shouts at the black man: It's your fault. And so the wheel turns century after century ad infinitum.

"I'd never understood women," he says between his tears. "The pain of love is harsh, but women put up with it day in, day out. Women only have one man and when they lose him, they never know whether they'll get another one, but they take their pain. I'm going to be left with four women, but I can't take it. A man wasn't made to suffer, I can't bear it, I can't take it, I'll die. But things aren't going to stay like this, no, oh no!"

He goes over to the cabinet and pours himself a drink. He drinks. He puts the glass down and leaves. He gets in his car and drives off at high speed. We guess what's going through his mind. There's going to be a festival of violence unleashed on Lu, that's what we all predict. I phone Lu to warn her. We lean on the

< 402 >

windowsill. We watch Tony getting into his car. Clutching the steering wheel with all the aggression in the world. Dear God, he's so furious, he's going to kill someone. He shoots off at high speed without any respect for the law of the road, priorities, or pedestrians.

I'm overcome by a wave of panic. Good God, he's going to kill someone! And if he kills Lu, I shall suffer remorse for the rest of my life, morally I shall be the author of her death. I take Mauá's car and head off in pursuit. I reach Lu's block and rush up the steps two at a time. The door's wide open. I look inside. I can't hear shouting or even voices. I clutch my belly. I feel dizzy. Lord! I came to give my help expecting to find a scene of violence, and all I meet is silence. Could it be I've got here too late? I tremble. I go in.

The two of them are sitting face-to-face in the lounge. I see Tony. Instead of shouting and blustering, he sits there stiffly, looking at her. I'm appalled. He looks spellbound, bewitched, and he's crying like a child. His heart pounding anxiously. Imploring. His male pride detached and floating in midair. All that's left of the man is a lump of flesh begging for pity. Dear God, I'd rather watch anything in life than my Tony humiliating himself for the love of another woman, before my very eyes. I'd rather he behaved like an injured male, I'd rather he yelled, beat her, bit her. But he's like a castrated bull. And he gazes at her with that look of an ox defeated by the plow. Lu's spirit is ascending. She's the angel floating on high. She's left for other embraces, she's gone for good. After a long silence, he opens his mouth and beseeches her.

"Why are you leaving, my darling Lu?"

"Because the time has come."

"You're mine!"

"Where's your certificate of ownership?"

"I paid the bride price."

"That's not enough."

"Give me back the bride price I paid."

"Certainly. Double, if you wish. But before that, give me back all the happiness I gave you."

"Leave me my children and go."

"What paternal rights do you want, if you were never a father in any sense of the word?"

"We built this home together, Lu."

"Home? It's a dove's nest at the top of the pine tree. Along comes the storm and the eggs get carried away by the wind. Your

< 404 >

hurried kisses were like morning dew, they didn't even moisten the tongue."

"I've got so much love to give you, Lu. So much love. If you want, I'll leave the other women and just be with you."

"Really?"

"Oh, Lu! You're leaving such emptiness behind. You're taking my heart with you. And my heart has so much love for you, don't go!"

"Yes, I'm going."

"I'll kill you!"

"Kill me then. What are you waiting for?"

"Why are you leaving me, Lu?"

"I want to be a legally married woman with a ring on my finger. I want to be led to the altar steps with a veil and everything. Give me all that, and I'll stay."

Tony searches for an answer to parry this blow. Never before had he felt the pain of rejection. He goes back in time and recollects. Lu wound round his body like a serpent. Her ardent body enveloping him in the struggle of love and death, until the game balanced out in a tie, two-two, four-four. He recalls the sighs, the pauses, the passion. Now another man is going to take possession

< 405 >

of that body. He becomes emotional and starts talking nonsense. His voice sounds like a toad's call. An old toad who has lost the best of his vocal tones serenading out on the marshes.

"How are you going to love someone else if I give you everything that is best? You have a house. Clothes. Food. Home. Children. A husband for a week in every four. Why are you leaving, without even consulting me? What bad have I done? Can't you see I love you, Lu?"

"I love you too, can't you see?"

"Ah, you wretched woman! Go if you want, you'll never find another man like me. You're going to remember me because you'll be unhappy. You'll miss me, you'll see. You'll beg to come back to my arms on bended knee, and when that happens, the one who'll spurn you will be me, you ungrateful strumpet!"

He tries to give her one last punch in the face. A farewell blow. To get his revenge and turn her into a bride with a swollen eye on her wedding day. His arm is a weapon. He closes his fist like a sling. He punches. But the gesture is slow and weak. His attack is silent, uninspired, without spirit. She dodges him and the fist is lost in the air. He holds both her arms and shakes her like a bush. But Lu is a spider. A scorpion. A wasp. She's the one who attacks.

< 406 >

She gives him a deep, vampire bite on his fat arm, which draws blood. He lets her go with a howl: Murderer!

It's a miracle, but he doesn't react. He feels the bite on his most sensitive side, that of the heart. The wound burns. The wound bites. The wound covers his weeping body with a red blanket. In despair, he raises his eyes to the sky, whose deep gray night contains tones of purple. He looks at the draft of air carrying bits of red dust. The red of his blood. He seeks help from Saint Valentine, who is lost somewhere up there along the heavenly pathways. But the sky is red. The clouds are red, and have formed a red barrier that has made Saint Valentine's image invisible. I look at Lu with surprise and rage. Her love never equaled that which was dedicated to her. But love is much stronger when one parts, just as the last kiss is the greatest of all kisses.

I take off my headscarf and turn it into a bandage to staunch the flow of blood. My God, it's a deep wound and is going to leave a scar. The mark of her teeth is a tattoo to remember her by. Each time he looks at it, he'll sigh: Lu, my darling Lu, whom I loved so much and who left for someone else's arms.

I feel an immense pain, as if that wound were mine. I'm overcome by a wave of jealousy, he loves this woman Lu more than he

< 407 >

does me. So be it, I accept. Love is sublime, it can't be manipulated by human hands. It comes, it touches us and marks our heart with deep scars. Love is a superior emotion, it flies loftily and perches wherever it wishes. Love is independent, it cannot be bought, it cannot be sold. It's a breeze that comes and goes, enters the breast and settles there without asking permission. It is born and dies wherever it pleases. It's the magical tone of a rustic flute that enchants and causes the soul to soar. It refreshes like the waters of a spring and fortifies the spirit. When it feels it is necessary, it can be more violent and destructive than storms. Love is a diamond. It is as ephemeral and eternal as a speck of dust.

"Rami!"

"Yes, Tony."

"You are the main culprit for all my suffering."

"I know."

"Do you feel sorry for me?"

"Sorry for you?"

I look at him with pity. His is a heart freezing over in the midst of flames. And he's asking for someone else's warmth in order not to be transformed into a statue of ice by love's fire.

< 408 >

"I know you came to help me. Well, help me. Take my hand before I fall. Let me lean my pain against your shoulder."

He's in the middle of a rough sea and can't weather the waves. He's sinking, moribund. I give him my shoulder to lean on. A woman is the tree trunk to which the victims of all shipwrecks cling for survival. A woman is nature's cycle. Perfect. Complete. In summer, she provides the leafy shade where great warriors may rest their weariness. In winter, her body gives off a vast warmth that covers the whole land. In springtime, she is the flower of all colors that lends joy to nature. In autumn, she is the seed that lies concealed, proclaiming future springtimes. The heart of the whole universe palpitates in a woman's womb. Every woman is earth, trodden on, dug over, sown with seed. Wounded by feet trampling on her, blows, punches, kicks. Fertilized. Unfertilized. A woman is our first home. Our final home. In a married couple, the man always dies first, so that the woman can cast the last shovelful of soil and the last flower on her beloved's grave. A woman is as strong as the rocks on Mount Vumba. As soft as meadowland grass. As giving and fertile as the black soil of the Zambezi Valley. Benevolent as a field of corn. As poisonous as the lava of Mount

< 409 >

Etna. As lofty as Mount Kilimanjaro. As unsettling and treacherous as the mists of the Sahara. She is the prophetess of eternity, capable of revealing the past, present, and future, when excavated good and deep by the sorcerous hands of a good archaeologist.

"Rami!"

"Yes, Tony."

"I'm crying, can't you see? In front of you I can weep openly. You've always been present at the moments when I've gone off the rails. You've always put up with my acts of madness. You're more than a wife. You're a friend. Would that all men had a wife like you. Devoted. Trustworthy. I'm a lucky man. I know I give you cause for bitterness, but what do you expect? Who's going to give you cause for bitterness unless it's me, your husband?"

"Yes, dearest Tony. Only you can crown me queen of thorns and of pain, because you're my man."

My answer is couched in resentment. Being a man is to be raised on high by the sacrifice of five spouses. One's gone and there are four of us left. But he doesn't want four. Four is a base line, it's a square, it's flat, it's a tabula rasa. He would rather have five. Five is a pyramid. It's space, It's the ability to look down on the earth from the height of a flight toward the horizon.

< 410 >

I take his arm and drag him along with me, and he is so weak that he obeys my every command. I get in the driver's seat of his blue car. I know how miserable he's feeling, I know men and their thoughts. They can't abide the idea of being abandoned. I know some who became impotent, who went mad or ended up alcoholics, just because they were cuckolded on a whim. Women are stronger, they overcome desertion with greater courage. They're exchanged each day. Betrayed. Seduced. Abandoned with babies in their arms. Bought. Beaten each day, but they resist. They put up with the magic jackknife and the chastity belts when the man goes off to war or on some adventure. When they get old, they're whipped by their own sons, and accused of witchcraft. And they pray and thank God for each of their torments. That's why they use any excuse for singing and dancing. *Those who sing, send their troubles packing.*

We women engender existence, but we ourselves don't exist. We bear life, but we don't live. We bear children, but we aren't born ourselves. Some days ago, I met a woman from the interior of the province of Zambezia. She's got five children, all of whom have grown up. The eldest, a slim and elegant mulatto, is the product of the Portuguese, who raped her during the colonial war.

The second, a black, strong and graceful like a warrior, is the fruit of another rape by the freedom fighters in the same colonial war. The third, another mulatto, as cute as a cat, is the product of the white Rhodesian commandos who pillaged the area in order to destroy the bases of the Zimbabwe freedom fighters. The fourth is from the rebels who waged the civil war in the interior of the country. The first and second were the result of rape, but for the third and fourth, she gave herself of her own free will, because she felt she was a specialist in rape. The fifth son is from a man she slept with out of love, for the first time.

This woman bore the history of all her country's wars in her womb. But she sings and laughs. She tells her story to anyone who passes, tears in her eyes and a smile on her lips, as she affirms: My four sons, without a father or a name, are children of the gods of fire, children of history, born from the power of a force armed with machine guns. My happiness was to have borne only men, she says, for none of them will experience the pain of rape.

< 412 >

38

It's two o'clock in the morning, and today is Saturday. I've got insomnia, I can't sleep. I'm scared of sleeping in case I dream. I've had ghastly nightmares. It's almost as if the here and the beyond combined together in a great circle of light and shade when human beings slept. Tony's beside me, and today he isn't snoring. His sleep is as translucent as a gentle breeze. His soul is out there yonder but his body is over here, moving to the rhythm of a nightmare's dance. He's moving his arms like wings in a squid's flight. I sniff around in Tony's dream world. There's a smell of roasting. It smells of a man burning. He's in the inferno and turning this way and that in the waltz of despair. He sweats. He shouts Lu's name. I'm alarmed. Men's dreams are a mystery.

He shouts and wakes up.

"Rami, what time is it?"

"Two in the morning."

"It's today that Lu's getting married, isn't it?"

"That's right."

< 413 >

"And you're going to the wedding, aren't you?"

"If you allow me, I'll go, but if you don't want me to go, I'll stay."

"Go. Go with me and help me to stop this marriage."

"Stop?"

"Yes. Go and shout at the top of your voice that Lu has a husband who loves her, she's got two children and a home, that she's leaving a man to his loneliness, waiting for her, that she's married …"

"Married?"

"Well, bride-priced."

"The bride price is a custom, a tradition, it has no application in law."

"I know."

"So, what then?"

"I'm a good man, Rami, I don't deserve such treachery. I can even understand that Lu might be passionately in love. Passion is a fantasy, it's a passing thing. Rami, tell me: Is it that I don't look after you all? Don't I give you all you want? There are men with ten wives and I've just got five. I've always given you your food, paid all your expenses punctually, I visit each of you devotedly, what more do you need?"

< 414 >

That's exactly what polygamous love is about. To have a man in your arms while he yearns for another. You wash the gentleman, darn his socks and underpants, polish the heels of his shoes, pamper him, make him smell nice, so that he can look good in front of other women. Loving a polygamist is to chew pain by way of nourishment, to fill your belly by swallowing your saliva. Loving a polygamist is an endless wait. Endless despair.

Tony is revealing the whole of himself to me. I nose around his open wounds. There's a smell of pain, there's a smell of love, there's a smell of fresh blood. I hear a crack coming from his chest. His heart clatters like a sheet of glass hit by a stone. I suddenly think of my mother. I think of my aunt, whose life ended inside a wild animal's stomach all because of a chicken's gizzard. How many times have I been the target of an attack in this home, I who am the first wife? I have to put up with this sort of thing every day, but I still can't get used to it. The invocation to my rivals prickles my spirit like pins in some voodoo session.

"Rami, help me hire a gunman to shoot my monstrous enemy to death. Help me find some magic to stop this marriage, some thunderbolt that will send him to kingdom come at the church door."

His speech takes on a horrific, superstitious tone. This unloved man starts planning incredible acts of revenge, howling on a moonlit night. There are no words capable of consoling an abandoned man. Ah, Tony, my scorned little crybaby. Despairing, selfish, yelling his blackmail threats in order to get his milk and pap. I'm sadly surprised. He's just proved he loves Lu more than he does me.

"You women know a lot about magic. Find me a really powerful thunderwitch."

"I don't know any."

"Yes, you do, Rami, of course you do. You just don't want to help me. You're from the south, you were born among the Ronga. You're from Matutuíne, you were born on the banks of the River Maputo."

"Yes, that's true."

"Well then? The thunderwitches are your aunts."

"I don't have any aunts with such powers."

"Rami, I beg you: Speak to your relatives and order three thunderbolts. Just three."

"Three?!"

"Yes. To wipe out the invader. One for the head, the other for the heart, and the strongest of all for his private parts."

"But?!…"

"Think about it, Rami, think hard. I'm going to lose a wife, and you are going to lose your best friend, your closest confidante, I know you're very fond of her, Rami."

"Yes, I like her."

She gave my Tony pleasure, but she was a friend and a sister to me. I'll no longer be able to enjoy that smile, that laugh of hers, so often. She was the spiritual flame from which I lit my candle. I'll no longer have that mirror, which reflected the image of what I was, of what I am not and will never be again. Lu's departure pains me, but we need to lose in order to gain. From now on, I'll have one less rival to share him with, and the waiting time in the conjugal rota will be one week less. If I lost Tony's love, it wasn't because of Lu. The one who took my husband away was Ju. That's why I'm so fond of Lu, because it was she who avenged my jealousy. And then she lent me Vito, who rendered me a service out of pity, giving a loving hand to an unloved woman in need. Thinking about it, Ju is much less of a rival. Lu is so powerful that she's taken the breath of life away from us. Ever since Lu arrived on the scene, we've been buried in Tony's heart.

"So, Rami, are you going to help me or not?"

Poor Tony. He believes women are devoid of reason, living purely on their emotions, incapable of any kind of revolution, who can be calmed in their weeping with a toffee, a promise, and who can be made to shut up with a good spanking.

"Rami, how can a woman leave a man like me? She can go and marry this man, but she won't find a better man than me in this world. I picked her out of the gutter and gave her a sumptuous home, I made a lady of her. How can she betray me?"

I feel like laughing. I feel like crying. I feel like doing something else that I can't even explain. Yesterday he spoke words of love to me that were honeyed. His lips close to my ear, he sang me beautiful songs. He seduced me. He inspired me. He drove me wild. Now he speaks words of love to me that are seasoned with bile. He's destroying me. Mistreating me. Driving me wild.

"I'm a good man, Rami, there are worse men than me. Everything I do, I do well. Having many women is a right that both tradition and nature confer on me. I've never mistreated Lu, I've beaten her occasionally, only to show her how much I love her. I've also beaten you sometimes, but you are here, you haven't abandoned me to go and live somewhere else. My mother was often given a hiding by my father, but she never abandoned her

< 418 >

home. Women of a previous age are better than the ones you get nowadays, who take fright at the mere sight of a whip."

"You're right, Tony, women nowadays just have no sense at all. Why don't you go and marry my grandmother?"

He raises his voice as high as the clouds. It stays there. My God, what are the neighbors going to think of us? But his voice can't withstand the lofty heights and plummets down vertiginously, defeated by the force of gravity. He gets out of bed and walks over to the window. He says he feels both hot and cold. He says he feels a tingling throughout his body. He says he's short of breath and the pain is killing him. He lets out a shout. A sigh. And he repeats his speech.

"Rami, get me a thunderwitch and order three thunderbolts, help me, before I die!"

His great body collapses like a tree cut down by a hurricane. He plunges into a world without sun or moon. He forgets his pain, he forgets Lu, he forgets betrayal and marriage. He forgets everything. He forgets himself. He escapes to another world. I stop crying. Thinking. Feeling. I jump out of bed in a flash. I bend over him and place my ear next to Tony's chest. His heart is humming in a whisper like a guitar being played quietly. I really am going to be a widow, I don't want to be a widow anymore, help me! I die at every one of my Tony's deaths. I don't want any more mourning, gravestones, I don't want to be kutchingered again.

Beto, João, Sandra, Lulu, all leave their bedrooms and help me carry their father out to the blue car. I defy death and the highway. I defy the silence of night. While I drive, I pray. Dear God, bring my Tony back to life!

We reach the hospital in a minute or two and Tony is placed on a stretcher as if he were a corpse. We hurry down a long corridor, too long for the tiredness I feel. Heartrending sighs from the dying upset my spirit with their depressing melody. Everywhere, there are broken, weakened people, like petals that have become detached by the strength of the wind.

We go into a consulting room. There's the doctor, smiling.

"What's the matter? What's happened?"

I explain.

"Doctor, the things he's been saying, the mad stories he's been telling, doctor, the bite on the arm, the sudden fevers, doctor, that beautiful woman, the marriage that's going to take place, doctor, all the hysterics, the shouting, doctor, the nightmares, the foaming at the mouth, doctor, the sweating, the shortage of breath,

< 420 >

doctor, my Tony, the pain in my heart, doctor, my rivals, we are five wives, doctor, the one he desires most, his favorite, doctor, if my Tony dies again, I'm going to be kutching …"

At this point, Tony comes to his senses and attacks me with all his strength.

"Shut that mouth of yours! How can you talk about my private life to all and sundry if I haven't given you leave to do so? As your husband, I refuse to let you behave like some fishwife. You're a woman, and you should stick to your place, because when it comes to my health, I'm the one who looks after that."

I'm indignant. I'm the one who tore through the early hours. I'm the one who defied the wind, cleared the clouds away, and chased off the storm. Now he comes back to life and casts me into the dirt. This Tony takes the sunlight away from me slowly and deliberately, and throws bundles of darkness on top of me, one sheaf at a time. There's a huge fire in the air that only I can feel. Memory mingles with tears that flow like gusts of wind. In a flash, I remember an old woman pushing her dying husband on a trolley. Barefoot, her heels cracked because, during the whole of her life, the soil had beaten the soles of her feet relentlessly. She was an old woman dressed in rags. Without a smile or any shape to her. A tree bearing soured fruit. An old woman who seemed to know all the secrets of a desert crossing. Who had drunk all the bitter flavors of the universe and survived all manner of poisons. Her soul stolen from her, she was like a ghost wandering the horizons of this world. That old lady abandoned her equally old husband right here, in this same consulting room, in front of this same doctor. I remember her words. I repeat them.

"Doctor, I've put up with this man my whole life. If he doesn't want me to speak, then let him die!"

I left the doctor's surgery like a gust of wind. All I wanted was to get out into the street. All I wanted was some fresh air. All I wanted was a bit of freedom from life's disappointments. From my past, or from some other dimension, I hear a voice calling me: Rami, come back here, Rami, don't leave me, Rami, listen to me, Rami, obey me, Ramiiii!…

Three in the morning. I get home and enjoy some restorative beauty sleep. I wake up at seven. I phone my dressmaker and ask her to iron my clothes so I can get dressed at nine. I call Mauá to get my skin seen to, and she sends over her best makeup artist. I take a foam bath. The makeup girl gets to work on my skin. First, there's a manicure and pedicure session. Then comes the mask, and she starts putting the cosmetics on: the base, rice powder, rouge, mascaras, shadows, and other products I've never heard of before. I go to the mirror and am ecstatic. I'm like a bird in full plumage. I sigh. I want to be the most beautiful of all the guests. I want to be the bearer of all the colors of nature. Today, I want to be blue like the ocean. I want to be the horizon where tired eyes can seek inspiration and those in despair can find repose. I want to be the sea into which all rivers flow.

My dressmaker arrives and helps me on with that sky blue suit of mine. I go over to the mirror again and feel dazzling. I turn this way and that in front of the mirror, and there's no doubt about it. I'm going to be the most beautiful guest at Lu's wedding. I can't even believe it's me I'm seeing. But it is me, reborn thanks to the cosmetics industry. Today, a man is going to covet me, for sure. Today, I'm going to kill the most distinguished gentleman with desire. The sun won't go down without someone loving me in silence. I call a taxi to take me to the church, for I'm not in the right mind to drive. Before going out, I phone the doctor.

"Doctor, how's my Tony?"

"He's out of danger. It wasn't a heart attack, but he mustn't get so excited."

< 424 >

39

I'm one of the first to arrive and I sit right in the front. There's a steady stream of people coming into the church. The place is so full that I fear there won't be enough room for so many people. All of a sudden the church is lit up. Fresh air circulates through the windows, through the dome, and through the hearts of hundreds of those present. The organ plays, the people get to their feet, the bride is arriving. I turn to look at the entrance to the church and sigh. Here's the bride emerging from among the thorns like a white angel descending from heaven. Here she is, blossoming as she advances. How long the journey has been up until this point! My tiredness is lifted. My soul soars into the air like the highest branches of a pine. I hear the whispers of all the fountains and the song of all the birds in the universe. The bride and groom are in each other's heart, king and queen on the sun's throne.

I'm in heaven and am swaying to the sound of the organ music. The guests' applause, the priest's voice, pull my soul along on the scent of the breeze, dear God, watch over my heart before my emotions kill me. I view a past of sweetness with bitter feelings. Lu wears a smile on her face that reminds me of when I was a bride. I was also once happy as she is now. I was also a queen in my day, but now, oh God, I'm a slave, dying of resentment. Life is a wheel, a day of thorns, another day of flowers, a day of sun, another day of storm. Dear life, how often do we weep and smile at the same time?

The bride and groom say yes and I weep. Yes, the source of all things. Yes to love and two hearts become one. Yes to sperm and to the egg so that a new race may be born. Yes to hatred, so that the world may be set alight with endless fires. Yes. It's in the word yes that all the mysteries of the universe are celebrated.

This bride is a river with reflections of the sun and the moon. She is a tiny particle of dew in the arid land that witnessed her birth. The particle started to grow, and gradually took the shape of a drop, a stream of water, a river. And she became a source. She journeyed through the dryness of the bush and knew monstrous cities, where women sell their bodies in order to eat. But she flowed round all the obstacles like a river in flood. Now she is celebrating her victory song, galloping through the skies on the wings of Pegasus. When I close my eyes, I hear this bride murmuring gently to my ear alone: Rami, it is possible to change the world. The world is within us!

The ceremony comes to an end, Lu is married. Everybody rises so that they can congratulate the couple. I'm the last one. She asks me in a whisper:

"How's Tony?"

"He had a deep fit of depression early this morning. He's in the hospital."

"Why?"

"Because of you."

"Is he very ill?"

"He's out of danger."

"Ah, thank goodness. It's good to know that a man really can die of love for me. This piece of news has made me doubly happy today."

"Congratulations, Lu."

"Rami, you're like a great mother to me, and I shall never forget you. You are a woman above all other women. I'm a successful businesswomen. A beautiful bride. A true wife. My happiness is your work, thank you, Rami."

"Praise be to God!" I sigh.

< 427 >

"There's something else, Rami. On this solemn day, I offer you a place in my family. I'm now the first wife. Thorns and pain. I want to give you the position of second wife, so that you may be pleasure and flower, at least once in your life. Vito is yours too. You deserve all the happiness the world can offer, Rami."

She smiles. We embrace. We kiss and weep with delight. Mauá and Saly join us and we all hug Lu in a great show of celebration. Everyone is here except for Ju. Mauá is so emotional, she can hardly contain herself.

"Rami, just look at how beautiful your work has turned out. What would we be if it weren't for you? You are our mother, thanks to you we have been reborn. You understood our suffering, our poverty. You adopted us like daughters and you improved our lives – she places her hand on my shoulder and whispers in my ear: "I'm the next one to get married, Rami, you're the first to know my secret."

Saly unleashes an endearing feeling straight from the heart that carries on the wind like honey in its fluidity. She declares. She sighs:

"If women join hands together, they can change the world, isn't that so, Rami?"

"Yes," Mauá adds, smiling, "with Rami's strength, we've managed to change the course of our lives. Thank you, Rami."

We take various photos at the entrance to the church. I sit down on the steps to capture the occasion with the camera that is my own eyes. I weep. For me. For the millions of women who drift helplessly through life's sediment. Who bear in their bellies the mysteries of creation and the seeds of eternity, to give birth to the light of life and illuminate the blindness of the world? It's we, the women, we women! Who comforts life? We do. Who makes the males feel more male, enables them to don the plumage of glory and triumph in all their struggles? We do. Who calms the spirit with a flower, after a day of toil? We do. We are night and morning in one star. It's we who sow the flower and the wind that carries the dark cloud that fertilizes the soil. We are the arc of the sky and the arc of the earth as they meet in the horizon's affirmation. We are the center around which all the curves of the universe wind. But it is we who face the storm. It is us that life slowly suffocates and buries in the belly of the distant mountains. It's us that men kill with thirst, ever so gently. It's us that the world forces to seek out a rich man so as to get the crumbs from his table. It is us that society fails to provide an opportunity for so that we may earn our own living in a dignified manner. Every day, we seek love only to find deceit. We seek a flower and only find thorns. We seek our daily bread and society gives us grains of stone. We seek air and all we find is ash raining down on us, extinguishing the breath of our existence. In our villages, we are taken to schools for sex at the age of ten, and we learn to lengthen our genitals, to become squid, prickly pears, octopuses, and turkey beaks. And while all this is happening, men go to school to learn how to earn their daily bread. While they learn how to write the word life on the map of the world, we go out in the early morning, following our mothers, in order to scare birds away from our plantations of rice.

I raise my eyes and I contemplate the world. In one corner, women join together in a circle and their voices burst out resplendently in song. The waves of sound increase in tone and snake through the heavens like wild horses. Hopes, strength, and joy spring from their sweet song and fall upon the earth in a cascade of flowers. My pain is transformed into joy by a stroke of magic. The verses of the song rise to my lips. I stutter. And then the song is released from my throat like some projectile. Why am I crying if no one has died? I expel all my pain and anguish. I expel the tears that gather on my lashes. I push aside this fearful rock that crushes my breast and prevents me from breathing fresh air. I abandon the solitude of the church steps and join the ring of dancers. I stamp the ground in complete abandon. The heat, the sound, the vibration, lighten my steps and I spiral like the wind. To the sound of the hands clapping and the songs, I turn this way, that way, upward, downward, to the left, to the right, in the dance of assuagement, the dance of prayer, the dance of freedom. The firm stamping of my feet raises the dust and the earth's fragrance, and from the ground, I receive the vital injection of fire and water. Sweat pours down my body, I'm in a sauna. All tension is released. I feel that I'm not alone, Mother Earth is lulling me. With sweat and tears I dance in prayer: God, make me the last of a suffering generation of women!

We interrupt our dance and advance down the road in a procession. Our song penetrates the clouds, and we colonize the heavens with our voices. We reach the moon, we rescue Vuyazi, the rebellious princess stamped upon its surface. We place a crown of palm leaves on her head, and at her feet we scatter flowers of all colors. We ask as of one voice: Why were you stamped on the moon's surface as a punishment for all eternity? Why were you condemned to the icy inferno of the skies? Her answer is a silence of love and tenderness, and we declare with one loud yell: We know everything, we know it all. You refused to have tattoos cut into you with sharp blades, just to please your master. You refused to carry out that act of cleaning his genitals on your breasts after love making, to show your obedience and submission in accordance with the duties forced upon women in our part of the country. You refused to give feet and bones to the girls and gizzards and good pieces of meat to the boys. You fought passionately for the principle of fidelity, and against the *licaho*, the chastity knife. You said no to the harem and to love by rota. You fought for the right to exist, whether in matters of love or those of food. All you wanted was to be a tree planted in the soil, swaying in the breeze, this we know. All you wanted was to be a secure nest for the birds of the sky, and that's why you were condemned. Today, we beg forgiveness for those who hurt you, together we cry, they don't know the harm they did you and the entire universe.

We plucked Vuyazi from her static position and danced with her over the moon's vastness. We soared into the heavens and discovered that each star is a woman scattered high above. The earth is made of clay and is shaped like a woman. The moon is

< 432 >

ours, we colonized it and it was conquered for us by Vuyazi, pioneer, heroine, princess and queen, the first woman in the world who fought for happiness and justice. The world is ours, every woman's heart can accommodate the entire universe.

We rescued her soul from the inferno of the skies and brought it back to the paradise of the earth around the fire, and with her we coiled our way through the streets of the city. Together we celebrated what was to come and we took an oath: From now on, we shall march forward on behalf of all women who have been left defenseless in their lives, we shall multiply the strength of our limbs, and we shall be heroines prepared to fall in the battle for our daily bread. Singing and dancing, we shall build schools with foundations of stone, where we shall learn to read and to write the lines of our destiny. We shall cross the sea on the ship of our eyes because we'll know how to sail to the other side of the ocean and we shall bear with us a message of solidarity and sisterhood to the women of the four corners of the world. We shall teach men the beauty of forbidden things: the pleasure of weeping, the taste of the wings and feet of the chicken, the beauty of fatherhood, the magic of the rhythm of the pestle as it grinds the grain. Tomorrow, the world will be a more natural place, and our babies, girls as well as boys, will have four years of suckling. At the hour of their birth, girls too will be greeted with five salvos of drumbeats, under the roof of their father's home and in the shade of their ancestors' tree. We shall march along with the men, as soldiers dressed in mud and sweat, in the plantations, the mines, the factories, the building sites, and we shall keep a honeyed kiss for each child's mouth. We shall be richer both in bread and in love. We shall look at men with true love and not for the numbers on the banknotes hanging from their pockets. Alongside our boyfriends, husbands, and lovers, we shall dance from victory to victory in the *niketche* of life. With our menstrual impurities, we shall fertilize the soil, from where a rainbow of scents and flowers will spring.

< 434 >

40

I celebrate waking up to yet another day. I gaze at the thick fog of a November morning. On the horizon, the sun spreads its newly born rays. Today, the heat is going to be intense. I am surrounded by all the signs of absence. I feel a warmth welling up from deep inside me and brushing the tips of my nerves. Have I slept alone? No. I've slept with my yearning, the queen of my nights. Yearning takes the form of a figure, a female companion, and has the invisible color of ghosts. I feel deep yearning. But a yearning for whom? For Levy? I've no idea! Maybe it's for Vito. No, it can't be for Vito, he's an honest man, a married man. It can only be yearning for Tony, that burden God has placed on my shoulders. I feel deep anguish for those days. I live in sorrow, I live in pain, and I don't even know why.

I suddenly envy Lu. Who has a husband all to herself. Who has a warm bed every day, and every hour. Who sleeps on a sheet of stars and has even forgotten the anguish of the weekly rota.

I envy the miniskirted women, who sell their bodies, who sell

< 435 >

their dreams, living each day, each instant, without a single worry. Who wander the streets, who drink, who smoke, who fall in love and out of love, who exploit and are exploited, who are the recipients of false love but who spread true illnesses. I envy divorced women, women who have assumed their solitude, acknowledged and endorsed in front of an attorney, who can freely choose their lovers. Who assume the role of both father and mother, who earn their daily crust with a man's fists, but who at night want to be women. Who mingle feminine and masculine in one single verb. Who still dream of a true prince, because their former husband changed from a royal prince into a toad after half a dozen kisses.

I'm envious of barren women, whose womb has broken the cycle of suffering. They haven't given birth to women for crying, or men for causing women to cry. I pity myself, a married woman. Suffering cruel treatment for no gain whatsoever. Used only to be exchanged later. Unloved but held in esteem socially. A woman camouflaged in her solitude, hidden away. I pity women who are widows, accused of having witches' teeth so as to chew up the corpse of their husbands in fantastic orgies. I pity little old ladies who are always alone, vanquished by life. I feel even sadder for the child women who play at being mother to their dolls, who are treated like pigeon's eggs, but who one day will be broken like clay and will follow a sad path, like mine, who will be slept with without knowing any pleasure, and who will give birth to other women and other tragic stories.

I'm scared of women who envy me, and there are many. You're blessed, Rami, you've got nice rivals, they say. Those northern women, when they steal a husband, it's for good, so you'll never see him again. They put such a spell on him that he won't be able to bear the sight of you, of your children, or even of the street you walk down. In your case, he comes and goes. He provides food for his children. He enters and leaves the house in order to keep up appearances and deceive public opinion. You're lucky, Rami. It's lucky to be loved, they say. How many women are born and die without ever knowing the color of love?

I laugh. Can a husband be stolen? How is the robbery carried out? An adult man introduces himself to a beautiful lady and exclaims: Steal me, my love, steal me from my wife's arms, go on, steal me, my treasure!

This love I feel seeks a return that is no longer possible. But why did Tony bring me here? At my mother's house, I had food and a bed, but he took me away from there. He told me we were going to face life together. Build a nest lined with soft wool. He even told me that together we would gaze at the ocean, count the stars in the sky and talk until morning, our heads resting on the same pillow. And here I came, fished like a mackerel, disposed to love and to build. And what did he give me? Only a sponge mattress and a plate of rice and beans. I need warmth, I need affection, but who is going to give me some?

I leave my bed, ravaged by the tempest of unsatisfied love. I go to the bathroom and look in the mirror. I go to the kitchen. I scrub the dishes with all the rage I can muster in order to chase away my anguish. The soapsuds grow in my hands like hillocks. I sing my mother's favorite song from when, pestle in hand, she would grind the corn.

How many times do I get hit in one day
Me, his first wife, oh yeah!

In the midst of my silence, I hear someone approaching quietly. They're a man's steps, I can sense the rhythm, I can sense the smell. I turn my head and see Tony, right behind me. I'm taken aback. What's he doing here?

"Rami."

< 438 >

"Yes, Tony?"

I stop washing the crockery and look at him, surprised. He gives me his roguish smile. He's got his hands hidden behind his back, he must have a present for me, but this time I'm not going to let that present seize me. I look at my watch, it's still only seven o'clock. I swear I can't understand this man, who sleeps in one woman's house and wakes up with his head in the other's. He holds out his hand and gives me a red rose, which I receive without any emotion and place on top of the sideboard. What do I need a rose for at this hour? If only the rose were a bit of firewood for my stove. If only it were a few leaves of green vegetables or a plate of rice and beans. But a rose?

"Don't distract me, Tony."

He gives me a hug and a kiss. He does his best to invest passion in that kiss, which to me tastes cold, metallic. Then he sits down in the chair opposite me and starts telling me stories.

"Rami."

"Yes!"

"I've taken a decision that'll please you."

"What's that?"

< 439 >

"I want to leave all my wives and just be with you. I've had enough of being a philanderer, a husband to all the women from the north and south of this country. Don't you agree?"

He thinks he's pleasing me with his lies. I don't applaud dishonest attitudes, oh no. Poor soul. He thinks he's feeding my vanity by saying I'll be the only one. He thinks he can buy my soul by offering the heads of my rivals on a tray. I'm an honorable person, I can't betray anyone, not even my rivals.

"Rami, I just want to love you and no one else."

"Just me? Can I know why?"

How many times did he swear he loved me, how many times did he betray me? How many times did he swear to each of my rivals he loved them? How many marriages did he promise, and how many did he fulfill? How many times did this miserable wretch lie in the name of love? Ever since he came back from being dead, our bed has remained cold. He would take me to parties, to dinners, he would chat away and encourage me. And he would kiss me gently. I'd get excited, awaiting something that never came. Whoever saw us like that, arm in arm, imagined fire, volcanoes, thunder and lightning, but our hugs were no more than icy cold. He pretended to love me, he sought in

< 440 >

me some public image, a convenient perch, a display of pretense to stop people gossiping. Those who see us walking down the street exclaim: Ah, what a lovely couple! Lately, Tony has been treating me like a leper, for reasons I can't fathom. It's not as if I've ever been unfaithful to him! With Levy, I made love out of sacred duty, and in the case of Vito, it was stolen love, without any intention on my part of betrayal. Our love is a game teenagers play, a hug here, a little stroll there. He lavishes me with flowers, gifts, innocent kisses, all because I was kutchingered and am impure. Poor me. Purified in my widowhood, sullied in my marriage. Why am I being punished with this sexual abstinence if Tony was the main author of the crime? Why does the idea of infidelity provoke endless cataclysms in men? I'm a woman, dear God, I'm a woman and am young, blood still courses through my veins, but this man insists on feeding me only with potatoes and flowers.

"Would you be capable of leaving Mauá? And the children you have?"

"Rami, I never had time to look at you, to feel you, let alone appreciate the world that lies within you. I must have turned into a horrible creature before your eyes."

I suddenly feel a need to get out of there, to get away from that lying voice and breathe some fresh air. Ah, dear God, the man I fell in love with has a double, triple personality, and lies nonstop!"

"Where did you get that idea?"

"We have five children, we've been married for twenty years, you're my wife and I'm your husband, but I've spent most of the time away from you."

From on high, he spills his load of sweet nothings like a fertilizer, I feel it. What type of a reaction is he trying to produce in me?

"Tell me, Tony, why do you want to deceive women and leave them saddled with your children? What did you want from them?"

"Nothing serious, I admit. It was pride, pride purely and simply. Having a woman here, a son there, feeds any male's vanity. I'm not the only one. A lot of men do that."

He plunges his hands into my breasts and destroys my heart as if he were uprooting a plant from the soil. I feel an immense pain, he's killing me, I'm dying, how often do I get killed every day in this home, I who am the first wife?

"Don't blame me, Rami. I'm not the one who invented the world and its traditions. Long before I was born, men were like this."

How right he is, my God! This situation was born out of the belly of the past, and women have been fish on the slab at the market stall forever: a kilo of this, two kilos of that, I'll take this one, I'll leave that one, I like this one, I'll take that now, I'll pay for that now, I'll use that one now, now I'll bake it, now I'll eat it.

"It was your idea to bring all these women together, Rami. You surprised me. You exceeded my expectations. You led the whole flock with incredible skill. I would only have used them and abandoned them without so much as thinking of the consequences. From street vendors, you managed to transform them into entrepreneurs."

"Tony, dear, you got tired of me and fell for them. You got tired of them and now you're coming back to me. Soon, you'll get tired of me again. I don't believe in you."

"The country is full of single mothers. Their case won't be either unique or the last of its kind."

I burn with terror and anger at the message being rubbed into me like pepper into an open wound. I feel my whole body ablaze,

I feel heat and thirst, and yet why? There's nothing extraordinary in his affirmation, indeed anything other than that would come as a surprise.

"What makes you think your decision will please me?"

"I know, Rami, I know you've always wanted me by your side and at peace. You embarked on this polygamy thing just to have me near you, I know."

I feel enraged. I grab a wooden spoon to give him a good beating and chase him away from there, but he seizes my arm in mid-air. Ah, how I wish I had a wolf's teeth to chew his tongue off and condemn him to eternal silence! I feel like smashing him over the head with a huge cooking pot and shutting him up for good. All my gestures are arrows fired in indignation. I'm surprised by myself. I'm not an aggressive person. I could assault all the men in the world, but not my Tony. He's sacrosanct, he's the father of my kids.

"Calm down, woman, calm down." He tries to placate me. "There's no need to get so angry. I'm being sincere, let me confess. I came to ask your forgiveness. I don't know how I was capable of abandoning such a beautiful woman, such a . . ."

"Shut that mouth of yours, Tony!"

< 444 >

He begins to talk feverishly. He hisses words of love and lays bare his monstrous character. He's completely unaware of the flames he's tossing in my path. Nor does he see the pain I feel when he fills my ears with lewd confidences.

"Where has this sudden inspiration come from?"

"From life. I saw the futility of all the things I was doing. I thought I was a man with wings and I sought my treasure on the wrong map. I was on the verge of death because of illnesses brought on by ill-managed love. Rami, I turned your life into a hell, but forgive me, Rami, I'm your husband."

He's knocking on the door to my heart, poor little soul, but my heart no longer exists, it's been eaten away by woodworm. He's knocking on the door to my soul, but my soul lives high up, in a stone fortress. All I've got is this kutchingered body that he rejects. Ah, my love, my sweet tragedy! Maybe I'll forgive you some other day, but not today.

"I think of you so much, Rami."

"Don't exaggerate, Tony."

"I'm not exaggerating, no, that doctor listened to my story and advised me to control my passion so as not to suffer from love's illnesses."

I'm infuriated and answer ill-humoredly:

"Ah, I've got it. You're here to protect yourself from love's ill-nesses. Go on, get out of here, go and look after your women, off you go!"

"Don't talk to me about the other women, Rami. They attached themselves to me because they wanted money. Now they've got their own businesses, they no longer respect me. One can't trust women."

"They don't respect you? How?"

"They don't kneel when they're serving me, like they used to, and they don't massage my feet when I take my shoes off. Lately, it's the houseboy who opens the door for me, because they're never at home. All they think about is their business ventures and they say they've got too much to do."

He gets up from his chair. He hugs me and gives me an affec-tionate caress, like someone rubbing a stone to produce a spark. My body is cold. It's marble, it's asbestos, it doesn't catch fire.

"Let go of me and, once and for all, go and see your women. I'm the one who doesn't love you anymore."

"Don't think like that. You're my security, my safe harbor. No

< 446 >

matter how much wandering I do, this is my home. It's by your side that I want to die."

Men are predators of air and wind. They fly around the world and only come home when their wings are broken. They expect their women to behave like rocks, even when they're buffeted by a huge whirlwind. Just take Tony. He asks me to open my arms and welcome him, he wants to return to the old dance down in the deepest branches of my nerves. Love is a murmur from one heart to the other. A palm and the breeze in the same waltz, a bee and pollen in the same honeycomb. Manioc and the oven in the same heat. Ah, Tony, our souls no longer sway to the same rhythm!

"At this hour, you should be having breakfast with Saly. What are you doing here?"

"She left very early, leaving me in bed. She says she's got to go and get some merchandise, goodness knows where."

"So you were frightened of being on your own and ran to mummy's arms."

"Why are you so hostile toward me, Rami, why?"

I feel like asking him: Who made me desire kisses other than yours? I who was a virgin and pure. My dreams were as white as the clouds floating through the sky, but they became dark and swollen as if a tornado were brewing. I also feel like asking: Who made me a bed of thorns and forced me to sleep in it? Who dressed my crimson heart in mourning? Who served me vinegar and bile and made my eyes weep? Who turned me into the widow of a husband who was still alive? Who obliged me to cohabit with rivals, like sisters?

"Oh, Rami, I'm your man."

I suddenly remember my maternal grandfather. When he got drunk, he would take his leave of his friends like this: Ah, my wife, my drum! I'm going home to play my drum. So that she may shed the tears I feel. So that she may provide blood for my wound, my anguish. So that she may lay to rest the anger I feel in my soul. So that she may enliven the sadness in my being by unleashing the lullaby of her weeping. Don't you beat your wife? Beat her, hit her, so that you can join in the dance of life. Beat her in your anguish, your pain, your joy, beat her, hit her. And when she screams, the sigh you give is orgasmic: Ah, my wife, my drum!

"Go and see Mauá, go on. She's your passion."

"That one's a mystery at the moment. I suggested we have another child and she turned up her nose. All she thinks about

< 448 >

is her beauty products, and her endless stream of clients. She's thought up ways of working on the weekend, she does hairdressing and makeup at people's homes for special occasions, weddings, baptisms, and all those women's things."

"You've got Ju, she loves your company."

"Ah, Rami, that one's turned out the worst of all of them. She's devoted to her work in a way I would never have imagined. And, my God, is she efficient! She's got a whole army of employees, fifteen of them. She spends her time shouting orders and she even shouts at me now. She doesn't even make me frothy coffee like she used to."

"You must understand, Tony, it's her work."

"It's not nice having to seek an audience with my own wives. I have to make an appointment timed to the very minute in order to enjoy their company. And what's worse, my children follow their mothers' example, they don't care about me. From having it all, I now have nothing. My wives fly off like birds out of an open cage, and I'm left looking on in alarm, while these women, whose wings I tied, after all know how to fly. Yesterday, they were selling things on the street corner. Today, they're businesswomen and no longer respect me."

"Now I understand. You want to die here because there's no more room for you over there. My love, the solution to your problem lies in a new marriage. You've got to buy yourself another woman."

"Don't even mention it, I don't want any more women. If I could turn the clock back ..."

"Turn the clock back? That's a useless, thoroughly exhausting notion. The sun that sinks doesn't come back. That story about the eternal return is nonsense. You can go back, of course, in some other incarnation, but you never go back to being exactly the same. You can even reincarnate as a monkey, a little bird, a tree. Did you never hear about a man reincarnating as a woman?"

I walk out of the kitchen and leave the house, abandoning Tony to wallow in the memory of something that never got as far as being built. I take a deep breath. I want to feel particles of air falling over my breast and to bury my pain in the deepest part of the ocean. I want to fall asleep on the banks of the river and let the melody of the fish comfort my tears. I want to walk barefoot over the loose sand, like a wildcat. Love a man? Never again! I shall get myself a man who will love me. I shall be someone's second wife, just as Lu suggested. Never again the first. I want to

< 450 >

be everything: the wind, a fish, a drop of water, a white cloud, anything else but a woman. I want to be a free spirit, to lean on the windowsill and watch the rain falling. To be a ghost and sit, invisible, on the top of a mountain to see the sun rising. I want to be a grain of sand in the wind and to dance my *niketche* to the sound of the flutes of all the breezes.

< 451 >

41

I've summoned my rivals to an urgent meeting in order to discuss our Tony. I've told them of his sinister plans to abandon them all and live only with me. They didn't reply. They laughed. They knew that old song. Tony's magic words, his trap and his bait, they told me.

"I never heard that one," I say.

"How would you hear it if you're the first wife?" Saly explains.

"He would always tell me: I'm going to leave Rami," Ju declares. "I've heard that song millions of times over the last nineteen years or so. He told me that he felt less of a man when he was with you. That you weren't a good cook. He would tell me your bed was cold. That, because you were fat, you didn't hurry to carry out his orders. That you're like a tank, hard to control, and that's why he was going to divorce you to be with me."

"He said the same thing to me about you and Ju," says Saly.

"He said the same thing to me about Rami, Ju, Lu, and Saly," Mauá concludes. "What he said to me about you, Rami, was more serious. He told me you were like a blank sheet, as flat as a prairie without any curves, dangly bits, or flesh to get a grip on. A dried-up tree trunk. A smooth fish he couldn't hold, slippery yet static. A creature that breathes but doesn't sigh. A heavy bulk that trundles by. A bird's feather that leaves no mark. A bit of salt water that isn't enough to moisten the face."

"Is that so?"

I drink a bitter glass of nothingness. I choke.

"What?"

I don't know where I find the strength to smile. I'm indignant. He uses my name in order to charm his mermaids when his mouth is devoid of poetry. Sitting with his friends over a few drinks, he teaches them all the tricks and ploys to hunt women, like some champion of love, and they all chuckle at our expense. Ah, but what an ugly thing a lying man is. How wicked my Tony is, what a liar! He serves us all a dish of love, seasoned with untruths. Ah, Tony darling, you incorrigible liar!

Suddenly, I begin to weep all the tears in the world. Dear Lord, why did you make me a woman? A woman has a serpent's tongue, which is why she carries the weight of the world on her back. A woman is bile, she is the mysterious creator of all the evils of the universe. A woman is someone you need, but whom you don't need at all, which is why when she dies, people shed a couple of tears and say with a sigh: Rest in peace, dear lady. Lay your afflictions and your tiredness to rest in the bosom of the earth. Sleep in peace. A woman is an eternal problem that has no solution. She's an imperfect project. She's made up of curves. There isn't a straight line in her, she can't straighten up. Is she surreal? No. Is she abstract? Also no. Is she Gothic? Yes, she is. She's got arches, domes, ogives. She's soft, she's weak, she's as obstinate as water that drips so much, it ends up making a hole. A woman talks a lot, and she talks too much. That's why she's silence, she's a grave, she lives at the bottom of a well, the endless abyss. Just look at her. She's greedy, a glutton. No sooner had she been made than she asked for a fat juicy apple and a nice big yam for her oven, for her stove. You can see she's got the allure of a good cook. That's why God showed her his butt straight after she'd been created. She's defective, which is why she's eternally seeking some concrete form. With hairpieces. Lace. Silks. Fashions. High-heeled shoes. Hairstyles. Massages. Lipstick and jewelry. Hardly has she learned to breathe fresh air than she rushes off to rituals of initiation so as to cover her body in tattoos and acquire the scales of a fish, so escaping the slipperiness of a catfish. She learns to lengthen her genitals every day, like someone milking a cow's udders. All this to gain the shape of a squid. Of an octopus. Of a turkey's beak and transform herself into a fearsome man eater. In a woman, there's no end to her blood. If it's not menstruation, it's childbirth, aggression piercing her heart like a thorn. In spite of this, she gives blood to save the dying and she produces the blood of her children, her grandchildren, and the great-grandchildren who will, one day, be born. A woman is as sturdy as a haystack and weeps over the merest straw.

A man is the one for whom all the bells toll. He's the one for whom all voices are raised, when death takes him: He was so good, how he'll be missed, my God! A man is the cause of the sadness borne by widows. Because he's a concrete being. Perfect. Soaring. The one who is forever sought, but never found. Every man is a success. Every man is a sun. He's a star, who speaks through silence and lives eternally. His whole being was constructed with the geometrical measurements of sanctity. He's made of straight lines. He is a tireless arrow piercing all the curves in the universe in order to straighten the world's paths. He's an animal threatened with extinction, but who merits preservation, who dies by the thousands on the field of battle because he can't control his greed for love, ambition, and power. Everything is his right: to kill, to love, to summon, to possess. He is the perfect monument. His image grows in the direction of the sun. Like the statue of Zeus, he has his feet planted at opposite ends of the world's diameter, which is why everything has to pass between his legs. Ships. The fresh water of rivers. The multitudes, cars, trucks. And all the women in the world.

My rivals console me and I stop crying.

"Rami, don't cry. All men are like that."

I calm down. All this man Tony does is confuse me, drive me to distraction. I thought I knew all of him, but the truth is I don't know him at all. Never before had I imagined hearing such cruel things said about me. One day, he's in love, the next day, he's out of love. One day, your ears hear one thing, the next day, another woman's ears hear something else. Occasionally, he sings the same song to all his women. The love he shows us is served up seasoned with lies, just as fish is served up with rice.

I regain my self-control and again assume the leadership of our conjugal parliament.

"What shall we do now, girls?"

"I haven't got time to cater to all his whims," says Saly.

"Nor me," says Ju.

"Me neither," says Mauá.

"The best solution is to suggest to Tony that he take a new wife," I propose. "What do the others think?"

There's a moment's silence.

"A new wife. Who's for it? Who's against?"

I miss having Lu there, for she's a tiebreaker. If this vote ends up without a majority, how are we going to break the deadlock?

"A new wife," cries Mauá.

"Agreed," says Saly.

Ju opens her mouth. She's going to vote against it, we all know.

"A new wife," Ju says at last.

We all look at each other, surprised.

"Decided unanimously. Tony must get a new wife."

"So where's this new wife going to come from?"

"I don't mind helping in the search," says Saly.

"Neither do I," says Mauá, "there are lots of free Makua women around."

"Not a Makua," Saly argues, "it's got to be a different ethnic group from ours. It won't be hard to find some nice young girl in this huge country."

I look around at all my rivals. Any enthusiasm for our common property has faded. They are cold and indifferent toward Tony's existence. What is love unless it's the grand dream, the great anguish, the never-ending wait? When love has been satisfied, it's all over, just as it is for the ravenous eater, who casts aside his bowl of soup once his belly is full. Love's only good when it's incomplete. Ours is a love that is satiated, without desires, diversions, or jealousy. Ah, who would have thought our best times were when we were busy fighting over our love? Now that it's all over, the magic has been lost. Each one of us is absorbed in our own preoccupations, our business ventures, our children.

"Girls, I can see you're no longer interested. You're deserting Tony."

"No, never. We're not going to abandon Tony," Saly insists. He lives in us, and we live in him. We built our world with him. It was this polygamous husband who gave us these beautiful children. It was this polygamous husband who loved us and humiliated us. It was this polygamous husband who brought us together in friendship, in solidarity, in this wives' club. And, my God, how good this union around a polygamous husband has proved to be!"

"We are women like our mothers and grandmothers," Ju argues.

< 459 >

"We want to maintain the good name of our ancestors, but let us be clear, Rami, life has changed. The verb 'to love' has changed its meaning, and is no longer used in the same way, nor does polygamy follow the same rules it once did. Culture isn't everlasting, although we do our best to preserve tradition. We'll do everything we were taught to do, just as our ancestors prescribed. We are women of courage, of respect. It's very hard to accept polygamy in an age when women are affirming themselves and conquering the world."

"Ju," I ask suspiciously, "why the long speech?"

"In polygamy, women watch over their man, you know this," Ju reminds me. "When the older wives get tired, grow old, like us, it's not because of their age, but because they are worn down, and so it becomes necessary to rejuvenate the home with the new blood of a virgin, as delicate as an egg."

I'm finding this meeting painful. I always believed love was forever. First it was Tony who shattered my beliefs. Now, it's these bees, with their momentary loves. They've bitten their pollen and are now fluttering off elsewhere, abandoning the faded flower. And they say they know how to love more than I do.

"Ju, I know you well, you don't want anything to do with this

< 460 >

polygamous husband anymore, and you're claiming your right to do other things."

"When it comes to his presence, having a polygamous husband is exactly like having a lover. He comes, he goes, you never know when he's leaving or when he's coming back, a polygamous husband is like rain. But he's worse than a lover. A polygamous husband is complicated, capricious, proud, idle. He sits on his throne all day long and issues orders like a king. After he's had his food, he takes a bath, perfumes himself, and leaves. And we remain as beggars, our hand outstretched, and we organize ourselves in a club, join together in our weakness and insist on our rights. Am I claiming rights? What rights? What is a polygamous husband if not an errant creature who scatters himself across the world, like a cloud, a seed, a feather, a piece of air? Can you, by any chance, claim rights from the wind?"

I look at Ju in surprise. Her words sound as vigorous as warhorses galloping into battle. From her mouth, a huge cloud of vapor billows forth, a hurricane of smoke and color. Of bitterness. Of the coagulated blood from all the wounds and knife thrusts she has suffered from the first moments of her first kiss right up until her current, thorn-filled love. The sentiment she expresses

< 461 >

today is one of rebellion and refusal to submit. Of maturity. I see the firmness of the brutal wound in her soul that contains the breath of life which will propel her toward the final onslaught. I see a bright flash in her eyes. It's good to see her explode, speak, may she free and purge herself, so that she can throw off her inner burden and go back to being a woman. A woman, purely and simply. Who laughs. Who dreams. Who raises her eyes to infinity and counts sheep among the clouds in the sky.

"What'll become of us when he's all hunchbacked and holding a walking stick?" Ju moans. "The rotas will get longer, a month here, a month there. If a week's wait is so painful, what will it be like later? He'll most likely live with just one, and live with the others in his thoughts. Which one of us will be the lucky devil who's going to inherit that heap of scrap metal when old age comes? Maybe Rami, the first wife and his owner, with her legally sanctioned property rights. Maybe Saly. Or maybe Mauá, whom he loves so much. The rest of us will live as solitary old maids and elderly widows. I don't want to be an old maid any more than I want to be an old widow. In some corner of this world, there must be a man just for me."

"If we'd studied more, we would have had a different fate. We

< 462 >

could have had the freedom to choose between love and a career. Between the cross and Calvary. Between the oven and the icebox. But as things are, we have neither one thing nor the other," I say.

"Study more in the village I come from? What for?" Saly comments sarcastically. "So as to count the number of birds pecking away at the grains in the rice fields? To count the missing teeth in the mouth of the old man you get given as a husband?"

"Oh, it's important to study, even if it's only so you can read the doctor's prescription, Saly," I reply.

"In our villages, life is pure, men and women are nature's twins, governed by the sun and the seasons of the year," Mauá confirms. "People are near to God. The hospital is twenty kilometers away, the school fifteen kilometers, there's no road, no jobs, no prospects. People have never seen a car or electric light. The most important thing is to procreate. The more children you have the better, some of them die, but there are always a few left to provide support when you get old. If I completed sixth grade, it's because my aunt was a teacher and lived near the school."

"You women in the south are luckier," Saly says. "In our villages, girls get married when they're twelve, as soon as they've completed their initiation rites. They stop school at third grade and have their first child before they're fifteen," she concludes in a doleful tone.

"Isn't school important then?" I ask Saly.

"My God, of course it is! That's why I've gone back to studying. I want to speak and write Portuguese well. I want to manage my business well. I even know a few words of Italian, but what I really want to do is to speak English too."

"Italian?"

We all look at Saly in surprise and fire questions at her. She smiles.

"I've bought a book..."

She's lying, and I know only too well why. Ah, fiery forty-year-old women. We women live in a deep, silent well and we think the sky is as wide as the hole we can see up above. But one day, we discover that the waters covering us have the color of the sky. Our dreams begin to soar as high as the stars. We discover that the shouts of men are the rustling of waves, and don't kill. And the greatness of men is no more than a peacock's crown. We discover that there are extraordinary things in the forbidden world that deserve to be experienced. We discover that the lilies of the field have a divine scent and that true love has the taste of freedom.

That's why we become children again. Walking the sandy paths barefoot. Tasting the raindrops deep in our throats. The colors of the rainbow rising to the immensity of the earth and the sea. And we want everything. Love. Illusion. Dreams. The smell of the earth and the smell of the ocean united in one aroma. Old age and infancy at one and the same point. We seek in vain our lost youth. And we try to salvage what remains of life with the talons of a hawk. We like to write poems in the romantic style. To receive love letters. To go to the carnival and ride the roller coaster. Eat cotton candy and lick ice creams. Throw ourselves with all our heart into the sea of adventures. Exchange kisses under the light of the moon. Walk hand in hand with the man we love along the seashore and count the stars in the sky.

"Girls, shall we go and find a wife for Tony?"

"Let's go!"

We embark on a frantic search. We crisscross the country by car and by plane. Our love is made up of self-sacrifice and sharing. It's altruistic and unselfish. We travel to the four corners of the world, seeking a beauty to charm our Don Juan. We're looking for a young wife for an old polygamist.

We've been looking for the ideal woman, the woman who

agrees to stifle her young girl's dreams without moaning or complaining. Who has a uterus disposed to give new life to the world. Who obeys and doesn't protest, who volunteers herself for torture. The ideal woman is a comet, all men yearn for her but can never reach her, there is nothing more difficult than to search for the ideal woman. We have risen to the challenge and are seeking her wherever the wind blows. We start off in the south. Here, girls are all beautiful, elegant, and slim. No sooner have they got married than they begin to expand, to explode like balloons filled with oxygen. They've got more money, and enjoy all their meals: bread, sausages and ham for breakfast, chicken and fries, peanut curry and corn porridge for lunch, crackers and butter for tea, delicious candlelit dinners accompanied by wine, and, between meals, there are hamburgers, popcorn, and hot dogs of the type sold on every street corner. They eat too much and don't do any serving.

We journey on to the central region of the country. There, we find young girls of smaller build. Short. Dark skinned. Neat and tidy, pretty little things. We spend a lot of time trying to find one that's worth the trouble. Some of them seem good and obedient, others more headstrong. They're no use. We head off to the north. We rummage around. The young girls parade before us, like the

< 466 >

jobless queuing up for work. Marriage really is a job, which is why the girls submit, obey, humiliate themselves, in the hope of being chosen for the position of wife to an old polygamist. I look at the poor teenagers walking, their eyes closed, toward the world's traps. That's how men want us: blind, ignorant, fearful, timid. I gaze at them from my lofty queen's throne, my throne of straw, of fire, of tears, and of thorns. I demand the impossible from them.

Open your mouth and show us your teeth. There's one missing, you won't do. Now you, get your clothes off. You've got blotches on your skin, you're no good. And you, come here, walk. You plod along like a mule. You're no good. Show us your hands, your heels, your fingers, the soles of your feet. You're full of calluses, you won't do. Show us your backside, your breasts, your belly. We would prod. Your tits are flaccid like sponges. You're no longer a virgin. Your rear doesn't have that ripe firmness to the touch, like that of a young girl. You're too old. And you've got a good figure, okay, but let's have a look at your fish scales and get the tape measure out. You're fifty kilos and dried up. You're seventy-five and fat, you're no good. You've got a beautiful face, but you're fat up above and skinny down below, you won't do. African elegance is pestle shaped: a narrow waist, fat down below, and slightly

< 467 >

skinny above. Now laugh, now sing. Now speak. You laugh like a witch, you talk like a donkey, and when you sing, it's as if you're buzzing, you won't do. Say all you know about culture. General culture, the culture of love. You don't know anything, you're not prepared, you won't do. Some of these girls smell of detergent. Others of soap. Very few of them smell of perfume and most of them just smell of women.

The mothers have joined the procession in order to sell their daughters' charms. I was delighted, moved, inspired by the look in their eyes. The looks those women gave were the world's reflection. We ordered their daughters to take their clothes off and they gave their consent, their approval. That's how women journey along their fateful road. Naked. Just see how they strip off for the beauty contest. Just see how they smile as they parade, like beef cattle on their way to slaughter. See how they seek their freedom and fame in the starkness of the catwalk. See how their perfect butts sway and how they willingly give themselves up to be prodded, assessed, tasted, and approved. The body of a beautiful woman is a detergent for the man to wash the dirt from his muddy eyes, the body of a beautiful woman is a good bit of flesh for a vulture to peck at.

< 468 >

We travel up to the north of the country, where we eventually find the ideal woman. Can it really be that she's ideal? To find the perfect woman, we need a magic mirror and the eyes of a clairvoyant. Popular wisdom states that any beautiful woman is a witch. If she's not a witch, then she's volatile. If she's not volatile, then she's lazy, dishonest, useless. Have all our efforts really been worth it?

< 469 >

42

My sitting room hosts the most important session of the conjugal parliament, which is why we've invited Tony. He's late, but he'll come. Leaders never arrive at the appointed time. While waiting, we've been talking in order to allay our anxiety. Today we're not talking out loud. We whisper in each other's ears as if not wanting to offend the air. We talk about modern marriages, and marriage in the old days. About feminist thought, which is changing the face of the earth. We talk about the rate of divorce, which is skyrocketing. We talk about our man. We talk about ourselves. We chat, we complain. We miss Lu to sweeten the atmosphere. To breathe life into the conversation. To give us the joie de vivre that always springs from her inner being.

Tony arrives and sits down in his favorite corner. He gives us his impassioned look. The look of a dreamer. Of a man fulfilled. He's got used to the loss of Lu.

"So, my little doves, are you going to tell me the reason for this meeting?" he asks, his voice as happy as it's ever been.

< 471 >

I begin to talk about little things. Flowers. Our children. I seem unable to talk about anything significant, and he doesn't suspect anything. I pluck up courage and try to get to the matter in hand. I feel a stone obstructing the sound of my voice in my throat. Suddenly, I stop, I feel a loss of breath. My God, I'm suffocating. There's no air in this room. There's no air in my chest, I'm going to faint. I make an effort and say:

"Well, we …"

I stutter. Dear God, I feel as if I'm going to lose my power of speech. I panic. I want to disappear, leave the place. I want a Makonde chain to lock my mouth up for a while. But I haven't got one. Even if I did, I haven't got holes in my lips. Ah, Makonde women know all about life. They prepare their mouths so as to force themselves to be silent because they know that someone who is nervous or angry can say silly things. That's why they have two holes pierced. One on the upper lip. The other on the lower. Then, they just buy a chain, padlock their mouth, and keep the key a long way away.

"This meeting is the result of …"

Oh, how I'd love to feel the silence of my speech. I yearn for

< 472 >

a tiny drop of courage of the type that dwells in the bottom of a wine glass. I make an effort. I'm the first wife, I'm the main one, I must exercise my right to speak and set an example. At first, I only manage to croak. Dead syllables. I close my eyes. When I open them, my words sound like thunderous, destructive gunfire. It's the start of the storm.

"Oh, Tony," I say, "we want you to know how much we admire you, and that without you, we are nothing. We want to safeguard the position you deserve, as a man."

Tony's looking out the window as the evening falls. Night approaching. He's not paying any attention to what I'm saying. Of course. Women never have anything to say and when they do open their mouths, they only talk nonsense. I give my voice a much more serious tone.

"In the olden days, women looked after the crops, the children took care of the livestock, while the sovereign husband rested on his throne. Nowadays, we also work and we often don't have enough time to look after you, which is an impossible situation. It has always been like this. It's nature."

My speech grows stronger, like a whirlwind. I feel its waves

< 473 >

spreading concentrically. I sense its hiss. It's full of obscure diversions, of the type that attracts disaster with the force of its suction.

"Man is a great tree that lives for hundreds of years. And in order to preserve his strength, he needs sap, new blood. Woman is merely a fruit, she ripens, rots, and falls. We are old, Tony," says Mauá, her head bowed, without much conviction in what she says.

He sits listening to what we have to say, one after the other. He seems both pleasantly and unpleasantly surprised. It looks as if there's a conspiracy. He gets anxious. He gets up and goes over to the sideboard and pours himself a whiskey. Alcohol is a good remedy for the emotions. He has heard some wonderful, astounding declarations. Gradually, his face takes on a worried expression.

"Looking after a man is a task for many women, we appreciate that fact," Saly concludes. "We carry out our role, but our strength is not enough. All this work and childbearing has made us somewhat tired. You need human warmth. You need some more affection. New love."

Now the words sound like the clink of chains falling into place.

He realizes he's fallen into a trap. He looks at us one at a time, and begins to weigh up what each of us has said. Our finely tuned orchestra. Our well-rehearsed choir. We have become an army of conspirators about to deliver the final blow.

"Being the wife of a polygamous husband is a huge responsibility," my words carry authority. "We want to have the honor of demonstrating to the world that we are adult women and know how to share. That we're not resentful. And I, in particular, wish to use the rights that polygamy has conferred on me, as your first wife. I've decided you must marry a new wife.

"I've put the matter to your younger wives, and we agree unanimously. You must have a new wife."

My dulcet words shoot through the air. There's a whiff of irony, there's a whiff of hypocrisy, which bombard him like hailstones. He smells the threat and is scared out of his wits. He throws us a glance which pleads for mercy. For the first time, he speaks in a low voice.

"God help me, you're killing me. I was always a man who was avid for life, but not any longer. I'm tired of so much loving and so much suffering. Please, I beg you, don't punish me with this.

I can't withstand strong emotions, you know that. It's about my life, my health. I've already done too much loving in my life. I married a lot of women, and now I've had enough."

"Men are strong, Tony, they can put up with the world's burdens, get married again," I insist.

"Oh, no!"

"A king can't refuse either a throne or servitude offered. If you refuse to accept our decision, you repudiate us. An extra woman in a polygamous home is always welcome," says Saly.

"I'm not ready for it."

"But we are. We've found the ideal woman, and now all we have to do is to prepare the ceremony. Mauá, bring in the bride," I order.

Mauá goes to the bedroom and returns leading by the hand a jewel, a pearl, a diamond made especially to be admired. This is the bride. She takes a few steps. We look at her. My God, I've never seen such a pretty girl. She walks like a gazelle. From every gesture emanate waves, sea birds, white clouds, breeze, perfumes, all of which complement her. She is perfection in movement. Even the steps taken by her bare feet go well with her. Even the grasses she treads are thankful for the gift of having been brushed by her perfume. She stops and looks at Tony. Even the pose she

< 476 >

assumes as she stands there looks good on her. Her eyes are Venus's diamonds, and when she blinks, each eyelash releases gold dust, and it all looks good on her. From her smile, doves, birds, flowers, are released, and they all suit her perfectly. Her backside looks so good, nicely wrapped in her blue-check *capulana*. Mauá invites her to take a seat, and my God, how she sits! She parks her butt on the chair like a bird lovingly protecting her eggs in the nest. Even the simple gesture of sitting down on the velveteen sofa suits her perfectly. The fragrance of her body, the movement of her chest in the gentle act of breathing, suit her perfectly. Her little cotton blouse that envelops her full breasts gives her a freshness that suits her perfectly.

Tony is left speechless. All passion begins with a simple gesture. The vast forest succumbs to a mere flame. This jewel has the power of fire. She has the color of the sun. She has the color of the moon. She is both moon and sun in the same heavenly body.

"Take this girl away from me before I fall in love," he says with some difficulty. "Protect her from my claws before I commit original sin."

We glance at each other and remain silent. A donkey that refuses its pasture, if it hasn't lost its teeth, must be ill.

"I can't think clearly with her around. She's making me dizzy. She's setting my body on fire," he bursts out.

Tony is suffering. Passion is giving his soul a horsewhipping as strong as hammer blows. He's dying of desire, but he's clutching the reins of his appetite with the strength of Hercules. Ardent love is powerful and brings all red-blooded men to ground. Vanquished, he declares his love.

"Girl, I'm going to pay your bride price with all the money the world contains. I'll give my entire fortune for you, all my life, my very being, for you, girl, you're so pretty! You're like the sea. You're like moonlight. You're everything, sea and sky."

Tony's voice is gentle because the music of love has penetrated his soul. Love is both a remedy and poison. It saves and kills in one go.

"Come here, girl. Sit down next to me. What is your name?"

"Saluá."

"That's a pretty name and it suits you. Where are you from?"

"From Niassa, I'm a Nyanja."

"Ah, you're from the lake that has good fish. What do you want?"

< 478 >

"To be your wife."

"You're still a child."

"I'm eighteen. I was damseled at fifteen. I know how to wash clothes and to wash the dishes. I don't know how to cook well, but I can learn, and I know the most important thing: I've got my fish scales and I've got my squid. I learned how to make love during the initiation rites."

"You were damseled?"

"Yes. To damsel is to celebrate the rites of initiation."

My God, Tony is driven crazy when Saluá opens her mouth and reveals those teeth that are whiter than grains of corn, more sparkling than pearls, and that produce a lunar reflection that suits her very well. When she speaks, the breath released from that flute suits her well. That skin of hers like a ripe cashew, those eyes of a meek cat, suit her down to the ground. That succulent body, like a fresh tomato, is perfect for the semi-toothless mouth of a fifty-year-old polygamist. This girl Saluá is perdition in the midst of paradise. The role of serpent in the Bantu Eden suits her well.

"Tony," Saly explains, "we know your desire to embrace the whole country through marriage, which is why we went to get this girl from the northwest. She talks Portuguese with a Nyanja accent, but we'll get her talking correctly in due course.

He takes a deep breath and sighs. He kneels at this young girl's feet and worships her like a goddess. His voice takes on a sweet, melodic tone. His mouth fills with words of sugar and passion. His eyes are agog with so much desire. The love he feels for her is both fire and torment. He takes her silky hand, and then let's go.

"Dear God, she's beautiful. She is a flower, and my hands are soiled, I'm scared of touching her in case she gets tainted. I feel old and tired of running from shelter to shelter like a crab. Do you think I should deflower this young girl, accompany her through her pregnancy, childbirth, menstruation, diapers, bibs, and babies' nighttime tears? No, I can't, I don't want to. When I was in the hospital, I saw men wasted away like ghosts. I saw wizened, skeletal women. I thought about life. The world has got AIDS. My sexual curriculum is abundant and enviable, it makes me imagine both truths and fantasies. I don't want to touch this flower in order not to sully her, please, take this girl back to her home."

We are left bewildered. He hides his face. The time has come for the snail to hide inside his shell. He's defeathering himself with his own beak, like an old parrot. He's abandoning love like a castrated ox and folding his wings in full flight. It's the first sign of autumn, winter is getting ready to make its entrance.

"Tony, are you still really a man? Are you still a man with a capital M?" Saly challenges.

"Why?"

"Ah, you're no longer a man, Tony, my darling. You're broken," she replies. "You've laid down your arms. Your arrow has gained the curves of a rounded mirror, dearest Tony, you're a weakling now."

"I'm sorry if I've disappointed you. But I like my love tasting of conquest, and I can't accept a woman placed in my arms. I'm a wolf. A shark. A hawk. I like to fight with my prey in the act of hunting. I'm still a red-blooded male."

"This is about polygamy, Tony," I cut in menacingly. "In this system laws speak louder than your desires. You don't have a choice. Do you accept her or not?"

This generates a moment of deep silence as if it were incubating a storm. What words can be uttered to break the ice? Who will win in this contest? He or we? There's stalemate. We say yes. He says no. But he can't even contemplate or imagine what it means to go against the wish of four women together.

"I can't accept the offer. No, I don't accept it."

"Is that your final word?"

"Yes. And let's not talk further about the matter."

Oh dear! The game's been lost. All we can do now is climb to the top of the mountain and unleash our curse.

"We respect your decision," says Saly. "You'll remain in your corner, then. You'll have all you need: food, care, and peace and quiet, but not our company. Your refusal is a declaration of sexual impotence, and so we'll summon a family meeting and inform its members of what is happening, so that we can then seek conjugal assistants. This is a right that polygamy gives us."

A firestorm explodes in Tony's soul that balances in the flame's dance. He suspects he's being consigned to solitude in the heart of the crowd. When love is offered him on a plate, the lover gets suspicious. Now he understands that he's not being the target of love, but of an amorous revenge.

Mauá looks down and appears to be concentrating. Then she opens her mouth and speaks. She gains courage and gets it off her chest in one go.

"I've already got a conjugal assistant who's going to be my husband within the next fortnight. Tony, I shall miss you a lot. It only

< 482 >

remains for me to thank you. You saved me from the trash heap and brought me close to Rami, who taught me lessons about life and caused me to be born anew."

Tony opens his mouth like a hippopotamus sighing. Words remain suspended between pain and surprise. Astonishment is transformed into a deadly wind, but no breath emerges to feed it, and it is made to dance around in a twister. Dark clouds descend from the skies and blindfold him. Mauá's attitude was expected. She was too tender a blade of grass for an old donkey. She was seeking a father and not a husband, and now that she's earning her own crust, she's found true love. Could she be considered self-seeking? Has she committed a crime by any chance? She knew she was being used, she played the game and won hands down.

Ju opens her mouth, she's going to say something, this Ju who never says anything, always immersed in pain and silence.

"I never speak, but today I want to talk. I need to talk. Tony, your black children have got a white stepfather, they've gone up in the world. Your nineteen-year-old son drives a Mercedes his stepfather gave him on his birthday. He no longer needs to point at his father's blue car speeding off down the road. My new husband is Portuguese. We love each other very much, really very much. He's ever so gentle, my dear old man. He's a widower, this man of mine. And he's got money. Lots of money. He's got bank accounts, shops, houses, cars, properties. I've got money flowing out of the pores of my skin now, Tony. I take baths in money. I breathe money, lots of it, all I tread on in my home is money. He's adopted my children as his own, and shows them a lot of affection. I'm soon going to marry him, veil and all. At last, I'm going to step up to the altar in a wedding dress, wear a ring, enter the church to the tune of 'Here Comes the Bride.'"

Her words are the fatal bullets that unseat the horseman and make him fall to the ground. Ju has left us in a state of shock, and we are flabbergasted. Tony's heart is left to bleed slowly, like a piece of turf that has been sparked and is gradually turning to ash. He tries to open up the ground to swallow him, but the ground rejects him. Like the ostrich, he hides his head under his wing and leaves his backside for all to see. We raise our eyes to Ju and contemplate this incredible miracle. The deceived woman who deceives her deceiver and rises from the ashes in a victory that's the size of the world.

"You're prostituting my children, Ju," says Tony with a sigh.

"Are you absolutely sure they're yours?"

"How long have you had this man?"

"Two years."

"How?"

"A polygamist only has two eyes, he can't see what's going on behind him. He's only got one nose and can't go sniffing around everywhere."

Ju's speech is caustic. It is searing. It is carcinogenic. Tony's body writhes in the dance of death. There's debauchery in Ju's tone of voice. There's vengeance and rejoicing in Ju's soul. She's carved out her own space and now enjoys the best cuts of steak, she eats chicken gizzard and fish heads as she relaxes in peace under the shade of the banana tree. How happy she is, our Ju! Ah, my Tony! Your castles at the top of the hill were built of sand. Your vulture's beak was made of clay, and it wore away at every peck. You were born a man, but you were given wings of wax, and when you flew up to your castles, the wax melted, you fell to earth and your snout was smashed like a hen's egg. Dearest Tony, everything that begins ends, like the wind that blows, like the sun that rises and then sinks, like the spring that comes and then passes. An octopus has many tentacles, but it can't grasp all the oceans of the world. The wild animal kills only to satisfy its

< 485 >

hunger, while you wanted to devour the entire world with milk teeth. Beautiful women are born every day, in every corner of the planet. You can't sleep with all the women in the world, but please, Tony, do give it your best shot!

< 486 >

43

My rivals leave, taking the rejected girl, Saluá, with them. Only the two of us are left. We reencounter each other.

"Rami!"

"Yes, dear Tony."

"Today, I'd like to speak words of remorse to you. But a man cannot show remorse. Everything he does is well done."

"Just as well."

"I'd like to tell you you're a great woman. But I can't do that either. Women are always small."

"I know, Tony."

"I adore you. I want to adore you, but I can't. To adore is to get down on your knees. A real man doesn't bow, he remains erect."

"Really?"

"I'd also like to say I trust you, but I'm also not allowed to. Men must always suspect women, and women must always trust men."

"I know."

"Today, I'd like to violate all the norms and tell you I admire you and hold you in high esteem. But I can't even do that. It's women who should feel proud of their husbands and never the other way round. Women are supposed to admire their husbands and never the other way round."

"What a pity!"

"Today, I want to cry, Rami, let me cry. All I've ever given you is the anguish of my passions, and I hurt you on a daily basis. I love you like no one else. I'm that restless sea, that cold, dark blanket that has covered your whole life. I'm the one who closed my ears at night to your song of love. I'll be yours forever, because I'm your lament, your breath of fire, your bitter memory. I tattooed your body with thorns of fire. When your soul wandered, desolate, it was my image that emerged before you like a ghost. When you felt the pain of abandonment, it was for me that you yearned. If one day you have a night of love with some other man, it's me you'll recall in the elegy of lost time.

I fold my arms. I look. I listen. A wave of blood crashes furiously in the deepest branches of my arteries. I tremble. Today, he seems to be telling the truth, but I don't believe him. How can I believe in a man who has spent his whole life lying?

< 488 >

"I don't understand your problem, Tony. Why so much sadness because of a new wife?"

He doesn't answer me. I look at him with pity and tenderness. He gets up and goes to the bedroom. He opens the wardrobe and picks out one or two items of clothing, which he places in a travel bag. He walks from one corner of the room to the other, he stops, sniffs loudly, sobs, raves: No, it's impossible, it's not true, no, no no … He seems to be in conversation with creatures from other planets, other spaces, other dimensions, that only he can reach. And they still say men are strong, when this one weeps and is frightened of taking a new wife. He makes his way toward the falling rain. He puts his hat on his head and lumbers out into the rain.

In my mind, I recall magical tales of people vanishing in water vapor, in a nocturnal thunderstorm, into the morning mist. I start to panic.

I give a fierce yell and set off after him. He stops for a second, looks at me, and sets off again. I catch up with him and block his way. Good Lord, his eyes are more than ruddy, as if his breast were ablaze and the flames were consuming his whole body. I'm a few meters away from him, but can hear the drumbeat of his vanquished heart. I've seen many men falling from the top of their pedestals, but I've never seen one fall from the ground into a ditch. How sad! I thought only women wept when they'd been abandoned. But why build pedestals if the ground is firm? Why complicate existence when life is simple? Why dream up terrible conflicts, impossible loves, if everything in life is mortal and comes to an end, like the trees, fire, diamonds? Why create traps to imprison souls, thoughts, feelings, if life is a mere puff of air, if it's as free as the water that flows, the wind that passes, the flight of a tiny bird? Why mistreat women, if they are existence, luster, stars, light, the Milky Way, paradise?

"Tony, come back, you're going to catch a cold."

"Let me leave for a world where there are no women, no temptations, no loves, no children. A world solely made up of men. But I know that such a world only exists in the confines of my imagination. That's why I'm going to the house of the only woman whose love has no equal: my mother."

"Tony, it's cold."

"I want to feel this rain, this wind, this coolness. I want it to penetrate my soul and calm this fever."

< 490 >

Rain washes everything: the sky, the ground, the horizon, the whole of nature. It extinguishes fire, but not bitterness. Sadness is made of stone, only time can eat away at it.

"Why so much sadness, dear Tony?"

"Now, when I close my eyes, I can see how life has stifled me. I have made a blanket of thorns to cover myself with. I'm bleeding. I've lived my whole life with a razor-sharp sword up against my neck. I never saw it."

"But why?"

He rummages around in his memory like a dog gnawing at an old bone. His delirium blows away like particles of air escaping through a broken window. His voice hisses like a whirlwind dragging up dead leaves, sand, and dust.

"I turned love into a suicidal game and your tears haunt me like ghosts. Having many women doesn't mean you're manly, it means you're grazing. I don't even know how these children were born or grew up. I never accompanied their mothers to the maternity clinic, I never held them in my arms, there are so many of them that I even get their names mixed up, I never went to their birthday parties."

"Those are women's tasks, Tony."

"All of you together are lionesses on the loose in the arena. You've defeated me, Rami. You've destroyed me."

"Ah, my dear Tony, don't be so sad. You are merely the stage upon which the theater of life is played out. You're a square through which traditions, cultures, principles, and tyrannies parade. Polygamy is a system with a philosophy of harmony. A woman enters a home, knowing she won't be the only woman. You led me to the altar and the oath you swore was fraudulent. You signed up to a law that was contrary to your desires. You entered this system ignorant of its norms, and you betrayed me and all the others."

"It was my fault that all this happened, I know, but you could have forgiven me, although I'm aware I don't deserve it, but making mistakes is only human, did you forget that?"

"Your problem at the moment is that you're lonely, dear Tony. Stay with Saluá and you'll be happy, you'll see."

We walk as far as the square. There's no one in the public garden. We're alone with the plants in that rainy paradise, displaying the fire in our bodies to the cold of the world. We remain in each other's arms for a long time, listening to the voice of God ordering thunderclaps, lightning, water, in his act of creation. We are clay

< 492 >

melded together into one hillock, he is Adam, I am the serpent, on the verge of original sin. He tries to tear a drop of love from me, a word of reconciliation. His dry mouth glues itself to mine in a divine kiss. Ah, dear God, this kiss is driving me crazy, its melting my heart, transcending me, never before has he given me such a kiss. He hugs me to him and he presses against my belly, which is as hard as a stone and palpitating with life.

"Rami, are you going to have a child?"

I look down. It's my turn to cry.

"But how, if …"

I don't answer, and continue to weep silently.

"Tell me it's mine, and save me."

A family in ruins. Lu, the desired one, has left for another man's arms with her veil and her posy. Ju, the deceived one, is madly in love with an old Portuguese man brimming with cash. Saly, the one he fancied, has bewitched an Italian priest who has abandoned his cassock out of love for her. Mauá, his beloved, loves some other man. I'm the only one left, the queen, the first wife, to save his manly dignity. All these women came and perched on my roof, one by one, like birds of prey. Now they've taken to their wings, one after the other. They all loved my man, they sucked all the honey he had and left. And now he's on the edge of the abyss. Trembling, he asks me to rescue him. My God, I'm powerful, I have the impression I could save him from his fall. I have the magic formula in my hands. Say yes, and redeem him. Say no, and lose him. But I lost so much before I met him. He ignored me long before he met me.

"I can't save you. I'm trying to save you but I can't, I haven't got the strength, I'm weak, I don't exist, I'm a woman. It's men who save women and not the other way round."

"Rami!"

"It's Levy's child!"

His arms drop like a heavy sack. The three thunderclaps he once tried to order so as to destroy Lu's bridegroom now attack his brain, his heart, and his private parts, and turn him into the calcified superman in the Eden of the local square. All he can see is darkness and rain. He stands there for minutes on end contemplating the emptiness. He was an island of fire in the middle of the water. I let him go. He doesn't fall, but he flies into the abyss, toward the heart of the desert, toward a hell without end.